PRAISE FOR THE SPLIT WORLDS

"Newman brings an intriguing
Regency England, and faery in
third volume brings a strong resol
worlds established in the first two

—*Locus* magazine

"A modern fantasy that playfully mixes magic and interesting characters into an intriguing mystery."

—*Kirkus Reviews*

"Newman renders the Split Worlds with verve and an infectious sense of fun, and presents in Cathy a strong and personable heroine."

—*The Guardian*

"Emma Newman has built a modern fantasy world with such élan and authority her ideas of why and how the seemingly irrational world of Fairy works should be stolen by every other writer in the field. Her characters are complex and troubled, courageous at times and foolhardy. This book of wonders is first rate."

—Bill Willingham, Eisner Award winner, and creator of *Fables*

"Emma Newman has created a reflection of Bath that reminds one that charming is not safe. *Between Two Thorns* shows the darkness beneath the glamour of the social Season. Learning to be a young lady has never seemed so dangerous."

**—Mary Robinette Kowal, Hugo Award winner,
and author of *Glamour in Glass***

"With a feather-light touch, Emma Newman has crafted a very English fantasy, one brilliantly realised and quite delightful, weaving magic, mystery and parallel worlds together with ease. Newman may well be one of our brightest stars, *The Split Worlds: Between Two Thorns* is just the beginning of a remarkable journey."

—Adam Christopher, author of *Empire State* and *Seven Wonders*

"*Between Two Thorns* is magical, exciting, and clever. It manages to conjure a world that feels completely natural but also mysterious, sometimes dangerous, sometimes funny, combining several different kinds of urban fantasy into one story, and capturing a lovely sense of modern Britishness that is reminiscent of other fantastic British fantasy. I'm eagerly awaiting the sequel!"

—Fantasy Faction

"I'm actually very glad this is the beginning of a series because I want more of this world, more of these characters and more of this insanity. Newman has created a great complex universe that seems to have a million different stories embedded into its walls. In a world full of supernatural and urban fantasy books, *Between Two Thorns* stands out as the start of a uniquely developed series that deserves everyone's full attention."

—Mandroid

"This novel draws you in from the very first, tempting you with magical creatures set against present day Bath. I tried only reading one chapter just to test the writing style, etc but found myself, a few hours later, having read a vast amount of the book … It sits beautifully within my favourite type of fantasy novel, fairy tale within the present day."

—SF Crowsnest

"An enchanting novel from Emma Newman, an urban fantasy that has no sign of tattooed women in leather pants. A headstrong scion and an investigator discover dark doings in the outwardly genteel world of Bath's secret mirror city."

—SF Signal

"*Between Two Thorns* really was an unalloyed pleasure to read and it's hard to write a review for it that isn't just gushing … Newman has created a unique blend of urban, historical, and crime fantasy clothed in a Regency veneer. *Between Two Thorns* is delicious, engrossing, and enchanting and, so far, my debut of the year."

—A Fantastical Librarian

THE SPLIT WORLDS
BOOK TWO

EMMA NEWMAN

DIVERSIONBOOKS

Also by Emma Newman

The Split Worlds Series

Between Two Thorns

All Is Fair

A Little Knowledg

Diversion Books
A Division of Diversion Publishing Corp.
443 Park Avenue South, Suite 1008
New York, New York 10016
www.DiversionBooks.com

For more information, email info@diversionbooks.com

First Diversion Books edition January 2016.
Print ISBN: 978-1-68230-376-4
eBook ISBN: 978-1-62681-315-3

For the Alchemist

1

Sam knew it was a terrible idea, but once he realised he had to go back to Exilium his course was set. It was like the time he and Dave decided to see who could drink the most tequila without throwing up or passing out. As they matched each other shot for shot he knew it was stupid—perhaps even dangerous—but once they'd had the idea it was impossible to ignore. It was like a cannon already fired; something was bound to be broken, it was just a matter of what.

As he walked out of King's Cross station and looked down the Euston Road, Sam doubted his plan. It wasn't much of one anyway: go to the last place the blonde girl had been seen and look for something...weird. The television appeal from her family was still raw in his thoughts. If he hadn't been watching the news over breakfast he'd be at work now, perhaps even successfully putting the events of the last few weeks behind him and doing what the Sorcerer had ordered: not telling a living soul about his entanglement with the Fae, and getting back to his mundane life.

But he had seen it and recognised the blonde as one of the enslaved dancers in Exilium. Cathy had said there was nothing he could do but everything had changed since then. The Rose had been broken, that's what they said. Those people might be free, but trapped on the wrong side of the Nether.

He'd tried to call Cathy but the phone went straight to voicemail. She was probably in the Nether and he had no idea how to get there without the Sorcerer's help. He couldn't go to the police. What would he say? "Good morning, officer. Those missing blondes—the ones you didn't seem to notice were being kidnapped—are being held in a beautiful magical prison created for the Fae." Sam knew they'd either laugh at him or have him sectioned. Neither would help those people.

Sam wasn't entirely sure he was still sane. At least Leanne had left without being tangled up in it all. She'd already moved to London and he'd promised to join her as soon as he could arrange some time off work. He would never be able to tell her anything about what had happened to him and he wasn't sure their marriage could survive the strain.

Ultimately he would have to hand in his notice—if he wasn't sacked first—and move to London. He'd never really wanted to live in the Big Smoke, but since the trip to Exilium he'd lost all motivation for his job. Perhaps a change would be good for the marriage too.

Perhaps he needed therapy.

He walked past the British Library with the slow pace of a lost tourist. He looked up at the higher floors of the huge buildings and down into the drains and gutter. What did he expect to find? A lock of blonde hair? A rose petal? A convenient note detailing instructions for the kidnappers?

"You twat," he whispered to himself. "What the arse are you going to do anyway?"

He headed back towards the station, thinking it might be best to abandon his childish attempt at heroics and go and visit Leanne at the apartment. He hadn't even seen it and he was supposed to be moving in soon.

Waiting at a set of traffic lights, he looked up at the huge hotel on the other side and then down the road he was about to cross. Surely they wouldn't take a girl anywhere near such a busy road? Perhaps they'd led her into a side street like the one he was looking down, away from the crowds and CCTV.

He crossed and turned left, keeping the hotel and station on his right. He'd never appreciated how far back King's Cross stretched. He passed dozens of waiting taxis and decided to do a circuit of the area immediately around the station. Further down Midland Road he was about to turn back when he saw greenery incongruous with the urban concrete around him. Remembering the intense green of Exilium's meadows he pressed on, finding a church set back from the road behind ornate iron gates.

The churchyard had been turned into a small park and Sam found its natural peace irresistible. He went through the gates and immediately felt better, as if the place had dropped a blanket around his shoulders to protect him against the quiet violence of the city. He strolled to an elaborate tomb, past an ornate blue drinking fountain and up to the church. He didn't go inside when he heard music coming from within, not wanting to interrupt anything, so he walked around the back and came across an oak tree with dozens of gravestones stacked at its base.

He stared at the way the roots had grown between the slabs until the stones and the tree looked like they'd always been one. There was probably a metaphor for life and death in there somewhere.

"Hello!"

He jumped and looked for the source of the high-pitched voice. It sounded like a—

"Down here!"

He crouched and peered into the dark crevice between two gravestones. A tiny face moved out of the shadow for a moment and then an equally tiny hand waved at him. It was the faerie from Exilium, the one who'd led him and Cathy to Lord Poppy.

"Bloody hell! What are you doing here?" he whispered. "I thought you guys were trapped in Exilium."

"We can come through in the oldest places, if we're very careful. How clever of you to come here."

"I had no idea…wait—what do you mean?"

"You want to come back, don't you? To Exilium?" When he nodded, it clapped its hands. "I'll take you. Close your eyes."

He hesitated. The first time he'd met one of them in Mundanus they'd Charmed the fuck out of his brain and practically ruined his life. The second time he met one, Cathy had walloped it with a plate. He was fairly certain this one was actually helpful in Exilium, but not certain enough.

"I promise I'm taking you into Exilium to help you," it said. "I won't take you anywhere horrid or turn you inside out."

Sam remembered the people he had to find. How else was he going to get there? He closed his eyes. There was a brief tickle on his left eyelid, then on the right, and his ears popped.

He was struck by a distinct change in air quality; the grim fumes he'd already become accustomed to in London had been replaced by the sweet scent of flowers.

"We're here!"

Sam opened his eyes. The blue of the sky made him ache for childhood summers, playing outside in seemingly endless sunshine, and the grass was so verdant it made him doubt he'd ever seen real grass before.

Then he remembered what Cathy told him: people could get lost there forever if they didn't stay focused. He looked at the faerie. "I don't suppose you've seen any blonde people here lately? They're from Mundanus."

The faerie flashed an excited smile. "Oh, yes! Would you like me to take you to them?"

"Yes! Brilliant!" Sam said, following as it set off. Maybe this heroic rescue thing wasn't going to be so hard after all.

Catherine sat in her nightdress. Her feet were cold; the slippers were still tucked neatly in their usual place just to the left of her bare toes. Leaden, she leaned back towards the welcoming divot her head had made overnight.

"Oh, no, you don't!" the maid dashed over to pull Cathy onto her feet. "Time to get up now, Miss Papaver! There's so much to do. The mistress said I need to wash you quick."

The nightdress was pulled off her and the sponge rubbed up and down her arms. Cathy watched the activity with complete detachment. "So much to do," the maid had said. That resonated.

"You must be so excited," the maid gabbled. Cathy wondered if she'd been talking all along and she just hadn't realised it.

She was about to ask why when the maid had already moved onto another subject. All she wanted to do was lie down and go back to sleep. Once she'd been washed and dried, an unfamiliar silk dressing gown was tied about her waist.

Cathy could feel a flutter of something unpleasant in her stomach. Had something bad happened? Was that why there was so much noise?

She could hear servants clattering up and down the stairs. The house was filled with the sound of orders being given and occasional shrieks from her sister down the hallway. The latter was nothing new.

"Come on, now," the maid said. She'd opened the door and was looking at her expectantly. Cathy assumed she wanted her to leave, but walking felt like a distant memory of something she once did to pass the time. "You're to be dressed in your mother's dressing room today."

"Why?" Cathy fought to form her lips around the word.

"It's tradition, isn't it?" The maid had resorted to pulling her along.

Again, that sense of something terrible, a long way away from where she was now. She felt a dull serenity as she watched maids carrying all manner of things up and down the stairs. One was running out of her sister's room in tears, a hairbrush flying out after her.

Then she was in her mother's dressing room. Aside from a huge mirror, the walls were filled with cupboards and wardrobes. A single red chaise-longue was positioned in the centre of the room.

Cathy was left looking at the pink glow lingering on her skin from the maid's earnest scrubbing. It was like looking at a painting of herself; she felt no connection to her reflection.

A woman bustled in with two assistants and, after a liberal application of talcum powder, Cathy found herself in the midst of efficient dressing. When she was in silk hose and bloomers, chemise and corset, her mother entered, wearing a blood-red dress with large black buttons. Her sister was close behind, hair half pinned up, a nervous maid trailing after her with a basket of hair clips and other accessories.

"You look well rested," Mother said.

Elizabeth sat on the chaise-longue. She was wearing a dressing gown over her underwear, judging from her tiny waist. "Now for goodness' sake get it right!" she said to the maid after taking the basket from her. She picked out a hairpin and passed it to the girl, whose hands were trembling. "What are you staring at?" Cathy realised she'd lost track of herself again.

"Now, now, dear," Mother said, inspecting her own hair in the mirror. "Today is the one day you have to be particularly nice to Catherine."

"Already? I thought that was once we leave the house."

"Elizabeth." Mother gave her a look that ended Elizabeth's pout.

"Once my hair is pinned I want you to tighten my lacing, Mama, you're so much better at it. I want to make Imogen look like an elephant next to me. And I need a new lady's maid, mine is hopeless."

Imogen. Imogen Reticulata-Iris. William's sister. Just the thought of him made that distant flutter spike into a brief burst of something bright and sharp.

"I think I…I was going to do something." Cathy realised she'd spoken aloud when her mother came over.

"You don't need to do anything except stand there and be dressed." She looked into Cathy's eyes as if checking that a long-lost cat was still missing. "Elizabeth, did you eat anything at breakfast?"

"I had a small cup of tea and not a morsel of food. I'd rather faint than be too full for a tight lacing, Mama. Catherine slept too late to join us. I expected you to be up before the rest of us today."

"Why?" Cathy asked, but Elizabeth was too busy slapping at the maid's hand for jabbing a pin into her scalp.

"Are you ready for your dress, Miss Papaver?" The woman was familiar, but it took her a few moments to place her as the dressmaker. "Are you feeling all right?"

"She's fine," Mother said. "Start dressing her now."

Cathy was guided, pulled and pushed into a heavy embroidered gown. It was white. She stared at it in the mirror as the tiny buttons were done up the back. Its crystal beads glinted in the sprite light. Through her muddied thoughts, two facts bubbled slowly to the surface: it was a wedding dress, and this was very, very wrong.

"Is she going to faint?" the dressmaker said as Cathy swayed.

"No." Mother took hold of Cathy's arm and clasped her hand tight.

"I had to do something," Cathy said, trying to shake off the wooliness. "I had to—"

"Hush now, dear." Mother patted her hand. "You're just a little lightheaded, that's all, it's perfectly natural."

Elizabeth came over and looked into her eyes. "Oh, Mother, look at her. She can't get married like that. Did you give her poppy milk?"

"Just so she would have a good night's sleep." Mother's smile was more smug than compassionate. "We'll make sure she's bright and wide awake when she needs to be. Now let me see to your lacing whilst they pin Catherine's hair. The carriage will be here soon."

As Cathy was steered to the seat, she remembered she'd intended to tear the bed sheet into strips and escape from the window of her bedroom. She wasn't supposed to be getting married, she finally realised, but the thought was as slippery as a melting icicle. Her eyelids drooped and she found it hard to keep her head up. Nap first, escape later, she thought. There would be time. There was always time for sleep.

Max watched Axon stitch the incision closed as Petra peeled off the latex gloves covered in the dead Arbiter's blood. In the silence of the cloister the only sounds had been those of the autopsy. Both Petra and Axon were clearly shaken by what they'd seen but

Max's emotions were safely locked away in the gargoyle back at the Sorcerer's house.

The Sorcerer came to the doorway holding a handkerchief over his nose and mouth. "All done?"

"Yes, Mr Ekstrand, all done," Petra replied, taking off the apron and washing her hands in a nearby basin of water. "Once Axon has finished, I suggest we repair to the house."

"Good idea," Ekstrand replied. "What are your initial impressions?"

Max could see Petra's hands trembling with fatigue. She'd been working solidly for two long days. Axon had noticed it too. "Perhaps that would be better discussed over a cup of tea, sir," he suggested, tying off the thick black thread.

"I'll open a Way," Ekstrand said. "Thank you for your hard work. An admirable activity for a Thursday, wouldn't you agree?"

"Indeed, sir." Axon pulled off his gloves. "I'll see to everything back here once refreshments have been served." That earned a grateful smile from Petra.

They left the cool sterility of the healing room at the cloister and walked straight through into Ekstrand's hallway. Petra excused herself, Axon promised tea and Ekstrand paced impatiently as Max hobbled to the sofa in the living room.

The gargoyle was upstairs and Max knew it was hiding from the gruesome task of discovering what had killed everyone in the Bath Chapter. Max assumed it was feeling unsettled, as his own emotional reaction to the autopsy was bound into the stone through the soul chain round the gargoyle's neck.

Ekstrand poked at the fire. "How's the leg?"

"Healing well, thank you, sir," Max said.

"Splendid, splendid. I spoke with the Master of Ceremonies this morning, whilst you were at the cloister. He's much better than when you first found him. He couldn't speak for long. His niece is getting married today."

"The puppet who helped us?"

"Was that her? I have no idea. Perhaps, although he has more than one niece. He's very happy to have his house back, even though he won't be able to use it in the same way again, of course."

"And what exactly did he use it for?"

"Secret meetings with his lovers. It seems the sister gets jealous. Strange bunch, the Fae-touched."

"Yes, sir." Max tried to flex his foot, as having the broken leg resting on a footstool was giving him pins and needles. A dull ache where the titanium pins and plates had been secured felt like it had set in for the day.

"Sorry to keep you waiting, sir," Petra said as she entered wearing different clothes. "Max, the gargoyle can read!"

"You didn't give it any of my books did you?" Ekstrand was half out of the chair before she had a chance to reply.

"Of course not. I gave it one of mine."

"*Wuthering Heights*," Max said as a sudden image of the title page popped into his mind.

She blinked at him. "You know it's creepy when you do that?"

"It houses his soul, of course he knows," Ekstrand said. "Petra, once we've discussed your findings I want to practise what one should say on hearing that a niece has recently married."

"All right." She had her notebook and pen and sat on the nearest armchair as Axon arrived with the tea. As Ekstrand was distracted by the impending refreshments, she leaned towards Max. "The gargoyle liked the sound of it. It almost went for *The Count of Monte Cristo*."

"It is Lapsang Souchong, isn't it, Axon?" At the butler's nod Ekstrand said, "I'll pour."

He handed a cup of tea to Max. "Lavandula told me that if we hadn't intervened, the Roses would have broken him and returned him corrupted. Before we could say, 'More Battenberg, please' they'd have used him to wheedle their way onto the Aquae Sulis Council and shut me out. That reminds me, where's the cake?"

"Here, sir," Axon said, bringing in a large plate stand. "Lemon drizzle cake sir, as requested."

"Did I really ask for that? Pop it down and give everyone a

slice, there's a good fellow. Now, let's discuss the details from the autopsies."

Petra flipped back a few pages. "The results are…unusual," she said after a few moments, and then took a slice of cake from Axon gratefully. "They all died from the same cause: their hearts were turned to stone."

Ekstrand's cake didn't reach his mouth. "I beg your pardon?"

"The hearts were literally turned to stone. We carried out ten autopsies including the two Arbiters, the Chapter Master and three of the people who had thorns growing out of them, plus four selected at random. Previous to the…incident all were in good health. They were taken from different parts of the cloister, so I think it's a reasonable assumption that everyone died from the same…ailment."

Ekstrand rested the fork and its morsel of cake back on his plate. "Maximilian thinks the mutual murders were staged. Would you agree with that?"

She nodded. "Yes. No one was strangled, and the angles of the knife wounds and the force applied don't match up with the people who were supposed to look like the assailants. I'll compile the details of those observations in my report. I believe they collapsed when their hearts were changed. They would have had a very short period of consciousness, whilst the blood in their brains was oxygenated, but then they would have died in a manner similar to a person having a heart attack. I can't imagine how it must have felt." Her voice wavered and she cleared her throat. "That's speculation, of course."

"This is most disturbing." Ekstrand picked up the fork again. "Do you think they all died at the same time?"

"As far as I can tell, yes. It's not possible to work out exactly when. It would explain why no one raised the alarm."

"What in the Worlds could change their hearts to stone?" Ekstrand wondered aloud.

"It doesn't sound like Fae magic," Max said.

"This is unlike anything the Fae would be able to do, even if they wanted to," Ekstrand replied. "I thought the Rose magic picked up by the Sniffer was a causal factor. Now I'm not sure. Perhaps it just grew the thorns."

"It seems a seed was forced down their throats after death and then grown, rather than a stem being forced in to choke the individual," Petra said.

"Hardly justifies the amount of Rose magic detected," Ekstrand muttered.

"Could a Sorcerer do it?" Max asked the question, seeing it as another tick in the column under "Sorcerer of Essex corrupt".

"No," Ekstrand replied without hesitation. "It's simply impossible."

"Couldn't a formula be written on the building and affect everything within it?"

"Maximilian," Ekstrand said, "your skills, whilst admirable, do not extend to sorcery. Formulae require exact definition of variables and parameters. Each person's heart would have subtle differences making it impossible to work one formula that could affect every single person's heart at exactly the same time."

"Even if it were defined by the common variables?" Petra asked. "Couldn't all of the hearts be expressed as the organ that pumps blood with four chambers, four valves—"

Ekstrand shook his head. "Far too vague. This is simply an impossible thing to achieve with either Fae or sorcerous magic. It is truly inexplicable."

"We'll carry on investigating," Petra said. "There must be a critical piece of information we're missing."

Ekstrand nodded. "We need to be thorough, that much is true. Every single body needs to be autopsied and tested for any other trace magic. I'd also like to have a go at one myself. It is Thursday after all."

Petra fidgeted. "I'm not sure this is the best time, Mr Ekstrand. There's so much to do. I can refer you to an excellent book on pathology."

"Jolly good." Ekstrand smiled and finally took a bite of the cake. "Excellent, Axon, excellent. Not too sweet, just enough tang to the lemon."

"Thank you, sir."

"The only clear lead we have is the Rose magic," Ekstrand said. "No one could replicate that residue."

"Perhaps a Sorcerer could," Max said. "It all points to the Sorcerer Guardian of Essex. The corruption is in his territory, and when—"

"Remind me about what happened in London," Ekstrand said, sliding a second slice of cake onto his plate.

"I was shot whilst collecting evidence, sir. They were turning a blind eye to kidnapping an innocent in broad daylight."

"Ah, that's how your leg got broken and your soul ended up in the gargoyle, yes, I recall it now. And they knew you had a deep connection open and the Chapter Master could see what you were witnessing, am I right?"

"Yes, sir, which is why I think the Sorcerer of Essex is responsible. To cover it up."

Ekstrand shook his head. "It makes no sense. Why make it look like the Roses are involved?"

"Maybe they were," Petra said. "Just not in killing them."

"We're definitely missing something," Max said. "They drop dead when someone or something turns their hearts to stone, someone arranges their bodies to make it look like they killed each other and then works some powerful Rose magic that only results in a few stems? It doesn't add up."

For a while, the only sounds were the crackling of the fire and Ekstrand's chewing.

"Just because the corruption in London is in Dante's territory, it doesn't logically follow that he is behind the destruction of our Chapter," Ekstrand said. "It may be that a third party has found a way to infiltrate the Chapters, thereby corrupting Dante's and destroying mine. If that's the case, no one is safe. And all indications are that the Roses are the infiltrators. Even if we don't know how those hearts were turned to stone, we know there was Rose magic used in the cloister, and that they're being given free rein in one of London's wards."

"They are the common element," Max agreed.

"I suppose Lady Rose is difficult to speak to at the moment," Petra said.

"I'll have to petition the royal family to interrogate her and the Brothers Thorn, but given the circumstances it shouldn't be too difficult," Ekstrand replied. "I'll do that tomorrow. Always better to deal with Fae royalty on a Friday, I find. And the wheels are in motion with regards to the moot with the other sorcerers. When I'm there I'll be able to gauge if Dante is aware of the corruption in his Chapter or not."

"Is there any way we can keep an eye on things in London?" Max asked.

"Too risky," Ekstrand said. "We don't have the resources to monitor things in any subtle manner, and we can't risk Dante finding out you're there, nor the Arbiters who tried to kill you."

"And what about the Chapter?" Max asked. "Are you going to rebuild it?"

"When I know exactly what happened to the last one," Ekstrand said, picking crumbs off his plate. "And not a moment before. Terribly tiring, I recall, building a Chapter and training a Master. Definitely not something for Tuesdays or Thursdays. Or Sundays for that matter. Now, Petra, I need to practise what to say to the Master of Ceremonies on his next visit when he mentions the wedding. I was planning on commiserating with him and offering a slice of something. I had thought a nice Victoria sponge, but now I think lemon drizzle cake, and perhaps a handkerchief. Dreadful business, weddings, dreadful. What do you think?"

Petra set down her notebook and picked up her cake plate. "I think we'll work on it, Mr Ekstrand."

2

Will sipped his morning tea and thought of Amelia Alba-Rosa instead of the woman he was marrying in less than two hours. Not that Amelia was an Alba-Rosa anymore; now she and her brother would be known as Amelia and Cornelius White. He wondered how well she was recovering from the trauma of the Sorcerer's revelations and the destruction of their place in Society. She and Cornelius would be back in Londinium by now, waiting at the house they'd always lived in. Now their home belonged to him.

"Another cup, Will?" Nathaniel asked as he poured his own tea. His brother was in better spirits than usual, which had surprised Will, seeing as he'd missed the opportunity to duel with Horatio Gallica-Rosa. Then he realised the good mood was for that very reason: Nathaniel was now seen as the best swordsman of his generation and he hadn't even needed to lift a blade to achieve it.

"No, thank you," Will replied.

"I wonder where Horatio is now," Imogen said. The Gallica-Rosas were on the minds and lips of everyone in Aquae Sulis.

We were only obeying our Patroon. How can this be happening? Horatio Gallica's words had transformed him, from a hateful, arrogant man hell-bent on ruining his fiancée's reputation, into a pawn on the losing side. If the Iris Patroon had ordered such behaviour Will knew he would have obeyed, just as Horatio had, and the thought haunted him.

"To think I actually danced with him," Imogen said.

"To think you hoped to marry him," Nathaniel said, stirring sugar into his tea.

"I did not," Imogen replied. "I speculated about his potential as a spouse, nothing more."

"I saw you huff and puff every time Elizabeth Papaver danced with him."

"Dear brother, there is a world of difference between wanting to keep in the race and backing the wrong horse altogether. Surely you of all people understand that."

Nathaniel dropped the spoon onto the saucer with a clatter and fired a dark glare at Imogen, promising retribution at a later date. The ignorance of yet another family secret filled Will once more, but by the end of the day he'd be married and moving out of the family house and none of it would matter. The thought both delighted him and killed his appetite. If only he were leaving to set up home with Amelia. He couldn't imagine having breakfast with Catherine. What would they talk about?

At least his fiancée was more interesting than he'd thought. Catherine had successfully navigated a mundane through Exilium, carried out a secret spying mission for a Sorcerer and smuggled a sorcerous artefact into the most controversial party of the season. She was clearly capable in a crisis, so why was she so inept at the easiest aspects of life in Nether Society?

"Lost your appetite, Will dear?" Imogen was still glowing from having scored a point off Nathaniel. She reached across and patted his hand. "Perfectly understandable. I do hope they dress Catherine in something decent. Surely they could manage that for her wedding day. After all, it's the only day of that girl's life that everyone will be looking at her."

"By the end of the day she'll be your sister-in-law," Will reminded her.

Imogen withdrew her hand, her sharp smile fading. "How perfectly awful."

"Don't worry, old chap, she'll be veiled," Nathaniel chipped in.

"Yes, just pretend there's someone else under there when you're in front of the Oak." Imogen smirked. Will knew perfectly well who she meant.

Neither Nathaniel nor Imogen mentioned the Albas openly, probably some nod towards discretion on his wedding day. No doubt everyone in Aquae Sulis was speculating about why he'd saved Amelia and her brother from the Agency, and he knew what most of them were thinking of his motive. They were probably right.

"William," his father called from the doorway, "a word with you in my study."

His father was already dressed for the wedding. Will excused himself and followed him in.

"Good morning, Father." Will smiled, trying to give the best impression of a man ready to face his fate goodnaturedly.

"Close the door and sit down. We don't have much time and I need to talk to you about something important."

"Wisdom for married life?"

The stern glare burnt the cocky smile from Will's lips. "I've just spoken with the Patroon. Everything is ready at the Oak. I know you were pushing to marry Catherine Papaver sooner than planned. No doubt you were surprised when I told you the new date."

"A little. I assumed it was because Horatio's accusations against her went public." Will felt the muscles in his neck knotting. He'd worried that the marriage was happening far faster than a polite request from him and the threat of scandal could explain. He hadn't told his father the real reason behind his desire to marry sooner than the end of the season, because he didn't want anyone else to know about the beating Catherine had suffered. It wouldn't do anything except increase the chance of her being harmed again.

"Well, that's true, and now his accusations have been made public I'm glad we moved quickly. Hopefully everyone will be too busy gossiping about the fall of the Roses to remember what he said about her." He paused. "You're certain the purity opal remained white?"

"Positive," Will replied and wondered again whether it did change colour when he'd pressed it against her neck. Not that it would have changed the fact that he wanted to get her away from her father as soon as possible.

His father nodded, satisfied. "There's something else, William. Once you're married, the Patroon wants you to establish your residence in Londinium."

"Londinium?"

"You've impressed him, and with the Rosas being rounded up by the Agency and their control of the city lost, this is the perfect time to further our interests there."

"But surely this is something for one of your generation? Or Nathaniel, as the eldest?"

"The Patroon is not easily impressed, William, and neither am I. You handled the Rosa debacle with subtlety and quick wits, both of which will come in useful in Londinium. We want you to secure the Dukedom and bring the Court under our control."

Will sat back, feeling the knots reach down his body and into his stomach. The Dukedom? It was beyond ridiculous. "I…It was a bit of a coup revealing the Gallica-Rosa treachery but it doesn't exactly mark me out for Duke material. I couldn't have done it without the help of the Alba-Rosas; they warned me about Horatio."

"Horatio said the Albas were just as guilty as he. Tell me, did they really come clean with you? Or did you lie to save them?" When Will didn't immediately respond, his mouth twitched. "You wouldn't be the first man to lie for the sake of a woman."

"In all honesty, Father, I don't think it's as simple as Horatio claimed. I wouldn't be surprised if there was some truth in it, but I think Amelia and Cornelius genuinely came to like me and didn't wish me any harm. Amelia certainly did not do anything to jeopardise the engagement. On the contrary, she made an effort to be kind to Catherine."

"Cornelius has cooperated with my staff but I don't think you should ever trust him, or his sister. They could be useful to you, if you choose what you tell them with care and verify anything they tell you before acting upon it."

"Surely it's in their best interests to be trustworthy?"

Father raised an eyebrow. "It's in their best interests to please you. That's not the same thing in all situations. Never trust a

Rose, William, you know that. And remember, a mistress can be very expensive."

Will looked away, not wanting to discuss that with his father of all people. "I'm flattered, Father, but I can't see how that one evening could qualify me for such a task."

"You made excellent use of the information you uncovered, you kept calm and you managed the crowd magnificently. The Lavandulas have sent me letters expressing how impressed they are with you and have ensured there is a magnificent property waiting for you and Catherine. The Patroon's staff are making it ready for your arrival after the honeymoon."

"I had no idea the Lavandulas owned property in Londinium."

"They've acquired several impressive houses as compensation for the crimes committed against them."

"So the house once belonged to the Rosas?"

Father nodded. "Best not to think too much about that. Our people will make sure no traces of them are left behind."

"But—"

"This isn't a proposition, William. The decision has been made."

Will put aside his doubts and irritation. They wouldn't serve him now. "What support will I have to take the Dukedom?"

"A generous income, and the Patroon has assured me that should you need extra funds we will take care of that as a family. Do whatever it takes to impress the Great Families in Londinium. Lord Iris himself is behind this."

"The Patroon said that?"

"He said enough. You know the Patroon was pushing for this marriage. He's taking a greater interest in you. I don't need to tell you how important it is that you succeed, do I?"

"No, Father." Will said it in his most confident tone, but he knew the odds were more than stacked against him. "Do you think that Catherine is still the best choice, given this new remit?"

"Nothing has changed on that front," his father replied, standing up. "I'm sorry, William, the agreement is too entrenched to change now. You'll have to do all you can to bring her up to scratch, but Dame Iris will help too. She takes all new brides brought into the family under her wing to make sure they know what's expected of them."

"Good," Will said, relieved. "I'm sure Catherine will be most grateful." He stood, needing what little time he had alone to consider what he faced. "I need to dress for the wedding."

His father stood too and reached across the table to shake his hand. "I'm proud of you, William. Don't let me down."

The faerie led Sam up a gentle hill, promising that the people he sought were very close. Just like before, exactly who he was looking for was on the other side. Four women and one man, all blonde, all looking dazed and horribly lost.

"Hey!" Sam waved from the top of the hill and they drew closer together fearfully. As he ran down the slope he could see the sparkling bands that had been around their ankles were gone.

"Who are you?" one of the women asked.

"Are you from home?"

"Can you help us?"

Sam grinned. "I'm here to rescue you." He'd always wanted to say that. "I live in Bath. I'm going to take you home, to your families." He scanned their faces, looking for relief and gratitude but seeing doubt and fear instead. "I'm like you, a mundane," he added.

"Have you got anything to eat?"

"I've got a packet of crisps and half a doughnut."

"We're starving," one of the women said.

He recognised her from the photo on the TV appeal. Her name was Clare and she was a model. They all were. It was probably why they were taken and why it hadn't bothered him that they were rather gaunt. He pulled his rucksack off his back and found the crisps.

"I wouldn't give those to them," the faerie said, zipping in between him and the others, who cowered away from it.

"Why not?"

"Don't believe anything they say!" the man said, snatching the bag of crisps from his hand and opening them. They closed around him like pigeons around crumbs.

In moments they were retching and spitting out lumps of chewed potato. The man threw the packet on the ground and the faerie dashed behind Sam. "You think that's some sort of sick joke?"

"I told you," the faerie whispered.

"Oh, no." Clare pointed to something behind Sam. "It's one of them."

Sam turned to see Lord Poppy strolling down the hill, swinging his black cane back and forth. He was exactly the same as the last time Sam saw him—long black hair and black eyes with skin like a lily petal—bringing back unwelcome memories of being licked in the ear and held by poppies as the Fool's Charm was broken. He wished Cathy was with him to step forward and handle it. He realised the models were hiding behind him instead.

"Ah! The little mundane my favourite brought to me! Did she send you back as a gift this time?"

"No, she did not!" Sam pressed against his wedding ring with his thumb. The last time they met he wasn't wearing it. "And before you try anything dodgy—" he thrust his left hand towards Poppy's face, fingers spread "—I'm protected by Lord Iron."

"How terribly exciting for you. Could you explain why that's relevant? Am I threatening your person?"

Sam lowered his hand, aware of the people cowering behind him as if he were the only thing protecting them from a rabid dog. "Um…"

"Irrelevant then, it seems. And it's such an ugly ring. Wouldn't you rather take it off and put it in your pocket so its ugliness isn't inflicted on everyone around you?"

Sam nodded, pulled it from his finger and did as Poppy suggested. He wondered why the people behind him were groaning.

Poppy's smile didn't seem to cheer them up. "Now tell me, has my faerie been helpful?"

The faerie fluttered next to Lord Poppy, giving Sam a hopeful smile. "Yeah."

"She brought you into Exilium, I understand."

"Yeah."

"And led you to these poor little waifs and strays."

"Yeah."

"And what do you plan to do with them? No one wants them. They're soiled now. They smell of the Rose. Never has a scent been so unfashionable."

"I'm going to take them home."

Poppy tittered and watched Sam for a moment. "You're telling the truth!" He flapped his free hand as the faerie accompanied his melodic laughter with its own soprano harmony.

"What's so funny? They were kidnapped!"

"But," Poppy said, dabbing at the corner of his eye with a slender finger, "they'll die if you take them back to Mundanus."

Sam glanced at the crisp packet at his feet. Would they be incapable of eating anything at home? Or was that something to do with being in Exilium? "We're willing to take the risk." He twisted to look at them. "Right?"

All of them nodded.

"So be it."

"And we're leaving now."

"So soon? But we've hardly had a chance to enjoy the day. It's a very special one. My favourite is being married to a very pretty boy." Sam had been certain Cathy had more time. "They moved the date," Poppy added. "She's captivated the Iris boy to the extent that he begged his father to marry them as soon as possible. Isn't that romantic?"

But she had been determined to find a way out. Sam jolted. That's what he needed to do! "We need to go now."

"Before we've settled my compensation?"

"Oh, no." Sam sighed. "Look, I told you—"

"Because it would be so dreadfully impolite to accept help from my faerie—twice—and simply leave without a token of your gratitude. Or rather two of them."

Sam folded his arms. "Like that time you took one of my memories?"

"Yes, but I don't want another. I took the one I liked the best, the rest are horribly dull. No, I want you to do two things for me, such easy tasks. It being my favourite's wedding day has filled me with generosity, it seems. You're lucky she likes you. Otherwise I would have cursed you to believe you'll die if you don't bray like a donkey and given you an irresistible urge to visit the ones you most want to impress in Mundanus."

"What do you want me to do?"

"Take a message to Catherine. That's all. And then in one month—or perhaps less—you're to deliver something to me."

"But I don't know how to find her."

"Then you'd better work it out. Otherwise I shall be displeased. Now, the message is this—and take care to recite it perfectly, otherwise your debt won't be paid." Sam nodded. "'Dear Catherine, Your friend accepted my help in Exilium. As payment, I require the painting you promised to me the last time he visited before the next Mundane new moon. It must contain an Iris secret. Your *true* patron, Lord Poppy.'"

"Hang on a minute!" Sam said. "You said my taking the message was payment, not her giving you a painting!"

"Ah, the painting is in return for not turning your fingers into hungry rats with a taste for your flesh. I think that's most generous."

Sam couldn't reply. He just blinked a few times, trying to drive the image from his mind. "OK…tell me the message again."

Poppy repeated it. Backwards. Sam's temples started to throb as the faerie giggled.

"Fine, I got it," he said, trying to sound confident. "Do I just take the painting to the church again?"

"No. That's such an inelegant way to bring my favourite's masterpiece. Simply stand in front of a mirror, say my name three times with the desire to come here and you'll be able to step through. Of course, should you wish to visit before then, or—" he looked pointedly at the people behind Sam "—bring me other gifts in return for saving certain doomed souls, you'll be quite welcome."

"OK. Thanks." He didn't want to thank him but he had to get at least one thing right. "We'll be off then."

"But how will you leave?" the faerie asked.

"You'll take me back, won't you?"

"Only if you give me something in return," Poppy said.

"Oh, for the love of...If you don't let us go, I can't give Cathy the message, can I?"

"I could find another way and give you an alternative compensatory task if you wish."

"No. No...I'll..." He looked at the faerie and at Poppy, understanding even more clearly Cathy's frustration with the Sorcerer and his unwillingness to help. He put his hands in his pockets in an effort to look relaxed and not at all panicky, and his fingers brushed the wedding ring. He clasped it tight, horrified he'd taken it off. "I'll find my own way out. Thanks." He started walking as Poppy laughed. "Come on then!" he called back to the others and they followed him.

"I'll join you," Poppy said. "A stroll before the wedding is just what I need. Do you know where you're going?"

Sam marched on but Poppy matched his pace effortlessly. "Out of Exilium."

"Oh, this is simply divine entertainment," Poppy breathed. "If only I could bottle it and save it for dull days. But Catherine would be upset if I rendered you into a few drops of hopeless optimism. I have no desire to upset her when I can't see it."

Sam tried to ignore him, pressing the ring painfully into the palm of his hand to keep his focus on it. There had to be a place he could get them out. Surely Exilium had a border?

"How long do you plan to walk? Your waifs look so dreadfully hungry. Poor little things. Perhaps I could take them in, I'll need something to play with after the wedding. I fear I might feel a little upset by the sight of my strange sunlit one becoming an Iris."

Sam had the urge to veer left. Was that Poppy, the faerie or something else? He slowly changed their direction and Poppy didn't seem to notice. He pressed on.

"Oh, look, over there is a patch of daisies in the shape of a teardrop. If you can guess what made it, I'll grant you a boon."

"No, thanks," Sam said. He was on to something, he could feel it.

"A missed opportunity is a dreadful thing. I could have given you the ability to know a woman's desire. Or a man's, should you wish it."

Sam shook his head. "Not far now," he said to the others. Then he saw something ahead: a huge pillar driven into the earth, the grass around it yellowed and coarse. A fogbank hung in the air on the other side of it as far as he could see, so dense the ground seemed to stop where it began, as if forming the edge of Exilium. The pillar looked like it was made of iron with copper bands riveted around it and was about six feet tall. It was covered in symbols and things that looked like algebraic equations written by an insane mathematician. Several thick iron chains ran from the top of the pillar and disappeared into the ground.

Poppy had also stopped and planted his cane in the ground. "Well, I need to go to the wedding now," he said, turning slightly so the shape up ahead would be out of his sight. "I look forward to your delivery—whichever one it may be. Time for you to leave."

He pushed Sam backwards with the tip of his cane, so hard it hurt. The panic of falling made his arms pinwheel and seemed to go on for longer than it should. There was a horrible pop in his ears, a brief pain in his sinuses and his stomach rose up like he'd fallen several metres instead of onto his backside.

One second he saw blue sky as he tipped back and the next a white ceiling. His hands sank into a deep pile rug and there was the scent of cologne. Before he could even take in the room Clare landed next to him and then the others, as if they had fallen through an invisible hole in the ceiling. One of them landed on a chaise-longue, the rest on the rug next to Sam.

"Good God!"

A man in his sixties was on the other side of the room with a butler tying a bit of white cloth around his neck like a weird tie.

Poppy's faerie appeared next to the older man and whispered in his ear as the servant came over and pulled Sam to his feet.

"Oh...I see," the man said. "Well...where should I send them?"

The faerie whispered something back and a twitch at the corner of the man's mouth made Sam nervous. He nodded and went to the door leading out of the room as the others were pulled onto their feet, just as disoriented as he felt.

"This way," the man said, opening the door and gesturing for them to go through. Sam couldn't see a room on the other side, just a haze.

"Where does it go?"

"Home," he said. "I have a wedding to go to. Will you please hurry along?"

Sam wondered if they were in the Nether, as the Sorcerer's house was, so he looked out of the window. The familiar silver mists confirmed his suspicion. "Come on," he said to the others. "We need to go. And I think we should all hold hands, in case something weird...I mean *more* weird happens." They did as he asked. Clare slipped her hand into his to join them together.

Wanting it to be over as soon as possible, he ran out of the room. His ears popped again, there was a rush of cold air and he found himself—and mercifully the others—in the central reservation of a motorway. It was dark and cold and he didn't have a clue where they were, but car fumes had never tasted so good.

3

The servants were lined up outside the house when the butler opened the front door. Everything was misty white through Cathy's veil. Her mother's hand cupped her elbow, steering her forwards, as Cathy's legs still felt as if they belonged to someone else. As they emerged, she saw the carriage waiting, decorated with red poppies, looking more like something to transport people to a war memorial in Mundanus. It seemed appropriate.

"Best wishes to you on your wedding day, Miss Papaver," the butler said with a bow.

"Health, wealth and happiness," the cook said, curtsying, and the same was repeated down the line.

The footman helped her into the carriage and her father was waiting inside. Once the train of the dress had been arranged under her mother's critical eye, the door was shut and there was a familiar lurch as the carriage pulled away.

Father was dressed in a black morning suit with a poppy-red waistcoat and one of the blooms buttonholed in the lapel. It suited him; the dark colours matched his black moustache and peppery hair. He wore his usual funereal expression as he took in her garb.

"You look very…nice," he finally said. Then he peered through the veil, studying her glassy eyes, and tutted. He lifted the gauze, which was edged with crystals, and planted a dry kiss in the centre of her forehead, whispering a few words as he sat back. A wisp of smoke reached towards his lips for a brief moment, then Cathy shuddered and felt like she expanded into her own body, as if she'd been dozing at the back of a room all morning.

"Take a few deep breaths," he said. "It takes a moment to wake fully."

She batted the veil up and away from her face, looking down at the white gown, taking it in properly for the first time. She could feel the crush on her chest of an impending panic attack, horrified that she'd been sleepwalking her way into the wedding day she desperately needed to avoid.

"You…you…" The terrible things she wanted to call her father were so plentiful she couldn't settle on one. "Sly, evil…"

"Don't say anything you may regret later, Catherine."

"How could you do this? You drugged me!"

"Your mother and I decided it was the best course of action."

"That doesn't make it right! My God, I knew you were both cold…evil people but this! Drugging your own daughter so—"

"Be quiet!" The commanding boom he'd perfected in the army was still with him. "I want to have a conversation with you, not sit here and be insulted. I could have waited until we arrived at the Oak to fully revive you, but I felt it was important we speak whilst we can."

"Am I supposed to be grateful?" She almost choked. Now she wasn't shouting, she could feel the anger trying to escape in tears but she was determined not to dissolve, and certainly not in front of him. The first and last time she'd broken down in his study he'd beaten her until she'd passed out.

"You have a choice, Catherine. Have a civil conversation with me now, and learn something in the process, or continue to demonstrate all of the qualities that have precipitated our treatment of you. If you insist on being rude, disrespectful and rebellious, you will be treated as a spoilt, worthless child with no sense of duty or honour. Which will it be?"

Cathy permitted herself one moment of fantasy, in which she punched him squarely in the face and shouted all the things that burned in her chest, then forced herself to think strategically. He was right: she did have a choice, just not the one he offered. She could rant and vent all her fury, or she could start looking for a way out.

"That's better," he said, interpreting her silence as a victory. "Now, I've been giving this journey a great deal of thought over the past day or so. It's the last time you'll be in my care. After today, another man and another family will be responsible for your wellbeing."

She sucked in a breath to cool the scream building in her throat. In less than thirty seconds he'd unknowingly summed up one of the roots of her rebellion: the idea that she was nothing but a delicate piece of property.

"As such," her father continued, "I felt I should say a few things to you that I have neglected to over the years. I'm a man of few words, as you know."

You prefer violence, she wanted to snap at him, but she kept that inside too.

"I confess I've struggled to comprehend your behaviour. It started early on, when you simply refused to delight in the things that all little girls like. You have a stubborn streak that is most unbecoming and, frankly, I had no idea it would result in the despicable way you ran away and hid from us for so long."

"You made your disappointment perfectly clear to me when I was brought home."

"I haven't finished. And you're doing it again. Just listen." He paused, waiting to see if she'd acquiesce. She focused on expressing all her hatred in her silent glare. "You know I've been angry with you, on many occasions. I simply could not understand why you continuously rejected every effort we made to give you the very best life. Dresses, dolls, the best dancing and singing teachers, all manner of things your sister adored, you threw back at us and simply refused to even try."

"That's not true. I did try to do all those stupid things you wanted and I can't! I'm just not made that way."

"You can't even speak in a civil manner." He shook his head. "I'm constantly ashamed that I have failed to make you into an accomplished young lady. We are so very lucky that events have transpired to make this marriage happen, otherwise I have no idea what would have become of you."

Her fists were clenched so tight Cathy feared she'd split her knuckles. She took a breath but he held up a hand.

"I haven't finished. Your lack of gratitude and your supreme lack of appreciation for the privileges you have enjoyed astound me. I have seen people suffer, Catherine, really suffer in the most unimaginably awful situations, and to see you pouting and refusing to participate and even be courteous when you have such a blessed life quite frankly disgusts me."

She looked away, feeling a sharp stab of truth in his words.

"I realised last night that one of the other reasons you have infuriated me so is..." He paused, and she looked back to see him searching for the right words in a way she'd never witnessed before. "...is because I believe we're far more alike than I've ever wanted to admit."

She gawped at him. "Really?"

"You know very little about me. You've never expressed any curiosity. I thought it might interest you to know that when I came of age and was presented to the Patroon to make my request, I too did not ask for what my parents expected of me."

Cathy blinked, unable to imagine even a shred of rebellion in the stilted, repressed rod of a man that was her father. She remembered his rage when she'd asked to go to university instead of the shallow beauty or grace Charm her mother had pressed for. He'd never once let it slip that he'd done the same.

"What did you ask for?"

"To fight in the First World War."

"But I thought that was a tradition for Rhoeas-Papaver men—to be in the army, I mean."

"The First World War was seen as too dangerous for active service. It was very different, what with the Gatling guns mowing down the officers in such numbers. Our family has served in many military campaigns over the ages, when our interests were under threat, or when some young blood wanted a taste of glory, but no one was permitted a commission when they saw what was happening in the trenches."

"But you wanted to go out there?"

"I turned twenty-one in 1916. I was desperate to get out there and give the Hun a damn fine kicking, but the pater said no. So I asked the Patroon, and he had to say yes."

Cathy saw a spark of something in his eyes that she'd thought impossible: spirit. "Were they angry with you?"

"Furious. Got a beating, but I took it. No doubt something will be said about it today."

Cathy remembered the wedding. There would be family there, her grandparents right back to her great-great-great-grandparents, possibly older. She didn't bother to keep track as they'd never shown any signs of being interesting. But having heard her father speak, she wondered if that assessment was correct. Perhaps they all hid their interesting quirks too well. Even though it was intriguing, she still didn't want to be there.

"If you knew what it's like to have to ask for something you need to do, even when everyone else says no, why were you so hard on me?"

He frowned as he considered her question. "I wondered that myself, I must confess. I realised it was because you asked for something selfish. I wanted to defend Albion, and England. I wanted to risk my life in a noble cause. You just wanted to rebel."

"Not for the sake of it!" Cathy realised he saw her as nothing more than a horrible child; he had no idea what it had been like for her. "You say I threw stuff back in your face but every time I tried to explain you hit me. Mother thought I kept messing up my embroidery deliberately but I was just rubbish at it. And then she'd tell you and then you'd beat me again. What was I supposed to do?"

"Take it on the chin," he replied, as if he were talking about being gently teased. "Try harder. It's your duty to represent your family in the best way you can."

Try harder. In the early days she did try so hard to please them but she gave up when she realised there was no way to be the child they wanted. Miss Rainer's lessons had increased the gulf between them by giving her other things to aspire to and revealing how stagnated Nether Society's attitudes were in comparison to Mundanus. "All this duty crap is just a way to control people, and keep control. If I'd been born in Mundanus—"

"You were not," he cut in. "You were born into one of the most respected families in Aquae Sulis. Why not accept your life and your role in Society?"

"But you didn't accept it when your father told you not to fight in the war."

He pursed his lips. "That's completely different. You're about to marry into one of the most wealthy and powerful families in Albion. You'll never want for anything, you'll have security for yourself and your children, respect in Society—if you don't destroy that with your wilful behaviour."

"But I don't even want children!"

He paled. "Catherine, that is the wish of every woman."

She wanted to drum the seat of the carriage with her fists but she wasn't going to waste her first opportunity to try and make him understand where she was coming from. "Just because women are capable of giving birth it doesn't make that the only thing we should aspire to. There are women in Mundanus who run successful businesses, who lead countries! Powerful, accomplished women doing amazing things, and you just want to trade me like a piece of bloody porcelain!"

"There's no speaking to you." He looked out of the window, though there was nothing to see except the mists of the Nether.

"You just can't handle it when I say things you don't want to hear and can't beat me for it."

She watched him struggle with his anger. Eventually he sighed, closing his eyes. "Catherine, this isn't just me, it's what Society expects of you, and what our patrons demand of us. I have always said that your wishes are irrelevant because there is no getting away from the fact that Lord Poppy has decided this marriage will happen.

You should be grateful your fiancé had the foresight to request an earlier date."

"Will wanted to marry sooner?" Cathy couldn't understand it.

"Yes, and Lord Iris himself must have sanctioned moving the date. I can't see any other way the Oak would be available, and everything arranged with such short notice. You gave us no choice but to accept. We had to make sure this happened, by whatever means necessary. I don't enjoy forcing you into this, Catherine. I'm simply doing my duty."

"But there must be a way to—"

"Enough! Turn all this energy into planning how you will make William happy, or I warn you, Catherine, he could make your life most miserable indeed. Any talk of avoiding this marriage is utterly futile."

"I managed to make a life in Mundanus and people would say that's impossible. It's not a crime to not want to marry a man I hardly know!"

"You think your mother and I knew each other? We met on two occasions before we were married, the first at a garden party, the second at our engagement ball. You've been infected by some romantic ideas from Mundanus. It just isn't like that here. We do things the way they've always been done, and I will not risk my entire family's honour just because you refuse to toe the line."

"Toe the line? This is slavery by another name!"

"That's it, if you—"

A flash of red at the window distracted them. One of Poppy's tiny faeries, in the same red petal dress as the last time Cathy saw her, was tapping on the glass.

Father knocked loudly on the roof of the carriage and the driver halted the horses. The door was opened and the faerie fluttered inside, clapping her hands joyfully at the sight of Cathy's dress.

"Oh! It's so exciting!" She twisted in the air to look at Cathy's father. He knocked on the roof to start the carriage again once the door was shut. "Are you the favourite's father?"

"I am." He inclined his head respectfully.

"What do you want?" Cathy asked, a thousand awful possibilities coming to mind with little effort.

"Lord Poppy wanted to make sure you looked perfect."

"That's very thoughtful of him," Father said.

"He said that when he sees his favourite arrive, he wants to weep bitter-sweet tears."

"Lord Poppy is at the Oak?" Father asked as Cathy felt nauseous.

"And Lord Iris!" The faerie pirouetted in the air. "That's why Lord Poppy sent me. Now close your eyes and I'll make sure he isn't disappointed."

"Have you ever met any Fae royalty?" Ekstrand asked.

Max shook his head. "No, sir."

"Well, it should be an education to you then. Do you have all you need?"

"Yes, sir."

"Then let's be off."

Using his silver-tipped cane, Ekstrand opened a Way from the ballroom to a familiar mundane field, the one where he and Axon had picked up the puppet after she'd been left there by the Censor of Aquae Sulis. It was early in the morning and the sun hadn't risen high enough to evaporate the dew off the grass or burn off the mist. Max took a deep breath of the fresh air as the Sorcerer then opened a Way into Exilium. He had not wanted to risk opening one directly from his house.

The mundane grass looked grey compared to the sun-soaked meadow Max saw through the opening. He stepped through first, checked that no Fae or faeries were nearby and then beckoned to Ekstrand to follow. Ekstrand closed the Way behind him, whispered something beneath his breath and struck the earth with the cane. Max felt the ground vibrate, like a little shockwave had rippled out from it, and the grass bent as if flattened by a brief gust of wind.

"Let's bring one of them here," Ekstrand said, adjusting his cape. "I have no desire to traipse across the prison, and the beauty of the Palace would be lost on you anyway. Besides, it's always good to remind them of the pecking order, wouldn't you agree?"

"Yes, sir," Max replied.

"Especially on a Friday," Ekstrand added.

Max leaned on his walking stick while Ekstrand only rested his hand lightly on his cane. The sun was gentle but Max adjusted the brim of his hat so he could see all around them without squinting. They were standing at the top of a hill. There was nothing but meadow and blue sky, a warm breeze and trees in the distance. He remembered victims talking about how Exilium looked like a dream of a perfect place, too colourful to be real. For Max, immune to such things, it looked like it could be anywhere in the Cotswolds.

Ekstrand was scowling. "I must raise this at the Moot. It's too pretty here. Damnable Fae."

Max was about to ask what he meant when a figure came into view, climbing the rise of the hill steadily, clearly one of the Fae. He was tall, slender, like they all were, dressed in a tail-coat and trousers, cut somewhat like those Ekstrand wore. He wore a circlet of oak leaves instead of a top hat, however, and his cape looked like it was woven from thousands of oak leaves, reaching down to the ground and spilling behind him for many metres.

"Only the Prince?" Ekstrand sniffed. "I'm insulted."

"Good day to you, Sorcerer of Wessex, King of the lands between the Tamar and the Arun, the Severn and the dividing sea, holder of the plains of Avalon and Salisbury, keeper of Avebury and Stonehenge and the ancient southern forest."

Max knew he would be ignored; the Fae found it impossible to see Arbiters as people. The Prince gave him the briefest glance, presumably to check he wasn't about to throw a copper net over him. The Prince's eyes were a vibrant green, no discernible pupil, iris or humour, just green. His hair was the colour of polished oak, rippling in long waves down his back.

"Is the King too busy to answer my summons?" Ekstrand made no effort to disguise his irritation.

"The King sent me, knowing you would wish to discuss the recent events in your domain. I am personally overseeing the matter and was judged to be of more help to you."

"I want to speak to Lady Rose."

"I'm afraid that's impossible," the Prince said with a smile.

"I beg your pardon?"

"She's being punished." The Prince spread his hands. "It's what you wished, is it not?"

"I left that to the King and Queen to decide. I merely made them aware of her crimes."

"And they were of such severity that she's been stripped her of her status, and her influence in the Court and the Nether destroyed. We can assure you, with confidence, that she and her brothers are unable to interfere with Aquae Sulis now."

Max studied the Prince's face, the soft voice, the smile that never left him. He could understand Lady Rose's status suffering as a result of the embarrassment of being escorted away from her own party by an Arbiter, but to strip her and her brothers of everything, even dominion over their own puppets, seemed more than merely harsh. It was disproportionate.

"I should imagine Lady Lavender was furious," Ekstrand said. "I had no idea the royal family cared so much for appeasing her."

The Prince remained silent, the gentle smile still present.

"However, I cannot imagine how an audience with me would interfere with Rose's punishment," Ekstrand continued. "On the contrary, I should imagine it would only deepen her misery. I want her brought to me at once."

"As I said, dear Sorcerer, that's not possible. But as soon as her punishment is over, I will gladly escort her to you. Personally."

"When will that be?"

"I cannot imagine it taking any longer than three mundane years."

"That isn't acceptable." Ekstrand twisted the cane in his irritation.

"That isn't negotiable," the Prince said. The Sorcerer's growing anger didn't seem to concern him at all. "I'm sorry if it's an inconvenience, but may I remind you that the treaty of the Split Worlds merely gives you permission to keep us from Mundanus. It doesn't extend to your making demands of our royalty when the matter in hand doesn't concern any innocents. This is, as you would say, an internal matter. Lady Rose is one of our own and we are punishing her ourselves. You have no right to interfere with that."

Ekstrand's lips were nothing more than a thin line. Max knew he wouldn't be able to push it further; to do so would reveal there was more at stake than he could risk the Fae royal family discovering. That, and the fact the Prince was correct. Ekstrand had the right to use Arbiters to keep the Fae out of Mundanus, and the right to stop any actions on their part that could lead to the kidnapping, death or exploitation of an innocent. Nothing more.

"I'll remember this," Ekstrand said.

"I'm sure you will," said the Prince. "As will I. I recall every conversation we have ever had, Sorcerer of Wessex, every slight, every demand, every wound. Whatever business you have with the Rose will have to wait. In the meantime it may be of benefit to you to watch the Irises. I understand they're powerful in your domain."

"The Irises have never been any trouble," Ekstrand said. "Unlike some of your people, they understand the need to obey the treaty and stay in the Nether."

"But a stone thrown in the Nether has ripples in Mundanus, dear Sorcerer, you know that. The Rose is destroyed, her power broken. Look to the Irises if you want to worry about a family's influence. Now our business is concluded, I bid you good day."

Ekstrand said nothing as the Prince walked away. Once the Fae was out of sight he opened a Way back into the mundane field and then another into the ballroom once he was sure no one else was there.

"No right to interfere," he muttered to himself as he unhooked the cape at his throat and left the room.

Max followed him and was about to ask for his orders when Petra intercepted them in the hallway.

"Mr Ekstrand, I was checking the data in the monitoring room when I noticed this." She handed him a piece of paper. "I thought you should know."

Ekstrand scanned it and clicked his tongue. "I told you we should have killed him." He turned to Max. "That mundane, the one who was Charmed, he's been back to Exilium. Unescorted. See to him would you?"

Cathy and her father rode the rest of the way to the Oak in silence once the faerie had gone. It was impossible for Cathy to tell whether the magic had done something spectacularly awful or wonderful; her father was inscrutable.

The lack of scenery made the silence unbearable. Every minute she came up with an argument to present, but then a predictable counter-argument surfaced just as quickly. Then she realised he would never help her get out of it, and the chances of escape had diminished to near zero. Two Fae lords were going to be there and both were highly motivated to see the marriage take place.

But she couldn't just give in and she refused to accept it was the end of her hope for freedom. Even if the worst happened, and there was no way to postpone the event and then escape before it could be rescheduled, she could still get away after they'd married. It could be worse, she thought, I could be marrying Ming the Merciless. Then the nervous giggling started, followed swiftly by the urge to cry.

"I understand it's natural for the bride to be nervous," her father said. "Just be brave, pay attention to when you have to speak and what you have to say, and the day will go smoothly, I'm sure of it."

"You make it sound easy."

"In many ways it is, Catherine."

She tried to imagine him as a rebellious young man. She failed. "Were you scared, when you went over the top in the war?"

He looked down at the carriage floor. "I was more angry than afraid."

"With the top brass?"

"No, my father."

Cathy frowned. "I don't understand."

"He Charmed me before I left. I didn't know about it until I first saw action. Made it impossible for me to be killed by bullets or small pieces of shrapnel. Of course, if I'd stepped on a mine, I'd have been done for, but it still did enough."

"I didn't think Charms like that existed."

"It was very powerful. He almost bankrupted the family and had to make a terribly serious bargain with Lord Poppy to get it."

"Why were you angry though? Surely it made it all a lot less scary."

He shook his head, he looked so saddened by her question. "It deprived me of true bravery. All of my men faced death with such courage, but I knew it was very unlikely I'd die out there. I felt like a fraud."

"So I suppose forcing me to marry someone is nothing compared to ordering men to their deaths."

"We all have our duties, Catherine. For some it is to fight and die for their country. For you it is to marry a man and guarantee our prosperity in Aquae Sulis and the favour of our patron."

What could she say to that? She kept her silence, exploring the world through her father's eyes. Finally, she really understood why he'd been so exasperated with her. "I'm sorry I'm not what you wanted me to be," she said, feeling the carriage slow down.

"Thank you." For the first time she could remember, he smiled at her. It made him look like a different man. "I'm sorry I didn't try to talk to you sooner. We're here. Hold your head up high, you look beautiful. And remember you'll always have Papaver blood, even when you have the Iris name."

She looked up, hoping the tears would spread out rather than fall. Her father reached across and pulled the veil back over her face as the carriage door was opened. He stepped out but she couldn't move.

She'd been to the Oak once before as a guest of a distant cousin's wedding. Cathy wondered if it was really as spectacular as she remembered. The tree was one of the oldest oaks in England and existed in Mundanus, the Nether and Exilium. As far as she knew, that was unique. In the Nether, a grand structure had been built around it where all of the marriages in the Great Families took place. In her memory it was cavernous and intimidating.

Father held out his hand to her and she knew this was it. She wondered whether tripping and gashing her face open or breaking her ankle would be enough to force postponement. When his hand clasped hers and he guided her firmly she realised the silliness of the idea.

The pale stone building was on the scale of a majestic cathedral but with an organic quality, like it had grown rather than been built. There were no visible joints between stone blocks; the Gothic archway door and the building around it appeared to have been shaped out of a single piece of stone. Only powerful Fae magic could make something so impossibly beautiful.

The doors were open. Cathy could hear something calm and lilting being played by a string quartet. In the silence of the Nether, and with the acoustics of the cavernous space, the murmur of the waiting guests also floated outside.

Her mother's carriage had arrived. She and Elizabeth emerged and the bridesmaid dress was duly fussed over. When they came over, their startled expressions told Cathy the faerie had done something noticeable at least.

"Oh, Catherine," her mother said. Was her expression…pride? Cathy couldn't be certain; she'd never seen it before. Glancing at Father, Mother asked "Did you…?"

"Lord Poppy sent a gift ahead," he replied. "I understand he and Lord Iris are inside."

"I think I shall faint," Elizabeth gasped.

"Don't be absurd." Mother gave Elizabeth a hard stare. "No dramatics today, Elizabeth. This is Catherine's day—yours will come soon enough."

"Oh, God," Cathy whispered as she saw Lord Poppy emerge, the faerie flitting about excitedly next to him.

Upon sighting her he clasped his hands theatrically over his heart and she saw a glittering tear roll down his cheek. "That's exactly what I wanted," he said, gliding towards her with outstretched hands as her family bowed and curtsied appropriately. "The bitterness of losing you, but the sweet pleasure of knowing you will be the perfect bride."

Cathy wanted to vomit and imagined heaving all over his immaculate morning suit.

"Thank you for your gift, my Lord," she made herself say, prompted by her father's glare as he straightened up.

"Only the first part." He swept the tear from his cheek with one of his long fingers. He kissed the sparkling droplet and it turned into a teardrop-shaped diamond.

Holding it delicately between thumb and forefinger, he pressed it against the base of her throat and she felt a tingle shoot around her neck. A tiny squeak slipped from Elizabeth's mouth.

"There," he said, pulling back, the diamond gone from his hand. "Now I will know where you are all day, so I don't lose you in the celebrations afterwards. I would hate to miss my opportunity to congratulate you."

She didn't miss the wicked glint in his eye. You bastard, she thought, reaching up to feel the diamond held on what felt like a chain no thicker than a strand of hair. You knew I wanted to bolt.

"Your generosity humbles us, Lord Poppy," her mother said.

"Oh, it's nothing." Lord Poppy smiled. "She is my favourite, after all."

"May I present my other daughter, Elizabeth, my Lord?" Father said.

"You're not at all like my favourite." Poppy sounded disappointed as he looked at Elizabeth. It was probably the first time her sister regretted that truth. "All of your prettiness is on the outside. Is there anything more interesting inside?"

Elizabeth, unused to her beauty being met with such uninterest, was unable to answer. "I play the piano," she managed to say.

"But do you allow the instrument to play you?" he asked. "I

fear not. But you're pretty enough to make a good match. Perhaps you'll surprise me as much as your sister did. Now that is something to aspire to, wouldn't you say?"

Her mouth opened but no witty retort or earnest pledge came out. Even though Cathy had wished her childhood inability to speak in public on Elizabeth a hundred times over, watching it actually happen was quite awful.

"Forgive me, my Lord, but has my brother arrived?" Cathy didn't want to appear eager but couldn't think of anything else to take his attention from her floundering sibling.

"Yes, with his teeny tiny wife. But you should be more concerned about whether your fiancé has arrived, no?"

"Has he?" Mother asked.

"Yes, and he is a handsome fellow. Well, I mustn't indulge myself a moment longer, otherwise Iris will get irritable, and we don't want that, do we?" He winked at Cathy, making her shudder. "I look forward to seeing you shine, my little sunlit one," he whispered to her before he went back inside.

Elizabeth's lower lip wobbled. "He hates me."

"Hush now," Father said. "He just wants to make a fuss of Catherine."

"Believe me," Cathy said, "If he hated you, he'd have made it much more obvious."

"Put it out of your mind," Mother said. "Look, there's Nathaniel to escort you up the aisle. You can see it as a practice."

Nathaniel nodded to them from the entrance. He was dressed in a similar dark frock coat to Father but wearing a waistcoat embroidered with tiny irises. The sight of him brightened Elizabeth, who slipped straight into her default mode of trying to garner the most attention. Imogen came into sight and was clearly judged to have the thicker waist of the two, speeding Elizabeth's recovery even more.

"She has to walk up the aisle with Oliver Peonia." Elizabeth waved at them. "How demeaning."

Mother took the bouquet from the footman who'd gathered it

from their carriage, and formally presented it to Cathy. "Carry this, and all of our best wishes with you," she said, and actually smiled. Probably the relief, Cathy thought as she watched her mother go ahead.

Elizabeth dutifully arranged Cathy's train and then went to Nathaniel, beaming as he kissed her hand. The bridesmaids and groomsmen paired off amidst a flurry of curtsies, bows and polite greetings. There was no best man or maid of honour for weddings within the Great Families.

Father looked at her. "It's time, Catherine."

She looked at the expectant faces of William's siblings who were supposed to become her own and heard the congregation's gentle murmur hush with expectation. Her guts cramped. "I can't do this," she whispered, the poppies in the bouquet quivering with her. She thought of Josh, the times they'd kissed, the evenings curled up next to him, laughing at bad sci-fi films and gushing about the best ones. How could she even think of marrying any other man, let alone an arrogant Iris who wanted nothing better than to rise in the Society she needed to escape?

4

Over a hundred pounds poorer, Sam unlocked the front door as the sun was coming up over Bath. He ushered his charges inside and closed the door, listening to their teeth chatter. He'd had to tell the taxi driver who'd picked them up from the service station on the M6 that they were a dance troupe and he was their manager. Their minibus had been stolen whilst they were in the toilets, he'd said, before they'd even had a chance to change out of their costumes. The taxi driver looked them over, uninterested, and turned the meter on. Thankfully he wasn't the chatty type.

"Front room's first on the right," Sam said. "I'll put some toast on. Tea all round?"

They all nodded and staggered through the door. Sam filled the kettle, worrying about what to do next. He'd managed to persuade them to come home with him to at least try to eat and get a story together before they went to the police. They were easy to convince: starving and in shock. After dropping a couple of slices of bread into the toaster he tried to call Cathy again.

"It's me, Sam, the one you took into Exilium. Um…I really need to meet up with you. I had to go back there and rescue those dancers we saw and I think I might've fucked up. Just a little bit. Call me. Please. It's urgent."

He made a round of tea, using, for the first time, the tray they'd been given as a wedding present, after wiping the dust off it. They were all slumped on the sofa and chairs and looked dreadful in the early-morning light. He wondered whether to call an ambulance.

All reached gratefully for the cups and cradled them, a couple starting to cry at the familiarity of it all.

Clare took a tentative sip and then spat it out. "What is this?"

"Tea."

"It tastes…poisonous. I can't drink this."

Sam looked at the others. "Try yours."

All of them were unable to keep it in their mouths, sending the weeping ones into hysterics. Sam heard the toaster pop up but didn't hurry to the kitchen, thinking of the crisps. "Fuckington Stanley," he whispered. Was Poppy right?

A noise in the hallway made him think the front door hadn't been shut. He went out and bumped straight into the gargoyle.

"'Ello, Sam."

He yelped. "What the fuck are you doing in my house?"

"Your front door was open," Max said, stepping out from behind the gargoyle. "You've been in Exilium."

"How did you know that?"

"It's against the agreement Mr Ekstrand made with you before you left his house."

Sam remembered promising not to tell anyone and the sting in his palm when he shook the Sorcerer's hand. He looked at the skin there, seeing a tiny red spot, as if he'd been pricked with a pin. "Did he put something in my hand? Is that how you knew?"

"This is serious," Max said. "You're already a breach. How did you get back there?"

"Look, Poppy's faerie helped me to rescue these dancers Cathy and I saw and there's something wrong with them. I need your help." He pointed at the front-room door.

Max poked his head round and returned to Sam. "The blondes," he said to the gargoyle. "They were taken a while ago," he said to Sam. "You shouldn't have brought them back to Mundanus."

"What was I supposed to do, leave them to starve in Exilium? Lady Rose took them and now she's gone down no one else wants them."

"I can't help you," Max said. "They'll never be able to live in Mundanus again."

"There must be something we can do!"

"Usually the tainted are taken to live in the Nether, but that's not possible."

"Why not?"

"The usual treatment isn't available anymore."

"Can't Ekstrand take them in?"

Max shook his head. "He'd never agree to having tainted anywhere near him."

"Stop calling them that!" Sam moved them to the kitchen and closed the door. "They've been kidnapped, had their bodies controlled…they're traumatised. You have to help them. Isn't that your job?"

"It's part of my job to stop innocents from being taken. They're no longer innocent."

"So what do I do now? Isn't there anything Ekstrand could do to help them?"

"Not that I'm aware of."

"You're seriously telling me the only chance they have to survive is in Exilium?"

"Yes, because of unfortunate recent events. A Charm from one of the so-called Great Families could help," Max said. "Theoretically. I've never had to look into it."

"Then take me to where Cathy is."

"I can't do that."

"Why the fuck not?"

"It's against the rules."

"Sod the rules," the gargoyle said. "Those people are going to die."

Max looked at it for a long moment. "It's not the only reason. If I take Sam to the puppets to save those people they'll know something is wrong with the Chapter. It would send them a message: if we don't have the resources to help the tainted, we don't have resources to police them. Then more innocents would be taken."

Sam rested against the countertop, feeling sick with fatigue. "Are you going to do anything?"

"Do you have a means of getting back into Exilium?"

Sam nodded. "I think Poppy knew this was going to happen."

Max looked at the gargoyle and it raised its stone brow at Max, almost like they were having a conversation Sam couldn't hear. "Then I'm going to leave here and forget what I saw. But if you go back there afterwards, or do anything else outside of Mundanus, Ekstrand is going to notice."

"It's not like I want to go back there. Anyway, if he's not going to help he sure as fuck doesn't have the right to bust me for having to go back there to do so."

"Actually, he does." Max said. "I'll check on you when you get back. At least you have some protection." He pointed at the wedding ring.

"Yeah," Sam replied. "Brilliant. Now I've got to break it to those people that they're never going to see their families again."

"I can't do this," Cathy said again but Father didn't seem to hear her, extending his arm with a silent invitation to slip her hand into its crook and stride on to her destiny. The air felt thick and the boned bodice too tight to draw a breath.

"Catherine." His voice was low and soft to avoid attention.

"I can't do this," she repeated, the thought bouncing around in her head like an echo in a cave. She looked at the waiting carriages and wondered whether she could sprint over, push the driver off and make her escape like a Western stagecoach thief.

A pinprick at her throat drew her fingers to the diamond. Poppy knew she was tempted to run and was reminding her there was no way out today. She imagined throwing the bouquet on the ground and stamping on it whilst screaming hysterically. Then she accepted her father's arm. The prickling faded as she took her first step towards the entrance, causing a flurry of final preparations from the rest of the wedding party.

Far too quickly she and her father were going through the doorway, the beauty of the vaulted roof and grand oak at the far end of the hall now fully evident. The walls running down the sides were more glass than stone, but they still didn't let in enough of the diffuse silver light of the Nether. Above them, huge globes of glass were suspended from the ceiling holding what appeared to be thousands of sprites. The worst day of her life was about to happen in the most beautiful place she'd ever seen.

Rows of seats were filled with people who as one turned and looked at her as she entered. Instinctively she slowed, her body betraying her desire to flee from their attention. Another prickle from the jewel at her throat and a tightening of her father's arm around her hand pulled her into the forwards rhythm once more.

She heard the ripple through the crowd and focused her attention on the hem of Elizabeth's dress in front of her. She couldn't look ahead, not towards William, it would make it too real. A tear slipped free, feeling cool against her hot cheeks and she bit her lip, fighting to keep the rest back. I hate you all, she thought, falling back on her rage to stop her from collapsing in a sobbing heap.

Then Elizabeth's dress veered to the left and Cathy realised she was almost at the end of the aisle. The Oak loomed ahead of her. Its russet leaves brought the memory of autumn into the great hall. She could see faeries flitting from leaf to leaf, peeping out to witness the marriage for the royal line. A terrible burning rose up from her stomach.

Her father stopped and gently held her arm so she followed suit. She was aware of people standing just ahead and her gaze fell from the Oak to two elderly gentlemen dressed in morning suits. One she recognised: the Papaver Patroon, Sir Papaver himself, who looked just as stern as she remembered. He appeared to be in his early sixties, but Tom had told her that he was rumoured to be over a thousand years old and had to have regular lessons in "modern speech". Her eyes were drawn to his unusually large earlobes, something she'd stared at whilst he'd lambasted her for asking to go to university.

The other elderly gentleman was presumably Sir Iris. He stood on the right, wearing an iris-blue waistcoat with his morning suit. He was taller and more imperious, with something of the hawk about his features, and he looked at her with undisguised surprise. No doubt he'd been warned to expect some plain Jane.

He was standing in front of William, who was now turning to face her. His smile was warm and his surprise was more subtle.

"Who gives this woman to be married to this man?" Sir Papaver asked.

"I, Charles Rhoeas-Papaver of Aquae Sulis, give Catherine Rhoeas-Papaver to be married to this man." Her father's voice was loud and strong.

"And do you vouch for her virtue in front of these witnesses?"

"I do."

Elizabeth took Cathy's poppy bouquet. Father relaxed his arm, and as her hand slid free he took it and passed it to the Patroon, who held it tightly, as if expecting her to run back down the aisle. With a small bow her father discharged his last duty and went to sit next to her mother.

The Patroon's hand was cool and dry, while hers trembled in clammy horror.

"Who gives this man to be married to this woman?" Sir Iris asked.

"I, George Reticulata-Iris of Aquae Sulis, give William Reticulata-Iris to be married to this woman."

Cathy hadn't even noticed William's father standing beside him. He bowed and sat down. Evidently it isn't necessary to prove the man's virtue, Cathy thought.

"Do you, Catherine Rhoeas-Papaver…" Sir Iris said, making her jump. Now she was facing the Patroon she could see Lord Iris and his striking white hair in her peripheral vision. She felt his scrutiny acutely. "…take William Reticulata-Iris to be your husband in accordance with the wishes of your family and patron?"

The moment stretched as her heartbeat became a thunderous roar in her ears. The insistent prickling at her throat faded into the background as she looked at William and tried to imagine him kissing her, touching her and expecting more than she was willing to give. She could see a white blob reflected in his dark-brown eyes and found it so hard to comprehend on a deep level that this was actually happening to her. After all she had done, after all she had tried to do, she'd failed.

But she still couldn't say the words. The pain at her throat increased and even William's studied serenity was showing signs of cracking.

But there was nothing to be done, and she suspected that if she didn't answer, Lord Poppy would take her over. She'd heard the Fae could do that. No doubt that was another reason behind the necklace. They're only words, she thought, trying to dilute the significance of it all. I don't mean them, they're just words.

"I do," she croaked, another tear breaking free.

She could hear her mother's sigh behind her and a rustling amongst the crowd accompanied the collective relief.

"Then repeat after me," Sir Iris said, glaring at her, "I do faithfully promise…"

"I do faithfully promise…"

"To honour and obey my husband in all things."

They stuck in her throat but she forced them out. Just words.

"To forsake all others and to bear my husband's children…"

Just words.

"And to strive to please my husband and my new family till death do us part."

The tears were rolling freely now. William was trying his best to look encouraging.

"Do you, William Reticulata-Iris, take Catherine Rhoeas-Papaver to be your wife, in accordance with the wishes of your family and patron?" said Sir Papaver.

"I do." Not a hint of reluctance. He was an extraordinarily good liar. She needed to remember that.

"Then repeat after me. I do faithfully promise to protect my wife, provide for her comfort and defend her honour, until death do us part."

He repeated it in one go and Cathy seethed. She'd pseudo-promised to bear children and give up her life altogether and all he had to do was ensure she had somewhere to live and duel anyone who badmouthed her.

The Patroons turned their backs and looked up at the tree. Two faeries burst out from the canopy, each holding a ring made of oak. As she watched them being dropped into the Patroons' hands Cathy couldn't recall ever seeing wooden wedding rings in Society.

Sir Papaver gave a ring to William, who took her left hand gently, waited for her fist to unclench and then held it at the tip of her finger.

Following the Patroon's guidance, he repeated, "With this ring, I thee wed. Let it be a reminder of your vows to me and my family as long as you live."

He slid it on easily, despite the clamminess, and she thought for a moment that it was far too large. She enjoyed the thought of being able to lose it easily. But when it reached the base of the finger, it tightened into a snug fit and gave off such a pulse of magic that she physically jolted. As she stared at it, the ring paled and took on a golden sheen.

Then the other ring was being held out to her for William. "With this ring, I thee wed. Let it be a reminder of your vows to me as long as you live." He didn't shudder when it shrank.

The Papaver Patroon stepped back and let Sir Iris take the centre. "I now declare you man and wife."

The hall was filled with polite applause. William lifted her veil and smiled at her, leaning in for a kiss. She stood rigid as his lips brushed hers. They were soft and he smelt of peppermint.

Imogen waited patiently, holding a new bouquet of brilliant blue irises. "Welcome to the Reticulata-Iris family," she said with a false smile and thrust it towards her.

After she took the flowers William extended his arm to her. When she just stood there, too dumbstruck to move, he gently took her free hand, tucked it in place and they set off back down the aisle as the congregation stood, still applauding.

Soon the din was behind them and they emerged into the

Nether. "Are you all right?" William asked quietly, feeling her violent trembling.

Cathy couldn't form words in any sensible order. She felt like she wanted to cry and throw up and faint all at the same time. He gently wiped the tears from one cheek and she flinched. "Don't do that," she said, disturbed by the intimacy of the gesture.

"I'm sorry. I just want you to feel better."

"I hardly think you're the one able to do that," she snapped and then the attendants were offering congratulations and all she wanted to do was push them away and run.

William used the opportunity to back off from her for a few moments, long enough for her to feel guilty. He'd been forced as much as her, he just dealt with it better. She reached for his hand and when he came closer she whispered, "I'm sorry," in his ear.

"Could I have a moment with my wife?" he asked, eliciting excited commentary on the first use of the word. He drew her away. "Thank you. We need to just get through today, all right? Just smile and nod, it'll pass, then we'll talk tonight."

The conjugal night. Her stomach flipped unpleasantly. "I'll try," she said.

"You really do look wonderful, Catherine," he said. "I want to try to make the best of this. I hope you will too."

She couldn't stop the tears. He turned her so her back was to the emerging guests, saying soothing nonsense whilst she sobbed as quietly as she could.

"Catherine, I'm sorry, but there's an Iris tradition we must observe now. You need to speak in private with my mother, before we can go in for the reception. She's waiting for you."

Cathy turned to see her new mother-in-law waiting nearby, holding a small gift-wrapped package. "I don't want her to see I've been crying."

"You're not the first bride to cry afterwards," he said. "She's harmless, go on."

Cathy walked unsteadily towards her. William's mother was smiling, but didn't exactly look happy. She had the demeanour of someone waiting to inform a relative of an accident, rather than give a gift to a new daughter-in-law. Cathy realised it probably wasn't far from the truth. She certainly felt the need for commiseration more than congratulations.

"Hello, Catherine. Come with me."

Cathy was led to a nearby building where the reception would be taking place. It was in the same style as the Oak's hall but on a smaller scale. They entered through a side door and went straight into a small room with two chairs and a table where tea was already laid out.

"Sit down," her mother-in-law said.

Cathy did so, wondering whether her makeup was magical enough to have not ended up in rivulets down her cheeks.

"Tea? I suggest you take some now, whilst you can."

Cathy nodded, worried that if she spoke her voice would crack. William's mother had the same eyes as her son and a quiet grace. She looked less than five years older than her. It was strange to think she'd borne children and been married longer than Cathy had been alive.

Cathy took the cup from her and it rattled in the saucer. "Sorry," she whispered, unable to bring the trembling under control.

"I understand. I sat where you are now, some years ago, talking to William's paternal grandmother, and I shook so much she commented on how loudly my teeth were chattering."

Cathy smiled as best she could, grateful at the attempt to put her at ease even if it was ineffectual. The tea was strong and hot and, despite everything, comforting.

"We're about to have the same conversation I had all those years ago but before we begin, I should like you to call me Mother from now on."

"All right." Cathy cleared her throat. "As you wish, Mother."

That earned another smile. "Good. I do understand how overwhelming this is. Your life has changed forever and it will take time to adjust. However, as a bride married into the Iris family, there's something you need to know about before the reception."

She held out the package. Cathy set down the cup and saucer

to take it from her. She untied the blue ribbon and unwrapped the gift. It was a pair of long evening gloves, beautifully made from iris-blue silk.

"Thank you," she said. "They're lovely."

"They are very important. You may have felt a little flutter when the ring was placed on your finger..."

"When it shrank to fit, yes." Cathy looked at the ring again. It was hard to believe it had ever been made of wood.

"It wasn't just the adjustment. A Charm has been placed upon you, as on all new Iris brides, Catherine, just as it was placed on me."

Cathy's tongue stuck to the roof of her mouth. Her heart, which had been settling into a normal rhythm, started to pound again. "What Charm?"

"Only an Iris man may touch you now. If a man other than William touches your skin, it will leave a mark on you and burn him."

"What?" Cathy sounded stupid in her shock.

"I was just as surprised as you were. Take a moment," Mrs Iris said, offering her the cup and saucer again. She set it back down when Cathy just stared at it.

"What if my brother kissed my cheek?"

"He must not."

"What if...what if the Shopkeeper shook my hand?"

"He must not, Catherine. You must always attend public functions gloved, and only ever present your hand. The mark, I am told, lasts until your husband chooses to lift it."

"This is awful!" Cathy stared at the ring. "Did he know?"

"William? No, his father will be speaking to him now."

But you knew, Cathy thought. She'd only met William's mother twice, very briefly, and had no idea what she was like. If her own mother was anything to go by Cathy knew it would be best to stay calm and not show any anger. That always closed down the conversation with her mother and set them at odds. Perhaps, if she did things differently right from the start, her mother-in-law could be an ally.

"I can see it's a shock but, as my mother-in-law said to me, only a woman who covets the touch of another man would be upset by this."

Cathy pressed her lips together, choking on the beginning of a tirade against the patriarchy and how that kind of thinking allowed this barbarism to continue. Could she keep it all in long enough to get through this conversation, let alone the rest of the day? The rest of her life? No, just today, she promised herself, just shut up and get through today and then you can find a way out.

Her silence was making Mrs Iris uncomfortable. "I suggest you drink your tea. When you're ready to go to the reception, put on the gloves and I'll escort you back in."

Cathy looked at the silk gloves. The thought of putting them on to go and smile and curtsy after this made her feel sick to the stomach. Holding in the rage and the urge to sob was making her chest ache. Shouldn't she say something? Wasn't quiet conformity to this misogynistic farce perpetuating the problem?

"I didn't want to marry either," Mrs Iris said gently. "In fact, I doubt any marriage that has taken place in front of that tree was entered into with a glad heart. It will get easier."

"How did you cope?" Cathy asked. "Didn't you feel angry?"

Mrs Iris picked up her tea cup and saucer again. "Anger is not becoming in a lady. I knew that pushing against the inevitable would only make it hurt more. Let it go. It's done, find new friends, find a hobby, bear your children and you will be left in peace."

"I'm not like you," Cathy said, unable to stop her voice cracking. "What if I can't just grin and bear it?"

"Then you have to learn, or your life will become insufferable very quickly."

Cathy broke down, unable to hold it in any longer. She expected a savage verbal attack, but instead felt a gentle hand on her shoulder.

"I can see how hard this is for you," she said, speaking softly, "and I'm not without sympathy. But I know there are plans for my son, and he will need your total support. Don't make his life more difficult. He's a kind, loving boy and, if you let him, he'll be kind to you."

5

Max leaned heavily on the walking stick, doing his best to ignore the terrible aching in his back as he held his position on the other side of the spy-hole. Petra sat beside him, ear pressed to the wall, making notes. Occasionally she shook her head at Mr Ekstrand's attempts to be sociable with the Master of Ceremonies in the living room on the other side of the wall.

Lavandula had come straight from his niece's wedding and had been full of details about it for the first cup of tea. Uninterested, Max picked up on the gargoyle's occasional bouts of laughter on the other side of the house. He hadn't realised *Wuthering Heights* was a comedy. Its foul mood at being unable to help the tainted seemed to have lifted once it realised there was nothing to be done for them without the Chapter to take them in and care for them. If the Chapter was still intact they would have been given a new life, becoming researchers and staff to support the Arbiters. Now they were doomed to be slaves of the Fae, forever.

"I should imagine that Londinium is quite different without the Rosas," Ekstrand said, bringing Max's attention fully back to the conversation.

"Yes, all scrabbling to decide who'll be the next Duke, no doubt," Mr Lavandula said. He was dressed in an oyster-coloured satin jacket and breeches and a lavender-blue waistcoat embroidered with silver and pearls. "Though, between you and me, dear Ekkie, I don't think things will change too radically. I wouldn't be surprised if the Rosas remain in control of the domain one way or another."

"But the Rosas must have suffered once their actions were discovered?"

"Oh, yes, the Agency rounded them up quite dramatically."

Agency? Petra mouthed to Max. He shrugged. For a moment he thought of the Judd Street talent agency that had snared those blondes. But that was connected to the Rosas, a front for their business interests and a means to lure in the right kind of innocents, not an organisation that would round them up.

"The ones they could find," Lavandula said. "That's the thing about the Rose, pull it up in one corner of the garden and you'll find it springing up somewhere else. The family is just the same. They have deep roots beneath the surface all over Londinium, nay, all of Albion. Apart from Aquae Sulis, of course." He sniffed, lifting a lace-edged handkerchief to his face to frame his smile. "My sister and I are certain of that."

"Won't the Agency have a means to find them? Your people have Charms for that very purpose."

"The Rosas have wealth; they can afford the very best means of hiding. Mark my words, my sorcerous friend, we have not seen the last of them."

"I suppose you aren't concerned about what happens in Londinium." Ekstrand poured more tea.

"Oh, I'm more interested than I used to be. My favourite niece has taken up residence there—the one who helped you to find me—so I've made it my business to find a little Londinium bird or two. In fact, just today I heard one of the minor Ranunculus family sons fell foul of an Arbiter in Hampstead. How embarrassing. Tell me, how is your broken Arbiter? Recovering well?"

"Yes," Ekstrand said with a nod, handing over a refilled cup. "It's good to know the Sorcerer of Essex is keeping London safe."

"Mmm." Lavandula sipped his tea. "It's certainly good to know that the hapless Buttercups are as harmless as they ever were. And may I congratulate you on the delicious drama you effected upon my return; it quite distracted those at the ball from my...condition. Why, not a soul has commented upon the fact my cravat was missing, nor the state of my clothing and general struggle to be conscious, let alone erudite. They were all looking at you being so magnificent. It was so thoughtful of you, Ekkie dear."

Ekstrand made an attempt to smile graciously. "I'm glad you're recovering so well."

"Indeed. Now, if you'll excuse me, seeing as we're all caught up and can put that terrible business behind us, I need to get back to putting the Season in order again." Lavandula finished his tea and set the cup and saucer down gently. He stood and held out his hand to Ekstrand. "I do appreciate the understanding we have. It puts the other cities to shame. Why no one else has such an understanding in their domains I have no idea."

"Perhaps they have more to hide," Ekstrand suggested.

"Perhaps the other Sorcerers aren't as charming as you." Lavandula patted the top of Ekstrand's hand as they shook. "Axon will see me out, ta-ta!"

"Taddles!" Ekstrand waved awkwardly.

Max waited for the front door to shut before following Petra into the room they'd been spying on. Ekstrand was flopped in his armchair, exhausted. At the sound of them entering, he opened one eye and looked at his librarian.

"You did very well, Mr Ekstrand," she said, helping Max sit comfortably. "Just one thing: it's 'toodles', not 'taddles'."

"I thought it was toodle-pip or not at all," Ekstrand said. "It's most confusing and by the end of our meetings I'm so tired."

"But we have the information we need," Max said. "The London Arbiters are still policing the other families, so it seems they had a deal with the Rosas in particular."

"And we know the Roses have either been rounded up or are hiding," Petra added. "Mr Ekstrand, do you know anything about this 'Agency' Lavandula mentioned?"

"Not a jot, and I'm not happy about it," Ekstrand said, alert once again. "I knew I should have stayed to see what the Censor did with them. Maximilian, I want you to find out more about this Agency. If the puppets have developed a group to administer justice in the Nether, I want to know about it. And we need to interrogate a Rosa. If this Agency has them, we have to find it."

"Or we could try and find one of the Rosas in hiding," Max suggested.

"That may be less complicated," Ekstrand replied. "I don't want to get tangled up with an organisation I've only just heard about. Why has no one told me about this?"

Max spread his hands. "I think the puppet who helped us before should be approached. Sam said she knew more about Mundanus than they normally would. The puppets don't usually let their daughters travel in Mundanus, or learn its ways. Only the wealthiest sons do that, from what I understand. I'm wondering if she has some insights into staying hidden. She may know more about this agency too."

"Good idea. I'll prepare an Opener, so she can come to us, and ask Lavandula to get it to her," Ekstrand said. "He'll enjoy the intrigue."

Will unlocked the door of the penthouse apartment hoping their cases had already arrived and the champagne supper he'd arranged was waiting for them. Catherine hadn't said a word since they'd left the reception. He was glad that his father had arranged for a temporary Way straight to the building. If he'd had to sit in silence with her all the way from Bath to London it would have been unbearable.

"In Mundanus the groom carries the bride over the threshold," he said as he pushed the door open to the scent of fresh iris flowers.

"You don't need to do that."

"After you then."

The apartment was in the centre of London within walking distance of practically every famous landmark. He'd almost forgotten what the constant rumbling of a city's background noise was like, and the smell of the polluted air. The sound of sirens and car horns took him back to his Grand Tour. He looked forward to exploring the city again.

Catherine walked in with slumped shoulders, radiating misery. Will drew in a deep breath and readied himself for the challenge ahead.

He locked the front door against the rest of the world and followed his wife inside. She looked so different, it was hard to believe she was the same woman he'd struggled to talk to during the engagement. She still looked like Catherine, only...better.

The reception had passed without incident. The two Fae lords drew so much attention it made it easier to get through than for most couples. He'd worried that Catherine would have been incapable of polite conversation, and she did seem to take a long time to emerge after the talk with his mother, but she got through it well enough. He suspected she was too shell-shocked to cause any offence.

He watched her drift towards the living room, the crystals in the train of the dress sparkling under the bright modern lights. It had been pinned up into a cascading set of ruffles and the veil was still attached to her hair. He tried to imagine unhooking all of those tiny clasps later that evening and wondered what she was like beneath all of the layers of silk.

"It's a nice place," she said.

"I told you we'd honeymoon in Mundanus."

"Honeymoon." She shook her head.

"It doesn't quite seem real, does it?"

"No, not even slightly."

They reached the candle-lit living room, its walls covered in art. The servants had arranged the supper beautifully and would now be resting in the apartment below until they were needed again. Will was pleased to see his instructions had been carried out, and he checked his pocket watch as she looked at the paintings. Everything was on schedule.

"I thought the reception went well," he said. She didn't reply. "Champagne?"

"No. Thanks."

"Do you mind if I do?"

"Go ahead."

He twisted out the cork and it opened with a perfect sigh. Pouring into a single flute seemed a tragic act so he poured out a little for her and carried the glass over.

"Let's toast the future, Catherine," he said, holding it out to her.

"I said I didn't want any."

"Please. For me."

She took the glass and he chinked it gently. "To our future. May we find success and happiness together."

She raised an eyebrow. "Did they put a Charm on you to have unfailing optimism in the face of doom or something?"

He drained the glass. "I thought I'd make an effort. We can choose to be positive or drive each other mad. I hope you prefer the former."

"What did you think when you heard about what they did to me?"

"You mean the Fidelity Charm?"

"'Fidelity Charm'? Is that what they call it? Oh, the joy of euphemisms."

"I was surprised. I thought about you. I knew you wouldn't like it."

"Do you agree with it?"

He took his empty glass back to the table, wanting a moment to gather his thoughts. "I can see why it's done. Lord Iris is most particular when it comes to children, I suppose it's a way to ensure they're...of our blood."

"I asked you if you agree with it, not why it's done. I understand that perfectly."

"I think it's a rather harsh way to guarantee trust."

"Yes, I had you down as one to seduce a woman into being compliant, rather than forcing her."

He poured a larger glass of champagne. Catherine still hadn't tasted hers. "I can see you're angry. You've been furious about this from the very start and this certainly hasn't helped."

"You bet your life it hasn't."

"But I'm not the one who did this to you. And I'm not the one who forced you to marry me."

"But you moved the date! My father said you wanted to marry sooner. That screwed everything up! Why did you do that?"

"Screwed what up?"

Then she downed the champagne.

"You were hoping to find a way out of it, weren't you?"

She shrugged in a most petulant manner and he had to consciously remind himself to remain patient. He was certain there was a way to bring her round. He needed her more than she realised and more than he liked to admit.

"I pushed for the date to be changed to get you away from your father," he replied, noting her surprise. "You didn't think I'd see those bruises and do nothing, did you?"

"I was scared you were going to tell someone. When nothing happened I just…I don't know, I thought you'd forgotten about it."

"You think I'm that shallow? I was outraged. I would have gone and demanded an explanation from your father, had he been anyone else. But he and my father are close, and besides, it's always best to make as few enemies as possible. I thought it better to remove you from the abuse by getting married sooner."

She was scowling at him. "Why didn't you talk to me about it?"

"I didn't want to embarrass you."

"So you just decided to rescue me instead."

He shook his head. "You're very difficult to please, you know."

"I would like it if once, just once, a man would not decide what's best for me without seeing how I feel about it first. Admit it, if it had been Oliver being beaten, you wouldn't have just engineered his rescue."

"It would have been much harder to marry him." He had hoped to crack the ice with a light joke, but she didn't appreciate it.

"The point is, it didn't even occur to you that I might have an opinion. I was just a helpless girl."

"Well, you were," he said, shrugging. "Otherwise you

wouldn't have had the bruises. You just don't like to admit that you needed help."

She rolled her eyes but remained silent.

"Why did he beat you?"

"He was angry with me. It happened all the time when I was a child."

"Why was he angry?"

She drained her glass. "None of your business."

"Was it because you were late to the engagement ball?"

"That was Lord Poppy's fault, not mine."

"But something was wrong; my mother spotted it. Was it because of what Horatio was saying?"

He watched a red flush creeping up her neck. "No," she said, but it was too late.

He had more questions but she was too defensive for him to get anything more out of her. He needed to put her at ease, then try to find out more. "There's a supper here that needs to be eaten. Why don't you come over and sit down? Let's get to know each other. We're going to be together for a very long time. Let's at least try to become friends."

"You just won't give up, will you?" She still walked over, despite the sarcasm.

"I asked your family's cook what your favourite foods are," he said, moving a chair out for her. She pulled out her own and sat down. He sighed and sat in the one he'd chosen for her.

"That's very thoughtful," she said. "But miniature custard tarts?"

"Oh, that's one of mine." He smiled.

"Do you think that if you're sweet enough to me, I'll be easier to manage?"

He offered her the pâté, and when she refused he spread some on a slice of toast. "I'm hoping that if you see that I'm actually not a horrifically awful chap, you might let me get to know you. And that, horror of horrors, you may also want to make a go of this."

"You don't want to get to know me. You want me to be pliable and bear your children."

"You won't give up either, will you?" He laid the knife down, took a bite. Perfection. "I think you're afraid you might like me."

"Oh please, stop, I might be sick."

"No, hear me out. If you actually started to like your husband, what would you have to push against? If you liked me you might actually start to like this life and you might have to accept all the parts you don't like about it, instead of rejecting it all in one convenient bundle."

"That's ridiculous." She stabbed a fork into a slice of ham and let it slap onto her plate.

She was pouting like his younger sister Sophia as she shovelled a spoonful of potato salad onto the ham, trying to ignore him. "Oh, Catherine, I know this isn't really you. Lucy told me."

"Told you what?" There was genuine fear in her eyes. Interesting.

"That you're a funny, bright and quite remarkable woman. That I should be patient with you."

"She said that?"

He nodded. "She took me to one side whilst I was waiting for you to finish with Mother." He regretted reminding her of that.

"About the Charm, William, can you lift it?"

"Why?"

"You said yourself it's harsh. I think it's barbaric."

"It can't be lifted. I'm sorry. And before you ask, I did check. I knew you would hate it. Only Lord Iris can undo the Charm in the wedding ring and, believe me, you do not want to make that case to him."

"Bastards, the lot of them," she muttered.

He chose to ignore that. He watched her push the food around her plate, locked inside her own furious thoughts. She took herself too seriously to be prodded into shifting her outlook. He munched on the toast as he considered his next move.

"I had an unpleasant surprise this morning, before the wedding," he said. "Father called me into his study and informed me that we're to move to Londinium and I'm to take the Dukedom."

"What?"

"That's what I said." He smiled. "The house is being prepared for us now. It will be ready by the end of the honeymoon. Do you mind missing the rest of the season in Aquae Sulis?"

She looked delighted. "Not at all!"

"It doesn't mean we won't have events to attend here, in fact, I anticipate we'll be very busy indeed. With all the upheaval of losing the Rosas, I imagine the Londinium notables in Aquae Sulis will abandon the season to consolidate their interests here."

"Hang on a minute," she said with a frown. "The Dukedom? They want you to be in charge of the Court?"

He nodded. "I'm under a huge amount of pressure, Catherine. After what happened with the Master of Ceremonies, they're expecting great things from me."

"Regret taking all the credit now?"

He smirked. "Not at all. You didn't seem to appreciate it."

"I didn't think you needed anything else to inflate your ego."

"I didn't neglect to mention your involvement with the Arbiter and the Sorcerer because I wanted all of the acclaim. I did it to save you the trouble of difficult questions and—"

"There you go again, saving me when I don't need it."

"Not just you, the Censor also. She was the one who sent you to help the Sorcerer, after all. I'm sure she wouldn't have appreciated that being revealed to your family, or the rest of Aquae Sulis for that matter. It isn't all about you, Catherine."

She tapped the potato salad with the back of her spoon and was quiet for a few moments. "Hang on. If you become Duke, then I would be Duchess. You don't have to go for the throne, do you?"

"Catherine, I'm not doing this because I feel like it. Lord Iris wants our family to take Londinium."

"Aren't you sick of everyone telling you what to do?"

He took another bite of toast and mulled the question over. "It seems to me that the higher up the ladder you climb, the fewer people can do that. Ultimately, we'll never stop being…guided by our patrons, but look at the benefits we have in return. If I become Duke, we'll have more freedom than ever. Wealth independent of the family for one thing, that's significant. And control over property in a way that's impossible in Aquae Sulis. They do things very differently here."

"But do you actually *want* to be Duke?"

The question made him pause. He hadn't even thought of it that way; all he'd considered was the difficulty of the task. "That's irrelevant," he said and her eyes widened.

"Holy crap, they've totally brainwashed you."

"I beg your pardon?"

"You haven't even thought about it that way, have you? They say jump and you say, 'How high?'" She shook her head. "I don't suppose you've heard that song." She dumped the spoon and leaned forwards. "What I don't understand is how you could travel all around the world, meet people—mundane people—and see the most amazing things, then just come back and forget about it all!"

"I'll never forget my Grand Tour, it was the best time I've ever had." He didn't want to admit how much he missed the Sicilian coast. He didn't want to think about that woman, her laugh, and kissing away the tiny white circles of salt dried on her legs as the sun set.

"But didn't it make you realise how much you're missing now?"

He pulled his mind back to her and realised how strange a question it was. "That's an odd way to see a Grand Tour. It isn't a chance to see all the things denied us. It's a chance to broaden our minds."

"Oh, yes, but for men only, because women don't have minds to broaden."

"Ladies choose not to lose the first bloom of youth."

"We don't choose anything. Trust me."

He sat back, aware that he was underprepared for her attitude. During their brief engagement she'd made it very clear she was unhappy about the match, but he hadn't discovered the root of her dissatisfaction. She'd apologised for her bad manners, and then repeatedly destroyed every attempt to have a civil conversation. The only time they'd actually agreed on anything was when he had to distract the staff at the Rosas' failed housewarming party so the Arbiter could enter the house unseen.

Memories of Horatio Gallica-Rosa's accusations returned with renewed clarity. He'd said she'd been living in Mundanus instead of being polished up at a finishing school abroad. The evidence supporting Horatio's claims certainly outweighed any of lessons in deportment.

"Didn't your mother prepare you for this life in any way at all?" he finally asked.

"All she did was demonstrate how—" She cut herself off and sucked in a deep breath. "They did all they could, in their own way. It just didn't…I just…I'm just…" She closed her eyes, looking very pale all of a sudden. "You'll want me to impress people if you try for the Dukedom. I can't do that. I'm no good at that kind of thing."

He reached across to cover her hand with his. "I'll do everything I can to help. We'll bring in tutors, we'll practice our dancing, I'll coach you on how to deal with these soirées."

She looked at him. "It won't do any good. Look, we need to figure out a way to make your family accept that this is a poor match and…I don't know, nullify the marriage or something."

"Are you mad?"

"No, I'm serious, it's the best solution for both of us. You can marry someone more suited to you and I can go and do what I want to do."

"And what exactly is that?"

She stared at him and he could see she was weighing whether to tell him or not. "It's not playing political games and pretending to be someone I'm not."

Evidently she needed to trust him more than she did. He pulled his hand away. "You need to stop thinking like that. You don't believe I can help you because you've never been helped."

"I don't want to be."

He gritted his teeth. How was he supposed to take the Londinium throne with a petulant child of a wife? The way Lucy had talked about her made him think she'd actually been referring to another Catherine. He had to make the marriage work. If it failed it would cause a rift between their families in Aquae Sulis and make his chances of taking the throne even more remote. The residents of Londinium would never respect a man who couldn't keep his wife.

"We just need to find a way to make life in the Nether more bearable for you," he said, trying to sound as light as he could. "It doesn't have to be as bad as it was with your family. In fact, I'll make a promise to you now that it won't be."

She just stared at the food.

"And I'd like you to promise me that if there's something about our life in the Nether that you find unbearable, you must tell me. Then we can improve it instead of letting it fester."

"What if it's everything about life in the Nether?"

"Well…then we'll address each concern one at a time until you're happy. We have time, after all. Which reminds me…"

He plucked out the pocket watch. Two minutes to go. He stood up and gently pulled her to her feet. "I arranged a surprise for you."

He guided her to the balcony. There was a blast of cold air as he opened the French doors. The Thames was a black ribbon glimpsed between buildings, the night-time city ablaze with electric lights and the thrum of urban life. He took off his jacket and placed it around her shoulders, then closed the doors behind them so it would be warm inside afterwards.

"It's an amazing view," she said.

"That's not what I arranged," he said, as the first rocket shot up into the sky and exploded into a ball of blue light.

"Fireworks!" Enraptured, Catherine was quite transformed and he realised how tense and defensive she usually was. Her thrilled exuberance actually made her quite attractive. Then he was caught up in the display, having only seen a handful on his Grand Tour.

"That was so brilliant!" she cheered at the end of the grand finale.

"Wasn't it?" He turned her face towards him and kissed her.

She moved away so fast she banged the back of her head on the glass of the French doors. "What did you do that for?"

"I can kiss my own wife, can't I?"

"Don't do that again." She scrabbled for the door handle and then dived back inside the flat.

Will's euphoric mood collapsed. Catherine pulled at the clips holding the veil in place as she stamped away from the doors, his jacket falling from her shoulders.

When he stepped back inside, the air felt oppressively warm. "Catherine," he called as she headed for the door. "What's wrong? Didn't you like the fireworks?"

She was scrunching the veil in her hands nervously. "They were wonderful. Why did you have to spoil it?"

"How can kissing you be called spoiling it? I wanted to because you looked beautiful and the moment was perfect. Do I have to explain?"

"Did you think I'd be so dazzled by the fireworks that I'd just melt in your arms?"

"I didn't—"

"Because I'm not going to do that. I may as well tell you now I'm not going to let you sleep with me."

He blinked. "I beg your pardon?"

"I know you're expecting it, but I think that would be wrong."

"How can it be wrong for a marriage to be consummated on the conjugal night?"

She threw the veil over the back of a nearby chair. "Look, I know this might be hard for you to grasp, but having sex with someone I barely know—and didn't want to marry—is not something I want to experience."

"But it's—"

"In fact, I think it's shocking that they put a Fidelity Charm on me to stop me running off and shagging the first man I meet, yet expect me to leap into bed with a man I barely know just because we said some words in front of a tree."

"You swore an oath to have my children. That will be very difficult if we don't share a bed."

"I swore that under duress. It doesn't count. And if you try to force me—"

He held up a hand. "I don't think you realise how lucky you are. Most men wouldn't listen to your feelings on the matter, and certainly wouldn't entertain a conversation with you on the subject."

"I'm not going to thank you for not raping me yet."

His fingernails dug into his palms as he struggled to contain his anger. "It wouldn't be rape. This is one of the most fundamental duties you have as my wife."

"What I choose to do with my body is up to me. I don't want to have sex with you, therefore if you try to force me it's rape, regardless of whether you're my husband. It's against the law for you to—"

"What law?" he demanded.

"In Mundanus it's—"

"Their laws don't apply to us!"

"I'm not just going to lie back and think of Albion!" she yelled, moving to put the table between them.

"How dare you force me into being monstrous just to take what is my right to have!" Will gripped the back of the chair in front of him, seething. This wasn't how it was supposed to be, not how he planned it at all. He must have been the first man in Society to be faced with such an unbearably difficult wife. "It's my duty as much as yours," he said, trying to sound calm again. "The first child is a critical milestone. They'll want to see you pregnant as soon as possible. If you refuse, you place me in an impossible position."

"Sorry." She folded her arms. "You'll just have to deal with it."

"No, *you* will." He took a step towards her, but the way she flinched made him pause. What was she turning him into? This wasn't the kind of husband he wanted to be. He shut his eyes, not able to look at her a moment longer. "You need to give your attitude some serious thought," he said, picking up his jacket from the floor, desperate to get out of the apartment and away from the way she was making him feel. "I'm not going to wait forever."

6

A muscle near Sam's eye twitched as Poppy stared at the five poor bastards he'd dragged back into Exilium. They were barely able to stand, their legs spattered with dried mud spots from the motorway, their hair lank and messy.

"Well…I suppose I could find a use for them. If they were cleaned up and dressed properly…"

"And given some food and something to drink, for Christ's sake." Sam was losing his patience.

"And if you're willing to give me something in return."

Sam knew that was coming a mile off. "Yes, if they'll be cared for and treated well."

Poppy's smile was broad and reminded Sam of an alligator eyeing up a lone water buffalo. "Let's see…there are five little waifs so I would ask for an utterly trivial five years of your life. One for each."

Sam clenched his fists. Clare was staring at him.

"It's such a generous offer," Poppy said. "Take this poor thing." He grabbed Clare's wrist and pulled her away from the others. She started to shake. "I'll have to feed and clothe her, give her somewhere safe to sleep—mundanes have so many needs—for eternity. Only one year of your life is a trifling amount in comparison, wouldn't you agree?"

Sam looked into her eyes. She was more than terrified, she was angry and blaming him for the latest indignity they were being subjected to. Five years off his life wasn't so bad. It would be easier to avoid some of the creeping misery of old age than the guilt of failing to make a deal to save them. His grandmother struggled for years with arthritis and the slow decline of dementia. Maybe it would be a blessing in disguise.

"Deal."

"Wonderful!" Poppy plucked a flower from those clustered about his feet and blew across its petals, sending a shower of sparkles deeper into the trees of his domain. "Follow them, little slaves. There will be food and pools of deep water for you to frolic in." He watched them leave and called, "I expect to see frolicking of the highest order when I arrive!"

"I'm going." Sam needed to be in a pub. He needed to be so drunk he couldn't remember what he'd done.

"Before you do, would you be so kind as to go and pick three blades of grass for me from over there?" Poppy pointed down the path out of the clearing.

"Why?"

"Please? It won't take you very long."

Sam set off. If a piano was going to fall out of the sky as he picked it, or the Lord of Grass turn up and demand his belly-button for payment or some other Fae crap, he just wanted to get it out of the way.

He returned with the grass held between thumb and forefinger and held it out to Poppy.

"How long did that take?" Poppy asked and before Sam could reply the faerie spoke from a little way away. Sam hadn't even noticed it was there.

"Four minutes," it replied and Sam followed the voice to spot it amongst the trees, sitting on an hourglass ten times its size. The sand seemed to be frozen mid-flow.

"So how many are left?"

"Ooooh, lots."

"How many exactly?"

It looked surprised by Poppy's question. "Exactly…in numbers?" When Poppy nodded it looked up for a few moments and then said "Two million, six hundred and twenty seven thousand, nine hundred and ninety six." It wrinkled its nose and coughed. "Urgh. Mathematics tastes horrid."

"Goodness." Poppy turned back to Sam. "When it's broken into the tiny bits you seem to value, five years sounds like much more time."

Sam realised what the hourglass represented. "Now just hang on one fucking minute—you mean I have to do whatever you want for a total of five years?"

"Yes." Poppy twisted his cane with a horribly smug look on his face.

"Not five years off the end of my life?"

Poppy frowned. "Goodness, no. Why ever would I want your worst years? Or did you think you would die earlier? Oh! What a fascinating misunderstanding. You were willing to die sooner for those waifs? How noble."

Sam pinched the skin between his eyebrows to stave off the headache spreading across his skull.

"Not all at once," Poppy said. "Every now and again. Half an hour here, five minutes there."

"That's it, I'm going," Sam said. "Fuck this. Fuck all of it."

"See you soon!" Poppy called.

Sam raised his middle finger and held it aloft as he left the clearing. Thankfully, it seemed the Fae didn't know what it meant.

When Cathy was certain Will wasn't coming back straightaway, she went into the bedroom and freed herself from the wedding dress. She ended up ripping some of the seams as she couldn't reach all of the tiny buttons at the back but the sound of the fabric tearing was wonderfully cathartic. When the dress was nothing but a pool of beaded silk around her feet she jumped up and down on it a few times and then kicked it across the room until she realised how childish she was being. The tears started.

She let them fall as she unlaced the corset and peeled off the stockings. She brushed her fingertips over the red marks the corset's bones had left in her skin and remembered the new curse they'd put on her. The one her father had placed on her had been removed that morning and she only knew that because she'd overheard a brief and cryptic exchange between her parents during the reception. She'd been curse-free for less than an hour.

An experimental tug on the wedding ring confirmed her suspicion; it fit too snugly for her to pull it off easily. She considered experimenting with soap and cold water but knew it wouldn't work.

She needed clothes in the mundane fashion and she needed to get out and walk. Cathy wiped the tears off her cheeks and pulled a couple of jewels from her hair as she looked at the wall of fitted wardrobes. The sound of a police siren going past the window reminded her that she was in Mundanus and it cheered her. Getting out of the Nether was half of the battle.

The food had been laid out before they arrived so she suspected the Iris machine would have selected clothes for her honeymoon, had them brought to the flat and unpacked at the same time. She opened the first door she came to and found dresses hanging with matching shoes beneath. She rummaged in drawers and found underwear but no jeans or sloppy tops of the kind she would prefer. The Irises didn't want her to wear trousers. They probably thought it was indecent.

"Fucking Irises," she muttered as she pulled on knickers made to delight a husband rather than be comfortable and a lacy bra that would itch like crazy. "Fucking Fae bastards," she added as she laddered a new pair of stockings and then abandoned them.

She pulled out the most comfortable-looking dress, even though it was one she would never pick out for herself, and put it on. It was too neat, too floral and far too feminine for her taste. When she looked in the mirror she felt sick at the sight of herself as the perfect little wife in the perfect little dress. "Fuck all of you," she said to the reflection, and went hunting for a clock.

She missed her wristwatch. In the Nether men had pocket-watches and the ladies relied on the clocks around the house and the punctuality of the staff to run their day. Thankfully the electric oven in the mundane kitchen had one. It was almost half past six in the evening, the darkness outside in keeping with the Novembers she remembered from her time at university. So many people moaned when the winter nights lengthened but she loved them as much as the days. Simply the change from light to dark and back again filled her with a gentle delight. Living in the constant twilight of the Nether was unnatural in the extreme. She had to get out and see the electric lights of the city and feel the fresh air on her face again. But she needed a plan too.

The table was still covered with food and, now that William had left, her appetite was returning. She unfolded a napkin and put in a few dainty sandwiches and tartlets that would travel better than the rest of the fare. Then she considered where to go first as she ate a boiled egg and the potato salad.

She needed access to the internet and her bank account. That would give her control over her mundane affairs again and make sure everything was ticking over until she could return. To do that she needed to call her friend Tanya and get her tech sent, as she'd arranged before Tom had taken her back to Aquae Sulis, so she needed a phone. She wanted her old phone back as that was the number she'd given Sam, and the one Josh knew.

Then she needed to go to the Emporium of Things in Between and Besides and see if the Shopkeeper could help. What exactly she wanted help with wasn't fully formed in her mind yet, but she planned to think about that as she walked. Tech first, magic second; he would be there until late anyway.

Before she'd left Manchester she'd memorised Tanya's number so all she needed was a public payphone. And cash.

"Shit."

She didn't have her bank cards—they were with the package left in her friend's care. The Shopkeeper didn't allow coins in his shop and he didn't keep paper money on the premises either.

Cathy thought about the way everything had been arranged in the flat. If the Iris servants had unpacked everything needed for a honeymoon in Mundanus, surely they would have left money somewhere?

She went back into the bedroom and looked in one of the bedside drawers. It contained a small bottle of scent and a neat pile of lace-edged handkerchiefs. So that was supposed to be her side of the bed. She dashed to the matching set of drawers on the other side and found a spare set of keys—presumably to the flat—an *A to Z* of London and a wallet. Jackpot.

There was a thick wad of notes inside; after a cursory flip through them she estimated there was over three thousand pounds in fifty-pound notes. She plucked two notes from the middle and dropped the wallet back in the drawer, then grabbed the keys and the *A to Z*.

A smart black winter coat was hanging on a stand near the door and fitted perfectly. It was belted, with too few pockets and no hood, but it did have an inside pocket in which she could secrete the notes and keys. One of the outer pockets was just big enough to hold the napkin of food. She didn't care about how the bulge looked.

She tested the keys first and once she'd identified the front-door key she left. In the lift down to the ground floor she wondered if she should have left a letter. If William returned to find his new possession gone, would a brief note saying "Gone out. P.S. You can shove this marriage up Lord Iris's arse!" make it better? Did the Fae even have—

"Focus," she said to herself, aware that her hands were shaking. It was the first time she'd been free to go where she pleased for weeks. Since Tom had dragged her back to Aquae Sulis she'd either been locked in her room, chaperoned or doing something secret, dodgy and stressful for the Sorcerer.

Cathy left the building and for a moment all she could do was stand on the pavement and take in the streetlights and cars, the crowds of people and the breeze on her face. She was filled with euphoria and renewed optimism. It took a minute to work out exactly where she was and that Covent Garden was just a short walk away. There would be shops there, and phones, once she had change.

Just walking down the street alone was exhilarating. People passed without giving her a glance and she revelled in true anonymity. No one was watching for her next mistake, no one cared about what she was wearing or how disappointing her face was. They were all just getting on with their own business. This was the world she wanted to live in.

A newsagent's caught her eye and a sudden craving for chocolate hit her. She went inside and glanced around for the sweets section, only to see Josh's face on several magazine covers.

Everything else greyed out as she headed for the nearest one and pulled it off the shelf. "What is Josh's secret?" was in huge letters underneath a picture of him in big sunglasses, caught mid-stride. "Serial monogamist leaves broken hearts in his wake, more on page 4," said the strap line underneath. Cathy flipped to the page to see a variety of shots featuring Josh and the redhead who'd knocked him down in Manchester and other women, all skinny and fashionably beautiful. She couldn't take in the text, her attention made scattershot by the shock of seeing him dressed so differently, his hair messy in a horribly trendy way instead of the hopeless geeky mess she remembered.

She stuffed the magazine behind another and picked up a second one, which gleefully described the latest cat-fight caused by two glamour models apparently quarrelling over whom he liked the most. A third speculated about a broken engagement between him and the redhead and a fourth suggested he was about to marry a brunette who looked like she'd eaten nothing but celery for the last decade. They were really all describing the same phenomenon in varying levels of sensationalist language: Josh was having no trouble whatsoever finding rich and beautiful women who wanted to be his girlfriend. And it was all her fault.

"Are you gonna buy one of those or just crease 'em all?" the bloke behind the counter asked.

She looked at him, still unable to form a coherent thought.

"I wanted chocolate," she finally said.

"Looks like you need more than that, love. D'you need to sit down?" She nodded. He pointed at the door. "There's a café across the road."

She put the magazine back on the shelf and grabbed a couple of bars of chocolate to take to the till. When she handed over a fifty, he didn't take it. "You not got anything smaller?"

"No, sorry, I need change to make a phone call."

"There's a mobile phone shop next door, get a pay-as-you-go, save us all some trouble."

She abandoned the chocolate, desperate to get away from the reminders of her botched wish, and did as he suggested. Twenty minutes later she had a phone and had abandoned the plan to call her friend until she knew her new address in London.

The café was her next stop and in minutes she was sitting down with a steaming hot chocolate in front of her. She was still shaken by Josh's fame and wondered if he was really as happy as the magazines suggested. The magazine coverage didn't fit with the Josh she knew. Did all those beautiful women love sci-fi films and books like he did? Had he opened up to them in the way he'd opened up to her? And what about his course? The pictures gave the impression of him being a London playboy—had he abandoned Manchester altogether?

Cathy stared at the new phone on the table in front of her. She knew his mobile number off by heart. She even picked it up, thumb poised over the keys, but she kept stopping herself. What would she say? And she still hadn't found a way to stay hidden yet, or protect him from the repercussions of her flight.

And there was the new curse. When she was with Josh her father's curse had made it impossible for her to undress near him. Now the Iris curse would make it impossible for them to even hold hands. Or kiss.

Just let him go.

The thought cut through the emotional mess and filled her with a sense of relief. Josh had moved on. Of course he had, why wouldn't he, especially with all those women to choose from? He probably didn't even remember her, and if he did it was probably the awful things she said to him just before that stupid wish.

The relationship she had with Josh had to be re-framed as something wonderful she once had but was now over, instead of something that was waiting to be rekindled if she could navigate the various obstacles between them. Besides, he'd be better off without her.

Cathy cupped her hands around the mug and blew across the top, watching the ripples on the surface of the hot chocolate. Hankering for an old love wasn't going to do her any good. She needed to focus on what she could do right now and what she could work towards whilst finding a route out.

She'd been so busy thinking about getting out and finding Josh that she'd lost sight of why she ran away in the first place. She didn't engineer an escape from life in the Nether so she could watch films, read comics and snuggle on the sofa with a fellow geek. And it wasn't just to find freedom—even though that was a big part of it. No, she'd wanted to find a way to make the best use of her mind, the best way to fulfil the potential that Miss Rainer's lessons had unlocked. The dreams of standing up for those without a voice and making all the difference to their lives had been lost in the panic and the upset and the wrench back into the Nether. There was no way she was going to sit around like bloody Rapunzel hoping that someone would come along and carry her off into Mundanus to resume her studies and pass all those exams. She already knew the mundane path towards fulfilment, impossible in the Nether with all the interference of the Fae and the patriarchal death-grip of the Patroons. It was just a matter of pursuing it.

The wedding ring chinked against the cup and reminded her of the marriage. Short of chopping her own finger off she couldn't remove it and the curse was offensive as hell but neither stopped her from resuming her studies. Would Will stop her if he knew what she wanted to do? She didn't know him well enough to predict whether it would be safe to tell him. He'd helped at the party in Aquae

Sulis, when she really needed an ally, but that was to save her uncle. Caution was probably the best option whilst she got to know him.

Cathy rose from the table with her body warmed by the hot chocolate and her spirit filled with a renewed sense of purpose. It was time to call Tanya and get the tools she needed for her studies again, call Sam with her new number and then visit the Emporium to see if she could resume her deal with the Shopkeeper. Anything was better than moping about, mourning a relationship that was long gone.

7

Cornelius Alba-Rosa took the stairs two at a time. He knocked on his sister's bedroom door, two quick raps then two slow ones.

"Come in," Amelia called.

She was seated at the dressing table, wearing one of her favourite dusky-pink brocade gowns, her dark-brown hair arranged in the style of a classical Greek beauty. Jewellery was strewn on the table and she was holding up a necklace against her throat.

"Hello, darling," she said. When she saw his reflection she twisted round, dropping the necklace into her lap. "What is it?"

"The Agency found Uncle Alfred."

She struggled not to weep. "How?"

"They intercepted a message, bribed a servant, I don't know. But that's the third Rosa in two days. I'm starting to wonder whether they're spying on us. I know Uncle Alfred was in touch with the others who were caught. I told my contact to stay away for at least two weeks, just in case any messages we send out lead them to Father."

"It makes sense. I had no idea they'd be so thorough."

"I think our enemies are putting pressure on the Agency to round everyone up," Cornelius said. "They're all too happy to get behind the Lavandulas' outrage."

"Even though most of them hate that family," Amelia said.

"Not as much as they hated ours, it seems," Cornelius replied, aware that he was dawdling his way towards delivering the rest of the news.

"If anyone knows how to benefit from disaster, it's the weasels in the Londinium Court," Amelia said, no doubt thinking of all the people they'd once dined and danced with, now gloating over their fall.

"There's something else." He came closer. "Someone tipped the Agency off about my business in Judd Street. They've seized the assets."

"Can they do that, even if we've been taken in by William?"

"Seems they can. William didn't know about the company, so he couldn't protect it. Even if he could, it would pass into his name, just like this house." He watched the flutter of her eyelashes as she blinked away tears.

"It could be worse," she said. "We could have been taken like everyone else. Better for us to live under William's protection than be subjected to that life."

"Is it?" he muttered, and then regretted it. "No, you're right, of course it is."

Amelia looked down at the jewels in her lap. "I was trying to decide which necklaces to keep and which ones to set aside, just in case."

He sat on the edge of the bed and rested his head in his hands. "I'm so sorry, Amelia."

"It's not your fault. Is that the last of your assets seized?"

"Yes. I'm officially penniless and homeless."

"Not homeless, darling—we're still in this house, aren't we?"

He tried to smile for her, but if he'd been alone he'd have been tempted to weep. He'd come close several times when lying awake in the silent house, wondering what had happened to their mother. The Agency had taken her from a dinner party in Grosvenor Square, dressed in a fine gown and diamonds. He'd heard whispers of what they did to the women, and his fists clenched at the thought of any of those Agency dogs laying a finger on her.

Amelia was putting on a brave face but their situation was dire. It was within William's rights to revoke his protection and turf them out onto the street on a whim, and for the first time Cornelius knew what it was to be helpless.

"Has William been in touch?" she asked.

"No, I've been dealing with his father's secretary regarding the house and the replacement of the staff."

She leaned towards him and lowered her voice. "I don't trust these Iris servants."

"Neither do I," he whispered back.

Even though they were still living in the house they'd known for years, having strangers attending to their needs was incredibly unsettling. Amelia was losing weight and neither of them had slept well since the night the Sorcerer destroyed their lives. With William's help. He couldn't forget that either.

"He's getting married today," she said, fingering the diamonds. "I heard the maids gossiping about it."

"I don't envy him having to marry that Papaver girl. She was awful."

"I don't suppose I'll ever see that Oak now," Amelia said, a tremble in her voice.

"One never knows what the future will bring." He knelt in front of her and took her hands in his. Even though he smiled and kissed the soft skin on the back of her hands, he knew she was right. She was an outcast now, and they both knew her fate.

"Still, I suppose being a mistress is better than the alternative." She was trying so hard to be strong for him.

"You weren't born to be a mistress," he said, the anger building in his chest. "You're too good for that. You should be Duchess of Londinium, as Mother said you would be."

"It's inevitable though, isn't it?"

He pressed a finger to her lips. His only sister, the one person in the world he trusted completely, buying their limited freedom with her flesh: that was not something he wanted to talk about.

"I'll find a way out of this," he said. "I promise. When all the fuss dies down and Society has a new family to destroy, our allies will come to the surface, I'm sure of it."

"We don't have any. If we did, they would have saved Mother."

"They didn't have the chance. If Father is managing to stay free, he's got to have someone helping him. He's just waiting until it's safe to make contact; that's what Uncle Alfred said and I believe it."

"But look what happened to him."

"We're not in the same boat. Besides, our uncle was hardly the sharpest thorn on the stem, was he?"

"I suppose we have a little time." Amelia kissed his hands back. "William will be away on honeymoon, and then there's the rest of the Season in Aquae Sulis. He won't have time to come here."

"That's right," Cornelius said as cheerily as he could manage.

"Do you think he believed Horatio?"

Cornelius silently cursed the Gallica-Rosa for the hundredth time. The way he'd tried to drag him and Amelia down with him had been unforgivable. He'd wondered the same as her in the days since the debacle, and hadn't come to a firm conclusion. It was possible William believed the claim that he and Amelia had been manipulating him, and still took them in anyway so that he could take Amelia as a mistress. But would a man as capable as William disregard such a betrayal just for guaranteed bedsport?

He looked at his sister, the beauty of Londinium, and suspected that William would. And his own life had probably been saved in order to secure her trust and gratitude. It made the bile rise up his gullet.

"If you can, you need to find out what he thinks," he said. "We need to keep him on side."

"I know," she said. "I'll do whatever it takes."

He pulled her into an embrace so she didn't see his face twist in disgust. He needed to work out whom he could trust and how the Agency was spying on them. Then he could get a message to his father. If his contact was to be believed, even the most powerful Letterboxer Charms could be intercepted.

The front door slammed and the gentle boom reverberated up the stairs. They exchanged a worried glance, knowing that no one was expected for the evening and their residence was firmly off the social circuit now.

"Not the Agency?" Amelia asked as he let her go and stood up.

"Who else could it be?" He put a hand on his sword.

She dropped the necklace down the front of her bodice, scooped up the jewels, crammed them into the jewellery box and shut the lid as footsteps came up the stairs and down the corridor towards her room.

"I won't let them take you," he said, drawing the steel an inch, readying the Charm he'd bought with the diamond cravat pin he'd worn at the last ball.

There was a knock on the door. He dropped the sword back into place, looking at Amelia. The Agency wouldn't be so polite.

"Amelia?" William called through the door. "Are you in there? May I come in?"

"Perhaps they didn't marry," she whispered and pointed at the wardrobe. "Quick!"

Cornelius darted over to it and got inside. He released the catch on the inner secret door that connected to his room before closing the wardrobe and losing the light.

"William?" Amelia called back. "Just a moment."

Cornelius waited. He wanted to hear what the Iris had to say first-hand, rather than an abridged version next time he and Amelia were alone.

He heard the atomiser and then a moment later smelt the Charmed rosewater even through the wood. The bedroom door was opened and William came inside. Cornelius wondered how he looked and wished he'd left the door open a crack.

"What a lovely surprise," Amelia said. "I thought it was your wedding day...you certainly appear to be dressed for it." The bedroom door closed. "Is something wrong? Has—"

She was cut off, for a moment Cornelius wondered if something had frightened her, then he heard the gentle sound of a kiss ending.

"I had to see you," William said. "I've missed you. Are you well? Are the servants to your liking? Do you have everything you need?"

"Yes, thank you," Amelia said with a notable breathlessness. "But why are you here? Did the marriage not take place?"

"Oh, it happened," William replied, accompanied by the sound of the bedsprings creaking as he sat on the bed. "But I just want to be with you. I want all of you, Amelia. Will you be my mistress? I swear I'll provide for you and your brother, I'll keep you both safe. I would have married you if I'd had a choice."

"I'm hardly a desirable match now," she said.

"I can't think of a better word to describe you," he murmured and they kissed again.

Cornelius battled the urge to burst out of his hiding place and throw William across the room. He buried his face in the silks of Amelia's dresses as the kiss went on and on. Why wasn't William with his wife, on tonight of all nights?

"You promise to keep Cornelius safe as well as you care for me?"

"Yes, I promise."

"And you promise to let us live here, as we always have?"

"Yes. I didn't want to take the deeds, Father insisted. Don't see the house as mine; it's your home, and Cornelius's too." He punctuated every two words with a kiss. Cornelius's fingers twitched at the thought of throttling him.

"Then yes, William, I'm yours."

Cornelius couldn't listen any more. He pushed the secret door open and left his sister to her fate, with only silent promises of revenge to keep the rage in check.

Sam watched Cathy pale to the point when he wondered if she was going to faint—if that was even possible sitting down. "Oh, fuck."

He took a long gulp of beer. She'd told him she'd been married off that day and narrowly avoided having to consummate a marriage to a man she hardly knew. For him to dump Lord Poppy's message on top made him feel worse than shit. At least he'd been in London, on the way to see Leanne, when she'd called with her new number.

"Are you sure he said by the next new moon?"

"Yeah. It's twenty-eight days. I checked."

"Shit. I can't paint."

"I'm so sorry. I really thought I could save them."

"It's not your fault," she said after what seemed like an eternity. "You didn't exactly come away unscathed. How the hell did you get there without me or the Sorcerer?"

He told her about the strange tree and the faerie who'd found him there. She shook her head. "They were watching for you, maybe cast some magic to draw you in, maybe even put the idea in your head in the first place. It's too much of a coincidence."

"At least I can get to the edge of Exilium by myself."

"You can?" She listened intently as he described the iron and copper pillar. "I have no idea what that's about. Doesn't change the fact Poppy has us both over a barrel. We are royally fucked here. There's no other way to put it."

Sam just nodded.

"Well…I suppose it puts this marriage into perspective," Cathy said, picking up her beer. "It's the last thing I'm worried about now."

"Will you be OK? Can anyone help you? Can I do anything?"

She took several gulps and put the glass down. "Bloody hell, that's gone straight to my head. No…I'll think of something. There must be a Charm…I need to go."

"Take care, Cathy, and I'm sorry."

"Just keep in touch," she said. "I'll check for messages whenever I can. And Sam? Don't try and be heroic again, OK?"

Sam finished his beer and then hers. It was time to go to the apartment and focus on the other thing he'd fucked up beyond recognition: his marriage.

He twisted his wedding ring as the lift to the fifteenth floor climbed. Free from the burden of passing on Poppy's message, he was now worrying about the call from his boss saying that he had to be in work at 8.30am on Monday with a damn good explanation for his repeated absences.

He was impressed by the building but a little intimidated. It was all shiny floors, glass and steel, the antithesis of their cosy Victorian terraced house in Bath. There was a concierge, which comforted him as he didn't like the thought of Leanne being alone in London. At least there was someone there to make sure dodgy people didn't come in.

The interior designers were too fond of metallic finishes for his taste. When he got to the door of the new apartment there were strips of burnished copper riveted to it in something they probably thought was an artful design. To him, it looked like a flattened basket with a warped horseshoe floating above it.

He hadn't really seen Leanne since they'd argued about her taking the job. He'd been pulled away from home by Ekstrand's interference and she'd been working all hours as usual. When she moved up to the flat it had been strangely insignificant as she'd only taken a couple of cases of clothes and left the house as it had always been. Sam wasn't happy about the move and the way she'd avoided any discussion about it but didn't feel he had the right to complain. That chance had passed and he had to adapt, otherwise their marriage would totally fall apart.

Even though she was expecting him, Sam's hand lingered just above the door. Should he pretend everything was fine or make it clear they needed to at least talk about the upheaval? Would she be cold and still angry with him about the way he'd ignored her calls whilst she'd been in Brussels? He couldn't explain to her the reasons behind his recent absences, any more than he could to his boss. Perhaps it was better just to move forwards, rather than say anything that would prompt awkward questions he wouldn't be able to answer.

He finally knocked on the door and Leanne opened it quickly, having been informed of his arrival by the concierge.

"This is a surprise," she said, all smiles. "Couldn't wait?"

"What do you mean?" he asked and pecked her on the cheek she angled towards him. Hardly the passionate kiss of a couple who hadn't seen each other properly for what seemed like weeks.

"You were supposed to come tomorrow."

"I was? You mean it's Friday?"

She nodded. "You got the day off work?"

Now Sam understood why his boss had sounded so pissed off. He'd lost track of the days with all the trips to Exilium and missing a night's sleep. "I'm lucky you're home."

Just the hallway said "wealthy executive apartment" with its shiny wooden floor and tiny halogen spotlights. It smelt faintly of paint, and the skirting boards looked like they were made of the same burnished copper. It was definitely Leanne's territory and felt like a domestic annex to her professional life. It wasn't the kind of place he could imagine himself living in at all.

"Marcus and I were nearby so we thought we'd come back here for a debrief instead of going all the way back to the office so late in the day. He wanted to make sure the apartment was OK."

"Marcus is here?"

"Yeah, come through, I can't wait to show you the place."

Sam clenched his teeth and left his rucksack near the door. He hoped "debrief" wasn't as literal as he feared. "I can come back later, if you're working."

"Don't be silly, we're just about finished anyway. What do you think of the building? Amazing, isn't it?"

"Yeah. Weird skirting boards though. I suppose it's trendy or something."

"Just wait till you see the view," she said, her heels clipping on the floor as she went to the furthest door and opened it. "Come on."

He closed the front door and followed her into a spacious open-plan living and dining room with the kitchen in the corner. Most of the wall in front of him was glass, allowing the panoramic view of the city to have the best impact.

"Wow," he said after a few moments. "That's cool."

"Isn't it beautiful? You can see the London Eye, the Houses of Parliament, and in the day it looks completely different again. I'll never get bored of this view. Make yourself at home." Leanne's heels echoed in the large space. "I've just opened a bottle of wine, do you want some?"

Sam dropped onto the corner sofa. It was less squishy than he'd have liked. "Go on then."

Leanne brought his glass of wine as he twisted the wedding band on his finger. He couldn't stop thinking about the way Ekstrand had reacted to it when he first met him, the way it had seemed to burn the Thorn brother's hand. He was certain it had also helped him to escape Exilium. The ring itself didn't seem anything special to him though. Perhaps the forge it was made in had something to do with all the weird shit.

"Love, do you remember who recommended that forge where we made our wedding rings? I was trying to remember the other day—a friend of mine wants to do the same thing."

"It was me." Her boss entered from the hallway. Sam hoped he'd been in the bathroom, rather than the bedroom.

"Marcus, this is Sam, as you know. Sam, meet Marcus."

Sam had only ever seen Neugent at a distance, usually in a car, or spoken to him on the telephone. Up close, he was struck by how old he looked: mid-fifties at least. There was more grey than blonde in his hair and the wrinkles around his eyes and mouth calmed Sam's primal competitive streak. His eyes were such an intense cobalt blue Sam wondered if they were contact lenses.

They shook hands. "It's good to meet you properly at last, Sam," Neugent said and Sam forced himself to smile, even though the sound of his voice set him on edge. It had been associated with whisking his wife away and ruining their plans for far too long to mean anything else to him now.

"Hello."

"Yes, I used that forge for my own wedding." Marcus smiled. Smug bastard. Sam wanted to punch him, then and there. "Much more romantic than something impersonal picked out of a jeweller's window."

"I didn't realise you were married," Sam said, spotting Neugent's wedding ring.

"My wife passed away some years ago."

"Oh." Sam took a gulp of the wine to fill the awkward silence.

"Good journey?" Neugent asked, sitting in one of the stylish armchairs.

"Not bad," Sam said, wondering when he was going to leave. The silence crept back like an unwanted dog.

"So I understand you're a computer programmer," Neugent eventually said.

"I code." He shrugged. "Websites though, not computers, mostly database-driven sites and server side scripts." He spoke quickly, hoping it would end the agonising small talk. He didn't come to London to chat with his wife's boss. Surely Neugent would realise he wasn't welcome?

"Well," Neugent said, standing up, "I'll leave you both to it. Have a lovely weekend. Good to meet you properly Sam."

"You too."

"I'll make sure I have those ideas for the Bolivian situation for you first thing on Monday morning," Leanne said, escorting him out.

"The meeting is 8am sharp but there will be breakfast there," Neugent replied. "Remember: don't be intimidated by their sabre rattling."

"Don't worry, it takes more than a few idiots with delusions of grandeur to bother me."

Sam looked at his wife, taking in her slender legs, her high-heeled shoes, the way her hair was perfectly straight, and wondered who the fuck he was married to now. He remembered a time when she lived in combat trousers and Doc Martens boots, her hair wild with bright purple streaks, and curves his hands could really roam over. Now she was too skinny with too many sharp angles. The way she laughed with Neugent, high-pitched and brittle, was the opposite of the throaty roaring guffaw that used to burst out of her.

He hadn't appreciated it as sharply as he did now, sitting in an apartment in which she looked right at home but which made him feel like an alien. This wasn't who they were, or who they used to be. The thought of leaving the home they'd scrimped and saved to buy and patched up in their first year of marriage felt like a betrayal. But it was clear she'd already left all that far behind.

She came back to the doorway. "What?" she asked.

I'm wondering if there's a marriage to save here, he thought. "Nothing," he said.

Cathy made it to the tube station, found the right platform, got on the train and then burst into tears. She should have known Poppy wouldn't let her go without one last attempt to make her utterly miserable, but to ask for an Iris secret too? Even if she did unearth one, how could she possibly hide Poppy's task from her new family? They wouldn't want her to have anything to do with her former patron.

A man sitting across from her asked if she was all right and she mumbled something back to deflect attention, horrified she'd lost control in public. It was the beer, it had to be. Come on, she thought, hold it together. There was no one to turn to, no one to protect her from Poppy or Iris or even her own husband, so she had to pull herself together and come up with a plan.

It felt better out in the open air again. Cathy remembered the last time she'd walked to the anchor property for the Emporium of Things in Between and Besides in Cloth Fair. She didn't know then that Lord Poppy was already waiting for her and the memory of being led into his trap almost made her turn around. But the Shopkeeper had promised he hadn't betrayed her, and besides, there was no one else in the Worlds she could go to. The only other person who would even be capable of helping her to hide from the Irises was the Sorcerer of Wessex and she had no idea where in Aquae Sulis his house was, thanks to his extraordinary paranoia.

She recited the Charm as she knocked on the door, making it echo into the Nether reflection of the property. Her feet were throbbing; the stupid shoes provided for her honeymoon had slight heels and she wasn't used to walking miles in them. "My kingdom for my old trainers," she said with a sigh and rested her forehead against the door.

There was the familiar sound of a key turning twice in the lock and the door opened. She could see the Shopkeeper through the haze marking the threshold between Mundanus and the Nether. His eyebrows shot up with surprise. "Catherine!" He beckoned her inside.

She took off her coat and hung it up before realising what she'd done. The Shopkeeper locked the door. As she'd hoped, the shop was shut to customers. "How are you?"

"I'm very well, thank you," he replied, returning to his usual spot behind the glass counter. As always he was dressed in a bow-tie and tweed suit, his white hair neat. A different leather-bound book was on top of the counter but she couldn't see the title on the spine. "And you?" He frowned at her. "Catherine…you're wearing a dress. With flowers on it."

She pulled a face. "I know. Things could be better. I…There are two things I wanted to ask you. First: do you have any Charms that could make me an artist?"

"Which medium would you like to work in?"

"Painting. And I have to be really, really good." It was doubtful she could find a way back to her life in Mundanus before the painting was due.

"Do you paint or sketch already?"

"No."

He pursed his lips. "I have various Charms that could help with certain skills but it sounds like you need everything…I do have a few things I could combine but there would be side-effects."

"I don't care, as long as I can paint."

"I can give you a combined potion for an eye for colour, form and beauty, increased manual dexterity, improved concentration and a substantial boost to your raw creativity, but I can't give you anything that will make you able to hold a brush correctly or make the best decisions in terms of subject and composition."

"But I don't have time to learn that."

The Shopkeeper peered over the top of his glasses at her. "This isn't just a new hobby, is it?"

Cathy shook her head. "It's really important."

"Well," he said, pushing the glasses back up the bridge of his nose, "I have heard about a very rare Charm that can supposedly make one truly artistic but it has to be made to order. I take it from the way you're looking at me you wish to place one?" When she nodded he went back to the counter. "It will take somewhere between three to four weeks. Do you still want the combined potions too?"

"Yes! I'll take…ten of them."

"Ten!"

"Well, they'll run out, won't they?"

"Each one will be effective for a number of hours. I wouldn't recommended consuming more than one per year, otherwise—"

"It's fine. Really. Ten. Charge them to my husband's account, unless there's something I need to pay myself?"

"You're in credit, actually," the Shopkeeper said, much to her surprise. "You overpaid me for the Luck Egg. A kiss of genuine gratitude and affection is worth a huge amount. They're very rare."

She almost kissed his cheek again, before remembering the curse. "I am genuinely grateful. Will it take you long to prepare the potions?"

"I'll do it straightaway and Letterboxer them to you as soon as they're finished. We'll settle up for the Charm once it's in. What was the second thing you wanted to ask?"

"I was hoping I could renegotiate with you, perhaps take my old job back and—"

"Wait a moment! I thought today was your wedding day. Am I mistaken?"

"No," she said, holding up her left hand.

His lips matched the colour of his hair. "What in the Worlds are you doing here?" It was as close to a squawk as she'd ever heard out of his mouth. "Have you taken leave of your senses? Where is your husband?"

"I have absolutely no idea."

"Does he know you're here?"

"Of course not."

He gawped at her. "What…why…what…"

"We had a row, he left and I—"

The Shopkeeper covered his ears. "I don't want to know, Catherine, I mustn't know, and I must ask that you leave, immediately!"

"Why?"

"Because I don't want them to find you here once they start looking for you. Bad enough that Poppy tracked you down to my shop. If Iris did as well they would ask very difficult questions indeed."

"But I don't have anyone else I can ask! I don't want to get you into trouble, but I wouldn't have risked coming here unless I really needed to. And this isn't any different to the time you helped me before."

"Of course it is! You're married now, Catherine, and not into just any family. Didn't your parents prepare you? The Irises are ruthless in their pursuit of perfection, in all things. I have no idea what William Iris thinks he's doing leaving you free to run away on your wedding night but I don't want to be caught in the mess if it's discovered."

Cathy didn't move. She couldn't. Where was there to go but back to the honeymoon flat? She looked down at the floor, not wanting him to see the despair in her eyes.

"I'm sorry." His voice was softer and she watched his shoes as he came out from behind the counter. "I genuinely want to help but I can't take the risk. And you can't either. You need to go back to… wherever you're supposed to be and hope that you get there before your husband discovers you've gone."

"I don't give a stuff if he knows."

"Catherine, listen to me. I once knew a young lady married into the Iris family and unhappy with her lot. She came to me for a sleeping Charm. I thought it was for her own use, but in fact she was using it to make her husband sleep as soon as he came to bed instead of fulfilling his—" he cleared his throat "—marital duty."

Cathy smiled at the thought of it, admiring the solution.

"They realised what she was doing," the Shopkeeper went on, his expression humourless.

"What happened?"

"They packed her off to the Agency and replaced her with a more obedient wife."

"Perhaps life with the Agency was preferable."

The look the Shopkeeper gave her turned Cathy's guts to water. "Oh no, Catherine. I can assure you, she has not improved her situation. Now go back to your husband before the same happens to you."

8

Will stroked Amelia's back, breathing her sweet scent in deeply. She was nuzzled into his chest, the bed was soft and they were both warm and relaxed. He could feel her belly against his hip, her right leg draped over both of his, her breasts pressed against his side.

Her skin was divinely smooth and free of blemishes, her hair long with a slight curl having been freed from its elaborate pinning. He explored the curve of her waist, brushed his fingers down her hip as hers traced the line down to his belly-button.

Will planted a kiss on the top of her head. She tilted her face up and stretched to meet his lips with hers. Her nipples grazed his skin and, seized with a pulse of passion, he grasped her about the waist and rolled her on top of him so her breasts would be squeezed against his chest. She giggled and let her hair fall around their faces, forming a secret world in which only their kisses existed.

Gradually, the realisation that he couldn't stay there all day as well as all night crept in and tarnished the gilded pleasure. This was how it should have been with his wife. He should have been tempted to tell Catherine that his plans for the day had changed and that they weren't to leave the bedroom until their marital home was ready. Instead, he found himself dreading seeing her again.

"What is it?" Amelia asked. "Do you have to go?"

He wrapped both arms about her, pressing as much of her skin against him as he could, wanting to have her leave an impression in his flesh that he could take with him. "Soon," he whispered. "I don't want to. But I should."

"It is your honeymoon, I suppose," she said, a twitch at the corner of her mouth waiting to break into a smile.

"Hardly," he muttered. "I'd rather pretend it was ours."

"I'm game," she said. "Let's pretend you're being called away to a function at Black's that you simply couldn't get out of. Whilst you're drinking cocktails, I'll bathe in milk and honey, and while you play billiards I'll wash my hair in rosewater." She kissed his throat. "And as you play cards, I'll brush my hair a hundred times with my sandalwood comb until it shines." She kissed his chest. "Then I'll come back to bed and warm it for you, so you can slip between the sheets." She kissed his belly. "I'll wrap myself around you and steal the chill from your skin."

He pulled her back up to kiss his lips, trying to control his baser urges. "If I'm not careful, I'll never leave."

"I've always preferred a carefree man," she said, smiling.

After a few moments locked together, he summoned all the willpower within him to slide her to the side and get out of the bed.

She pouted at him as he reached for his shirt. He was ashamed by the strewn clothing he'd have to reclaim and wear again. "I'm sorry, my love," he said softly, watching her hand stretch across the sheets towards him. "I have to go."

She heard the conviction and flopped onto her back, though even that was graceful. Her hair spilt across the pillows, she stretched, languid and the very epitome of temptation. As she stared up into the inside canopy of the bed, Will struggled into his underwear, embarrassed by the effect she still had on his body.

"I never thought I'd be a mistress," she said as he pulled on his trousers. "I was taught how to be a wife in charge of a household and oiling the wheels of Society for my husband's success."

He twisted round to face her. "I'm sorry."

"Don't be." She smiled, and he couldn't help but reflect it. "If I'd married, I never would have been with you and I wanted that, secretly."

"I wanted to be with you," he said. "I resented other people for taking my time, I kept waiting for when I could see you again. I never dreamt I'd have anything like this with you. I'm sorry you won't have the life you deserve, but the selfish part of me is glad we can have this."

He leaned across and kissed her again, then brushed his lips down her throat, skimming her breast until he reached a nipple and sucked it into his mouth. He felt her back arch as she gasped and cupped the other breast in his hand as he nibbled playfully. When he pulled back, her green eyes were bright with lust, her cheeks flushed and lips deep red. She grabbed at his collar but he pulled back before she could catch it, wagging a finger.

"You're a cruel man, William Iris," she said, pulling the sheet up to cover herself as he resumed his dressing. "You do that to me before you leave? Am I to assume you want me to do nothing but lust after you all day?"

"I would like nothing more," he said, truthfully. "I like the thought of you lying naked and restless under these sheets, needing me to return and quench that fire. I always knew something burned in you."

"And I you," she said. "We were meant to be together. Perhaps fate conspired on our behalf."

"Perhaps." He wondered why fate would be so unfair as to place Catherine in the role of wife.

Will did the best he could with the cravat, knowing he looked dishevelled and guilty of a night away from home. He ran his fingers through his hair in the hope of calming it into a neater tumble on the top, and took a last look at her. She'd rolled onto her side, propped up on one elbow, the sheet clinging to her curves beautifully. Her eyes were coaxing him back into bed.

"No," he said, as firmly as he could. "I'll be back as soon as I can, I promise."

"When?"

"Soon."

He tried to leave, then kissed her once and forced himself to walk out of the room. When he shut the door, the rest of the world came crashing in: the guilt at not consummating the marriage, the worry over what Catherine was doing now and where they could go from here. He leaned against the door for a moment, wishing unreservedly that Amelia was his wife, that Cornelius was his brother and that Catherine was off living her strange life in her own strange way with someone else.

Sam dropped his keys onto the shelf in the hallway and slung his rucksack on the sofa. The house felt horribly empty and was lit only by the orange glow from the streetlights outside. He switched on the light and went to the fridge only to find lumpy milk and something unrecognisable that smelt awful. He rescued a lone tin of beer from underneath a rotting lettuce, poured its contents into a glass and leaned against the kitchen worktop.

He knew he had messages from work to pick up and emails to check but he just couldn't face them. He was probably going to get dragged over the coals by his boss in the morning and rightly so; his productivity and attendance had nosedived. He'd wanted to talk it over with Leanne but she'd been obsessed with showing him the sights. It was as if she was trying to sell him a lifestyle whilst keeping him at arm's length, and he hated the way it felt. Every time he tried to have a proper conversation with her something came up. Either the bloody light started flashing on her Blackberry or it was time to get to the tube station to do the next "fun" thing on the list. He'd felt like a relative visiting, someone to keep busy and dazzle with success whilst ensuring there wasn't enough time to have a meaningful conversation.

Sam rummaged in a drawer and pulled out a takeaway menu. There was a noise from the hallway and he assumed he'd not shut the front door properly. He took a menu with him to read as he went.

"Evenin', Sam."

Sam yelled. The gargoyle was standing in the middle of his hallway with Max behind him.

"Don't you know how to use a bloody doorbell?"

"We came to make sure you're not dead," the gargoyle said in its smoker's voice.

"Why would I be dead?"

"You disappeared," Max said, reaching into a pocket and pulling out a small octagonal box. "After you went back to Exilium. I take it you took the tainted there?"

"I had no choice."

"But you disappeared the day after. Has the puppet been in contact with you? Did she take you into the Nether?"

"What? Look, I didn't disappear, I was in London. And what puppet?"

"Catherine," the gargoyle replied.

Sam felt the churn of guilt again at the memory of her face when he passed on the message from Lord Poppy. But they had met in Mundanus. "I haven't been in the Nether, I don't know how to get there and anyway I don't ever want to go there ever again."

"You're certain?" Max asked.

"Course I bloody am, it's a bit hard to miss, isn't it? Even I would notice if the sky turned silver and night never came."

The gargoyle and Max looked at each other. "Something's not right," the gargoyle said.

"On Friday evening shortly after eight you went somewhere else, correct?" Max asked.

"Yes. I went somewhere else."

"Where?" asked the gargoyle.

"None of your bloody business."

"This is important, Sam," Max continued. "You were taken somewhere outside Mundanus several times over the weekend and that shouldn't be happening. Even though we've had dealings, as far as anyone else is concerned you're an innocent. If someone has been taking you out of Mundanus that's against the rules of the Treaty, so I have to investigate. You may not like it, but it's my job."

The Arbiter and gargoyle both looked out of place in his house and showed no signs of leaving. "Whatever your Sorcerer did to keep tabs on me must have something wrong with it," he said. "I visited my wife's new flat which is very definitely in London, not the Nether, and I would have noticed if it was because it has bloody great big windows that look over the city, OK?"

The gargoyle's muzzle wrinkled. "Could've been a glamour, to make you think you were still there."

"But we watched the telly. There were proper lights and a kettle that worked. So it couldn't have been in the Nether. And I got a mobile phone signal there, for God's sake, so just admit it, your Sorcerer is barking at the wrong postman."

Max had wound up the little box in his hand, Sam expected it to open and show a tiny ballerina twirling to music. Instead, when Max held it out on his palm, the top opened and a tiny horn like that of a vintage doll's house gramophone emerged and turned slowly.

"Has your wife been acting any differently to usual?" Max asked.

Sam sighed. "Come into the front room. Can I at least get some food in? I'm starving."

He led Max and the gargoyle into the front room, hastily closed the curtains and then phoned through an order for sweet and sour chicken and rice.

Max was looking at him expectantly whilst the gargoyle was sniffing around the room like a bored bloodhound hopeful for some action. "You didn't answer my question about your wife."

"Leanne acting differently? Differently to what?"

"The usual."

Sam shrugged. "She's changed a lot since uni but I suppose that doesn't count."

The box and horn on the palm of Max's hand gave a gentle *ping* and he checked something on its side before closing it and returning it to one of his pockets. "Did something happen after university?"

"She got a job. We got married. Well, it was the other way round. We married right after we graduated." Maybe that was it, Sam thought. Maybe their parents had been right and they had married too young.

"Does she have the same job now?"

"She's a lot higher in the company." Sam folded his arms when he realised how far beyond his comfort zone he was. He didn't want to give anything more away. "Hang on, why are you asking me all this?"

"Has she lost weight?"

"Yeah. But she's busy."

"Does she wear different kinds of clothes to the ones she used to?"

The room felt cold. Sam shivered and closed the door to the hallway. "She's changed since she got this job but that's normal… isn't it?"

"Have you changed a lot since you got your job?"

Sam sat down, his legs feeling more unsteady than he wanted to admit. "No," he finally said. "Not as much." Perhaps that was the problem with their marriage. But he couldn't just turn into another person, not like she had.

Max rubbed his chin and then pulled a notebook from the inside pocket of his coat, slid the tiny pencil out from its spine and thumbed to a particular page. "I want you to listen to these times and tell me if you know where you were."

Max listed all the times he'd been at Leanne's apartment. Sam felt nauseous by the end. "I was at her new flat—our new flat—in London. I'm supposed to be moving up there. Theoretically."

"I wouldn't if I were you." The gargoyle looked up from the corner of the rug he'd been snuffling around. "Must be something bloody wrong with that place."

Sam reached for his beer and realised he'd left it in the kitchen. He unpeeled his tongue from the roof of his mouth. "Do you think the Thorn brothers are…I dunno…doing something to Leanne? Or the flat?"

"It's not them." Max sounded confident. "They're going to be in Exilium for a long time. Your wife wears a similar wedding ring to yours, I assume?"

"Yes, we made them together. I made hers and she made mine. Oh, fuck. Is this something to do with the wedding-ring protection thing?"

"Perhaps. Do you remember where you made them?"

Sam nodded and dug his phone out of his back pocket. "I've got the number of the forge here. I got it off Leanne this weekend, turns out her boss recommended the place to her."

"Is this boss of hers involved with the new flat in any way?" Max asked.

"It's a company flat and he chose it for her. He said it had the best view in the building. Fuck, is Neugent dodgy? Is he a fucking Fae?"

"Unlikely, if he recommended making those rings."

"But something is definitely dodgy," the gargoyle said. "We need to check that apartment out. Have a sniff about and see what's what."

"Agreed," Max said and looked at Sam. "You need to take me there."

"Now?"

"As long as your wife won't be there."

"She will be there now, but she'll be out at work tomorrow. I've got a key." Sam stopped. What was he saying? He shouldn't tell Max where Leanne lived—where he might be living himself very soon.

"Good." Max stood up. "I'll come here at dawn. Don't leave the house. We'll go to London together, you can show me the flat, we'll come straight back."

"But what about—" the gargoyle began but Max held up a hand.

"We'll talk later," he said to it.

"I'm not sure this is a good idea," Sam said as Max positioned his walking stick.

"It's not open to debate. You and your wife are at risk," Max said. "We'll see ourselves out."

The gargoyle gave a terrifying grin as it passed Sam. Max closed the front-room door behind them. There was the sound of movement, then silence. However they got in, they used the same way to get out.

Sam retrieved his beer, tried to think of any solution to the problems ahead and came up with nothing. He belched. "Fucksticks," he whispered as he realised there was another problem: there was no more beer in the house and there was no way he wanted to spend the rest of the evening alone and sober.

9

Will moved away from Amelia's door and walked slowly to the top of the stairs. The smell of bacon and fresh bread made his stomach rumble. He'd barely touched the honeymoon supper and had hardly been conserving his energy overnight. A bite to eat before he left wouldn't make a great difference, surely.

He followed the smells to a dining room where Cornelius was seated alone at the table. When he entered, Cornelius stood, making William all too aware of the power he had over him now.

"Sit down, old chap," he said cheerfully, heading towards a table laden with covered silver dishes. He filled a plate, his back to Cornelius, imagining the baleful stare being directed towards him. It was inevitable: he'd just destroyed his sister's virtue. He had to tread carefully.

Will sat across from Cornelius and the butler offered tea, which he accepted. The bacon was just crispy enough to be perfect, the toast still fluffy on the inside, the butter creamy and satisfying.

"I'm glad I caught you," Will said after a few mouthfuls. "I wanted to see whether you have everything you need."

"Yes, thank you. We've wanted for nothing."

"I trust the servants meet your expectations."

"Yes, thank you."

Will turned to the butler. "Could you leave us in private, please?"

The butler bowed and closed the door behind him. Will set down his cutlery to sip his tea.

"I'm keen to talk to you about the future," he said, aware that Cornelius hadn't yet looked him in the eye. "We haven't had the chance to talk since that awful night in Aquae Sulis. I should imagine it's been the most terrible time for you and your sister."

"Yes." Cornelius abandoned his toast. "It has been rather unpleasant, but not as much as it has been for the rest of our family, thanks to you."

Cornelius was doing his best to hide it, but Will could still detect the anger beneath the polite words. "Dreadful business," he said. "I couldn't let the Agency take you and Amelia, not after we'd become friends."

"Despite what Horatio said about us."

"Those were the words of a desperate man," Will said as lightly as he could. He'd believed every single one, but it didn't serve his interests to tell Cornelius that. "You were a good friend to me, warning me about his character. I couldn't allow Amelia to be rounded up and carted off by those awful people." He watched Cornelius considering his words. "But it does make things rather awkward now, wouldn't you agree?"

Cornelius simply nodded.

"Which is why I wanted to talk to you," Will said, pausing to take another bite of toast. "I don't like things to fester. Better to be straight with one another, wouldn't you agree?"

Cornelius looked at him properly for the first time. "That's not an approach favoured by many people in Londinium."

Will grinned. "I'm not breakfasting with them. And I wouldn't necessarily be like this with anyone whose regard meant nothing to me. But I value your respect, and would like to think our friendship could endure this tumult. I believe a frank discussion is just what we need."

"I'm listening." Cornelius was still guarded, no longer the man who, less than a week before, had been a self-assured elder brother escorting his sister in a foreign city.

"You're no fool, and my rather disgraceful appearance this morning will no doubt confirm your fears for your sister. I imagine you expected I would take her as a mistress, given the circumstances."

Cornelius looked down at his plate. "I hadn't realised how frank you intended to be."

"I know I'm bordering on the indecent," Will said. "But hear me out. It pains me that the only way Amelia and I can be together lowers her status and robs her of honour, but I wanted to assure you that I don't see her as a mere plaything. I have the utmost respect for her, and have every intention of fulfilling my responsibilities towards her, and you, with as much decency as I can."

"But you still take her virtue, sir," Cornelius whispered.

"Only a saint could resist Amelia in these circumstances and that I am not. But I'm no monster either. I want to beg your forgiveness and seek your blessing."

"How can I grant it, sir? She's a fallen woman, excluded from Society and destined to be nothing more than your private whore."

"Please, don't call her that," Will said, his voice hard. "My desire for her does not exclude her from Society. On the contrary, it keeps her as close to it as she can be. Her fall was the work of the Gallica-Rosas and your patron, not me. But I beg you, permit me to nurture the love between us and find something beautiful in this mess we find ourselves in."

Cornelius scowled at the table. "She was destined for great things. You must understand how difficult this is."

"I can only imagine how I'd feel in your place and that's why we're having this conversation. We have a choice, Cornelius. We let this destroy our friendship, with you living a shadow of a life, kept here only to save your sister's heart. Or you embrace me as a brother-in-law and treat me as her husband for all intents and purposes, excluding a life outside this house. I have so much I can offer you, if you do this for me. For Amelia."

Cornelius stared at him, the cleft between his eyebrows deep. "You genuinely love her?"

"I do," he replied.

"Then I give my consent," he said, looking away again.

"Thank you." Will poured himself another cup of tea in the absence of the butler, and poured one for Cornelius too. "Now, we need to talk about the future. I'm to move to Londinium by command of my Patroon. The family wishes me to take the Dukedom, and if you help me to do that, I'll make you Marquis of Westminster and give you a place in Society once more."

Cornelius's eyes widened. "You'd do that, even though my family no longer exists?"

"You're an intelligent man with an intimate knowledge of this city and its residents. I need someone I can trust, someone who needs to succeed as much as I. Besides—" Will smiled "—before all of this I got along well with you and I can beat you at cards."

"Would I have the right to property again?"

Will could see he was tempted. "I would see to it personally that the deeds to this house would revert to you and you'd have the right to own other properties and invest in any businesses you wish. I don't want you to feel beholden to me and I don't want you to feel dependent. There's no worse thing for a capable man."

"And Amelia?"

"Would be a marchioness and we'll hang the gossips." Will pushed his plate aside and leaned forwards. "What say you? Together, we could forge a path back into Society for Amelia and elevate you above the ones who turned their backs on your family. You would be free of worrying about your survival, and I would have a man I could trust, free of an agenda from a rival Patroon."

Cornelius nodded slowly. "I see it. Yes, it could work. I know enough, and you're capable with a wealthy and powerful family behind you." He extended his hand across the table. "I am yours, brother. I pledge my service to you as adviser."

Will clasped his hand with both of his. "Excellent. Now, more bacon, a brief rundown of the families to watch and then I must leave."

"I have a question," Cornelius said, his voice steadier and more like Will remembered. "If you don't mind, seeing as we're not ignoring any elephants in the room this morning."

"Go ahead." Will speared another rasher and dropped it onto the plate.

"I heard the servants say it was your wedding day yesterday. Is that true?"

"It is."

"Is it not customary to breakfast with one's wife during the honeymoon?"

Will sighed as he resumed his place. "Indeed. We've not had the best start. In fact, I fail to see how it could be worse."

"Forgive my saying so, but how do you expect to take the Court without a solid marriage? They'll want stability from a new Duke, and if they don't respect her, it will be all the harder for you."

Will's appetite ebbed away. "All you say is true, and I don't have an answer yet. Catherine is...different to anyone else I've known in society. But I'll get through to her. Now, tell me, who will put themselves forward once the dust settles? What was the old Duke like?"

"Horatio's grandfather was not a popular Duke but he was a strong one," Cornelius said, dunking a sliver of toast in the remains of his egg yolk. "His loss will shake up the Court immeasurably. He was Duke for over two hundred years, and his father held the title for three hundred before him."

"What happened to the father?"

"Madness, so they say." Cornelius shrugged. "I hear it happens to the very old ones. As for who will step forward, the first will be the head of the Semper-Augustus-Tulipa line. A regal lot—William of Orange was one of theirs, so they claim, and they haven't lost the notion that they should be rulers. Other than them, the only other large family with any clout are the Violas, but they won't be a problem."

"Why?"

Cornelius smiled. "You'll see. Your main competitor will be the Tulipa chap, but you have at least a fortnight or so to find your feet. The Marquis of Westminster won't call the Court to convene with everything in chaos as it is now."

"Why not? Surely this is the time a Court and a Duke are needed most."

"Everyone will be terrified of a war, so they'll all be speculating about who to back," Cornelius replied. "They prefer to do all that behind closed doors. I suspect they'll all be hoping that the strongest will step forward, declare his intention and be backed by such a majority it will be over quickly and painlessly."

"Could the Tulipa achieve that?"

"Perhaps. It's the most likely outcome, as things presently stand. When the Londinium residents hear about your intentions it will change the playing field."

"Let's dine together, once I've moved into my new house," Will suggested. He wanted to pay full attention without being distracted by day-old clothes and a poorly tied cravat. "I'll send a carriage for you." He stood. "Thank you for hearing me out, Cornelius. I'm greatly heartened by this turn of events."

Cornelius also stood and shook his hand. There was a reassuring warmth to his smile. "Thank you for your honesty. I have hope for our future once more, and I never thought I would. Before you go, there's something you may not know about Londinium. Travelling between Nether properties can be dangerous. The roads between them are unprotected and people have been robbed in their carriages."

"Highwaymen!" Will chuckled. "How quaint."

"But with modern weapons from Mundanus," Cornelius said. "Be careful. Some of the more paranoid travel in Mundanus and enter the Nether closer to the property. When you declare your intention to stand for Duke, I don't think it would be a bad thing for you to do the same."

His warning echoed in Will's thoughts as he sat in the mundane taxi back to the flat. Londinium was a challenge on many levels, and Will regretted rushing straight into Amelia's bed. He should have walked for an hour, cleared his head and gone back to talk it through with Catherine and try to build some sort of trust between them. He didn't want to force her into anything but there were expectations that could rapidly become problematic if he didn't win her over.

The family would be waiting for the announcement of a pregnancy and Cornelius had been right about the need for a solid marriage.

The argument with Catherine pressed upon him and made him sink lower in the seat. He'd been exasperated with her because he expected her to just consummate the marriage as a simple matter of duty. He hadn't considered her feelings or whether the assumption that he now had a right to her body was even acceptable. He wouldn't have dreamt of behaving so reprehensibly whilst on the Grand Tour so why should he treat Catherine so poorly?

But even as he considered her feelings there was an undercurrent of anger bred into him by his privileged life. This wasn't the sort of thing he should need to worry about. Catherine should know what was expected of her and—

No. That was the voice of his father, not him. He looked out on the mundane crowds wrapped up against the cold and unaware of the mirror city he was soon to live in. He didn't want to be Duke. He didn't want to make Catherine miserable and himself in the process. She'd said with such bitterness that women didn't have choices, but she didn't realise that so few of the men did either.

10

Back in a corset and back in the Nether, Cathy sat in an elaborately decorated iris-blue day dress, looking out of the carriage window. William sat across from her but she tried to ignore that fact.

She was tired and nervous, an unpleasant combination. William hadn't told her anything about the house they were about to move into, only saying that it was supposed to be a "wonderful surprise". That made her more nervous than the prospect of meeting new servants and having to begin the farce of married life; his idea of a wonderful surprise was highly unlikely to bear any resemblance to her own.

She'd barely slept since the wedding. The first night had been lost to despair and pacing up and down the flat as she tried to think of some way out before he returned. She had exactly the same problem she'd had before they'd married: she could bolt, but the Irises would be able to find her anywhere she went in Mundanus or the Nether. The second night she'd laid awake next to him, crammed over as far on her side of the bed as possible, utterly freaked out by sharing a bed with a husband she didn't want. At least he hadn't tried to touch her, and hadn't mentioned the argument.

If married life was going to be all about non-conversations, her family had prepared her well. He didn't ask her where she'd been or what she'd been doing, which both surprised and relieved her, even though she had a cover story all worked out. Instead, he focused on making the most of the rest of the day. They'd visited the National Gallery, which did nothing but send her into a silent panic about having to produce the painting for Lord Poppy, had afternoon tea at the Savoy, walked in St James's Park, gone out for dinner and then on to a show. It was a textbook romantic day out in London. Just with the wrong man.

She sneaked a peek at him, bored with the silver mists of the Nether. He was too handsome to be married to her and she expected whispered comments about that at the first social event attended together. He was clever, well-mannered, graceful and confident. All of his strengths would make her failings all the more apparent. Why couldn't they have married him to Elizabeth? Her sister would decorate his arm and not bruise his toes when they danced. She would know exactly what to say and when. This match was a disaster.

"What is it?" he asked. She'd failed to notice he was looking back at her.

"Nothing." She looked back out of the window.

"You're very quiet."

"I was just thinking."

"I still have that last song stuck in my head," he said, smiling. "It was a very strange show."

Cathy couldn't think of anything to say so she just nodded and looked back out the window. She consoled herself with the fact that she at least had a mobile phone. Once she knew their new address she could arrange for the rest of her tech to be sent and she could get in touch with her course tutor and look up her reading list. Above all she needed to work out a way to make contact with the Sorcerer of Wessex again so she could earn the boon he'd promised her. Being dependent on a Sorcerer hundreds of miles away who had no interest in helping her wasn't an ideal situation, but it was the best she had.

"What are you thinking about?" he asked. "It seems very serious."

"That show," she lied. "Musicals are weird. No one seems to mind when people randomly burst into song."

"I feel that way about opera," Will replied. "Oli made me sit through a performance of the Ring Cycle whilst we were on the continent, all those people blasting arias at each other for hours on end." He grimaced. "At least last night's show was only a couple of hours."

There was a pause. She fiddled with the beading on her dress.

"I thought yesterday was very pleasant, didn't you?" Will asked.

"Yes," she said, trying her best to be nice. It wouldn't be helpful to comment on how she had found it socially agonising to make small talk and steadfastly not address the dire situation they were in. She'd come to two conclusions. One, she had to find a way to be replaced by the Irises that didn't involve her death or the Agency. Two, she would probably have an easier life in the meantime if she was civil with William.

It helped that she felt sorry for him. It wasn't his fault, any more than it was hers, and as long as he didn't force himself upon her she would find a way to try and make things easier for him too.

If she could find a way to persuade him that a replacement would be best for both of them, he could become an ally, and the only way that was going to happen was if she found a way to make him really listen to her. If they became entrenched and even more alienated, he would just shut her out.

"Please don't look so worried," William said, leaning across to pat her hand. "You'll love the house, I promise."

"I'm not worried about that," she said and cursed her inability to think first when worried. "It's the…servants, I won't know them."

"There won't be any, just the handover staff who've cleaned it and removed any trace of the previous owner. And my valet, of course, I didn't want to leave him in Aquae Sulis. I was given to understand you didn't have any attachment to your previous lady's maid."

"No." She didn't want to take any staff from her parents' household with her. They'd only report back to Aquae Sulis about every tiny detail and, besides, she didn't want any reminders of that imprisonment. "So we're not having other staff?"

He laughed. "Very funny." He frowned when he saw her confusion. "Catherine, as lady of the house you'll be hiring the staff. In fact, a person from the Agency will be there later this afternoon."

"Oh, God." She sank in the seat. "You're going to expect me to handle all of that kind of stuff, aren't you?"

"Why wouldn't I?" He seemed genuinely confused. "Weren't you taught how to run a household?"

She thought back to her lessons with Miss Rainer. They always started with a nod to some aspect of domestic management then rapidly moved on to more interesting subjects like revolutions or the Suffragette movement. Should she declare ignorance now and provide another excellent reason to replace her? Was it too soon? "It'll be fine," she said, trying her best to sound confident. She didn't want to arrive at the new house in the middle of an argument.

"Good. I'm going to be in a meeting for the afternoon, I have correspondence to catch up on and then I'll be dining with Cornelius, so feel free to have dinner whenever you wish."

It hadn't occurred to her that he would set the mealtimes. She could feel disaster looming and knew it would be caused by her ignorance of some minor detail, something any wife would know. "You're having dinner with Cornelius? Is that a good idea?"

The memory returned of the Gallicas being dragged off by the Agency, and along with it her sister's speculation about why William had saved the Albas. She was reassured to discover she still didn't care whether he had a mistress, but it seemed a risk to dine with someone who'd lost everything and had Will to blame.

"Why wouldn't it be?"

"I know they're indebted to you, but won't they see you as responsible for what happened to Lady Rose?"

"I made sure we understand each other. But I'm heartened you thought to ask the question, and I thank you for your concern."

He looked pleased. She silently admonished herself and decided to keep quiet for the rest of the journey. She didn't want to give him any hope that she could polish up into a decent wife; she had to tread a fine line between incompetence and being minimally polite, so he would advocate a replacement.

A tap on the roof of the carriage indicated they were soon to arrive. William pulled on his gloves and recovered his cane from the holder in the door.

Like a good Iris wife, Cathy was already covered by gloves reaching up to her shoulders and a cape over the top. For the tenth time that day she silently cursed Lord Iris.

They turned a sharp corner and an impressive neo-classical building came into view, welcome after the void of the Nether.

"Here we are." William smiled broadly. "The beginning of a new life."

She pretended to fuss over a glove to cover up her inability to be falsely enthusiastic. The carriage door was opened and he got out first to help her out onto the cobbles.

Cathy looked up at the columns of the pedimented portico, trying to place where she'd seen the building before.

"You recognise it?" He took her hand, something she still found irritating. Why did he have to touch her all the time?

"It's familiar," she said. "But I can't work out why."

"We walked past here yesterday. I confess I had the driver bring us round a different way, to keep the park a surprise."

"This is Lancaster House?"

"It is indeed."

Cathy spun around to see gardens and then behind them the trees of Upper St James's Park, known as Green Park in Mundanus. So that was why Will had chattered about it so much the day before, explaining that both St James's Park and Green Park were reflected in the Nether. The famous Londinium park was the envy of Aquae Sulis and their new home overlooked it. "Is the whole building ours?"

He laughed. "Yes, all of it. Of course, residents of Londinium hold keys to the park gates, but there are few properties that have such a fine view over it, not to mention private gardens reflected in the Nether. Let's explore, shall we?"

"We don't need a house this big," she whispered as she reluctantly took his arm.

"On the contrary, this property is fit for a King. Or should I say a Duke and Duchess? Even Queen Victoria called it a palace."

She looked away, feeling like somebody had dropped her into the wrong life. The house was magnificent, too magnificent for her to live there; its grandeur made her feel all the more inferior and ill-suited for the life William was steering her into.

He led her towards the entrance. A butler was waiting with a handful of servants in a line. He stepped forward and bowed.

"Welcome to your new home Mr Reticulata-Iris. Ma'am," he said, with a slight bow to her. "My name is Shaw and I've been personally overseeing the renovations. I give my word that all traces of the previous owner have been removed."

"Thank you," William said. "May I see your credentials?"

The butler extended his left arm, palm upwards and pulled back the sleeve of his jacket and the shirt cuff. William inspected something Cathy couldn't see from her angle and then nodded.

"The items sent from Aquae Sulis have been unpacked. Of course, should our choice of master bedroom and personal suites be erroneous we'll move your belongings post haste. Would you like me to give you a brief tour and show you to your study?"

"Please do," William said, his right hand folded over Cathy's, holding it tightly tucked into the crook of his left arm. "My wife and I are eager to get settled right away."

Am I? she thought, but didn't say. Just as her father had always spoken for her, now her husband felt he could do the same. Don't make a fuss, she thought, pressing her tongue into the roof of her mouth lest some acerbic comment fly out before she realised. Just wait for the right moment and then act.

They were escorted into the entrance hall and both of them stopped to take in its grandeur. Cathy's eyes swept up the gilded staircase to the lantern-design roof two storeys above. The cavernous gilded space was breathtaking and she could imagine how much more dramatic the effect would be in the anchor property with sunlight to make the gold leaf glow. The butler waited patiently and then showed them the ballroom, the green room and the dining room.

"In Mundanus this part of the anchor property is used for state visits and can be hired privately," the butler said. "The building is closed to the public. I've taken the liberty of preparing a dossier of relevant information and an evaluation of mundane security for the anchor property."

"Thank you," William replied.

"As you can see, alterations to the décor have been minimal in these rooms as they're simply reflected from the anchor property and not heavily adapted to an individual family line," the butler continued. "However, the lesser rooms have had to be stripped more thoroughly and await your choice of redecoration."

There was the smell of iris flowers. They liked their vases full of blooms just like any of the Great Families. It was strange to see the delicate blue petals instead of blousy red poppies everywhere. It added to Cathy's sense of dislocation.

"Who were the previous owners?" she whispered to William.

"Horatio's parents," he whispered back. "I'm amazed they had enough restraint to not interfere with the state rooms too much. It's up to you to make the rest of the house beautiful for us, Catherine."

She swallowed, trying to force her tight throat open again. Interior design? Management of staff? This wasn't what she was supposed to do with her life. But then, what was that supposed to be?

Lord Poppy had implied she had the potential to be a great artist after she'd made her third wish. She didn't agree. What if the Charm didn't arrive on time? Would Poppy turn Sam's fingers into hungry rats as he'd threatened?

"Catherine?"

He'd stopped and was looking at her. "What?"

"Are you all right? You've gone quite pale."

"Oh, yeah, yes. Thank you. Just...I'm fine."

She focused on following the butler, trying to ignore William's attentiveness. Surely with only one other person present, who had his back to them, he could drop the show for a moment?

"And this is the master bedroom suite," the butler announced, opening the door onto a huge bedroom with plain walls and a bed at its centre. "The bed is new," the butler said, "and can be changed if not to your taste."

"Indeed," William said. "Dressing rooms through there, I take it?"

"Yes, sir."

"And through there?"

"We took the liberty of keeping a private corridor to a suite of rooms in the mundane property, Sir," he said, leading them both down the connecting hallway and opening a stout door at the end. "This is the nursery."

William pulled her in. The scent of fresh mundane air was unmistakeable after the feather-like brush of crossing over into Mundanus. It was the only room she'd seen redecorated so far and the paint smelled fresh. She scanned the pastel walls and the frilly curtains that framed windows overlooking the park, glorious in the sunshine. The room was dominated by an elaborately carved cot covered in stylised irises and fleur-de-lis.

"This arrived today, sir, sent by your mother. I understand it's a family heirloom."

"It is indeed," William said, beaming. "Isn't it lovely, Catherine? What a perfect nursery. Soon our firstborn will be sleeping in there."

Max adjusted the cap, making his forehead itch. The rucksack was uncomfortable and the straps kept trying to work their way off his shoulders as they approached the apartment building. It felt strange to be walking down a mundane street without the flap of his raincoat around his knees.

"You know, you look like someone in disguise," Sam said. "I thought you were like a detective. Surely you know how to be under cover."

"I'm an Arbiter, I don't normally hide in the line of my work. In fact it's usually the opposite."

"So you just dress like a private detective, rather than being one?"

"I wear what I feel comfortable in, and what's acceptable in public."

"Don't take this the wrong way," Sam said as they reached the lobby, "but have you seen any men wearing a fedora on the way here?"

"I wear a trilby."

"Whatever, have you?"

"I can't say that I have."

"That's because men stopped wearing them over fifty years ago. Sorry, but when you walk down the street, you look weird."

Max mulled this over as they crossed the lobby. He was used to innocents staring at him but he'd always assumed it was because of his unpleasant face and total lack of emotion. The possibility that it was because his clothes were out of fashion was revelatory. He wondered what the gargoyle would have to say about it when he got back to the Sorcerer's house. It seemed to have an opinion on everything these days.

Now wasn't the time to focus on his sense of fashion or lack thereof. He needed to identify what had caused Sam to disappear from Ekstrand's tracking bug. When he'd reported that the cause seemed to be the wife's apartment, Ekstrand speculated whether the wife was connected with the Sorcerer of Essex, whose wards could block the tracer. With the corruption in London, and their suspicion that the Sorcerer of Essex was behind the murder of the Bath Chapter, it was of the highest priority to investigate.

He looked around the lobby as Sam wished the concierge good morning. The apartment building was modern and the security was good. The lift felt smooth and reliable as it carried them upwards.

"There's no chance your wife will come home whilst we're here?" Max asked once more.

"She's at work, I checked again this morning. She won't be home until tonight." Sam leaned against the lift wall, hands in pockets. "This feels weird though, like I'm breaking into my wife's home."

"I thought you had a key. The concierge recognised you."

"I do. She doesn't know I'm here though. Oh shit, the concierge will tell her."

"Tell him not to mention it to her because you're organising a surprise."

"Good idea," Sam said, jangling the coins in his pockets with nervous energy. "You know I'm probably going to lose my job because of all of this crap?"

"If another agency is interfering with your wife, surely that's more important to you?"

Sam nodded. "Yeah."

The lift doors opened and the first thing Max saw was the copper detailing. He'd never say he was a man of instinct—it wasn't a quality associated with having a dislocated soul—but he did have a good eye for the unusual.

He checked for residents as he stepped out. The brightly lit corridor was empty. He examined the nearest strip of copper running parallel to the floor like a dado rail. A scrape with his thumbnail revealed it was only copper plated, with a thin layer of lacquer to prevent verdigris, covering a different metal underneath.

"Which is your wife's apartment?" Sam pointed and Max followed him to the door.

"What do you think of the décor?" Sam pointed at the stylised horseshoe, pulling a face. "I'm not sure I like it."

Max examined it and verified it had the same copper covering as the rail. "I think it's very interesting."

They went inside. "I've got to make a couple of phone calls," Sam said, heading towards the living room and its light at the end of the corridor. "My boss will be in the office by now."

Max observed the continuation of the décor in the apartment and how the bands of metal crossed the door with only a millimetre's gap where it sat flush in the frame. Taking out his knuckle-duster, he reached up and scored into the plaster work near the top. As he'd suspected, there was a strip of metal sunk into the wall and covered over, meaning the metal continued unbroken around the doorway and down the other side of the hallway.

He confirmed it was present in all the rooms as he listened to Sam stumbling over an excuse to his boss. In the bedroom Max noted a large metal light-fitting hanging over the bed and suspected it was connected to the rest of the metal.

Max switched on the light, moved behind the bedroom door to a place where the rail wouldn't be in constant view and scratched the layer of copper and lacquer off a small section. He rummaged in his backpack—it was hard to find his tools when they weren't in the correct pockets on his person—and found his mini-screwdriver kit. The magnetised tip was enough to confirm his suspicion that iron lay underneath the copper.

After dropping the tool back into the bag and checking for mundane bugs and cameras, Max went to the living-room window and examined the gap between the triple glazing and a fine mesh laid between the inner two panes. It was only noticeable at a certain angle thanks to the sunlight breaking through the winter clouds. "Very subtle."

He sat on a chair opposite Sam, plucked a small notebook from the depths of the rucksack and pulled out the pencil tucked into the spine.

"So how does it look to you?" Sam asked, trying to see what he was drawing. "Anything dodgy? Cameras hidden in the bedroom?"

"There are no hidden cameras," Max said.

"Well, that's something," Sam said. "You checked everywhere, right? And you know what to look for?"

"I did and I do. Who does your wife work for?"

"Pin PR. They do all the communications and marketing for loads of different companies. She's not one of those PR bunnies though. Leanne's high up and runs international campaigns."

Max flipped onto a new page in the notebook.

Wife works for Pin PR
High up in company
Who do they promote?
No rabbits

Then he went back to the original page. "And you're certain her boss recommended the forge where you made your wedding rings?"

"Positive. He told me himself. He said he used it for his own wedding. So what's with all the questions? Is there something else wrong with it?"

"Is there anything about her work that makes you uncomfortable?"

"You know you're starting to freak me out now, right?" Sam moved to the edge of the sofa.

"I'm sorry," Max said, "I need a little more information before I can decide what to share with you." He tried to look reassuring, but as it always had with any innocent, it just made Sam squirm nervously. Max let his face fall back into its natural position.

"Anything about her work…Well, they make her work crazy hours, but she enjoys it. This apartment is top-notch but she pays a tiny rent because it's subsidised by the company."

Apartment provided by employer

Max added to the list. "Go on."

"Her boss is called Marcus Neugent. Look, you said you're not a private eye, but you know how to investigate people, don't you? I mean, you do that to protect innocents, right?" When Max nodded, Sam leaned forward. "Then I think you should look into Neugent. I've never liked him."

Max added his name to the list. "I'll do that. What does he look like?"

"He's in his fifties…greying hair, really blue eyes. So is there something weird about this place?"

Max jotted down the description and then looked up at Sam. "This apartment has been warded."

"Warded? What's that supposed to mean?"

"It's protected against other influences. Now, I don't think they've warded it specifically against sorcerous magic, I don't see any of the markers for that. It seems to be warded against the Fae."

"Eh?"

"The copper strips, the horseshoe design on the door…copper renders the Fae's minions inert if they come into contact with it, and the Fae themselves hate it."

"That's why you put on those weird plated gloves before you went through to grab Lady Rose that night we got Cathy's uncle back?"

"Yes, it makes them weak. The copper design here is only plating though. There are bands of iron underneath."

"Do the Fae not like iron either?"

"There's a lot of superstition about it protecting people against the Fae, but it's less effective than copper in our experience," Max said. "There are traditions that still persist in some parts of England, horseshoes on doors being one of them. It could be that the iron is there to be thorough, or there could be another reason that I can't determine yet." He wondered if it was something hidden in the iron that was blocking the tracer, or something about the pattern of the metal bands that was beyond his knowledge.

"So you're telling me it isn't for show at all?"

Max sketched and then showed it to Sam. "This shows what the apartment would look like if you took away the walls and only the banding wards were left behind."

"It looks like a cage!"

Max nodded. "Yes, it does."

"Those bastards have put my wife in a flat that's really a cage? That's beyond fucked up!"

Max decided it would be wise not to mention the bedroom light fitting, and his suspicion that they were particularly concerned about when she slept. "I'm given to understand," Max said, his voice flat in comparison to Sam's panic, "that the cages at London Zoo are as much to protect the animals from the visitors as the visitors from the animals."

"You're saying they want to keep her safe? But why?"

"Lord Iron's protection has been placed upon both of you, as we already know. This is no surprise, Sam, it simply confirms that, for some reason, one of the Elemental Court wishes to keep your wife safe. If anything, it demonstrates they're more interested in her than in you. We just need to determine why."

"Yes, we bloody well do!" Sam stood. "I don't want to stay here, this is creeping me out."

"I'll look into Neugent, and the company your wife works for," Max said, putting the notebook away and following him to the door. "If it's any consolation, the members of the Elemental Court aren't like the Fae. They don't toy with innocents and they don't destroy people's lives."

"Not much of a consolation," Sam muttered, and they left.

Cathy woke with a cold compress on her forehead and the cape gone from her shoulders. She was lying on the new bed in the master suite, William sitting next to her.

"You fainted," he said before she spoke.

"I don't faint." Her head was woolly and her lips were tingling. "My sister does silly things like that, not me."

"Well, you did it very dramatically. Lucky it was just the butler there, if it had been a lady's maid there would be gossip about a pregnancy rushing through the house."

"No worries on that front." He was holding her hand again. She tutted and pulled it away. "You don't have to do that when we're alone, you know," she said, pulling herself up and trying to ignore the way the room span.

"I was concerned," he said stiffly and helped her onto her feet.

"I'm just tired." She held onto one of the posts to steady herself. "Obviously there's no other reason." She wondered briefly if Lord Poppy was interfering, but the teardrop diamond had turned back into a tear as soon as she had left the Oak with William. And why make her faint anyway? The possibility that it could have simply been too upsetting to see the place she was expected to populate with babies made her horrendously ashamed of herself.

"You were pale at the top of the stairs. Is something troubling you? Is it the house?"

"No. We'll rattle around inside like marbles, but there's nothing wrong with it."

"Good." He smiled. "Only you could say that. Most women would gush with excitement."

"I don't gush either," she said. Not with you, anyway, she thought.

"Will you permit me to approach you?" he asked.

She frowned. "What for?"

He moved closer, rested his hands on her shoulders. "Welcome to your new home, Catherine Reticulata-Iris," he said softly, and gently kissed her cheek.

A blush competed with the frown. "Will you please stop that."

"At least you have some colour in your cheeks again," he said, and she pushed him away.

She was about to make some kind of excuse to extricate herself from his non-magical charm offensive, when the bedroom door rattled violently.

"Letterboxer," they said simultaneously and a gilded letterbox appeared in the door. A letter shot through, skidding into the middle of the floor. As William picked it up, another came through, then, just as the letterbox started to fade, it reappeared again, precipitating a burst of letters as if they were being fired from a Gatling gun. After a brief pause the letterbox stretched and a large package wrapped in brown paper and tied with string tumbled through.

"Something from the Emporium for you, and these first two letters are for you too," he said, handing them to her. "The rest are for me."

"Oh, Mother said a gift was going to come straight from the Emporium." Cathy was relieved to see the Shopkeeper's seal on the back. She didn't recognise the calligraphy on the first letter, but then the scent of lavender floated up from the fine paper. She flipped it over, noting that her uncle's coat of arms had been pressed into the wax seal at a forty-five degree angle. It was the same code her mother still used, even now she was a Papaver. *Open only when alone.* "I suppose the time for correspondence has officially begun," she said as he gathered up the dozens of letters. "Good grief, who are they all from?"

"It seems our arrival in Londinium has already done the rounds in the gossip circles. Impressive. I was expecting at least a week to settle in before all the invitations arrived."

"I suppose it's better than being snubbed, seeing as you care about that sort of thing."

"They're all desperate to know my agenda, no doubt. Now that's interesting." He inspected a seal. "Looks like this one is from a Tulipa. I'll be in my study should you need me."

Cathy opted to sit on the bed to read her letters. She had no idea what the time was, but her solitude would be short-lived and she didn't want to waste time trying to find her way to the room that had been allocated to her. At first she was delighted that she'd have her own space with a desk and bookshelves to be filled, but when she realised it was provided for her to run the household affairs the delight had faded.

She opened her uncle's letter first. It contained a second smaller envelope with "Catherine" written on it, which she held as she read the single sheet of sweet-smelling paper.

> *Darling Catherine,*
>
> *I do hope you are positively delighted with your new home, for if you are reading this, you are surely chez toi. Has your delightful new husband told you Lancaster House was my wedding gift to you both? I hope its Bath stone makes you feel at home and that you settle quickly. I feel it was a suitable means of expressing my gratitude to you both for the parts you played in securing my return to Society. Fancy being rescued by the ugliest man in Albion, will wonders never cease?*
>
> *In all seriousness, though, my darling one (I fear I have under-appreciated you over the years, permit me to correct that) I do know how brave you were to speak to an Arbiter and deal with the Sorcerer.*

From what he has told me, your new husband has a talent for taking credit where it is not entirely due, but I won't tell a soul, I promise.

It seems you have also impressed the Sorcerer, for he begged me to contact you and send the enclosed letter. I have not peeped, for to do so with a letter from a Sorcerer would be unwise indeed, so I cannot warn you or praise you for its contents. May it suffice to say the Sorcerer did seem to believe it was of the utmost importance that you receive it promptly and whilst alone.

I find it all rather thrilling, and trust that should I have occasion to visit Londinium, you will regale me with tales of intrigue and adventure, as long as it won't damage your standing in society.

Needless to say, sweet niece, should you or your husband wish to return to Aquae Sulis at any time you will stay as my honoured guests.

With the greatest affection and eternal gratitude,
Your loving Uncle Lavandula

P.S. I've heard tell that some of the Rosas are evading capture by the Agency. Should that be true, you must take care, as I believe your husband is seen as the architect of their downfall (they never were fair nor reasonable).

P.P.S. Do not travel the Londinium Nether roads alone, under any circumstances.

P.P.P.S. Lemon is strictly out of fashion amongst the Londinium Ton, however I understand that honeyed shades of gold are most popular amongst the fashionable elite. Avoid ringlets and square-toed shoes. Ta ta!

It was the first letter Cathy had ever received from a member of her family that had made her smile and it was a strangely pleasant feeling. She laid it on the bed and opened the small envelope from the Sorcerer, half expecting it to emit a puff of smoke and creepy music. But it was just a small card and a piece of paper folded twice.

I will be available to speak to you at 7pm tomorrow evening. When alone and free to converse with me, unfold the enclosed piece of paper and press on an interior door, formulae against the wood. Until then, keep the paper folded and out of sight.

She turned it over to see if there was anything else, but it was blank. So her uncle had passed on a note from the Sorcerer. Was that a good or a bad thing? It certainly suggested a great deal of trust between the two of them, but then the Sorcerer had engineered his rescue, which counted for something. Cathy grinned. That solved one of her biggest problems: how to get in touch with him. She tucked the folded piece of paper into her bodice, slipping it between her corset and the dress so it didn't touch her skin.

As she was opening the other letter, a fine smoke wafted up from the Sorcerer's card and in seconds it had crumbled into ash. "Show-off," she muttered and read Lucy's letter.

Dear Catherine,

I hope you are well and settling in your new home. I haven't stopped thinking about you since the wedding day, I'm so sorry we didn't have the opportunity to speak in private, so I thought I would write you instead.

I could see how hard it was for you and Tom was so upset when we got home. He misses you. I wanted you to know that I'm here for you, and to reassure you that married life can be better than you might think. The trick is to look for the best in him, and in doing that, he'll find the best in you. This isn't just Californian hokey, please believe me.

I would very much like to visit you as soon as you are receiving visitors—there's so much for us to talk about. Let me know when it would be convenient. And I promise it will get easier.

With love,

Lucy x

Cathy laid it next to her uncle's letter. Lucy was sweet but what on earth did they have to talk about? The only thing they had in common was being married off, and Lucy didn't exactly share her feelings about that.

The door opened after a single knock and William came in with the bundle of letters still in his hand. She moved Lucy's letter over the patch of ash.

"We're having dinner at the Tulipas the night after tomorrow." He held out the invitation.

She didn't take it. "Who are they?"

"One of the most powerful families in Londinium. The man who has invited us is tipped to be the next Duke. No doubt there will be other important people there."

"I'd prefer not to."

William raised an eyebrow. "It wasn't a request, Catherine, but a note for your diary."

"I hate dinner parties."

"Do you have something suitable to wear?"

"Didn't you—"

He held up a hand. "Non-negotiable. We must attend as a couple, for goodness' sake. It's obvious."

Cathy took a breath to argue, but where would it lead? "I'll go if I can have tomorrow evening to myself."

"There's nothing planned for tomorrow," he said irritably. "Though if you insist on negotiating every time an event comes up this simply won't work."

"My uncle tells me that lemon is strictly out of fashion," she said with a sigh, knowing this wasn't a fight to be won and looking back at the letter. "But 'honeyed shades of gold' are very popular. What's that supposed to mean anyway? Honey isn't a verb."

William chuckled and she jumped at the unexpected noise. "It is if the Master of Ceremonies deems it to be so. That's most useful, thank you."

"It is? I thought it was drivel myself."

William sighed and looked up as if hoping for divine intervention. "I'll get a dressmaker onto it right away, shall I? Seeing as we have no one engaged here."

"There's no way they can make a dress in two days. Actually—"

she held up her hands "—I don't care. I'm sure your family has all kinds of clever ways to do stuff like that."

"Indeed. Just don't speak like that when we are in company, please," William said. "And the chap from the Agency is waiting for you downstairs. Good grief, I feel like a butler, organising you like this."

"You'd make a rubbish butler," Cathy said, sweeping the letters off the bed in the hope that the worst of the ash would come with them. "They always bring tea with bad news."

11

Cathy was shown to a sitting room in which two chairs and a table for tea had been placed. She wondered where the furniture had come from and whether she'd ever learn where all of the rooms were, before concluding that neither mattered in the grand scheme of things. If she had her way, she'd be gone before the house was fully decorated.

She had time to settle and smooth down her dress before the man from the Agency was shown in. She was struck by his lack of chin, giving his head the appearance of a partially inflated balloon held fast by his collar.

"Good morning, Mrs Reticulata-Iris." He bowed with a gentle click of his heels. The dark-grey wool of his Edwardian-style suit matched his close-set eyes perfectly. "My name is Mr Bennet."

"Good morning," she said and realised he was waiting for an invitation to sit down. "Please take a seat. Would you like tea?"

"Yes, please."

As he set down his briefcase Cathy felt like a child pretending to be her mother—something she'd never done in her actual childhood—making the experience all the more bizarre.

"On behalf of the Agency, may I offer our congratulations on your recent marriage, and welcome you to the fine city of Londinium."

"Thank you."

"Well, I imagine you are extraordinarily busy, so I will endeavour to keep this as short and uncomplicated as possible." He set the case on his lap, opened it and extracted a notebook and pen as the tea was brought in and served.

"There is a lot to do," she said, taking the cup and saucer handed to her gratefully. "It's not just recruiting staff, as you can see, most of the house needs to be redecorated and furniture bought." Was that her talking? She was slipping into role. The tea and context were probably—hopefully—making her behave this way. She fidgeted, wondering whether she should say something desperately inappropriate, just to make sure she was still herself.

"I can help with all of these concerns, in fact, it is my pleasure and privilege to do so." The more he talked, the less she liked him. Any minute he would rub his hands and give the oily smile of a man thinking about money. "However, I suggest we begin with the staff. I understand that in addition to this, may I say, *magnificent* residence there are several anchor properties and their Nether reflections which pay a tithe to the estate, three carriages housed in outbuildings and a shortcut to stables owned in Bathurst Mews near Hyde Park."

He knew more about the house than she did. A shortcut to mundane stables; that was something to note. Animals couldn't cope with prolonged periods in the Nether. She'd be able to cut across town and into Mundanus with the easy excuse of seeing to a matter in the stables. It was better than her rudimentary plan of using the nursery wing to access Mundanus, which would have involved sneaking though the anchor property to get out. Her uncle's warning about the Londinium Nether roads came back to mind; perhaps that was why the Rosas insisted on interconnecting their properties, to avoid the need to travel between them. Presumably the Iris cleaners had severed all those doorways. But where were Cornelius and Amelia being kept? Would the whereabouts of Will's mistress qualify as an Iris secret? Cathy decided it wouldn't be enough to satisfy Lord Poppy and, besides, there was still the tiniest chance that Will planned to be faithful.

"Ma'am?"

She blinked at him. "Sorry, I have a lot on my mind."

He gave a weak smile. "I asked if you've brought any staff with you."

"My husband brought his valet, that's all."

He made a note of that. "And do you have any plans to bring staff at a later point, or will the valet be the only one?"

"Just him," she replied, wondering what the Sorcerer wanted. She had to remember to bargain hard; she might not get another chance to see him.

She focused back on Bennet. He was scribbling away at something and muttering a little as he did so. She sipped the tea and planned to write back to Lucy inviting her to visit. Being married into Albion Society, having been born in America, must be tough. Giving her sister-in-law a legitimate break from the social pressures of Aquae Sulis was the least she could do.

"I think that's everything on the staff front." Bennet finally looked up from his notes. "When would it be convenient for you to interview the candidates for the positions of steward, butler and housekeeper?"

Her mother would be pleased that her wayward daughter now had an estate large enough to merit more than just a head butler. "Haven't we missed a bit out?" she asked.

"I'm sorry?"

"Don't we need to discuss the other staff?"

"Generally our clients leave all the arrangements to us." He closed the notebook. "There's no need for you to concern yourself over the trifling details. Once you have chosen the right steward, butler and housekeeper for your household they will ensure the staff settle in and work according to your desires."

Cathy set her cup down. Whilst she hated the thought of having to deal with running a household, she had to be careful that her family didn't bribe the Agency to bring in staff to spy on her. Perhaps her family didn't care about her now she was safely married off, but a bit of healthy paranoia wasn't going to do any harm. "But I'm interested in the details."

"It really isn't—"

"Mr Bennet, I may be a new bride, but please, don't make me feel like you're trying to give me the brush-off."

"Give you…? Of course not, madam, I simply assumed you'd

like to make an appointment for our interior designer to visit and discuss your requirements."

Cathy folded her arms and mustered a glare she'd learnt from her mother. "I want to know the details of the staff who will be sent to work in my house. It's not an unreasonable request."

He raised his eyebrows and looked down at the notebook, noisily sucking in a breath to convey his disapproval without openly offending her. "As you wish." He flipped through the pages one by one until he came to the most recent. "For a household of this size and status, I calculate you'll require just under one hundred servants in total, broken down into—"

"How on earth did you reach that number?"

Mr Bennet pursed his lips, making his non-chin recede even further. "Am I to understand you would like me to list every single one?"

"How about you just show me your workings-out?" She held out a hand for the notebook.

"This is highly irregular, I will contact you in writing and include a full list of staff to be sent."

"Well, I'd prefer to know why we need so many *before* they arrive. That doesn't seem irregular to me at all."

Reluctantly he handed over the notebook. "I see the error," she said as she scanned the list.

He coughed. "Error? I've been working in my capacity as procurement manager for over eighty years and I have never once made an error in my staff requirement calculations."

"That makes today an interesting day for you then." Cathy smiled at his discomfort. "You've assumed all of the bedrooms will be in use. Quite why fails me. Even if the small army of staff you propose were to live upstairs it would be less than half full."

"But—"

"And you've calculated that we'll be having huge banquets twice a week, which isn't going to happen any time soon—we've just moved here. And I don't see why we would have people assigned to clean the rental properties—surely the residents take care of that and we just maintain the building?" Living in Mundanus and paying attention to details to avoid scams that landlords and rental agencies employed to exploit students had prepared her surprisingly well. "I suggest we start with a basic assumption that, at any one time, somewhere between one and five per cent of the rooms need to be maintained for ready use. The rest can be left empty until needed. I can't imagine us ever having enough guests to fill the house anyway. How ridiculous. I think that would take the entirety of Aquae Sulis Society and that's never going to happen."

"That is irrelevant," Bennet flustered, "everyone will expect the house to be maintained as if it were full."

"Everyone? Who?"

"Society. You wouldn't wish them to think you were penny-pinching. Madam."

"Oh, for goodness' sake, I couldn't care less what they think, and quite frankly it's none of their business. So, based on a more realistic usage, that means instead of that absurd number of chambermaids and laundry staff, we're likely to need this many." She crossed out his number and replaced it with twenty-five. "That makes the salary bill too high, and that's a crazy estimate for the cost of fuel and water..." After a few moments she handed it back to him and watched him pale.

"This is most irregular." He slapped the notebook shut.

"That may be so, but I have more questions about how you break down the cost of the other expenses listed," she said, amazed that this household management business was so much more satisfying than she'd ever imagined it could be. She pulled herself up, not wanting to be sucked totally into the role expected of her. No, the management wasn't satisfying, it was the pleasure of catching Bennet out. The day she started to enjoy picking curtain fabric was one to be worried about, not this. "But first, perhaps you'd like more tea? And some cake too, I think. You are rather pale."

As she poured, it occurred to Cathy that the Agency must have sent Miss Rainer to her parents' household to be the governess. With a jolt she realised that she could find out where Miss Rainer was employed now and request that she be transferred to her household. A fantasy rolled out ahead of her, vivid and enthralling, of being able to debate and discuss books with her governess once more whilst they worked towards an escape. Then they could both flee to Mundanus and be free to pursue their own lives and ambitions and remain friends.

"Mr Bennet, I'd very much like to employ a member of staff formerly of my parents' household. She was my governess, called Miss Rainer, but I don't know where she's working now. Could you find out for me?"

"Ah." Bennet, having recovered his composure, rested his notebook on his knees. "I took the liberty of looking up who your governess was before I came today. It's a common request, you see, many clients like to have the same staff teach their own children."

The look on his face made Cathy's excitement curdle in her stomach. "Where is she now?"

"I'm afraid Miss Rainer passed away a couple of years ago."

"How? She was young and healthy!"

Bennet cleared his throat. "I understand it was a complaint of the heart and there was no suffering. I am sorry. There are other excellent governesses who can be sent when you require one."

He accepted his cup of tea as Cathy struggled to take it in. Miss Rainer died whilst she was at Cambridge. She never had the chance to tell her that she'd managed to break away and live a new life in Manchester, let alone give her freedom too.

A memory of a lesson about Aphra Behn returned with sudden brightness. "This is what Virginia Woolf wrote about her," Miss Rainer had said as words appeared beneath the graceful turn of her fountain pen. With a smile she slid the small piece of paper across the table, like a conspirator sending a secret message.

Cathy, fifteen at the time, picked it up and read it aloud. "'All women together ought to let flowers fall upon the tomb of Aphra Behn, for it was she who earned them the right to speak their minds.'"

Even now Cathy could remember that glint in Miss Rainer's eyes as Cathy returned her smile. "Have you done that, Miss Rainer?"

"Oh, yes," her tutor replied. "And you will too. She has a gravestone in the east cloister of Westminster Abbey. It's easy to find."

And Cathy did. The first day she went into London to sneak to the Emporium and start work for the Shopkeeper, Cathy went to Westminster Abbey with a posy of sweet peas and laid them on Aphra Behn's gravestone next to a bundle of tulips tied with blue ribbon. The fact there was someone else in Mundanus who felt moved to do the same made Cathy's chest swell with happiness.

She had to find out where they'd buried Miss Rainer but she didn't want Bennet to know her need. It was a private thing and Cathy didn't want to tarnish her personal pledge by exposing it to the air in clumsy words. She would lay flowers on Miss Rainer's grave and thank her for giving her the courage to not only speak her mind but act too.

Max sat on the wooden chair in the ballroom, waiting in a pool of light cast by the lantern near his feet. "No," he called through the door.

"Oh, come on," the gargoyle's voice rasped. "I can help."

"You'll be a distraction."

"Exactly. She'll drop her guard if I'm in there with you. You saw what she was like the night we got the Master of Ceremonies back. She couldn't keep her hands off me."

Max folded his arms, eyes fixed on the wall ahead. "She scratched behind your ear. Don't exaggerate."

"We could do the good cop, bad cop thing."

"I don't even know what that means," Max said, but as he finished the sentence a sense of two interrogators playing off each other surfaced in his mind.

"You need to read more. And let me in."

Max pulled himself up with the help of his walking stick and opened the door. "Don't get carried away," he said to the gargoyle as it grinned at him. "Let me do the talking."

The stone creature stalked into the room, lowering its head as it sniffed the floor and gave it a predatory look. Max closed the door and locked it again, even though he knew Mr Ekstrand would be arriving shortly. He wanted to make the point that he took security seriously. Max pointed at a corner and the gargoyle went and hunkered down in it, grumbling.

Moments after Max had sat back down, the door was unlocked and Ekstrand entered, wearing the same suit, cloak and bandanna across the face as he had the night they rescued the Master of Ceremonies. He carried his magnifying glass instead of the cane and noticed the gargoyle. "Should that be in here?"

"The puppet seemed to like it, sir, and it may make her drop her guard."

"Don't let her inspect the formulae too closely."

"I won't, sir."

As Ekstrand nodded, an outline of a doorway burned into the wall opposite him. Max reminded himself of the objective, got to his feet and readied himself for any foul play.

The door materialised, opened and the puppet stepped through and closed the door quickly behind her. She was dressed in mundane clothes with satin gloves that looked out of place.

"Good evening," Max said.

"Hey," the gargoyle called from the corner.

She looked at Ekstrand, swallowed and then waved in the gargoyle's direction uncertainly. Her eyes flicked about the room before she looked at Max properly. "Good evening, Mr Sorcerer, Mr Arbiter."

"You know the drill," Max said, approaching to frisk her, but she took a step back.

"Just make sure you don't touch my skin, whatever you do."

"I'll check her," Ekstrand said and beckoned her further into the room. "Close your eyes."

"Why?"

"So we can be more civilised than before," he replied and she did so.

He went behind her and peered through the magnifying glass. "Good grief," he muttered, and then moved the inspection across her left hand. "Damnable things, wedding rings."

"You're telling me. You can see it through my gloves?"

"It's cursed."

"I know. I daren't take it off. I'm not wearing anything else that's dodgy. Actually, can you tell if it's linked to Lord Iris?"

"Not actively, not this moment," Ekstrand replied. "But it's tied deeply to your soul. I'd be unsurprised if he knew when it was removed. Fascinating. The Irises take their marriages seriously, it seems. Other than that she's clean." He stepped away, tucked the magnifying glass under his cloak. "You can look again now."

She peered up at him, seeming braver. "I don't know why you're bothering with the face-mask thing. I'm hardly going to run off and tell people we've met, am I? And it's not like I could bump into you on the street."

"It's standard procedure when dealing with your kind," he said, and Max noticed her wince.

Ekstrand sat on an empty chair next to Max and gestured to the one in front of them. She scanned the shadows as she crossed the room and sat. "Is this where I was before?"

Max ignored the question. "We have a lot to discuss, and I'm sure you don't have a lot of time."

She nodded. "True enough. Why did you want to see me?"

"You said the last time we dealt with each other that you wanted my help," Ekstrand began. "I'm giving you the opportunity to earn it."

She folded her arms and crossed her legs. "I'm listening."

"We need to talk to one of the Rosas," Max said. "We know some of them are hiding in Londinium or possibly London."

"Why do you need my help to find them? Don't you have sorcerous means to do that?"

"It's not possible, in this instance," Ekstrand said.

"Why?"

"That's all you need to know," Ekstrand replied.

"The first time we met, you said you wanted protection from your family," Max began. "You said you weren't like them. Then when you returned from Exilium Sam told us you knew about things one of your kind normally wouldn't. Can you explain how?"

"I lived in Mundanus for a while."

"That's not usual for a female puppet," Ekstrand said.

She swore under her breath. "Look, if we're going to actually work with each other you need to stop calling me that. I have a name, it's Cathy. It's not my fault I was born into Society, it's not my fault the bloody Fae are constantly screwing up my life. I'm a person, and not like all of the other people who live in the Nether."

"I apologise," Ekstrand said.

"Point taken," Max acknowledged. She would always be a puppet though, regardless of how she chose to delude herself. "Can you explain why you spent time in Mundanus?"

"Look, let's get to the point here, I don't have time to justify myself to you both. We need to make a deal and quick, before someone notices I'm gone. I ran away from my family, I lived in Mundanus for about three years. Lord Poppy, the bastard, found me and dragged me back into Society. I had a plan to make a deal with you guys that day you took me, so I could escape before I was married off. But because you were so busy playing your Us versus Them game and wouldn't listen to me, I've been married off to a man I hardly know. Now, if you want my help you need to get me out of the Nether and protected from Lord Iris, Lord Poppy and the rest of the so-called Great Families before my husband rapes me in the name of consummating a marriage, or I'm going to be a lot less inclined to help you. Clear enough?"

"We'll get you out," the gargoyle said, coming out of the shadows. "Right?"

Max gave it a steady stare, willing it to back off. "You've made your point, pup...Cathy. You hid from your family, so you know the best way to hide using the Charms and artefacts available to those in Society, yes?"

She nodded. "You want me to tell you how I did it?"

"Yes," Ekstrand said.

"No," Cathy replied. "I can't do that."

"But you need to help us so we help you," Ekstrand said. "What harm could it do to—"

"No," she repeated, more forcefully. "I can't tell you, I'm sorry. It would break a promise. But I can still help. Do you want to speak to a particular Rosa, or just any?"

"We want to speak to the head of the Gallica-Rosa line or the Alba-Rosa line," Max replied. They were complicit in the plot against the Master of Ceremonies, and the two most powerful families in the Londinium Court. It stood to reason that one of them would know something useful.

"If I tell you where you can find them, I want you to free me from this curse and hide me from the Fae in return. You can do that, right?" She was looking at Ekstrand. "I mean, you're probably one of the few people in the Split Worlds who'd know how."

"I could," Ekstrand said. "But I'll only do that when I know I no longer need you in Fae-touched Society."

"But she needs to get away from them now!" The gargoyle's voice was half-growl.

"One more word from you and you're out," Ekstrand said, pointing a long finger at him. He looked back at the puppet. "This is just the first step to finding out what we need to know. The information you provide will help, but not solve the issue. If I'm to free you from the ties of your blood, you need to work harder than that."

"You're all the same," she muttered. "You don't give a shit about people, we're just the proverbial pawns on the chessboard."

"It's the way of the Worlds," Ekstrand said, without sympathy. "There is far more at stake than your happiness."

The puppet fidgeted for a moment and then said, "All right then, if you insist on being just the same as the Fae, how about this: I'll tell you where to find the head of the Gallica-Rosa line but in return I want you to find all the information you can on an employee of the Agency. She was a servant, not a member of one of the Great Families, so it shouldn't be hard to find out. Then if you need me to help with your Rosa problem, I will. In return you help me to get out of the Nether and hidden away from the Irises for good. Deal?"

"Who do you want to find?" Max asked.

"Deal?"

"Yes," Ekstrand said with an impatient wave of the hand.

"She's called—or was called—Miss Rainer. She was my governess for about ten years. She died about two years ago."

"She was involved with the Agency?" Ekstrand asked.

"Duh, of course she was," the puppet replied, and then her eyebrow twitched. "You do know the Agency provides all the staff, don't you?"

"Of course," Ekstrand said, but the puppet looked unconvinced. She was sharp.

Max whispered in the Sorcerer's ear, concerned that the longer Ekstrand stayed, the more of their ignorance he'd give away. "I think I should take it from here, sir."

Ekstrand nodded and stood up. "The Arbiter will deal with the details. I'm needed elsewhere."

The puppet nodded slowly, watching him leave, then looked at Max once the door to the rest of the house was shut and locked.

"All right," Max said. "So where do I find the Rosas?"

She smiled. "At the Agency. They were rounded up the night we all spoilt their party."

"I knew that already," Max said. "I need more."

"If that's the case, why not just go and demand a search? Why bother to ask me for help?" She leaned forwards, the smile widening. "You don't know anything about them, do you?"

"No, we don't," said the gargoyle.

"Go outside," Max said to it.

"She knows already, stop treating her like an idiot. There's no time for this crap," it replied. It went and sat next to her. It smiled and lowered its head, inviting a scratch behind the ears that she gave readily whilst smirking at Max.

"He's right," she said. "OK, how about this: I tell you what I know about the Agency and help you to track down their headquarters and in return you bring me the information on Miss Rainer."

"There's no other way to get to a Rosa?"

"No," she replied, but he didn't believe her.

"It would save time if there was."

"There isn't." She said it firmly enough to convince him she'd have to be persuaded in an unpleasant way to tell him. "Look, this way is mutually beneficial and we can start as early as tomorrow. I'll send a note to their rep. Give me something to put in his bag or pocket, something you can track through the Nether. Have you got something like that?"

He nodded. "I'll get one and send it via your uncle, with instructions. I take it that method is still secure?"

"Yep. OK, the Agency…"

He listened as she described her understanding of the Agency and her interactions with its representative. He didn't ask any questions or request any clarifications, letting his silence prompt her to speak more. When she was done, the puppet stood, brushed the gargoyle's cheek with her thumb and went back towards the place in the wall she came through. "Are you going to open a Way for me?"

He retrieved the Opener from its resting place under his chair and struggled to his feet.

"We'll do this as quick as we can," the gargoyle said as Max hobbled over. "Don't let that husband bully you into anything."

She didn't reply, just looked sadly at the stone creature. "You're sweet," she said finally and kissed the top of its head as Max drove the Opener's pin into the wall. She gave him one last glance after he opened it and went through.

When the Way was closed and the Opener was back in his pocket, Max turned to the gargoyle. "I'm not sure that's how good cop, bad cop is supposed to go."

The gargoyle's shrug was made impressive by its huge stone shoulders. "I felt sorry for her."

"That's what they're good at making people do. It's called manipulation."

The gargoyle shook its head. "It's called empathy, you cold bastard," it said, and left Max to hobble out alone.

12

Will watched Catherine fiddle with the fingers of her gloves, newly made in a warm shade of gold silk. "Try not to be so nervous."

"You say that after spending most of the afternoon coaching me and saying how important it is every five minutes."

"Well, I felt you should know." He twisted the cane; her nervous energy was leaching into him. "And you learned practically everything the first time so there's nothing to worry about on that front."

"A bunch of names and anecdotes is hardly quantum physics. Sorry, you were trying to be nice again, weren't you?"

He sighed. "I'm trying to reassure you. You seem to need it."

"Look, I told you that I was a bad match. I told my family and no one listened. Just don't go postal on me when I screw something up tonight, because you've had ample warning."

"'Go postal'?" He waved away the explanation, noticing she said *when* rather than *if*. "Just don't discuss politics or pick out any flaws and you'll be fine."

"I know. I stick to fashion—" she mimed being sick in a most uncouth manner "—the joy of being newly married and the 'delicious challenge' of decorating our grand new house. You'd be better off paying a professional actress to pretend to be me, rather than me pretending to have any interest in these topics. Actually, that's not a bad idea."

"Catherine."

She went back to glove-fiddling.

"Do you like your dress?"

"Well, I know what honeyed gold looks like now. If only my uncle could see me he'd weep with happiness."

"You look lovely."

"The *dress* looks lovely, William," she replied. "Whereas you look handsome."

It was the first time she'd genuinely complimented him. "Thank you," he said with a smile. If only she could accept a compliment given to her.

At the tap on the roof from the driver they both readied themselves for arrival. Whilst he was taking care not to show it, Will was nervous too. They both had to make an excellent impression and also weigh up the opposition. Cornelius had given him vital information that would make it easier for him, but Catherine's social skills were a concern and she would be on her own after dinner.

The carriage slowed and he peered out of the window at the entrance to Hampton Court, dismayed by how much it looked like a ducal residence, even if it was out in the middle of nowhere.

He got out of the carriage and helped her down the steps. The Tulipa butler greeted them and led them through a beautiful formal garden. "This is the reflection of the Privy Garden created in the reign of William III," he said with pride.

Of all the routes into the grand palace, Tulipa had picked this one. They were being reminded of the fact it was once owned by a King who was a puppet of the Tulipas.

They were led into the grand Tudor buildings, guided through a variety of breathtaking chambers and then shown into a relatively humble receiving room. A man he recognised from Cornelius's description as the Tulipa was handing a glass of sherry to one who was presumably the Viola. He wondered if he and Catherine had been given a slightly later time on the invitation so as to enable the Londinium residents to observe their entrance.

"Mr and Mrs William Reticulata-Iris," the butler announced and the doors were closed behind them.

"Ah, excellent, now we are complete." The host smiled and approached. "Permit me to introduce myself. I'm Bartholomew Semper-Augustus-Tulipa." He gave a formal bow which Will duly returned.

"Thank you for your kind invitation," he said. "May I introduce my wife, Catherine."

He watched Tulipa kiss her gloved hand, taking the opportunity to study him. The host was tall and most handsome, with dark brown hair tied back in a ponytail by a short black ribbon and eyes so brown they were almost black. He wore clothes in the late-eighteenth century style, and wore them well. His elaborately embroidered red jacket and long waistcoat glittered in the sprite light. Cornelius had reported his true age to be over two hundred and fifty but Bartholomew looked like he was in his thirties. Will had felt nauseous when he'd heard the true age, realising he was to be pitted against a man who'd lived ten times longer than he.

"A pleasure, Catherine," Bartholomew said. "I welcome you both into my home. This is my wife, Margritte."

He was joined by a fairly attractive woman with auburn hair. When she smiled, her blue eyes sparkled and her cheeks dimpled in a most becoming manner. Will kissed the soft skin on the back of her hand.

"And this is Mr Frederick Persicifolia-Viola." He gestured to a barrel-chested man who appeared to be in his late forties, with greying black hair and dramatic mutton chops.

"Call me Freddy!" he said cheerfully, coming over to pump Will's hand up and down. "Bloody mouthful that name is. Here's the wife too then, how do you do?"

He grabbed Catherine's hand and for a moment Will thought he was going to bite it off, but instead he kissed it in a way that made her recoil and left a damp mark on the silk.

"How do you do," she said as politely as she could in the circumstances.

"M'wife is over there." He pointed rather rudely at a woman half his size who also looked half his age. "George, come over here, there's a good girl."

She glided over gracefully with no embarrassment showing on her delicate features. Her hair was ash-blond, her eyes also blue. She was attractive, but nothing about her appealed to Will. There was something too mask-like about her face.

"I'm Georgiana. *Enchantée*," she said as Will kissed her hand. He didn't like the way she smiled at Catherine, as if having decided her superiority over her already.

"Sherry?" Bartholomew offered.

"Please," he replied.

"I'd like another," Freddy said, thrusting out his empty glass. "Helps build the appetite, what?"

"Indeed," Bartholomew replied, his smile perfectly polite.

"So, Aquae Sulis not good enough for the man who destroyed the Rosas, eh?" Freddy swallowed the sherry in one shot and waited for a response, along with everyone else in the room.

"Well, the Season peaked," Will replied nonchalantly. "After that evening, I knew nothing interesting could possibly happen there for at least another ten years."

It earned a smile from Tulipa and a guffaw from Viola and he felt the first test had been passed. As he sipped the sherry, he heard the Tulipa wife complimenting Catherine's dress, the colour in particular.

The butler announced that dinner was to be served and they went through another set of doors into a dining room, sparkling with silver and crystal but smaller than he expected.

"We prefer to dine in a more intimate space when meeting new friends," Margritte said, as she guided him gently towards his seat.

The Tulipas were, as hosts should be, seated at either end of the table. Will was placed at Margritte's right. Georgiana sat on his right, between him and Bartholomew. Freddy dropped into the chair directly opposite him, Catherine to his left and on Bartholomew's right. He had the feeling she had the worse deal, and didn't like the fact that she would be under Tulipa's scrutiny all evening. However, the fact that they had both been placed to the right of the hosts, considered to be the place for honoured guests, was a positive sign.

It started well enough. The soup was good, eliciting a flurry of comments, and wine was served, which distracted people for a few moments.

"So are we to understand that you have taken permanent residence in Londinium?" Georgiana asked.

"That's right," Will replied.

"What a difficult time to move here," Margritte said. "Everyone is still in shock about the Rosas. So many social events have been cancelled."

"Especially the ones the Rosas were planning." Freddy emptied his glass before the starter had even been cleared. "Of course, the Agency are having a bloody field day, nicking all their properties and raking it in."

"Where are you going to be living?" Georgiana asked.

"Lancaster House," he replied and watched the reactions with interest. Only Bartholomew was truly inscrutable, the rest were both impressed and envious to varying degrees.

"That's a beautiful property," Margritte said.

"What a challenge for a young bride," said Georgiana, smiling at Catherine.

"The most challenging thing isn't choosing the new décor," she said and Will's stomach tensed. "It's finding one's husband when there are so many rooms."

The ladies tittered. Freddy twisted in his chair to look at her more closely. Will admired the way Catherine ignored his disgraceful behaviour.

"So which family were you from before the Irises got hold of you?" he asked.

"The Rhoeas-Papavers," she replied.

"Ah, the red poppy lot, yes." Freddy waved one of the attendants over since his glass remained empty. "Well, the thing you need to know about Londinium is that there's no Master of Ceremonies or Censor, which means we can have a lot more fun."

"What Freddy is trying to say," Georgiana cut in, "is that Londinium is less socially prescriptive than Aquae Sulis."

"Oh, I don't believe that for a moment," Catherine replied and a chill descended over the table. Seeming oblivious as she winkled another sliver of lobster out of its shell, she continued, "It just won't be so blatant. Every social group has implicit and explicit rules about behaviour, but without a Master and Censor, the most influential of the Ton will control Society instead. It will be just as rigid, only less open."

She looked up when no one spoke, right at Georgiana. Then she glanced at Will and added, "That's what my uncle said anyway."

"Well, he would say that, wouldn't he dear?" said Margritte. Will gave Catherine as discreet a smile as he could. Good catch, Catherine, he thought. He noted that their hostess knew Lavandula was her uncle. She'd done her research.

"And your uncle is…?" Freddy asked, who clearly hadn't.

"The Master of Ceremonies," she replied. "He's my mother's brother. Of course he has an opinion on absolutely everything."

She was more able than she thought herself to be. Will felt a rush of relief and hope for the future. If he could just bolster her confidence, she was intelligent enough to be a real asset.

He noticed a look from Bartholomew when she said it. Yes, he thought, that's how I got the property. He could imagine the calculations Bartholomew was making: strong family with wealth on his side, massively influential and powerful uncle and aunt on her side…was he being reconsidered as a threat?

"The city has been shaken to the core by the fall of the Rosas," Bartholomew said. "We're still coming to terms with it all. It's a very uncertain time."

"It's about bloody time if you ask me," Freddy said after tipping the last dregs of the second glass down his throat. "Bloody Roses had their fingers in everything. We couldn't fart without one of them claiming the right to tithe it."

Catherine laughed at that, whilst Margritte took a sudden interest in her wine glass and the slightest sigh escaped from Freddy's wife.

"It will be interesting to see how things settle," Bartholomew said and the third course was brought in.

The conversation skirted around the Rosas a little more before

Will gently steered it towards safer topics such as their honeymoon and the delights of London.

"Wonderful place," Freddy said. "Owe every one of my grey hairs to it. M'wife says I visit it too much but every time I go back there something has changed. Fascinating." He turned to Catherine. "Soho is a very different place now, of course."

"Full of media companies and restaurants now, I understand," she said breezily, but Will noted how Freddy had dabbed at his mouth with the napkin, laid it back down on his lap but not brought his hand back up to his cutlery. Moments later Catherine's back straightened and her jaw clenched.

Just as Will was about to say something, Freddy sniggered to himself and the left hand came back up to take his fork again. Catherine was frowning at her meal, a gentle flush in her cheeks, and it took everything in him not to yell an accusation at Freddy.

"What exactly is a media company?" Margritte asked.

"Another mundane way to make money out of something utterly incomprehensible," Georgiana replied.

The conversation then divided. Margritte, Freddy and Georgiana sucked Will into a discussion about what the mundanes got up to in the city, whilst Bartholomew spoke at length with Catherine. Will did his best to maintain a presence in the former whilst listening in on the latter. It seemed mostly about Aquae Sulis at first, and the Lavandula connection, then he heard the names of some composers, and as the meat was served it sounded like they'd moved onto philosophy. Catherine was bright-eyed and animated by the time the fourth course was over. She seemed to be actually enjoying the conversation with the host. Will just prayed she wasn't saying anything inappropriate.

He suspected she was eager to hold a close conversation with Bartholomew to exclude Freddy as politely as possible. He was gulping down the wine like a man just rescued from a desert and had the table manners of a goat. How his wife could stand it, he had no idea.

Just as the salads were being served he noticed Freddy's hand below the table again. Margritte was consulting the butler about wine, while Georgiana was drawing Bartholomew's attention away from Catherine, who was also looking at Freddy's hand out of the corner of her eye. Catherine met Will's eyes across the table and he tried to convey that he knew what was happening. Catherine slowly and deliberately looked down at a fork, drawing his gaze. He watched her slide it beneath her napkin and then, with impressive subtlety, lower both below the table line. Freddy was too busy pretending to listen to Margritte to notice what Catherine was doing.

Will considered saying something, but was too captivated by the way Catherine held his eyes. Then, as Freddy's hand moved too far to the left, she raised an eyebrow as if to say, "Speak now or never," and then jabbed the prongs into Freddy's flesh.

He roared and his hand flew upwards, overturning his plate. Will kept his attention on Catherine, who was putting the fork back calmly with a satisfied smile.

"Frederick, really!" Georgiana shrieked. "Whatever is the matter?"

Freddy looked at Catherine, who turned to look at him, the smile not leaving her lips. "Is something wrong?"

"Did you manage to get any sleep?" Petra asked from the doorway as Max discarded the blanket.

"I did, what time is it?"

"Three in the morning. We had to put the gargoyle in the scullery for a few hours, it was wearing the carpet out." She passed him his walking stick. "I think it was excited. Mr Ekstrand is just fitting it with some new bracers now."

Max stood, ready for the familiar twinge whenever he moved his leg after a period of rest. "What for? Is something wrong with the old ones?"

"No, I'll let him explain. He's waiting for you in his study."

"Which one?"

"The one he lets people into."

Max followed her down the hallway, past the assortment of decorated doors and the monitoring room, to one near the end. It was made of plain wood with "Private, no apprentices, no owls" engraved upon it. Max wasn't aware there'd been any problems with owls. Nothing had filtered through to the Chapter anyway.

Petra knocked. "I have Maximilian with me, Mr Ekstrand," she called through the wood.

"Bring him in!"

Max followed her, finding the Sorcerer lacing the left bracer of a new set on the gargoyle's wrist. "Just wait till you see this," it said with a grin.

"Keep still." Ekstrand tied the last knot in the leather. "Good. Walk over there."

He pointed at the far side of the room. On first glance it looked like an average study with its large desk, shelves of books and comfortable chair, but Max's trained eye spotted the tiny lines of formulae inscribed on the bookshelves and the slight discrepancies in wear indicating there was something concealed beneath the silk rug. The gargoyle walked across the room to the far bookcase. Silently. Over rug, over wooden floorboard, the usual clunking of heavy stone was gone.

Ekstrand beamed and looked at Petra, who rewarded him with a delicate round of applause. The gargoyle appeared to be equally delighted.

"Very useful," said Max, nodding.

"Well, it is Thursday after all, technically speaking," Ekstrand said, looking very pleased with himself.

"Now you can take me with you," the gargoyle said. "When you check out the Agency."

"I was planning on going alone," Max said, but Ekstrand shook his head.

"I read your report on what the puppet told us about this Agency. I don't like it, not one bit. We're not going to visit these people in the usual way."

The usual way, the one that Max had been trained in and that had been used by the Chapter for over a thousand years, involved walking up to the residence in question, in either Mundanus or the Nether, and knocking three times slowly whilst wearing the knuckle-duster he always carried in his pocket. Everyone in the Great Families knew what it meant, the rules associated with it and the penalties of refusing access.

"Can I ask why, sir?"

"Something one should never do, when dealing with something completely unknown, is make assumptions," Ekstrand said. "I too planned to send you there to demand entry and see what in the Worlds they get up to, but when I saw the Tracker's resting location, and put it together with the facts in the report, I concluded that we cannot assume these people respect the rules."

"They're of Society, and therefore not innocents, so they're still bound by those rules," Max said. In the Split Worlds there was no such thing as exemption; the Treaty bound Society, the Fae and, in their own way, the Sorcerers.

"But that's another assumption. Why do we not know about them? Have they deliberately hidden themselves from scrutiny? If so, why? What are they hiding?"

"You want me to go in covertly?"

"Yes."

"With a walking gargoyle?"

"Yes. It's much quieter now, aren't you?"

The gargoyle nodded earnestly. "And I can hit hard too. Not that we'll need to hit anyone. Hopefully."

"And what if we're discovered?"

"Well, then it's time to hit them with the full force of the rules and remind them of your status."

Max nodded, understanding perfectly. Apply the rules when most convenient to him. Not usual, but hardly unheard of. And with no innocents involved, he wasn't going to argue.

"You said something about the location making you worried. Where will I be going?"

"Three quarters of a mile from the northernmost border of the Heptarchy, near Stirling."

"It's an area under dispute, a no-man's-land," Petra added. "The Sorcerer of Northumbria still has occasional skirmishes with the King of Caledonia. There's an uneasy truce that hasn't been broken for the last century, but neither seems willing to back down over a stretch of land between them."

"Which just happens to be where the Tracker ended up?" Max asked and both Petra and Ekstrand nodded. "I can see why you're being cautious, sir. You suspect this Agency might be exploiting the conflict and preventing either side's claim to win out?"

"Exactly," Ekstrand said.

"It would be a way to have a location outside any formal jurisdiction," Petra added. "It would also explain why this Agency has escaped attention for so long."

"They have enough resources if the puppet is to be believed," Max added.

"Cathy hasn't lied to us at any point," the gargoyle said, eliciting a raised eyebrow from Ekstrand.

"There's just one issue with this, sir." Max wanted to keep everything focused on the task ahead rather than on any inappropriate attachments being formed by the gargoyle. "If the Agency is located in a place outside anyone's jurisdiction, won't that make it difficult to fall back on the rules if we're discovered?"

Ekstrand rubbed his chin. "Good point. Better not be detected then, not until we know more about them. They may be utterly harmless, nothing more than a supplier of staff and furniture."

"You don't actually believe that, do you?" the gargoyle asked.

"No. Not for a moment. So be on your guard, don't get caught and if you do...don't mention me."

13

Once the roving hand was back in its rightful place, Cathy enjoyed the rest of the meal much more. Bartholomew was every bit the perfect host and she had the feeling he was actually enjoying their conversation. Freddy had laughed outrageously and clapped her on the back as if she were a fellow member of a gentlemen's club. He didn't try to touch her again.

William seemed to approve of her solution to Freddy's behaviour and yet again she found herself noticing how handsome he looked in his smart frock coat and cravat. She endeavoured to focus on Bartholomew for the rest of the evening and, whenever she caught herself glancing through the candlelight to check on William, she reminded herself that falling for her husband would not help her plans to graduate and carve out a career in Mundanus.

Once the dessert dishes were cleared, the last moment Cathy had been dreading arrived: the retirement to the drawing room whilst the men smoked cigars and drank port. With only two other ladies, both of whom knew each other well, Cathy knew there would be a horrible amount of attention focused upon her. She didn't want to make a mess of it, but if she truly didn't care, why be worried?

The lavishly decorated drawing room had chairs that were comfortable enough.

"Now, tell us truthfully," Georgiana said, sitting next to her. "Are you settling in well? Is there anything we can do to help?"

Cathy didn't believe the offer for a moment. She'd fallen for the same trick played by her sister too many times; Elizabeth would pretend to offer help in order to discover a weakness and then exploit it at the first opportunity.

"That's very kind," Cathy replied. "But nothing has proved insurmountable yet."

"Well, the Agency make it all so easy, don't they?" Margritte said, sitting opposite them. "As long as one has good taste and a good judge of character, they take care of the rest."

"They definitely make it easy—easy to be conned," Cathy said.

"Whatever do you mean?" Georgiana narrowed her eyes and Cathy wondered if she was about to make her first catastrophic mistake of the evening.

Will declined the offer of a cigar, not wanting to reek of smoke in the carriage and give Catherine another excuse to keep him away. He accepted the port with thanks as Freddy stumbled over to a cupboard in the corner of the room. He opened it, and the front of his trousers, and began peeing into the pot within. Freddy couldn't even do that without grunting like a warthog.

"May I compliment you on your wife, William," Bartholomew said, port glass in one hand and cigar in the other. He was leaning back in his chair, relaxed and able to speak as if Freddy wasn't there.

"Thank you."

"She's very intelligent. And not afraid to debate. Most refreshing."

"And good to get a plain one," Freddy said as he slammed the cupboard shut. He sat down again and tipped his glass back as far as he could to get every drop of the port.

"What do you mean?" Will asked.

"Good of the family to pair you off with a plain wife. Always better in bed, the plain ones, always so grateful."

Will set his glass down and was on his feet but Freddy didn't notice with his head still tipped back, looking up at the chandelier as he waved his empty glass around.

"Better than being saddled with a beauty," he drawled. "They're so demanding."

"I say, sir." Will, not getting a response from Freddy, turned to the host. "I must protest."

"Must you? What? Why?" Freddy tipped himself upright again. Some drool was shining in his muttonchops and his eyes were unfocused. "Barty, what's he all worked up about?"

"My apologies, William," Bartholomew said, raising a hand slightly to assure him it was under control. "Frederick, it's time for you to go home."

"Really? Haven't started playing cards yet though."

"It's time," Bartholomew said firmly.

"Oh." Freddy looked remorseful. "Have I caused offence, old chap?"

"You have indeed, sir. I demand an apology," Will replied.

"You have it, old boy! I lose my tongue sometimes and I mean no harm, no harm at all. And your wife is a delightfully spirited filly, I'll wager she—"

"Frederick." Bartholomew cut him off with an imperious bark. "Get his cloak and gloves," he said to the butler and then to Will, "Please accept my apologies too."

Will gave a curt nod and sat back down as Freddy struggled to his feet.

"Where's m'wife?" he slurred.

Will watched him with disgust, realising that it wasn't just form that had elicited his protest. He'd felt genuinely affronted.

"And by questioning his calculations I saved the household over one hundred thousand of the Queen's pounds per year."

The ticking of the clock seemed very loud. Both Margritte and Georgiana were speechless, making that awful nervous giggle build in Cathy's throat as the two women looked at each other. Cathy wondered if there was a social equivalent of chicken being played out silently in front of her. Who would react first? And which way should it go?

"They're exploiting the fact we would never talk openly about this kind of thing," she went on, trying to tip the tension over into something in her favour. "And whilst I may have committed a faux pas in being so truthful about it, I hope you see that it's in our best interests to do so. They have a monopoly so they feel they can bully us into doing things the way they want, but it shouldn't be that way."

"Monopoly?" Georgiana asked.

"They're the only service provider. They know there's no other agency for us to go to, so we feel we have to keep them happy. It all happens subliminally in the social setting, and then, when the meeting's over, everything's geared up to make it difficult, and embarrassing to ask questions or make complaints, do you see?"

"I do!" Margritte said, and slapped her closed fan against her palm. "Georgiana, don't pull that face, she's right! We shouldn't let pride interfere with common sense."

"The thing about common sense," Georgiana began in a tone that reminded Cathy of a character in an Oscar Wilde play, "is that—"

The door opened and the butler appeared. "Begging your pardon, milady, but Mr Viola has asked for his wife. I understand he's about to leave."

"Oh, he's drunk and belligerent again." Georgiana sighed as she stood up. "Really, the man is insufferable."

She spoke only to Margritte, as if she'd forgotten Cathy was there. The hostess didn't look surprised and gave Georgiana a sympathetic smile. Hasty goodbyes were made and she left, the sounds of her husband's bellowing echoing down the hallway.

"Does that often happen?" Cathy asked and Margritte nodded. "Then why do people still invite him? In Aquae Sulis he'd never see the inside of another person's dining room ever again."

"Well," Margritte said, sitting back down and inviting Cathy to do the same, "it's probably because he's disgustingly rich."

Cathy laughed at her plain speaking and Margritte smiled. "Catherine, I believe you may be just the breath of fresh air the Londinium salons need. I would be delighted if you could come to a soirée we're planning for a week from now. Something gentle to get people back into the mood again after all of this upheaval."

"Thank you, that's very kind."

"Seeing as the Violas have left, perhaps we should rejoin our husbands and play a game of cards a little earlier than usual. I'm sure Bartholomew won't mind—he seemed quite taken with you, and your husband is a delight."

"A delight?" She was about to make a comment about telling him that later when she felt the strangest sensation, deep in her stomach, as if she had just been in a very fast lift and reached the top floor.

"Yes, don't you agree?"

"Well..." It happened again and she gripped the edge of the sofa, squeezing her eyes shut against a pulse of vertigo.

"Oh, my dear, are you feeling unwell?"

"I do feel a little odd."

"Catherine?" William was at the doorway. Bartholomew was already in the room, though she hadn't noticed him enter. "Are you all right?"

"I'm so sorry," she said to the hosts, "but would you mind if we—" She stopped, the vertigo making her feel like she was about to fall off the sofa, this time accompanied by a twinge in her left hand.

"I'd like to take Catherine home. Will you permit me to thank you for a most pleasant evening?" William said as he crossed the room to her side.

She took his hands gratefully as the worst of the latest wave faded. He helped her to stand and she hoped she wasn't going to make a habit of fainting in his arms. That would just be too much.

"It was a pleasure to meet you both," Bartholomew said. "Catherine, I do hope you feel better soon."

After a flurry of capes and hats, Cathy found herself in the carriage once more. "I'm sorry," she said. "I don't know what's wrong with me, I've never been like this...must be married life." There was another awful lurch in her stomach. "Oh, God, do you think it was the lobster? I can't stand being sick. Do you feel strange?"

He moved across to put his arm around her. She found it comforting and then tried to ignore it.

"I know what it is," he said, resting a hand over hers and kissing her gently on the cheek.

"If you say it's something to do with starting to fall in love I swear I will vomit all over you."

He pulled a face. "Good grief, Catherine, you do say the most awful things. Does your stomach feel like it wants to move in the opposite direction to where you're going?" When she nodded he said, "And you feel dizzy, it comes in waves and there's…a tension, underneath it all?" She nodded again. "You're not ill. You're being summoned."

"That sounds bad," she whispered. The rocking of the carriage was making the vertigo worse. "What does it mean?"

"Lord Iris wants to see you."

She felt a lot worse. "You're saying he's doing this? How can he make me feel ill?"

He brushed her wedding ring with his index finger. "I'm sorry. It must be this. You're an Iris now."

"Oh, for fuck's sake, this just keeps getting worse! What else does this bloody ring do? Suck my soul out?"

"I don't think it does anything else. And whilst I understand your distress, please don't use that language."

"Sorry," she whispered. "I'm upset. Hang on, you know how it feels…it's happened to you?"

"Once, just before I left on the Grand Tour. He wanted to speak to me."

"And you felt like this until you saw him?"

"If you speak his name and say you're on your way, it eases, for a time."

Feeling foolish, and distinctly unsettled, she said, "Lord Iris, I'm on my way."

The tug in her gut disappeared and her head cleared.

"Better?" he asked.

"Will he hear what I'm saying now?"

William shrugged. "He's very powerful, but I don't know if it works like that. I imagine he's able to detect your desire to comply with his wishes."

He didn't move his hand when hers formed into a fist. "I don't know how you can bear it. This is worse than being a Poppy. All those years I thought it was hell but even when I was locked in that damn room I had more freedom than this." She caught the build-up to a rant and shut up. "I'm feeling better. You can let go now."

"I don't want to." He smiled. "I wanted to say how impressed I was."

"The food was very nice. Now, please, go and sit over there for goodness' sake."

He did so, but only after another kiss, its gentleness at odds with the fury she was trying to contain. She wanted to rant and rave and punch the seat cushions, cursing Iris and the entirety of Society, but he was so happy it felt absurd to show any of it.

"I wasn't impressed with the food, but with you." He slid down in the seat; it was the first time she could remember him seeming even remotely relaxed. "All that worry and you impressed them immensely, particularly Bartholomew."

"You don't mind that I stuck a fork in one of the guests?"

"Absolutely not. Freddy deserved it, disgusting man. If you hadn't handled it yourself I would have had to call him out. I almost did when we were having the port." He looked distant for a moment, his brow furrowed and cheeks pink. "He did howl though, didn't he?" He laughed.

The rage tipped over and she burst into laughter too as she recalled Freddy's roar. The carriage filled with the sound of the two of them laughing.

"Why do you think Lord Iris wants to see me?" she said once they'd settled down.

"I have no idea."

"Have I done something wrong?"

"Not in my eyes. The only thing we need to do is make a go of it. I think it really could work between us, do you see? You're clever, you're funny, when you're not being irritating or offensive, that is." He said it with a smile. "I felt proud of you this evening. Bartholomew complimented you most highly. I think that's an achievement in and of itself."

She felt a quickening in her chest: excitement. This is what it was to get it right, then, the feeling that Elizabeth must have had countless times in her life, one that until now had been alien to her. Feeling her cheeks grow hot, Cathy couldn't look at him as she tried to hold onto the feeling before it was destroyed by someone or something. Her gaze drifted downwards and she saw the ring, the thing they'd forced onto her, the tiny chains about her all held in that single band.

She was disgusted with herself. One taste of success, one bit of praise and she was ready to delude herself into thinking it actually meant anything other than the reinforcement of her slavery.

"What?" he asked.

"I nearly fell for it," she said. "I nearly started to think like they do."

He massaged his temples. "Why does it all have to be so complicated? Has it occurred to you that Londinium may just suit you in a way Aquae Sulis never could? Can't you appreciate that what happened this evening was a triumph and let yourself feel good about it?"

"Obtaining your approval, and that of Society, is not something I ever want to aspire to, so I shouldn't let it feel good when I get it."

He groaned, throwing his hands into the air. "You are simply determined to be unhappy!"

"You're determined to mould me into something I'm not. You and Iris, no doubt." She felt a flicker of anxiety at the thought of him.

"I know you're afraid." He reached across, but she pulled her hands back and he withdrew. "I was, when I had to go to him."

His unrelenting kindness irritated her. "I don't even know how to get into Exilium."

"Now you've been summoned, all you need to do is stand in

front of a mirror, alone, and speak his name three times." William's voice was quiet and his fingers were laced tightly together.

"You're worried too," she said.

"Of course I am," he snapped. "You're my wife."

The words were like a slap. She sank into silence, oscillating between the desire to scream and the need to weep with fear. She hated the feeling of being like a cork bobbing in the ocean, lifted up and down by them all.

"He's very precise," William said after a while. "He won't accept anything less than total obedience and deference. Your manners must be impeccable."

"All right."

"You don't need to pretend to be delighted about the marriage, not in the way Lord Poppy seemed to want you to be at the Oak. I think it's irrelevant to our patron. All that matters is that you do as you're told, regardless of how you feel about it."

"My father would approve," she said, wondering whether he'd had any idea of the life he'd forced her into. Not that it would have changed anything.

"And I assume you know not to eat or drink anything, and to be wary of—"

"I know how to survive in Exilium."

"Good. You should go there as soon as we're home. And wear that dress. You look very fine in it."

She felt remorseful then, for throwing everything back in his face all the time. "Thank you," she said, but he just looked out of the window. Perhaps he was right, perhaps she could make a go of it in Society, if that evening was anything to go by. She had actually started to relax in Margritte's company and was sad to leave so suddenly. But was it even possible to make a friend in the Nether?

14

Sam scratched his neck and felt the stubble. He'd been wearing the same clothes for three days, hadn't left the house in the last four and was watching daytime television. He grabbed the remote and killed the show. His life was never going to be enriched by a discussion about which man had fathered which baby. "You slob," he said to himself.

He got up and stretched, doing his best to ignore the pile of unopened post he'd dumped on the chair. It had been building up for a while and yet he just couldn't face opening it. He was supposed to call an estate agent, probably at least three, and get the house on the market but he couldn't face that either.

He trudged up the stairs, peed and stood in front of the sink, trying to muster the energy to have a shave. He was out of routine and with no job; being clean-shaven had lost its importance.

He pulled a stray hair from the sink as he revisited over and over again in his memory the moment of being sacked. He couldn't deny that his work had suffered and important deadlines had been missed. He hadn't argued when his boss had accused him of being irresponsible and neglectful and letting the rest of the team down. It was all true. He just didn't care anymore.

He'd packed up his personal belongings, said goodbye to Dave, who was too shocked to insult him, and came home. That first day he hardly moved as he tried to work out when exactly he'd stopped caring.

He wondered if Exilium had done it. After seeing a place like that, its colours and beauty, everything else had felt dull in comparison. But his memories of the place had already faded again, like the places he'd visited as a backpacking student.

"You're a slob and terrible husband," he said to the grotty face in the mirror. He'd been unemployed for less than a week and already looked like he'd never earned an honest wage in his life. He still hadn't told Leanne either.

He shaved and showered. By the time he was towelling himself off he felt a little better. He'd decided he should make the most of the time, eat better, get a little exercise. At least he didn't have to serve out a tedious notice period. He put the toilet seat down and sat in the steam, shaking his head. Who was he trying to kid? He felt like shit.

His mobile phone rang and he reached it just in time. "Lee?"

"Hi, Sam."

He checked his watch. Eleven thirty in the morning. "You OK? Has something happened?"

"I called your work phone."

"Oh."

"Dave said you've been sacked."

He chucked the towel on the bed and sat on top of it. For a few seconds there was no sound except the pattering of drips on the carpet. "Yeah, about that…I was waiting till I saw you."

Her high heels were clicking down a corridor, then there was the quiet squeak of a door opening and it sounded less echoey. "When did it happen?"

"Couple of days ago."

"And you didn't tell me?"

"Like I said, I was waiting till I saw you this weekend."

"Are you going to move to London now?"

"I…" He didn't know what to say. He couldn't explain that he was waiting for an Arbiter's report on her boss, the company she worked for and the dodgy apartment they'd given her.

"Have you at least got the house on the market?"

"Well, the thing is—"

"I don't think you want to move to London. I'm beginning to think you don't want to be with me anymore."

"I came to see you, didn't I? I wanted to talk but you just kept—"

"I've had enough."

"Of what?"

"This. Us, the marriage. You're not committed, you—"

"*I'm* not committed? You're the one who moved to London at the drop of a hat!"

"I want a separation. This hasn't been working for a long time and we've both been deluding ourselves. You don't want to live with me anymore, otherwise you'd have jumped at the chance to move up here sooner."

"Bloody hell, it's been two days! I needed to come to terms with it."

"What's there to come to terms with? You were going to hand your notice in anyway, weren't you?"

He paused. He hadn't planned to do that. He hadn't planned any of it, not the Fae, not the Fool's Charm, not the kidnapping or the weird wedding-ring business, none of it. The sharp pitch of her voice reminded him of the new Leanne, the skinny, driven, joyless woman he'd barely recognised at the flat. Why bother to fight for the marriage anymore?

"If that's what you want," he said and she ended the call. He listened to the silence for a moment, then let his hand drop to his lap and the phone slide to the floor.

The wedding band tingled as Cathy approached the mirror. William watched from the doorway to their bedroom. She looked at him as she spoke Lord Iris's name three times, making the glass ripple, and then Exilium was revealed in its hyper-coloured glory.

"Good luck," he mouthed silently.

The worry in his eyes made her hesitate and the tingling strengthened until it became uncomfortable. She stepped through, taking the hint. The trees of Lord Iris's domain were straight in front of her, which reduced the risk of running into Lord Poppy. She breathed in through her nose, released the breath slowly out of her mouth to steady herself, and then walked forwards.

Just like Poppy's domain there was a path leading deeper into the copse. The trees were more densely packed the further in she went, making it feel more like a tunnel. Soon she caught sight of splashes of iris blue, then some of the flowers edged the path. As she passed, the blooms turned as if they were watching her. She tried not to think about that.

She expected to reach a clearing, but instead the path led to a structure made of saplings. They'd been woven into a complex latticework half-dome, its apex twice the height of her. Lord Iris was seated within it on a chair carved out of a large tree stump. His long white hair was perfectly straight and his eyes the same blue as the flowers surrounding them, freakish in their lack of pupil, iris and humour, just a solid blue. He wore a black frock coat and trousers, very similar in cut to what William had been wearing that evening. His waistcoat was embroidered with golden thread, each tiny iris flower beaded and sparkling with the small amount of sunlight that reached them.

Cathy shivered under his gaze, dropped into a deep curtsy immediately and waited to be invited closer. Again, all of the flowers were turned towards her and she felt as if she were being watched by dozens of creatures, not one Fae lord.

"Come here." It was the first time she'd heard his voice and there was no warmth in it. At the wedding, he'd spoken only with Lord Poppy and the Patroons.

She straightened herself and walked forwards. He watched her with a terrible intensity. When she was a few feet away she slowed, now beneath the half-dome, but he pointed to a spot just in front of him. She clenched her chattering teeth and moved closer until she was mere inches from his hand. It felt too close. He looked down at the ground beneath his finger most deliberately and she realised he expected her to kneel. She planted her left knee exactly where he pointed and knelt on ground soft with fallen leaves.

Now she would have to look up to his face, which was of course what he wanted. There was none of the chaotic danger she felt around Poppy—instead she felt chilled to her core. If he carried on staring at her like that he would bleach the colour from her hair as well as her cheeks.

"Your hand," he said, pointing to her left.

She extended it towards him, trying to stop it from quivering. He mimed turning it palm up, which she did and he slid his hand beneath it until her wrist rested on his palm. His cold fingers curled around it. All of the tiny hairs on her body stood on end as he touched her and her heartbeat went from fast to frantic. His thumb curled until it was a couple of inches above her pulse point, then the nail elongated and sharpened into a talon. She gasped and reflexively pulled her hand away but his grip tightened just as quickly, his fingers holding her fast.

"Look at me." She forced herself to look into the intense blue, feeling the deep primal fear of being exposed to something so alien. "You are one of mine now," he said. "Poppy no longer holds dominion over your blood and bones."

She was certain he could feel her shivering. "Yes, my lord," she stammered. What else could she say?

"In all the time I have known Poppy, one as plain as you has never caught his eye, let alone stolen his affection. Never have I seen him so enthralled by such an unremarkable creature. There's only one conclusion to be reached: you're not as unremarkable as you appear to be."

"Or..." Cathy ventured, "he could be mistaken, and his affection misplaced."

"I did not invite you to speak," he said. "Poppy may have delighted in your opinion, but I am not he. You are here to answer my questions. Do you understand?"

"Yes, my Lord." She spoke with as much deference as she could but it had never come easily to her.

"Why did Poppy value you so highly?"

The last thing Cathy wanted to do was tell the truth, but she didn't know if she could bear to lie under his scrutiny. "I impressed him, my Lord. And amused him."

"How did you impress him?"

"I…I managed to humiliate a Rosa."

A tiny movement at her wrist tore her eyes from his; the thumbnail was closer to her skin. "How?"

"By helping a mundane man beat him in a duel."

"A Rosa duelling a mundane? What precipitated this?"

She hesitated, and the talon moved closer. "A wish I made, my Lord. It resulted in the Rosa losing a mundane woman he'd been promised. But it wasn't my fault."

"Who granted you a wish?"

"Lord Poppy."

"Only one?"

She could hear the shortness of her breath as the nail moved closer. "Three, my Lord. I was tasked to impress him with my choices, which I did."

"You told me humiliating the Rosa impressed him."

"It…it was complicated." She struggled to speak, the fear tightening her throat as the nail hovered above the vein. It was dark blue and she could see her pulse making the skin quiver up and down.

"Poppy was never complicated. He hasn't granted any of his pets three wishes for five generations. Why give them to you?"

"A whim?" She didn't want to reveal what had really caught Poppy's eye.

The nail touched the skin, as sharp as a pin, making her jolt and the breath fly from her lungs. She couldn't take her eyes off it and felt his intense focus on the top of her head. As the seconds passed the pressure increased, so slight she thought she was imagining it, then she saw the skin being pushed inwards and the pain increased.

"I asked to go to university at my coming of age," she blurted, but the pressure didn't ease. "And then I ran away from my family and lived in Mundanus." She felt the skin break. "I hid from them for over a year," she cried as a deep-red bead rose and started to trickle up the nail in a most unnatural way. "I hid from Poppy too until he found me, I don't know how!"

The blood ran back down the nail, pooling where its sharp tip was still pressed. Her heartbeat was roaring in her ears, she could feel sweat rolling down her back and she shook violently. It was hardly a wound, yet she felt as much distress as if it had been a knife driven deep.

"Always better to tell me the truth as soon as you speak." He tilted his head, studying her discomfort. "Such fragile reluctance…" The nail drove deeper and the bead of blood elongated into a narrow rivulet, sliding down the side of her wrist onto his fingers. "There is something you cling to, a vain hope perhaps."

He squeezed and she cried out in pain, frustrated by her impotence and enraged by his casual cruelty.

"That's better," he said. "I can hear your secret now. Did you really think that learning of your little rebellion would concern me? Did your family lock you away once you were returned?"

She nodded, watching the blood and wanting to run.

"And you think that now I know your plan to do it again, I'll do the same?"

She looked up from the nail to his eyes, closer than they were before. How did he know? A good guess?

"A mortal says so much when in crisis, and they rarely use words," he whispered, answering her silent question. "Answer me."

"Yes," she said, doing everything she could to hold in the gathering tears.

"And that hope endures even after I summoned you. I have no concern about your fantasy, for that's all it can be now. You felt my summons. There is no magic in the Split Worlds that can hide you from me, should I discover you've disobeyed your new family." The fingers holding her wrist curled and she saw their nails growing too, felt them prickle her skin but not pierce it yet. "But now we have met, I'm sure you are more keen to please my family."

"Yes, yes, of course," she said and screamed when the four other points drew blood.

"Not very intelligent. Lie to me again and I will write this lesson into your flesh with scars only you can see."

Tears splattered on the leaves in front of her. "I'm sorry," she whispered.

"There's something Lord Poppy holds over you. He mentions it when we see each other. He seems to think he still has some claim to you. Is there a contract between you?"

"He…he made me promise to paint him the best picture of my generation."

"You're an artist?"

"No, my Lord, but my third wish was to reach my full potential. After I made it, he told me to find paints and canvasses." She didn't mention the new deadline, fearing she'd suck Sam into Lord Iris's schemes as well as Poppy's.

He looked at her, *into* her. She shut her eyes, the urge to withdraw too strong for a moment, but she could still see them, like twin blue suns burnt into her retina. When she looked again his left hand was reaching towards her head and she twitched fearfully.

Lord Iris plucked out a hair—the brief sting barely registered above the pain in her wrist—and then tipped his head back and dangled the hair into his mouth like a length of spaghetti. He closed his lips around it and pulled it back up and out as if he was sucking something off it. As the strand emerged, no hint of the natural brown remained. He let go when the entire white length was free of his lips and the strand became a powdery dust that drifted to the forest floor.

"Lord Poppy may be mercurial, but he's no fool," he said, taking her chin and directing her attention back to him. "Now I know what it was he saw in you, and it was not artistic talent. There's no capacity for art within you. Even if you struggled for years you would produce nothing more than the mediocre." His thin lips formed a smile. "Very clever. I won't underestimate him again." Still holding her chin, he tipped her head back slightly, exposing her throat, then moved her from side to side, taking in every detail of her face.

As his words penetrated her fear, she wanted to ask questions and demand to know what her potential was if not artistic in nature. Why had Poppy lied? But she didn't dare open her mouth, especially with her wrist still skewered.

"How many days have passed in Mundanus since the wedding?"

"Four, my lord." And she still hadn't had a chance to find someone to teach her how to paint. If the Shopkeeper's special Charm didn't arrive in time—

"Instead of hankering for a life that's not yours to lead, obey your husband and focus on how to serve me to the best of your ability. As for this painting nonsense, your loyalty is to me now, not Poppy. Now it's time for you to go back and be a *good wife*." He punctuated the last words with a slight squeeze of the nails into her skin, before releasing her.

She swayed, the blood tickling her wrist as it flowed from the puncture wounds. Fearing he would be angry if she soiled her dress, she struggled to her feet, holding her arm out at the side. She curtsied inelegantly and then backed away, head still bowed, like a medieval courtier knowing better than to turn her back on the King.

When Lord Iris looked away it felt so different to be free of his intense stare. She reached the edge of the clearing, turned and hurried along the path, grateful to see a Way open before she even got to the edge of the copse. She could see the bedroom and staggered through, lightheaded and clumsy.

"Catherine!" William had waited the whole time, out of sight from Exilium. "My God." He paled as he took in the blood, grabbed a neatly folded handkerchief from his pocket and rushed to her side.

"Go away." She glanced back to see the Way closing. She sank to her knees, her legs too watery to stand. William knelt in front of her, wrapped the silk around her wrist and pressed tight.

"What happened?" he asked, but she couldn't speak. He drew her into an embrace and she pushed at his chest briefly then accepted the comfort. She sobbed into his frock coat, the two of them kneeling on the floor of the bedroom.

After a few minutes the worst of it was over. Her wrist throbbed dreadfully beneath his makeshift bandage and the hand that was still wrapped tightly around it. His other hand was rubbing her back gently as he reassured her she was safe.

She pulled back until she could see his face, ashamed to be snivelling like a child. He wiped away a tear with a thumb and stroked the back of her neck before kissing her on the forehead. "You need tea, and a rest," he said, in such a gentle voice she started to weep again. "And we should put a proper bandage on this."

"God, what is wrong with me?" She sniffed. "Honestly, William, I'm not like this."

"Shush, I don't mind, it must have been terrifying. Did Lord Iris do this?"

She nodded. "To make me talk about Poppy." The words unravelled as her chest heaved and the memory brought fresh tears with it.

"You're home now," he said, kissing her forehead again. "Let me take care of you. You've had a terrible shock."

"I don't want to—"

"For God's sake, Cathy," he said, standing and picking her up to carry her to the bed. "Stop fighting for just five minutes, will you?"

She rolled onto her side and curled as much as she could in her evening gown. She cradled her injury as he pulled the bell cord and then slipped her shoes off her feet. It felt too intimate and too demeaning to be cared for like this, like a wife. She should be keeping him at arm's length and the barriers up but she was so tired and wrung out she said nothing.

"Can you tell me what he said?"

"I don't want to think about it." She started to shiver again.

He sat next to her, stroking the wayward strands of hair away from her face. Where did he learn this compassion? How could he be capable of kindness, coming from a family so rigidly controlled and so cold?

He let her eyes search his, seeming happy for the moment to stretch. He gave the butler instructions for tea and the medical box to be brought, his hand never leaving her hair.

"I promised you I'd find a way to make this life bearable," he said. "I haven't forgotten that."

She thought of ten different ways to shoot his words down but spoke none of them. She could feel herself drawing inwards, no fight left. Iris had made it clear he could summon her back even if she did find a way back to her mundane life. There was no hope of escape any more, and, without that, what was there to push against? "You called me Cathy," she whispered.

"Do you mind if I do?"

"No. Only the people I hate most in the Worlds call me Catherine."

His smile was beautiful. "Then call me Will." The butler returned with a box and a maid set tea out on a nearby table. Will sent them both away. "I shall now impress you with my bandaging skills," he announced, opening the box. "All you need to do is watch with admiration and be thankful that Oliver Peonia is one of the clumsiest companions one could ever have on a Grand Tour."

She managed a smile, even though she could see his false cheeriness was just a means of covering up his fear. But wasn't that what they were all condemned to do with patrons such as theirs?

15

The Way closed behind them and Max shivered in the cold air of Mundanus. They were standing at the bottom of a hill and the lights of Stirling cast an orange glow on the distant cloud base. The bitter wind blasted through his coat, and he fastened the top button and pulled the compass out of his pocket. As his eyes adapted to the darkness he could just make out the needle's gentle glow.

"The Tracker should be at the top of the hill," he said to the gargoyle.

They both looked up and saw nothing but different shades of black. "I'll go and have a look," the gargoyle offered and Max nodded. He didn't want to struggle up a grassy slope with his walking stick unless absolutely necessary.

The gargoyle bounded off like an eager dog that had been shut indoors all day. Max quickly lost sight of it so he turned his collar up against the wind and looked at the town's lights. The gargoyle returned swiftly.

"We got a problem."

"Guards? Magical defences?"

"No. There's nothing there."

He checked the compass needle again. "The Tracker is up there somewhere. Are you sure?"

"Come up and see for yourself."

It was slow going and the gargoyle got more and more frustrated as the climb went on but Max went as fast as his aching leg would allow. At the summit there was nothing but a strengthening of the wind. Leaning on the stick as the gargoyle snuffled about, Max examined the needle and slowly closed in on the Tracker's location.

"Why are you doing that?" he asked the gargoyle. "Can you even smell anything?"

"I don't know," it replied. "I get this urge to sniff at things. It's been coming on stronger lately."

"Have you told the Sorcerer?"

"No." They looked at each other for a moment. "Do you think we should?"

"I've found it," Max said, distracted by the needle spinning round. "Have a dig about here, will you?"

The gargoyle did as it was asked and Max pulled out a penlight torch. He pointed it where the gargoyle rooted in the grass and a sparkle ended the search. The gargoyle scooped out a divot and handed it to Max.

Max plucked the Tracker from the clod of earth. It looked like a tiny clockwork ladybird with a brass shell. Max dropped the compass in a pocket and rummaged in another for his jeweller's loupe. He tucked it under his right eyebrow to inspect the details.

"It's a wonder you don't clank like a tinker's cart with all that stuff in your pockets."

Max ignored the gargoyle as he checked the Tracker was still intact, then inserted the tiny key he'd been given, which looked like a pin to the naked eye. The Tracker's shell opened and the workings inside looked in order as far as he could tell. Nothing was broken; it all seemed to be in the right place and when he pressed the minute nubbin at the heart of the workings with the key the six legs-cum-hooks extended and retracted exactly as they should.

Trackers were used for covert ops. They were designed to hook into clothing, or even sometimes into the hair of an animal, and stay hidden to monitor the movement of the target in and between Mundanus and the Nether. The formulae, too tiny for Max to read even with the loupe, could be altered to effectively programme the Tracker to alert the Chapter to whatever variable they needed. This Tracker had been set to wait for the target to stay in a location for more than three hours, then detach, leave the building and slip back into Mundanus to send a signal by arcane means beyond

Max's understanding. Ekstrand told him that wherever the Tracker was would be less than two metres from the anchor property, but the top of the hill was devoid of any structures at all.

"Don't blame this on Cathy," the gargoyle said.

"I wasn't even thinking about her."

"You were about to. She wouldn't have screwed up with the Tracker, I know she wouldn't."

"Why are you so keen to defend her?"

"Because no one else will."

"I'm not sure she'd appreciate that. She seems capable of fighting her own corner."

The gargoyle wrinkled its muzzle. Max focused back on the Tracker. There was no way to tell if it had failed or not, so he closed it up again and put it into the pouch Ekstrand had given him to bring it back safely.

"What do we do now?" the gargoyle asked.

"We could go back to Ekstrand and verify if the Tracker failed," Max said, "but we'd miss the perfect time to look around. Everyone will be asleep now. So, let's assume it has worked but has ended up further away from the anchor property than it should have."

"Maybe it mostly worked, then crapped out at the last moment," the gargoyle suggested.

"The Tracker couldn't have moved all the way up here, to the other side of the country and outside of the Heptarchy, all by itself."

"Perhaps the guy found it and attached it to something else to lead us to the wrong place."

"That's possible. Or he could have come through the Nether to a place in Stirling and walked up here to dump the device. I doubt that."

"Maybe they were watching the hill, saw me and thought, 'Bloody hell! A walking gargoyle! I'm not touching this with a six-foot bargepole,' and went home again."

"Perhaps…" Max looked around the hill. "But why here?"

"No witnesses."

"True. But what if the Tracker did work? Ekstrand was right

when he talked about assumptions. We're assuming that, just because we can't see an anchor property, there isn't one here. What if there's a place hidden inside this hill?"

The gargoyle grinned. "I like it. Where shall we start?"

Max pointed to a spot close to where the Tracker was found and shone the torch at it. The gargoyle started gouging out huge clumps of earth until there was a scrape of stone against stone. "Found something!"

Max directed the torch beam, peered in and saw a large block, buried. "Dig around it a bit, see if you can work out some dimensions."

The gargoyle dug a shallow trench quickly, exposing more of the stone and a couple of new ones. Max inspected them. "This isn't the top of a bunker," he said as the gargoyle groaned with disappointment. "These are old foundations. There was probably a fort here a long time ago. That disproves my theory."

The gargoyle shook its head. "I've got a feeling there's something here."

"You just don't want to go back to the Sorcerer and admit defeat."

"No, it's not that." It dug another couple of feet down. "You got that Peeper you used on the stolen house in Aquae Sulis?"

"Of course."

"Use it on this stone."

"Don't be daft."

"It'll only take two minutes."

Max shrugged, located the Peeper and gave it to the gargoyle. "Let's see if you can use it," he suggested, not wanting to struggle down onto his belly and lay his leg against damp, cold earth.

The gargoyle nestled down in the hollow and pressed the Peeper up against the stone.

"You'll have to adjust the lens to cope with the thickness of the stone," Max instructed.

"I know."

Max expected the Peeper to detach after alignment, as it would with any mundane surface without a Nether property anchored to it. Then they'd be left with no choice but to force the puppet to reveal how she'd stayed hidden.

"There's something there!"

"A bunker?" Max asked.

"No, I can see the floor, this is at ground level. The room goes up about another eight feet."

It made no sense; the gargoyle was looking through the side of the stone as if it formed a wall, not a ceiling. "But that's impossible, there's nothing above that stone for a room to be anchored to."

"Come and look for yourself."

The gargoyle helped Max to lie down and the cold penetrated his clothes immediately, making him all the more aware of the stubborn ache in his leg. Max peered through the circular device and saw a polished wooden floor stretching ahead of him. There was a row of desks, like an office rather than a schoolroom, and filing cabinets lined one of the walls, with shelves and shelves of huge ledgers above them. It was all visible thanks to the familiar pale grey light of the Nether. Max noted the lack of curtains on the windows. It wasn't like a private residence where heavy drapes were used to give the illusion of day and night. It looked like whoever worked in that room still kept a day/night schedule, however, because all the chairs were neatly tucked under the desks and it was empty of staff.

The gargoyle was right; the stone formed part of an anchor wall, close to the floor, but only the foundation seemed to remain in Mundanus. He'd never seen or heard of anything like it before. In fact, he wasn't sure how it was possible. Buildings owned by the puppets could only exist if anchored to a property in Mundanus. The cloisters that housed each of the Chapters were sometimes combinations of several reflections, but all of the parts were still anchored to a physical property in Mundanus. As far as he knew, the Fae were incapable of doing the same and the Sorcerers had taken great care to ensure it remained that way.

Had a Sorcerer revealed a secret technique? With the corruption in London the Sorcerer of Essex was the prime suspect. But why provide the Agency with that knowledge? If it became widely available to the puppets it could undermine most of the techniques used by the Arbiters to keep close tabs on Fae-touched society.

"This is big, isn't it?"

"It's big," Max said and detached the Peeper. "Just goes to show that it pays to be thorough."

"How do we get in?"

Max got the Opener and pushed the pin into the place the Peeper had been, the powerful formulae making it as easy as pushing a stick into mud. He twisted it and watched the familiar burning outline of the doorway form in the stone. He expected it to fail once it tried to progress past the stone but instead the outline continued upwards, as if a thin line of the air itself began to burn. The doorway formed just as it would have if the anchor property had been there. Max made mental notes of the details as the gargoyle jumped up and down, gushing about how it hadn't expected that and how exciting it all was. Max found it hard to believe it really was his soul trapped inside it.

The door formed. Max opened it and pulled out the Opener. He let it close behind him once the gargoyle was inside too. At least it had the sense to shut up.

The air inside the room had the familiar staleness of any Nether property. Max went to the one internal door that led to the rest of the house and gestured to the gargoyle to stay out of sight should anyone be walking past outside. It dropped low on all fours and slunk between the tables to lie beneath one of the large sash windows.

Max listened for movement on the other side of the door but all he could hear was the ticking of the clock above his head.

"I think they're all asleep," he whispered to the gargoyle.

"We should go outside, see what the whole place looks like," it replied. "These windows are too big for a fort, I want to see what kind of a building it is, and how big."

Max shook his head. "We only do that if we have time. We need to prioritise finding the information about the Rosas."

He went to the nearest filing cabinet. There was a small card in the holder on the first drawer he came to, with the letters "Y—Z" written on neatly. Max walked down the row to the one with "Ra—Re" written on it and moved down the drawers until he got to one labelled "Rosa". It made sense that one of the largest family lines should have an entire drawer dedicated to them.

He glanced up at the shelves above the filing cabinet and saw "Rosa" plus a range of numerals inscribed on the spines. "Come and get one of those down," he said to the gargoyle, pointing at a ledger on the nearest shelf. "Look through and tell me what's recorded in them."

He opened the drawer as the gargoyle did as it was told. It was stuffed with files, all labelled with names in alphabetical order, making locating the Gallica-Rosas very easy. He pulled out the one on Horatio Gallica-Rosa first, knowing he was involved intimately with the kidnapping of the Master of Ceremonies. There was a yellow dot next to his name on the file tab.

There were only two sheets of paper inside. One was a yellow slip with "Archived: HGR2475-L" written on it. The second listed his name, gender, family line, height, weight and physical description, even down to locations of scars and birthmarks. It read like a processing sheet at a mundane hospital or police station. Beneath the basic data, in a box labelled "Preliminary assessment" there were a few lines of cryptic notes.

> *Emotionally unstable without int & man.*
> *GTs—good rfs, nat. athl*
> *PSs—fencing, chess*
> *T—Strategy*
> *VS—8*
> *Sf AS? = 0*
> *Sf An? = High*
> *Recommended for: BP AP1 & An. entry prog.*

Focused on the information, Max stretched out a hand to rest it on the gargoyle's shoulder. "This is a report to the head of Chapter intelligence, to be filed under—"

"What are you doing?" The gargoyle twisted round to look at him, the open ledger resting on top of the filing cabinet.

Max shook his head. "Habit." He felt a flicker of irritation, then sadness before breaking contact. "It was trained into me so hard, I wasn't even thinking. We need to get this data back to Ekstrand for analysis."

"We need a Chapter, we can't do this by ourselves. Look at all this stuff. This would take our Chapter months and months to process."

Max nodded. "I bet there's a file on every puppet in Society here. It could revolutionise how we monitor them."

"I know, it's very cool." The gargoyle grinned. "I think these ledgers list everything the Agency has provided, and what they've been paid in return."

"What do the puppets pay with?"

"I don't understand most of it, a lot is in code, but they use the Queen's coin sometimes, which is interesting."

"Very," Max agreed. "And important."

"And worrying. It just goes to show how little we know about Fae-touched society. If all of this has been going on, what else are we missing?"

"Let's just gather the data and leave the wider implications to the Sorcerer," Max said, not wanting the gargoyle to get any more anxious. "I'll make some notes—you put the ledger back and take a look outside. Get a sense of how big this place is but just look, don't go out there, in case someone is looking out of a window. We need to get as much information as we can back to the Sorcerer so we can better prepare for the next time we come here."

Whilst the gargoyle obeyed, Max copied the notations listed in Horatio's file and that of his parents. Flipping through the rest, he theorised the yellow dot next to the names indicated they'd been brought in by the Agency. At a glance, he saw that several Rosas were still unaccounted for and their files were still fat. He settled for making a note of their names for now. The sight of a couple of white dots in the Alba-Rosa section drew his attention and he pulled out the files on Amelia and Cornelius Alba-Rosa, the other roses who'd been in Aquae Sulis that night.

Their files were also practically empty, both containing a yellow slip detailing where their previous information had been archived. But there was a piece of white paper in each with a simple form detailing how Amelia and Cornelius were no longer formally of the Alba-Rosa family, to the extent they'd been given a new surname: White.

Max read the note underneath, the same in both files. "Exempt. Taken in by William-Reticulata Iris. Formerly AS, now L."

"What!" the gargoyle exclaimed as if Max had read it out loud. "Why didn't Cathy tell us her husband saved those Rosas?"

Max put the files back. "I told you the puppet can't be trusted. She's been hiding those Rosas from us all along."

"There must be a good reason." The gargoyle sounded a little desperate. "What do we do?"

"I'm going to see if I can find the information about Miss Rainer, then we need to take this all back to Ekstrand and plan the next move."

"So you're still going to keep the deal with Cathy?"

"No. But I want the information on this governess if I can get it. It could be useful in more ways than one."

"Mrs Lucy Rhoeas-Papaver," Morgan announced, and Cathy did all she could to make the smile fixed on her face look genuine. At least the new butler seemed nicer than the interim one.

"Catherine." Lucy entered, dropped a reticule and a small package wrapped in brown paper and string on the nearest chair, and reached towards her with both hands.

Cathy stood reluctantly and accepted the kiss on her cheek. Lucy's blonde hair was pinned up and she was wearing a green travelling dress with gold detailing that suited her fair skin. Lucy was so petite that Cathy felt Amazonian next to her.

"It's so good to see you again," Lucy said as Morgan brought in the tea.

"And you," Cathy replied, but she wasn't sure how she felt about it. Since her return from Exilium everything seemed dulled. Even now, sitting down as Lucy retrieved her package and arranged her skirts, Cathy felt like she was watching everything through a pane of glass.

"Tom sends his love," said Lucy with a smile.

"How is he?"

"Oh, fine. He's a little worried about you, I guess."

Lucy sought eye contact so Cathy busied herself with the tea to avoid it. "How's Aquae Sulis?"

"Things are settling down again. The Master of Ceremonies hosted a soirée last night and he seemed very well." She accepted her cup with thanks and handed over the package in exchange. "I brought you a gift. I almost bought an ornament, for house warming, but Tom advised me against it."

Cathy let Lucy's gabble wash over her as she untied the string and pulled off the brown paper. When a corner of the hardback cover was revealed her heart quickened, but when the title was exposed Cathy's expectations collapsed. "*Mrs Beeton's Book of Household Management*," she said, barely able to keep the disappointment from her voice. "How… thoughtful."

Lucy grinned. "Look on the title page. I wrote a little something there."

Cathy struggled to contain a deep sigh as she opened the book. Lucy's handwriting was extravagant in its loops and curls. "Sometimes the most remarkable things can be found in unexpected places" read the dedication. Cathy wanted to drop it on the sofa and go back to bed but then her eyes flicked up to the title printed above Lucy's words. She untucked the front flap of the dust jacket and lifted it to reveal the true identity of the novel: *To Kill a Mockingbird.* It made her genuinely smile for what seemed like the first time in days.

"Have you read it?" Lucy asked.

"No." Cathy folded the dust jacket back into place. "I fell for your trick."

"I thought I should play it safe. I was at a dinner party a couple of weeks ago and these two women were talking about how the novel constitutes one of the greatest threats to the moral fabric of Aquae Sulis. Can you believe that?"

"Which novel?"

"Any of them. If they come to visit and poke around your bookshelves they won't disapprove. Honestly, Cathy—may I call you Cathy?" She didn't pause for an affirmative. "Between you and me, I think the ignorance of some ladies in Aquae Sulis constitutes the greatest threat to the city's moral fabric."

Cathy didn't know what to say to that even though she agreed. Was Lucy testing her?

"This house is so beautiful," Lucy said, snapping the strand of silence growing taut between them. "How are you finding it here?"

Cathy shrugged. She couldn't think of anything to say. All of the words that would have so easily tumbled out had sunk to the bottom of her since Exilium.

"That good, huh? How about William?"

"What about him?"

Lucy sighed and put her cup down. "Are you both OK? Are you settling into married life?"

Cathy picked up one of the small plates. "Would you like a sandwich?"

"I'm sorry," Lucy said. "I thought…I overstepped the mark, didn't I?"

"No, not at all." Cathy didn't know where to look or what to say.

"I thought we could talk like normal people do, you know, because of what you told me that night I first met you about Mundanus."

"Of course we can." Cathy regretted that confession. It seemed like it was years ago but was only a few weeks. At least Lucy hadn't reacted badly.

"Are you sure you're OK?"

Cathy checked the sleeve of her dress was covering the bandage.

It was so tempting to make an excuse and send Lucy back home but she didn't want to be rude. "I'm fine. It's just hard."

Lucy nodded. "I know. That's why I wanted to see you. I know how weird it is. One moment you're alone and the next you're supposed to fit in with another person's life. And knowing what I do about…before…I figured it would be even harder for you."

Cathy just nodded, fearing that if she spoke she'd weep. She didn't want to let Lucy in, she didn't want to talk about how she felt and what was going on. She wanted to curl up in a ball and sleep until it all went away.

"Is there any way I can help?" Lucy asked.

"I don't suppose you have a kick-ass Charm to make the Irises forget I ever existed?"

Lucy shook her head.

"Damn," Cathy muttered. "I suppose I'll have to make do with cake instead."

"You don't want to run away again, do you?" When Cathy said nothing Lucy came over and sat next to her. "My God, you do, don't you?"

"If I could I would."

"But what about William?"

"It wouldn't break his heart. He could marry Amelia. Then she'd be Duchess. I'm sure she'd love it and he'd be much happier with her."

"The Alba-Rosa?"

"*Former* Alba-Rosa."

"But what would you do in Mundanus?"

"What I was doing before." Apart from the Josh part, Cathy thought. "I'd go back to my studies and get on with the original plan." Lucy's expectant gaze was hard to resist. "I want to be a human rights lawyer."

Lucy glanced at the book. "I think you'll like that novel. I hear the Irises are pretty strict about—"

"I don't want to talk about them." Cathy didn't want to talk about any of it. She didn't want to be reminded of dreams that seemed so unobtainable now. Would Lord Iris know she was thinking about running away again?

"There's something I don't get." Lucy's voice penetrated the fog of worry. "You say you want to stand up for people who don't have a voice, but what about the ones you already know?"

"Who?"

"The women in Nether society."

Cathy twisted to face her sister-in-law fully. "Eh?"

"Jeez, you're something, Cathy."

"What's that supposed to mean?"

"You think you're the only woman who hates the way we have to live? I didn't think you were so—"

"Now just wait a minute." Cathy abandoned her tea cup. "All of the women I've met in Society seem happy as Larry with their dresses and powerful husbands. They like the way things are."

Lucy's eyebrows arched high. "Really? You've asked them?"

"Well, no."

"So you've just assumed that because they're behaving the way they should in public?"

Cathy looked away.

"Listen." Lucy's hand touched her arm gently. "I don't want to make you feel bad. I just don't understand why you feel the need to fight for people in Mundanus when there are plenty in Londinium and in Aquae Sulis who don't have a voice either."

"You're seriously telling me that there are women in the Great Families who hate the way we're treated?"

"Yes."

"I don't see you leaping up to champion them." Cathy regretted the words as soon as they'd left her mouth. "Sorry. That was rude of me."

If Lucy was offended she didn't show it. "Honey, no one is going to listen to someone from the colonies who's been here less than a year. But they do sometimes let their guard down with people they don't care about impressing. Like me."

"But I've never seen any hint of anyone being angry with it all like I am."

"But I bet you've never looked for the signs and I bet you've never asked them. It's not the done thing here. How many women do you really know?"

There were none and Cathy felt like a fool. She'd spent all of her life pushing against Society, completely convinced she was the only one who felt out of place, when it made perfect sense for there to be other women just as unhappy as her. How many times had she tried to just fit in and keep quiet to avoid attention? What if they were doing the same thing out of fear of being the only one who felt there should be more to life than what was allocated to them by their husbands and fathers?

"Albion sure is a strange place." Lucy didn't seem to like silence. "It's like it's stuck, it just can't seem to evolve."

"Are things very different in America?"

"Hell, yes!" Lucy laughed. "I think you'd like it there much more than here. Seems to me that Albion needs something to shake it up and knock the dust off all these ancient Patroons who don't realise how much things have changed." She looked at Cathy. "Or someone."

Cathy shook her head. "There's no way I could do anything. Who's going to listen to me?"

Lucy looked like she was about to answer but then just smiled. "I didn't come here to give you a hard time. How about a tour of the house? Tom will want to know all about it."

Cathy nodded but it felt like Lucy had just dropped a bomb in the room and then wanted to talk about anything but the things it had broken. The dream of escape was now tainted with the creeping fear that achieving her goal wouldn't be a glorious triumph of successful rebellion but instead a cowardly act. Was it right to leave others to quietly suffer the fate she couldn't accept for herself?

Like you could do anything anyway, she thought. But there was no comfort in reminding herself of how worthless her father had always considered her to be.

16

The butler closed the front door after the last of the guests left with smiles and promises to meet for tea. Will smiled at Cathy who sighed with relief.

"That went well," he said. "Are you tired?"

"More relieved than tired," she replied and then whispered, "I have got to get out of this dress."

Will watched her go upstairs as he loosened his cravat. The first soirée they'd hosted since their arrival had gone well. Bartholomew had talked to Cathy at length for a portion of the evening and Will made a mental note to ask her what they'd discussed. When Cathy was out of sight he put his hand in his pocket and brushed the small glass bottle with his fingertips. It had been in his pocket and on his mind all evening.

"Will that be all, sir?" Morgan asked.

"Could you bring two cups of hot milk to me in the drawing room?"

Morgan bowed and Will was left in the hallway. He looked up the stairs and decided to have a brandy in the drawing room first.

"What a bloody palaver that was," said a maid in one of the receiving rooms. He could hear the chink of glasses being put onto trays, and the general bustle of post-party tidying.

"She did it though, didn't she? Don't look much, but she kept her head."

Even though he'd been taught from an early age not to pay attention to the servants he found himself lingering at the doorway.

"She asked me if I was all right earlier," the first was saying. "Fancy that."

"I think that's strange. She don't know how to be the lady of the house, that's her trouble."

"I think it's nice. I was dead on my feet from all the lifting and she noticed. She—"

Will stepped into the doorway. The two parlour maids froze for a moment, then bobbed curtsies.

"Begging your pardon sir, we won't be long," the first one said with a blushing smile. She was very young. He couldn't remember either of their names; they'd only arrived the day before with over a dozen other servants.

"Palaver?" he asked, and their cheeks blazed.

"With the furniture, sir," the second said.

"Was there a problem?"

They looked at each other. "It didn't arrive, sir," the first said eventually. "The Agency said it would be here this morning, but by the afternoon there was still no sign of it."

"The furniture in here?"

"Yes, sir, and the red drawing room. You was out. Mr Morgan tried to get a message to the Agency but we didn't get a reply."

He'd been with Amelia overnight and with Cornelius most of the day, discussing the guests who'd spent the evening with them. He'd only had time to bathe and dress before the first ones arrived. "I had no impression of there being any problems when I returned this evening."

"Well, Mrs Iris had solved it all by then, sir. We don't know how she did it, but it was all delivered and in place before you got back."

"Not even Mr Morgan knows how," the second one said. "But he was very impressed, sir, we all were."

"We was worried you'd get back to empty rooms and the guests would have to be turned away." The first had clearly enjoyed the drama.

Cathy hadn't mentioned anything. She'd greeted him as if she'd spent the afternoon resting, as he'd hoped she would, not rushing around saving them from social death. When he'd been kissing Amelia goodbye, greedily stealing a few minutes with her in private as the carriage was prepared, Cathy had been dealing with a crisis and sought no credit for it when he'd reappeared.

He left the maids to their work, needing the brandy more than ever. Over the first week of their marriage, Cathy had impressed one of the most powerful families in Londinium, become the object of inappropriate affection from another, endured a harrowing experience in Exilium that she still couldn't bring herself to talk about, and had executed every wifely duty—save one—with unexpected success.

Her steadfast refusal to carry out that one duty was making him consider something terrible. He'd been patient but that was easy when he had Amelia, who was all too happy to slake his thirst. He'd done everything he could to ease Cathy into every other aspect of married life as gently as possible. They'd actually started to have proper conversations instead of just arguments; she was adapting to him and he, in turn, to her. When she was debating something passionately with Bartholomew or Margritte, or laughing at some comment he'd made, he'd been attracted to her. But every time he tried to kiss her in anything other than a brotherly way, she rejected him and then retired to her rooms. Whilst it was far from unusual to sleep separately, everyone else did that *after* consummating the marriage.

Will poured the brandy, giving himself a generous measure. When he saw the blood after she'd returned from Lord Iris, he knew there had to be more than interrogation behind it, and her refusal to talk about it only made the suspicion stronger. It was no surprise when he was summoned four days later.

"Your milk, sir," Morgan said, entering through the open door with a tray. "Is there anything else you require?"

"No, thank you, Morgan. Oh, one thing, I understand the Agency let us down today."

"Abominably sir, but Mrs Iris instructed me not to trouble you with it."

"Did they explain themselves or send an apology?"

"No, sir," he replied. "I've never known anything like it."

"I see. Goodnight, Morgan."

"Goodnight, sir."

Will waited until the door was closed and took the bottle out of his pocket. "I've been patient," he said to himself. "She's being unreasonable."

He took another swig of the brandy but its warmth didn't comfort him. He inspected the plain green glass bottle, unlabelled in case it was found by a servant or—worse—his wife. It wouldn't hurt her. He would be as gentle as he could, he even hoped she might enjoy it. He'd been told it was rare for the woman to fall pregnant the first time and he didn't want to have to resort to this again.

He put the bottle on the tray and swilled the last of the brandy around the glass, irritated with his procrastination. His father wouldn't have given it a second thought—then again, he wouldn't have listened to her protests on the wedding night. But he wasn't like his father.

"It's wrong," he muttered and picked up the bottle to put it in his pocket. But then he remembered Lord Iris asking why she was still virginal. How did he know? Had she admitted it under duress?

Will had never experienced the wrath of the Fae and didn't want this to be the reason for the first time. He slammed the brandy glass down, uncorked the bottle and dumped its contents into the cup on the right. Then he gulped down some of the milk from the other cup so that at a glance he would know that hers was the fuller of the two.

The milk soured in his belly as he carried the tray up the stairs. With every step, he tried to convince himself it was the best for both of them. Once she realised it wasn't going to be awful, perhaps relations would be better between them. He'd heard tales of girls reaching their wedding night and having no idea what was supposed to happen with their husband. Perhaps Cathy's ignorance was fuelling a fear of it. That didn't seem right though; she seemed more worldly than him sometimes.

Her lady's maid was leaving as he reached the top of the stairs. Upon seeing him she curtsied and left the door open when he gestured that he was on his way to Cathy. He knocked and went in. She was perched on the edge of the bed, sitting unnaturally stiffly. The pillow next to her was crooked and he wondered what she had stuffed under there so quickly.

She was dressed in a blue silk nightgown and robe that brought out the colour of her eyes. Her hair had been let down and the elaborate pinning for the soirée had left loose curls that rippled down her shoulders. There was a slight flush to her cheeks as she watched him set the tray down on the dressing table.

"I brought you some milk," he said.

"Oh. Thanks."

He left it on the tray, not wanting to appear too keen for her to drink it. She was tense and seemed more so when he closed the door. "I heard about the furniture."

"I told Morgan not to—"

"I overheard the parlour maids talking about it. How did you solve the problem?"

"You don't honestly want to know, do you? It's very boring."

"They didn't make it sound that way."

She shrugged. "They just don't understand it, that's all. I went into Mundanus, I made a few phone calls, it's no big deal or anything. When you're in London and very rich there are very few domestic problems that can't be solved with money."

How in the Worlds had she known who to call? It certainly wouldn't have occurred to his mother to solve the problem in that way. But it wasn't the time to ask. "I wanted to thank you. It sounds like you handled it all brilliantly."

"Oh, for God's sake, it's not like I saved a man's life. It was some sofas, tables and chairs. You make it sound like I was some superhero."

He approached her slowly. "May I sit next to you?"

She nodded after a beat, wary. "Aren't you tired?"

"No. I need to unwind after those kinds of events." He sat—not too close—and she pulled her legs up and tucked her knees under her chin, making the silk pool over her toes. When he glanced at them she tucked the fabric underneath her feet. "What was Bartholomew talking to you about?"

"We were discussing the Enlightenment."

"All that time?"

"It's interesting. And we talked about the student strikes at the University of Paris when the church tried to stop them learning logic and rational thinking. You know, oppression, control of intellectual pursuits in patriarchal societies, that sort of thing."

"The Tulipas have been speaking very highly of you in Londinium circles," he said, letting his pride show.

"I like them," she said. "I never thought I would ever say that about anyone in Society, but they're interesting, and they don't mind if I show that I actually know something more than which colour is fashionable."

"It's very different to Aquae Sulis, isn't it?"

She agreed and scratched her wrist. "I'll be glad when this bandage can come off."

"May I see?"

She extended her hand and he gently slid the silk up her arm to reveal the neat white bandage. Unlike the first few days it wasn't stained with blood. He carefully undid it and inspected the wounds. "This is healing nicely," he said. "Do you have a clean dressing?"

"I'll get one." She slipped off the bed and went into the adjoining dressing room.

He lifted her pillow and found a paperback novel with some sort of bizarre contraption on the cover. It appeared to be in outer space, heading towards a planet. He replaced the pillow and when she came back he re-dressed her wrist. "This will be off by the end of the week. Lucky we haven't had a ball to go to yet." He tied off the bandage and caught hold of her hand. "Are you all right, Cathy?"

She just looked at him for a few moments. "Why do you ask?"

"You haven't been the same since you went into Exilium."

"For the worse or the better?"

"You seem less angry."

She didn't reply, easing her hand from his grasp. "I suppose I've been trying to be a good wife." She spoke with such sadness it was as if she were talking about a bereavement.

"And you have been."

"I'm not looking for reassurance. I know what I have to do." She looked towards the window, eyes shining. "Running a house isn't so hard."

He looked for some sign of stubbornness or blatant defiance but there was none. "What did he say to you?" he asked, moving closer. "What happened there to make you so different?"

"He...he made me realise there's no point fighting you or the family." She looked down at the bandage, distant. "He's not like Lord Poppy."

"Cathy." Will slid closer to her, took her hands and kissed the back of them. "Our marriage doesn't have to be like a death sentence. I think we could be happy in Londinium. You said yourself you like the Tulipas. That's a start, isn't it?"

"I suppose so."

"And I know there's a book under the pillow," he said and she started, then looked fearful. "Why are you hiding it?"

"I'm not supposed to read books like that."

"Books like what?"

"Science-fiction," she whispered, ashamed.

"Of course you can. You can read whatever you like, you're the lady of the house. I'm not going to stop you. How absurd."

She gawped at him. "Really? You're not going to freak out and burn them if I have some in the house?"

"Burn books? What kind of savage do you take me for?" Then he realised why she said it and winced. "Did your father do that by any chance?"

She nodded. "All of them. He made me watch."

He stroked her fingers with his thumbs, moved a bit closer. No wonder she was so guarded all the time with a father that destroyed what she loved, and beat her brutally..."Is that why you didn't want to marry me? Did you think it would be beatings and censorship?"

"It was a big part of it. I thought all men in Society were like that, I thought you would be, and if not now, eventually. I thought the more you got to know me, the more likely you'd be to do the same." She saw his horror. "Oh, I realised pretty quickly you're not like that, really! You've been kind actually. Not what I expected at all."

He wanted to kiss her and initiate something physical to build on this new intimacy. But there had been times in the past week when she'd started to talk openly with him and then closed up in seconds at any hint of his demonstrating his affection. So he held back, mindful of the potion waiting in the cooling milk, hoping the right moment would reveal itself.

"I'm glad you could tell me about what happened with our patron. Please don't feel you have to hide things from me. We shouldn't have secrets between us."

"My mother once said to my aunt that a marriage was only as strong as the secrets kept from the husband," Cathy replied.

"You're trying to change the subject," Will said, but she kept silent. "Secrets are poisonous things. I trust you to keep mine as much as I hope you could trust me." He knew it was a gamble, but perhaps if he placed his trust in her first, she would let her guard down a little more. "I'm going to tell you something that is a secret in my family, one that could cause harm if it were to reach certain ears, to prove my trust in you. In the Iris family, there's a tradition of having three children each generation."

"Three?" She bit her lip.

"Lord Iris is fond of the number. I say it's a tradition, but it's more than that; it's one of those unwritten rules. My mother had a fourth child whilst I was on my Grand Tour, and no one outside of my immediate family knows."

"Not even the Patroon?"

"Especially not the Patroon. The poor girl doesn't even have a proper nanny. She's called Sophia and she's a sweet little thing."

"You miss her," Cathy said softly.

"Yes," he said. "Very much. My siblings refused to play with her so she got rather attached to me."

"What would happen if the Patroon found out?"

"Nothing good."

"I promise I won't tell a soul about Sophia."

He thought of the strange way she spoke sometimes, the accusation that Horatio made against her. "Is there anything you want to share with me?"

"Well…I was thinking about asking Margritte if she'd like to go to some of the museums and galleries in London with me. She loves art, we talk about it a lot, and—"

"That would be fine," he said. "Just be careful how much time you spend out of the Nether. It adds up. Look at Freddy."

"I'd rather not," she said. "An afternoon is hardly going to turn me grey, is it?"

"No, but afternoons here and there over a few hundred years add up."

"I'll bear that in mind," she said. "And I was thinking about seeing if there are people in Londinium who might like to meet and talk about literature. And maybe other subjects too."

"A book group?"

"Yes, do you know of any?"

"No, but I met someone on my Grand Tour who invited me to one. It was a very strange evening. I can't see any harm in you making friends here. In fact, that can only be a good thing. It would never take off in Aquae Sulis, but they do seem to favour intellectual pursuits in Londinium. Perhaps you'll start a trend."

She raised an eyebrow. "You'd like that, wouldn't you?"

"The Duchess of Londinium is one of the most influential people in Society, a natural trendsetter. It would be good for you to get a taste for it early."

She frowned at that. "You're still set on the throne then."

"Of course, nothing has changed. In fact, I think my chances are better than I thought they'd be."

"But don't you think Bartholomew would be a good Duke?"

Her comment triggered a flash of jealousy, even though he knew she didn't mean offence or anything more than truthfulness. "I think he would be an excellent Duke," he finally said. "But that's neither here nor there. Our patron demands I take the city. And you know how insistent he can be."

She nodded, the brief brightness he'd rekindled ebbing away at the memory of the Fae. "Will…I appreciate you giving me time to…get used to you. And I know there's pressure to consummate, as much upon you as there is me. I wanted to say thank you, for not pushing it. I know you must be worried."

"If we're to be truthful with each other then I have to say I am worried and, yes, I'm under pressure." He searched her face for the impending barbed remark but there was no sign of it. "Is there something about it that you're frightened of?"

She shook her head. "Not of the act, no."

"Are you so repelled by me?"

"No," she said, "you're very handsome. And kind and, well, it's just me."

He could see she didn't want to go into it any further. He could give her the drink now, talk to her for a while as it took effect…his duty could be done within hours and the pressure would be gone. But holding her hands—for the first time she hadn't complained about it—and seeing her genuinely trying to find a way to live her new life, he simply couldn't bear the thought of using magic to overpower her free will.

"I should let you get some sleep." He kissed her hands again, whilst he could.

"Oh, I forgot about the milk."

"It'll be cold now. I can have Morgan bring a fresh cup if you wish."

"No, thanks." She settled, giving his fingers an affectionate squeeze. "I don't really like warm milk, to be honest. I like cocoa more."

"Goodnight then." He kissed her on the forehead, deciding to give her another day or so. The inner struggle quietened now he'd decided not to go through with it, but he still noted her preference, should it be needed in the future.

17

Amelia sat at her dressing table, holding the atomiser up to the sprite globe. Less than a quarter of the perfume was left. She put it back, fingering the tassel as she remembered making the rosewater with her mother. They'd talked about Horatio and what it would be like to be Duchess. Amelia had said she hoped her sons wouldn't inherit his large nose. Her mother commented that, large-nosed children or not, marrying him was the surest way to the Londinium throne and, besides, the contracts had already been prepared.

Now that contract would never be signed, and she would never be Horatio's wife. Some days she feared she was going mad, the number of times she replayed those last moments as Rosas, the sight of him frozen by a Doll Charm and carried out on the Collectors' shoulders. When she remembered the Charms failing she'd thought that was the end of it. Not only had their plan failed catastrophically but they were going to be carried off to the Agency too. Every time she pulled herself out of the memory she was shaking. Each time she heard a thud downstairs or the front door close, she imagined Collectors running up the stairs. She'd taken to sleeping with a chair jammed under the door handle for the first few days but now William turned up at all hours she couldn't do that anymore.

Amelia tried not to think about Horatio but it was impossible. Unlike many destined to be married, they knew each other well. Or as well as any man knew her, which admittedly was hardly at all. But they had shared games of cards and enjoyed secret meetings in the lead-up to the Aquae Sulis Season during which they ate Turkish delight and plotted how to destroy the Iris-Papaver alliance. The hardest thing about the weeks before that awful night was having to play nothing but the girlish coquette. She'd been homesick for Londinium and her own secret life. To be back at home and yet cut off from the things that truly enriched her life was a gentle torture. It was impossible to feel settled and safe, despite William's promises, and the boredom was almost unbearable.

She'd known from a very young age that she would be married to the future Duke. As the families were agreed and relations good between the lines, it took the pressure off; the best match had already been made for her. It didn't alter the fact that she liked to ensure as many men and women as possible in the Londinium Court were in love with her. That was just good planning. She knew when she became Duchess she would need every ally she could get in order to maintain their power. To think that the plain, awkward idiot Papaver was the one William planned to sit by his side drove Amelia insane with anger. The stupidity of it! The waste!

She pulled the bell cord. She wasn't thirsty but tea would break up the interminable afternoon. She'd embroidered until her vision had blurred, had arranged her outfits into a dozen combinations that she would likely never wear and wept for her mother. That had drawn her to the table and the atomiser. At least they'd chosen a Charm derived from another source, purchased at the Emporium, rather than using one of the staples in her mother's repertoire. They'd been worried the Irises would suspect her and be vigilant for Rose-based Charms. That one bit of planning meant she still had a means to control William. But what would she do when the perfume ran out?

The maid brought in the tea, set it down, asked if she required anything else and was sent away. They were used to her taking afternoon tea in her bedroom now; she spent most of her time there. She couldn't bear the sight of the drawing room anymore; it reminded her of her mother too much. The empty places in the dining room made her think of the dinner parties they no longer had.

Amelia poured the tea, wondering whether William would still love her when free of the Charm's influence. It wasn't the first time she'd used it but the majority of the victims were mere mundanes.

Once she'd taken everything she needed she tossed them out of her life without bothering to see if their infatuation continued without exposure. She regretted that now and wondered whether the mundane manager of her secret company was still infatuated with her. She couldn't risk going to see him; even though the Agency wouldn't expect her, as a lady, to hold business assets, they might still be watching her for signs of their father's hiding place. After taking so many years to establish her business and working so hard to keep it safe from discovery by anyone in Society, she couldn't allow it to fall into the Agency's hands. And there was the artist she'd recently snatched from Neugent's grip. Would he be as susceptible to suggestion now? Would Neugent be able to tempt him back?

Footsteps on the stairs made her jump but it sounded like Cornelius so she relaxed. His coded knock confirmed it and she called him in.

He looked serious, as he always did these days, but also purposeful. "Darling, I need to talk to you. Is this a good time?"

"The tea is still hot," she said with a smile, setting aside her own preference to be alone in favour of ensuring he was at peace. She knew he was working hard in his own way to keep them safe, just as she was in hers.

She poured as he settled himself. "I can't believe I'm getting used to taking tea in your bedroom, Amelia."

"These are strange times we live in," she said, passing him the cup and saucer. "Now, what is it?"

He drank first and set the saucer on his knee. They were almost savages these days. "I've just had a note from William. The Marquis of Westminster has declared the Court will convene in two weeks' time."

"And what of the new Duke?"

"Whoever believes himself to have a claim is to declare as much on the night."

"So it's as we thought—a complete mess."

He raised an eyebrow. "It's not the most elegant way to acquire a Duke, but at least it will be over quickly. Only the most confident will put themselves forward and the chap with the most support takes the throne."

"Only those confident of support or irretrievably arrogant will step forwards," she corrected.

"That may be so, sister, but it still results in a new Duke."

"Will must be disappointed. Two weeks isn't enough time."

"He's been doing surprisingly well. He's going to be sponsored into Black's for one thing."

"Darling." Amelia shook her head at him. "I know you all like Black's very much, but it's not exactly a guarantee of power."

"But it's a sign he's doing the right thing. You know how hard it is to get in there."

"I know it's much easier to be thrown out and forgotten."

"What is it? You're not usually so negative. Has something upset you?"

Her fingers twisted the pearls at her throat. "It just seems so hopeless. Will cannot possibly take the city in such a short period of time. The Tulipas will be on the throne by the end of the month and we'll be charitable cases for the rest of our lives."

"You've been spending too much time on your own, darling." He moved his chair closer to hers. "You hardly leave this room…it's not good for you."

"Where else can I go?"

He looked down. "I'm sorry. I'm occupied with helping Will, I don't miss our old life so much. You always thrived on the latest developments in the Ton. But that's why I'm here. I've been thinking about Will's promise to elevate us, should he become Duke, and it's clear we have to act."

"What's the point? He's feeding you false hope. You'll never be Marquis of Westminster, darling."

"That's enough of that," he said, putting the cup down so hard it tipped in its saucer. He pulled her to her feet and marched her over to the mirror. "Look," he said.

She took in her face, her dress. Same as always.

"At what?"

"You are not destined to sit in this room and wait for William to call. You are the next Duchess of Londinium, you always were and you still will be." When she opened her mouth to protest, he pressed his forefinger against it gently, wrapping his other arm about her and holding her tight. "Listen," he whispered. "If we play fair and act honourably, we'll rot in this house whilst William and his wife enjoy a mediocre success in the Court. If we act decisively and with courage, we'll not only put William on the throne, but you beside him."

Her eyes widened. He didn't remove his finger.

"I received a message from an old friend today, with some very interesting news. One of the Thorn brothers has escaped his prison in Exilium and I have a means to contact him. I'm certain I could use him to destroy the Tulipas and put William on the throne, widowed."

She pushed his hand away from her mouth. "What are you talking about? Thorn will never want him on the throne."

"It will only be temporary. Once you're established as Duchess we'll be sure to tell Poppy his favourite was murdered thanks to Will's neglect and—"

She clamped her hands over her ears. "Don't tell me anymore, you fool! I don't want to give anything away."

"You won't oppose me?"

"Of course not." She turned and embraced him. "Do what you feel you must, you have my total support. Just don't get it wrong. We've had the only second chance we're ever going to get."

Cathy sat at the desk in her study looking at the sketch and comparing it to the picture in the book. She'd asked one of the footmen, a young man called Coll, to go and buy her paints, pencils, paper and all the other trappings of an artist, including books purporting to teach people how to draw.

They lied.

She tossed the pencil onto the desk. She had less than three weeks to come up with a masterpiece. Now she had an Iris secret but wasn't sure if she could bring herself to use it, after seeing the way Will spoke of his secret sister. Nothing about the commissioned Charm had arrived from the Shopkeeper and she was starting to panic.

She unlocked the drawer in her desk, pulled out one of the packets from the Emporium and rang for tea. Once she was alone again, she unstoppered the phial and sniffed at it tentatively. It didn't smell of anything but she could hear it fizzing like mundane lemonade. She dumped the contents into her tea. She needed to make progress fast and it was one of the few days when she didn't have anything in the diary.

She waited, listening to the clumping footfalls of the delivery men from the Agency. They were carrying hundreds of items into the house and filling the remaining receiving rooms with all of the furniture and ornaments that people seemed to think were important.

The Agency insisted her instructions for the previous day's delivery had specified that the items be brought with today's batch. She knew what she'd instructed, and it wasn't what they said, but they were never going to admit the error. She wondered if Bennet was petty enough to alter the date to spite her, seeing as her brief calculations at their first meeting had deprived the Agency of a sizeable amount of money. She suspected Margritte had been checking her accounts and dealings with the Agency too. Cathy knew it would be weighing on Georgiana's mind, though she'd never admit it. If other billing queries had flooded in after his meeting with her, Bennet would know she'd broken a cardinal rule of Society: never talk about money.

Whether the Agency had deliberately tried to make her life difficult didn't matter; she couldn't summon the passion to care about it. It was nothing compared to the challenge imposed upon her by Lord Poppy.

Will had barely been present. The conversation they'd had the night before in her room was the lengthiest since her return from Exilium. As she'd drifted off to sleep, she imagined inviting Margritte on a museum trip and bringing in books from Mundanus bookshops without fear for the first time in her life. But the next day those desires seemed distant and felt like silly daydreams she'd once had.

Then she remembered the latest piece of magical paper sent to her via her uncle to open a Way to the Sorcerer. It was tucked in a book at the bottom of the one lockable box in her bedroom. Surely they would have tracked Bennet to somewhere useful by now? The Arbiter would be wondering why she hadn't gone to them to collect the information on Rainer.

Cathy laid her hands on the table in front of her and looked at the wedding band. If Lord Iris could summon her, could he tell when she left the Nether? Did he know that she'd been in Mundanus yesterday, just for half an hour? There hadn't been any repercussions, but perhaps he'd known she was only there to solve a domestic problem, and therefore permitted it. She was staring at it so intently the band started to blur. I can't go to the Sorcerer, she thought. I can't take the risk.

The sprite light was reflecting from the band so beautifully that the fear of Lord Iris started to melt away. She moved her hand off the desk and onto the blotter, fascinated by the difference in colour, that point of transition from flesh to paper. She stared at the texture of her skin, the point where it met the wedding band. Perhaps she could draw that.

A knock at the door made her straighten. "Come in."

Morgan entered. "My apologies, but Dame Iris is here to see you."

She jumped to her feet. "What?"

Morgan repeated himself, adding, "I took the liberty of showing her to the red drawing room. It's one of the best presented and furthest away from the stairs the delivery men are using."

"Oh. Thank you. Is my husband at home?"

"No, ma'am, I understand he is with his tailor."

"Oh, God," she whispered. Morgan had already learned to

ignore her more inappropriate responses. "Well, I suppose I'd better get this over with. Do I look tidy?"

Morgan's left eyebrow twitched. "I couldn't possibly find fault with your appearance, ma'am."

She followed him out, checking that the long sleeve and lace edging were tugged down sufficiently to cover the bandage, then she remembered she should be gloved and ran back to the study to fetch them. She had to stop herself staring at the way the light played off the sheen of the silk.

She'd met the Dame very briefly after Will's mother had broken the news of the curse to her. The Dame was the most powerful woman in the Iris family and, being married to the Patroon, the last woman in the Worlds that Cathy wanted to have as a guest.

Morgan opened the door for her and she found the Dame inspecting the ornaments on the mantelpiece. Her elegant midnight-blue dress was cut in the late Victorian style, though with fewer bows and frills than the mundane Victorians favoured at that time. Cathy wished the trim was in a slightly darker shade. A petite woman, the Dame's waist was tiny and the bustle only accentuated it. Cathy would have guessed her to be in her mid-twenties if she hadn't known the Dame of the Iris line was rumoured to be over a hundred and fifty years old. All Cathy knew about her was that she was Sir Iris's second wife and nobody talked openly about what had happened to the first. She'd be happier to paint that secret, if she could discover it.

Dame Iris didn't turn at the sound of her entering and Cathy didn't know what to do as she lurked near the door. Whilst she was mistress of the house she was still mindful of the Dame's status.

The Dame adjusted the alignment of an ornament with a gloved fingertip. Cathy wondered who'd presented her with gloves on her wedding day. Was she bound by the same curse, or was a woman trusted by the time she'd risen to be the matriarch of the entire family?

She finally turned towards Cathy. She was a very attractive woman, beneath the haughty contempt. She had a delicate nose with a slight upturn at the end, all the better for giving the impression she disapproved of everything she saw. Her eyes were a dark blue, her hair a pleasant brown and artfully arranged.

"Well, don't just stand there, girl!" she said in a voice pitched at the perfect level to make Cathy jolt as if she'd been rapped on the knuckles with a ruler. "Invite me to sit and offer me tea, for goodness' sake!"

"W-would you care to take a seat, Dame Iris?"

"Why, thank you," she said and planted herself firmly in the middle of the most comfortable sofa, not once having to adjust her dress or bustle as Cathy always did when wearing that style.

"And would you like tea?"

"Please." The Dame smiled, as if starting from the beginning again.

Morgan gave a nod of acknowledgement and closed the door, leaving Cathy to sit opposite the Dame.

"Now, I had hoped to visit several days ago, but events conspired to make that impossible. Firstly, I would like to welcome you personally into the family. I'm certain you are delighted to be brought into one of the most respected families in Albion and the Frankish Empire."

"Thank you, Dame Iris."

"It's my responsibility as Dame to ensure you settle into the family well and execute your duties with perfection. The Iris way accepts nothing less, and I expect your total devotion to learning our family traditions and becoming an expert on our history."

Cathy took a sudden interest in the rug beneath the table. She was captivated by the way the variations in the direction of the pile affected the colours.

"Over the next three months," Dame Iris continued, "I will spend time with you to undo any poor habits you may have carried over from your previous life, and ensure you're behaving correctly. For the six months after that I'll see less of you but expect regular visits and twice-weekly letters detailing your movements and achievements. For the last three months of your first year, I will permit you to socialise independently and write to me fortnightly."

There was a pause. Cathy looked up from the rug and saw an expectancy on the Dame's face that made her squirm. "Oh," she said, not sure of what she was supposed to be saying.

"Oh! Is that how you thank a matriarch of my stature for devoting valuable time and effort to you?"

"Sorry, I mean thank you."

"Evidently you need a firm hand to lift you to our standards." The Dame paused, examining Cathy's face and dress. "Quite why you were chosen over your younger sister I have no idea, but one must make the best of what is given."

Anger flickered in Cathy's chest, the first time in days. "Lord Poppy and Lord Iris seemed to believe I was preferable," she replied. "Do we not have to accept their better judgement?"

The Dame's eyes widened until there was white all around the blue irises. She opened her mouth, presumably to chasten her, when Morgan knocked lightly and opened the door to bring in the tea.

Cathy smiled at him; her mouth was paper-dry and her stomach needed to be settled. The pouring of the tea was enough to weaken the Dame's frustrated reprimand until it was simply an irritated sniff as Morgan left.

"I can see there is a lot of work to be done, so we will begin straightaway," Dame Iris said after a few sips of tea. "Firstly, please explain to me why you are dressed as you are."

Cathy looked down at her clothing to remind herself of what she'd been buttoned into that morning. It was a simple green day dress with a black trim, one of the more comfortable as it was in the Edwardian style, and didn't require a huge bustle. "I…" She tried to fathom what the Dame meant. "I like green?" she said. And she really did, more than she ever had before.

"Do you? Why respond with a question? Regardless of the colour, why are you dressed so inappropriately?"

"I'm sorry, I don't understand."

The Dame tutted and set the cup and saucer down. "Really,

child, you are astoundingly ignorant. Is that or is that not the same dress you breakfasted in this morning?"

"It is."

"Then why in the Worlds did you think it was acceptable to come to me dressed so? What an insult!"

"I beg your pardon, Dame Iris, I had no idea you were planning to visit." Had I known, I wouldn't have wasted that potion, she thought.

The Dame sniffed. "That is irrelevant. After breakfast is over and the most pressing concerns regarding the staff have been addressed, you should be changed into your receiving gown."

"My what?"

The Dame's mouth drew into a tight pucker beneath her nose. "I find it difficult to believe that one of the most influential families of Aquae Sulis would live as savages. Back to basics it is then. A gown for breakfast, then a receiving gown, then in the afternoon, after 3pm, a tea gown should be worn and then the appropriate choice of gown for the evening event. And of course, should you choose to visit another household or promenade in St James's Park, you will wear a suitable gown."

"But that would waste hours!"

"Waste?" The Dame's voice was getting shrill. "How on earth can it be considered a waste to ensure one is properly attired? Did your mother not change her gowns to suit her activities?"

Cathy tried to remember. "I've no idea," she admitted.

The Dame was reduced to silence. She retrieved her tea and they both restored themselves. "What your mother chooses to wear is of no matter now," the Dame said, calmer. "You will abide by my rules, and I will see to it personally that your wardrobe is filled appropriately. I assume your dressmaker will be seeing you this week?"

"Yes, Dame Iris. I'm seeing her quite regularly to ensure my evening gowns are the height of fashion."

"Well, that's something, I suppose. Have your butler note down the dressmaker's appointment time for me before I leave. I will be here to ensure you order everything you need. Certainly nothing more in the Edwardian style, it's so unbecoming. You need to wear something that draws the eye down, to your waist, not above your shoulders."

Cathy slammed her cup down in the saucer as another burst of anger surfaced. "So I've been told in the past, Dame Iris."

The Dame fixed her with a stare but said nothing until Cathy looked back at the rug. "Now, on to your daily activities. Show me your embroidery, please."

"I don't have any." Cathy dreaded the response. "I don't like sewing."

"This won't do at all," the Dame said. "I require more tea."

Cathy poured her another cup. "It's not like I have time for it anyway," she said. "What with redecorating the house and—"

"I've heard enough. Two mornings a week you will accompany me to tea at various houses in Londinium, and you will not speak unless asked a question. You will watch and listen and learn how to behave appropriately. One morning a week you will host a sewing circle, attended by young ladies of my choosing, and you will practise your craft."

"My craft? But I—"

"Every Iris lady embroiders beautifully, and expresses her creativity, dedication and attention to detail in her work. There's no better way to pass one's time, aside from hosting dinner parties and soirées to further your husband's opportunities in Society, but having met you I pray there have been none so far."

Cathy's mouth hung open for a moment. "Actually," she managed to say, "we've already hosted one and it was a great success."

"By whose standards?"

"My husband's." Cathy hoped that would silence her.

"My dear girl, your husband may be one of the new bright young things everyone is so hopeful about but I doubt he has enough experience to be an adequate judge."

Cathy didn't want to speak to this awful woman a moment longer. She had a sudden moment of clarity and saw herself perched on the edge of her seat, being insulted and verbally abused by this twisted relic of another time. The Dame was making her feel utterly worthless again when she thought the worst of that was over.

"You are forbidden to go into Mundanus, of course."

"What!"

"How dare you raise your voice in my presence!" The Dame sharpened hers to its most imperious pitch. "Under no circumstances will I endorse frivolous trips into Mundanus. If you are too thick-headed to safeguard your youth then I must preserve it for you. You're not a beauty, Catherine. Were you to lose your youth it would only make things more difficult for you."

"That's it." Cathy stood up. "I don't have to sit here and be spoken to like this in my own house! I'm doing perfectly fine already, thank you. The Tulipas like me and Will thinks I'm handling everything brilliantly."

"Sit down and be quiet." The Dame didn't raise her voice, but Cathy sat back down again as if someone had pushed her. "Lord Iris warned me to keep a close eye on you and now I see why."

Cathy felt like she was being pressed down and her jaw muscles strained as she tried to speak. Dame Iris had used a Charm, one so powerful she didn't even see or hear her use it. Fear crept in at the edge of her anger.

"Yes." The Dame stood. "That's better, show some respect. I speak with Lord Iris on a regular basis and I'm sure you don't want me to report your appalling behaviour to him. I have little regard for what the Tulipas think of you, all I care about is the way it has inflated your pride and given you a false sense of accomplishment. When one is successful, Catherine, one cares not for what others think, but only whether they do as one wishes. And, by the way, there's nothing less attractive than a woman who thinks she's intelligent and inflicts her opinion on others." She adjusted her gloves, looked Catherine up and down with contempt and went to the door. "The butler will see me out. I suggest you reflect upon our conversation at length and obtain embroidery silks and canvas post haste. I expect to see a marked improvement in your behaviour by tomorrow morning, otherwise I will have to resort to similarly uncouth measures. It does not do to be an inconvenience to the Dame of your family. Good day."

Cathy remained seated as the Dame went into the hallway, had a brief conversation with Morgan and left. As the bang of the front door echoed through the house Cathy felt light again and was back up on her feet, jumping slightly now she was unimpeded.

Working her jaw again, she picked up the nearest thing to hand, the fine china cup in front of her, and threw it against the wall. "Bitch!"

Feeling better, she sat down again. She was going to pick up her tech to resume her studies and then see the Arbiter to get that file on Miss Rainer. Damn the risk.

There was a gentle clearing of a throat at the doorway. "I think I need more tea, Morgan," she said. "And the most inappropriate cake you can find."

Perhaps Lucy was right. Surely other women in the Iris family felt that the Dame's expectations were absurd? The thought was uncomfortable; if that were true, the argument for staying to fight was strengthened. She remembered her father's anger at having been denied the opportunity to be brave in the First World War and wondered if she'd have felt the same in his position.

She didn't have to make the decision straight away; she still didn't have the means to escape and stay hidden. In the meantime the file on Miss Rainer could be useful. What if she'd taught other students before her? Perhaps there would be some clue or previous assignments listed so she could identify others who'd be likely to feel the same way. Surely that's what Miss Rainer would have wanted?

18

Will stretched out in the carriage and thought ahead to the meeting he was about to have with Bartholomew. There was no doubt Tulipa had invited him over to talk about the letter from the Marquis, the one that had made Will's stomach sink. Two weeks was far too little time to make stable alliances with the various groups in Londinium, but Lord Iris would only care about the result, not the odds stacked against him. He feared it would come down to frenetic bribery and the vagaries of luck.

He needed to learn more about the Court than names and properties. No one wanted to organise a grand event so close to the fall of the Rosas, fearful it would be seen as bad taste, but it was what he needed to do; true power structures and patterns of alliances could be gleaned from just one evening at a ball. Could he depend on Catherine to support him well, though? She was hopeless at the larger events in Aquae Sulis and the last thing he wanted was for her to jeopardise his chances when he'd been making such progress with her. He smirked at himself. Yes, well done, he thought. Now you're actually able to converse with your wife. What an achievement.

He'd never known anyone so changeable and so confusing. Cathy could evidently hold her own in a conversation at a dinner or an intimate soirée and had managed to win over the Tulipas, yet the very simplest of social situations seemed to fox her. She seemed incapable of seeing that she was making progress too. Every time he tried to point out a success she shot him down as if she refused to believe she could ever achieve anything on her own merit. No doubt her father's violence was a factor in her lack of confidence but how had a family as respected and successful as the Aquae Sulis Rhoeas-Papavers created such a strange daughter?

A pressure was building behind his eyes. If only he'd been married to Amelia, it would be so much easier.

The carriage stopped and Will focused on the meeting again. This time he was escorted through Hampton Court Palace by a more direct route, having already been suitably impressed.

Bartholomew was waiting for him in a richly decorated drawing room, wearing a wine-coloured tailcoat, cream breeches and waistcoat. His cravat was perfectly tied and Will struggled to deal with a brief feeling of inferiority.

"William," Bartholomew said warmly, shaking his hand. "Thank you for coming. Sherry?"

"Please."

"I trust you're well?"

"Yes, thank you. Catherine has asked me to pass on her regards."

Bartholomew smiled as he handed him the glass. "I'm sure you know why I asked to see you."

Will nodded. "A certain letter, I presume. Anything else and we would have met at Black's."

"Indeed. I won't waste your time with small talk; I intend to stand for Duke, Will, and I'd like to have your support."

Will took a sip of the sherry. It was the one conversation he didn't want to have. "I believe you would make a fine Duke," he said, weighing up what to say next. Lying and saying he would support him, only to step forward as a candidate on the night, was too despicable to contemplate. Simply telling Bartholomew he was unable to support him without explanation would imply he was planning to support another. Tempting as it was to leave the Tulipa to fret about who that might be, it hardly seemed the behaviour of a gentleman. Besides, with only two weeks to go, Will was going to have to make his intentions clear to those he wanted to win over, and it would be all over Londinium before the week was out. "However, I'm not free to offer my support, as much as I would like to."

Bartholomew was surprised, just for a moment, but Will saw it flash across his eyes. "Have you decided another is more worthy?"

"Quite the contrary, I fear," Will said with as charming a smile as he could muster. "I'm putting myself forward, you see."

"You? But you've been resident for less than a month! I didn't think you were so arrogant."

"I'm not, sir, believe me. We've only known each other a very short period of time, but I've already come to have a great deal of respect for you. I'd like to speak frankly, if we can agree it goes no further than this room."

"You have my word."

Will didn't believe him. He wanted to, but with so much at stake, he knew the Tulipa would use every piece of information at his disposal. But Will had to plan for the possibility—nay probability—that he was going to lose. Duke Tulipa would remember his honesty.

"Were I to have a choice in the matter I would support you wholeheartedly. However, my family have tasked me with standing for the Dukedom, and as a loyal son I must obey."

"The Irises are interested in Londinium?" Bartholomew set his glass down on the mantelpiece. "It's a compliment they put so much faith in you, Will."

"Or perhaps their interest isn't so serious," Will replied. "If they really wanted Londinium, they have many more experienced sons to send. Perhaps they just wanted me out of Aquae Sulis."

"Perhaps."

Will was pleased he'd managed to muddy the water with a little self-deprecation. "So you see my hands are tied. I hope you take my being truthful with you as an indication of the high esteem I hold you in. When I'm forced to step forward on the night, you'll know why and not see it as a personal rejection of your candidacy."

"Is there no way we could persuade your family to release you from your obligation? I'd very much like to have you in my Court, in a high position. Standing against me is futile, and it seems such a waste to have your first Court appearance be a failure. Why not support me and avoid the embarrassment?"

"You're certain you'll win?"

"I'm certain there are no other serious candidates. Please don't take offence. I'm established in the city and have the support of the most influential people here."

"And you have many more years of experience than I," Will added. "All this is true. But what can I do?"

"Indeed. It's a shame, but I appreciate your candour. I do urge you to discuss this with your family. I'd be amenable to coming to an agreement."

"I'll put it to them. No doubt that would be far more beneficial than my humiliation." Will smiled and shook hands with him, settling into the role of dutiful son with no hope. By the time Will left, Bartholomew was back to smiles and gentle humour, unaware that Will was more determined to win than before.

Will looked out on the mists of the Nether, planning the letters he'd write once home, considering his options now Bartholomew knew of his ambition. If Lord Iris himself hadn't been behind this push for Londinium, he would have approached his father to discuss terms he could take to the Tulipa, knowing his chances of taking the ducal seat were next to nil. For the first time since they'd arrived, he permitted himself to consider failure and really look it in the face. What would Lord Iris do when Tulipa took the throne? Surely the family's Patroon would defend him, make it clear how impossible a task it was? Would the Fae listen?

He had two weeks but even if he had two years it wouldn't be enough time to win steadfast support from the Court. He was still learning their names, let alone their strengths and weaknesses. Cornelius was a great help, but acquiring dry information wasn't the same as forming true alliances.

It had always been an impossibility. Perhaps he'd been right, perhaps his family did want him out of the way. No, that was ludicrous; they'd never wilfully put a son forward for guaranteed humiliation. Perfection and success in all endeavours were expected, and if they couldn't be achieved, an attempt was not made. But then again the family hadn't proposed this, Lord Iris had, and the Fae weren't known for their realism.

There was only one option: Will had to play the game whether he wanted to or not and fair play would not bring a win. If he was going to sacrifice his principles to keep the favour of his patron and Patroon, how far was he willing to go?

He closed his eyes and rested his head, letting himself be rocked by the carriage. He heard a gentle pop and the scent of irises filled the air.

A faerie dressed in blue iris petals was hovering in front of him. It smiled and waved. "Hello."

"What a pleasant surprise," he said, holding out the palm of his right hand so it could alight. Practically weightless, it felt like two cold peas resting on his skin. "You look as beautiful as ever."

It giggled, hiding its mouth behind its hands like the Japanese schoolgirls he'd waved to on the Grand Tour. "And you are too handsome to live anywhere but Exilium."

"If I were to live amongst such beauty I would fade in your eyes and I would hate that to happen." Will smiled, all the while preparing himself for the message she was about to deliver.

"You're definitely the best of the crop. I'm sure if I asked my Lord—"

"But Lord Iris needs me to take Londinium, and who are we to go against his wishes?"

Its tiny pointed ears drooped slightly. "True. I have a message from him. He expects a son by the end of the first year of your marriage."

"A son? My wife and I would be delighted to be so blessed, but these things are notoriously difficult to predict."

"Without our help they are." It smiled and fluttered up to his nose to kiss it lightly, making the tip tingle. "There, a little help from me, just between us, you understand. You still have to do your bit." It giggled and smiled provocatively at him. "But when you do and your wife's belly swells, you can be happy in the knowledge it will be a boy and a fine one too."

"Thank you. I have no idea what I've done to be worthy of such kindness but I'm deeply touched by your generosity."

"So there shouldn't be any problem with satisfying my Lord now, should there?"

"No, thanks to you."

It fluttered higher, until it was level with his eyes. "Really? Is she being a good wife?"

"Catherine is surpassing my hopes and expectations in every way," he replied smoothly. "I'm sure our marriage will only get better and better."

It clapped. "Oh, how exquisite. I'm quite envious of her. She doesn't deserve you."

He opted for silence. Why was Lord Iris paying so much attention to their marriage and, more specifically, its consummation? Why had he insisted they marry in the first place? Whilst it was normal for every Iris generation to hope for sons, it was rare for the Fae to actively intervene. Charms to influence gender were incredibly expensive and used only after two daughters had been born, not before the first had even been conceived.

The faerie waved and disappeared, the air rushing in with a pop to fill the space it had occupied. Would Lord Iris summon Cathy again soon? It had taken her days to recover from whatever ordeal he'd put her through and if she returned to Exilium as a virgin they could both be in serious trouble.

He rapped on the roof of the carriage with the tip of his cane and it slowed to a stop. He opened the window and called up to the driver who leaned over to listen.

"Take me to the Emporium of Things in Between and Besides," he ordered, and the driver touched the brim of his hat.

Will settled back in his place as the carriage turned on the Nether road, hating the decision he had been forced to make.

• • •

Max sat on the chair in the Sorcerer's ballroom waiting for the puppet to arrive, the mask resting on his lap. He remembered the lesson his mentor had given him in how to use it.

"Our mentor was one hell of an Arbiter," the gargoyle said. It'd been so quiet in the corner Max had forgotten it was there.

Max nodded, remembering the sight of his dead body at the Cloister. Just an image, no grief and no anger.

The dry rasp of the gargoyle's attempt to weep filled the space. "We need to stop fucking about at the edges of this," it said. "Let's just go into London and bash some heads together until we find out what's going on."

"You know it's not that simple," Max replied. "I know you're finding it frustrating, but the Sorcerers have their ways. We can't force Ekstrand to hurry Dante into a meeting. Anything like that could precipitate a war. You know how twitchy they are about their sovereignty."

"It just seems like a waste of time. And *we're* finding it frustrating. You just get to sit there calm as a dead parrot whilst I'm feeling all of this. *I'm* the one who has to deal with it."

"If you can't handle this go and wait in the scullery."

"Piss off," the gargoyle growled. "I am handling it."

"You're still upset about her lying to us, aren't you?"

"So what if I am?"

Max had decided it could work to his advantage if the puppet saw the gargoyle was no longer on her side. It would put her on the back foot and he would exploit it.

The burning outline appeared, forming the Way, and in moments the puppet stepped through. She was wearing the same mundane clothes and long satin gloves as before, but now he knew why.

She opened her mouth to greet them as the Way closed behind her, but before the words emerged the gargoyle had covered the length of the room in only four bounds. It launched itself at her with a ferocity Max hadn't anticipated. She was slammed against the wall and her arms were pinned by its stone claws. She looked utterly terrified.

"Why did you lie to us?" it snarled.

"What?" Her confusion seemed genuine, but Max knew puppets were masterful actors.

"Why didn't you tell us your husband has two pet Rosas? You knew we needed to speak to a Rose, urgently, and you didn't tell us?"

"I..." She was breathless. "You're hurting me."

"Do I look like I care?" The gargoyle's stone teeth were an inch from her cheek. "You think we want to find the Rosas to have tea together? Have a nice little chat and a catch up? Every day we're delayed by you pissing us about, people are at risk. *Innocents*, not the likes of you."

"You think I could just ask my husband where they are? I don't know where he keeps them, I've never wanted to know. She's his mistress and I'm the wife—there's no way to ask that kind of question without it being dodgy as hell."

"Not our problem." The gargoyle didn't let go.

"Yeah, it's always mine, isn't it? If I found out where they are and you went and interrogated them do you think that would be the end of it? Who else is going to lead an Aquae Sulis Arbiter to his bit on the side? You know what Iris men do to wives that don't toe the line?" The gargoyle stayed silent. "They replace them."

The gargoyle drew its face back an inch. "You should have told us anyway."

"And hope you'd be sensitive to my circumstances? You think I'm that stupid? Your...handler over there thinks I'm worth less than horseshit, and wouldn't have given a second thought to blowing my life up into more of a disaster than it already is. Now, will you please let me go, you're really hurting me."

The gargoyle released her arms and returned to all fours, prowling in front of her as it considered what she'd said. She rubbed her arms where she'd been pinned.

"I thought you were being straight with us," the gargoyle said after a moment.

"I have been as far as I can be without getting myself killed or enslaved, OK? Can you please just try to see how hard this is for me to get away with? I'm already taking a huge risk just being here."

"But it's not an altruistic act," Max said. "You're only here because you need us."

She looked in his direction and saw the mask on his lap. She paled further. "What's that?"

"It's a Truth Mask," he replied.

"There's a clue in the name," the gargoyle added.

She looked like she was trying to press herself back through the wall. "There's no need for anything scary, OK?"

"Isn't there? As the gargoyle said, we thought you were being straight with us, when all this time you've been withholding information critical to our investigation. We've been polite. And patient. It's got us nowhere. Now you need to tell us the truth and this is the only way we can be sure."

"That's not true, I gave you loads on the Agency," she said, her voice higher pitched. "I bugged that man, didn't that lead anywhere?"

"It did, but, as we said before, that's only one part of the investigation. We need to make some serious progress and your games are getting in the way."

"I'm not playing games." She stared at the mask and its rivets gleaming in the lantern light.

"We need to speak to the Rosas still in Londinium. We can't hunt them so you need to tell us how to find them quickly. Tell us where your husband has stashed away his pet Rosas."

"I can't."

"Then tell us how you hid from your family."

"I can't do that either."

"Right." Max picked the Mask up and made a show of checking the straps, giving her a good look at the metal face with a shaped nose and nostril holes. There were no holes for the eyes and a metal grill that would fit over her mouth.

"I really can't!" she yelled. "Look, someone took a huge risk helping me, I don't want to put him in any danger."

"Not my problem." Max got up.

"I swore I'd never tell anyone how it was done," she said, palms flat against the wall as she tried to keep as much distance between herself and the mask as possible. "I can't break that promise."

"How many promises have you already broken?" the gargoyle asked, ending its prowling to stand in front of her, poised like he was about to pounce on a mouse.

She slid sideways, fumbling along the wall, looking for the doorknob that was no longer there. "There's no way to leave this room without my say-so," Max said. "There's nowhere to go, puppet."

She reached the corner. "I haven't done anything wrong. Don't do this, please." Her pleading eyes fell on the gargoyle. "I told you as much as I could, I led you to the Agency. That was the deal: Agency for Miss Rainer's details. Not this."

"We got the file on her," the gargoyle said. "All you have to do is tell us how or where the Rosas are hiding and you can have it."

"Hold her still." Max was close enough to see the sweat sheen on her face.

The gargoyle grabbed a wrist and pulled her towards it roughly. As she moved away from the wall it stepped behind her, raised itself on its haunches again and wrapped its stone arms around her in a bear hug.

"You see the studs on the inside?" Max asked, the puppet's eyes huge with terror. "Apparently they hurt but don't leave any permanent marks."

"Wait!"

He took a step closer.

"Wait!" she yelled. "If you put that thing on me, I'll never help you again. You said yourself this is just the start. How far can you get without me on the inside? It's obvious you can't act in London, or Londinium for that matter—what're you going to do when you need to bring these people in?"

Max stopped. "You need us more."

"Do I?"

She seemed bolder, as if a switch inside her had flicked from terror to absolute calm. The gargoyle was frowning. It had looked less happy from the moment it had grabbed her.

"Who else can help you?" Max asked. "You need a Sorcerer."

"There must be other Sorcerers," she replied, now staring him in the eye. "I'll find one. I'd rather get you the information without screwing over the one who helped me. I will, I swear it, on my blood if you need me to, or whatever way you people do it. All I need is twenty-four hours. Then I want the information on Rainer."

"Why didn't you offer this before?" the gargoyle asked, eyes narrow, its teeth brushing against her ear as it spoke.

"I didn't think of it. I haven't been planning this out like a game of chess, you know. And this isn't the only shit-storm in my life right now, OK?"

"If I let you go now, without using this, we're back to square one and there's no guarantee you'll see it through," Max said. "The way I see it, we use the mask, we get what we need before dinner."

"And be left without an insider," she reminded him. "And I reckon if you put that thing on me, and it hurts me, Lord Iris would know and kick up a stink. Then my uncle would find out and that would make things awkward between him and the Sorcerer. Do you want that?"

"Shit," the gargoyle said and let her go. "She's right."

She staggered and hit the wall again. "Look, if it's any consolation, I'd much rather deal with you than anyone else."

Max pulled the folded piece of paper from his pocket that Ekstrand had given him in case Cathy needed to come back. "If you don't come through the Way this opens at midday tomorrow, everything's off. No second chance. You'll get the file on Rainer when we know your information is legitimate."

"I'll be here," she said. "I promise." She looked at the gargoyle, as if about to say something, then didn't.

Max opened the Way and she left. The gargoyle sat next to him, staring at the place she passed through. "We need whisky," it said.

"I don't drink."

"I know. I definitely have the worse half of this relationship. I feel like shit now."

"Why? She wriggled her way out of it, just like any other puppet would."

"No, not like any other. I believe her. I don't think she was trying to pull one over us; she's not like that."

Max turned to face it fully. "Were you here just now? Didn't you see what she did?"

"I saw her keep it together when being held by me and threatened by you. Not many could do that. And don't get angry with me, there's no denying she's—"

"I'm not angry."

"You are, and now I don't know whether to admire her or be pissed off with myself. Thanks."

Max shrugged. "We'd better report to Ekstrand and hope he sees it the same way."

19

For the fifth time on the journey Cathy opened her reticule to be sure that her tiny digital camera was inside. She pulled it out, checked the battery level and that the flash was set to activate in dim lighting, and put it back in her bag again. She was alone in the carriage travelling on the Nether road to the Emporium of Things in Between and Besides, something her uncle had advised her never to do. She had no choice; she had to be alone at the shop.

Cathy chewed a thumbnail as she went over the plan again. If it didn't work she'd be back to square one and wouldn't get the file on Miss Rainer. She had no idea how many Sorcerers there were, let alone how to find another, and didn't want to have that problem on top of all the others. As time went on it would only get harder to avoid Will, especially once all the silliness over the Dukedom was over and no longer distracting him. The days had been rushing by in a blur of social engagements and hours had been wasted with Dame Iris. She'd tried to get the Dame to agree she'd be better suited to painting but it had achieved nothing.

The carriage soon stopped and she reined in her impulse to climb out straightaway. The footman opened the door and lowered the step. She accepted his help climbing out; the last thing she needed was a sprained ankle.

"I won't be long," she said to the driver.

"I'll wait here, ma'am," he replied, and the footman walked ahead of her to the shop's door.

Even though the basic building was the same as the anchor property, the Emporium's Nether frontage looked very different with its traditional signage in elegant script above the door and window display of bottles and packets. The footman knocked twice and then entered. Having worked there, Cathy knew that those two knocks activated a Charm that adjusted the clock above the door inside to indicate that Londinium clientele were about to enter, as opposed to those from Aquae Sulis, Oxenford or Jorvik.

Cathy walked in as a customer for the first time in years and was relieved to see that the shop was empty. The Shopkeeper looked up from his book and smiled before tucking in the bookmark.

"Mrs Reticulata-Iris," he said with the briefest glance at the footman before the door was shut behind Cathy and the two of them were alone. "Catherine," he said more softly and came out from behind the counter. "How are you?"

"Oh, you know," she replied, feeling very strange standing there in a late Victorian style dress replete with trimming and bustle, not dissimilar to the one Dame Iris had been wearing. "Things could be better."

His smile was sad, then it faded as he laced his fingers in front of his chest. "I've been told the Charm you ordered should be delivered next week."

That would leave less than a week to paint something to satisfy Lord Poppy. She hoped the Charm was worth such an agonising wait. "Great. Thanks. I was hoping to buy some of that...what was it you called it...atmospheric mist of beautifying?"

"Do you mean the Beautifying Mist of Atmospheric Improvement?"

"That's the one!"

The Shopkeeper frowned at her over his glasses. "Really? I recall you disliked the name and the scent, two rather critical elements of that product."

"Well, I wanted to give it another chance."

"In fact you described it as smelling of cut grass and almonds, and it made you sniffle like a mundane street urchin in February."

"OK, I'll come clean," she said. "I want it for a parlour game. I didn't want to tell you in case it offended you."

"Oh, well, that makes sense now." He smiled and she breathed out in relief. "I'm afraid it's in the stockroom, I won't be a moment."

It was exactly what she'd hoped for. She knew the Shopkeeper never threw anything away; there was a box tucked away on one of the highest shelves in the stockroom for failed products. He hated heights, so it would take him a few minutes to collect himself after the trip up the ladder and re-emerge.

Once she heard the door of the stockroom shut Cathy scurried behind the counter and through to the cubbyhole office which contained the ledger. There was barely any light to see by, and she couldn't strike the globe to wake the sprite as it would indicate she'd been there. She fished out her camera, switched it on and felt for the ledger. Mercifully it was open and in its usual place. Cathy took a close-up picture of the two exposed pages, checked it and took another in a slightly different position. She flipped a page back and took a couple of photos of those pages too. She risked repeating the process a couple more times, taking care to count how many times she'd turned the page so she could leave it open at the correct place. It was worth the risk; the more data she had, the easier it would be to crack the code used by the Shopkeeper to track sales and purchases. All she had to do was work out who'd been buying the most expensive Shadow Charms since the night the Rosas fell and she'd know where to send the Arbiter.

The camera was in her reticule and she was back in the main part of the shop before the Shopkeeper returned.

"Here it is, I'll wrap it for you," he said and she smiled, hoping she didn't look flustered. "I'll charge it to your husband's account."

"I suppose that's one of the few advantages of being married." She wondered if she was convincing.

He tucked the tissue-papered atomiser in a small box, then wrapped that in brown paper and tied it with string. "I do hope you can find some happiness, Catherine," he said as he handed it over.

"I'm not giving up yet," she replied. "Take care."

"You too, my dear, you too."

Unable to wait until she got back to Lancaster House, Cathy

looked at the pictures on the camera's small display screen whilst still in the carriage, but the Shopkeeper's scrawl was too small to read. It wasn't until she'd got back to her bedroom and uploaded them to her iPad that she was able to start work, after she'd told Morgan that she wasn't to be disturbed.

The Shopkeeper only wrote the customer name in code and listed an abbreviated product name alongside it. Just a glance at the latest page confirmed her suspicion; a lot of Shadow Charms had been sold recently. However, without any dates entered alongside the sales, there was no way to know whether she was looking at sales over the last week or the last month. Flipping back and forth through the pictures she'd taken it was clear the Great Families had a lot of things to hide.

She had to narrow down the entries; the Shadow Charms likely to have been procured to conceal rogue Rosas hiding from the Agency would have been bought in the last two weeks. Based on her memory of the accounts she could make a reasonable guess that no more than the last two pages would cover that time.

Cathy made a list of all of the coded names of those who'd bought Shadow Charms. There were four different people, but only one that had bought more than one Charm, so she focused on that name.

"'Nasal Climber 6-1-L'," she muttered.

The Shopkeeper had made all sorts of comments about his customers whilst she'd worked for him but she couldn't recall anything about one having nasal problems. She realised that cracking a code without a reference point was going to take far too long and then hit upon the idea of finding an entry that she could tie to a person. It could give an insight into the numbers and letter after the pseudonym, at least.

With no date reference and only the product names to go by it seemed an impossible task at first. Then she remembered the day Tom had found her and how they'd rushed to the Emporium to find something to save Josh from Horatio. The Shopkeeper had given her a Luck Charm and it had only been a couple of days after she'd reconciled the accounts at the end of her vacation.

Cathy flipped back to a picture of the earlier entries and scanned the list until she saw the entry "Luck Egg—short duration". It was only a few rows beneath the last product she remembered tallying up. Under "payment" the Shopkeeper had written, "One kiss of genuine gratitude and affection", and she knew it was the charm he'd given her to protect Josh.

Her name was entered as "Flanders cockerel 5-2-L (AS)" and when she scanned up the list she spotted "Flanders cockerel 5-1-AS" against a purchase of a Seeker Charm. She deduced that was Tom, as the Shopkeeper had warned her he'd bought another Seeker Charm just before Lord Poppy found her. That meant "Flanders cockerel" was the code for their family name and that the second number was an indicator of where in the sibling pecking order they came; Tom was 1 as the eldest and she was 2 thanks to being the middle child. After a few moments of chewing the end of her thumbnail, Cathy hazarded a guess that the first number was the number of generations down from the Patroon, or at least something along those lines to identify which set of siblings the second number related to. AS was most probably Aquae Sulis and the L against her name was because they'd entered the shop from Londinium, even though officially she was an Aquae Sulis resident. She wondered how he kept track of cousins but his memory was incredible—perhaps he only needed the prompt.

If she applied the same logic to the one who'd recently bought the shadow charms, that person was the eldest child of their generation and a Londinium resident. "Well, that's bloody useless, I need to know the family."

Flanders cockerel…how could that signify Rhoeas-Papaver? The Flanders part was probably because of the First World War association with the red poppy, but why cockerel? Then she recalled a painting by Monet that hung in the drawing room of her childhood home, one of a woman and child walking through a corn field dotted with poppies, and it was called *Les Coquelicots*. Could cockerel simply be a play on the French word for the red poppy?

"'Nasal Climber…'" Cathy whispered the epithet. People often referred to the Wisterias as climbers; it was a rather pathetic pun, the plant named after their line being a climbing vine and the family constantly trying to climb higher in social circles. Did any of them have a particularly large nose? Could the Shopkeeper be that childish with his nicknames?

She tried to remember the names of the Wisteria families resident in Londinium and recalled one that had been on Dame Iris's list of people she should know about: the Sinensis-Wisteria family. "Sinensis" was fairly close to "sinuses" and the eldest son did have notably large nostrils. She shook her head. Surely it wasn't so simple?

If it didn't turn out to be the right family there would be no real harm done. With nothing better to offer him, it was time to contact the Arbiter and hope the Wisteria was buying the Shadow Charms to keep an illegal Rosa hidden. She needed to keep the Arbiter and Sorcerer on side. Even if they couldn't get her out of the Nether by the time the painting was due, perhaps they'd get her out before Poppy realised how bad it was.

Max handed the piece of paper to Ekstrand and the Sorcerer scanned the information he'd copied from the Gallica-Rosa's file. He would have given him the information sooner but the Sorcerer had been having one of his bad days.

"I have absolutely no idea what this means," Ekstrand said. "There were lots of files?"

"Enough to store information on every single puppet in Albion, past and present," Max replied. "Including detailed records on what the Agency provides for them. We've always assumed they've found their own ways to live in the Nether but I think we were wrong. This Agency arranges everything for them in return for payment."

"Payment in charms or money?"

"Both, as far as we could tell, but there's something more to it than that. I think the coded information is an evaluation of some kind, I just don't know what Horatio Gallica-Rosa was being evaluated for."

"Most worrying. This is far more complex than I'd anticipated and we're under-resourced."

"I pulled the file on that Miss Rainer," Max said. "Seems she used to be the puppet's governess. She was removed from the Rhoeas-Papaver household following a complaint from the puppet's mother. Apparently Miss Rainer smuggled seditious materials into the household and exposed her student to 'dangerous and inappropriate' ideas."

"So that's why she's different from the other puppets?"

"It seems so, sir. She requested asylum the first time I met her."

"She's still one of them though," Ekstrand said, "whether she likes it or not. If she doesn't produce the information we need, use whatever means necessary to determine where the hidden Rosas are. I want them found before the Moot."

"Yes, sir," Max said and left his study.

Axon was waiting in the corridor with the gargoyle. "Samuel Westonville is waiting for you in the sitting room," he said.

"Thanks." Max found Sam in front of the fire, slumped forwards, face in his hands. "Sam?"

His eyes were bloodshot and circled by shadowed skin. He had new stubble and the dishevelled state of his clothes suggested he'd been wearing them for a few days. "Axon picked me up earlier, he said you wanted to see me."

"I've been looking into the forge where you made your wedding rings. I think you need to know what I found out."

"It's bad, isn't it?"

Max didn't say anything until he was sitting down with the gargoyle next to him. "You weren't the only couple Neugent recommended the forge to. There were ten others before you, and all of them made their own wedding rings like you did."

"What a romantic guy," Sam said. "So you gonna tell me they're all dead now or something?"

"How did you know!" The gargoyle's mouth dropped open, making his face look like a grotesque designed to have water pour from it.

"What?" Sam broke out of his misery and jolted to the edge of his seat. "That's not what you found out, was it?"

"Not exactly," Max said.

"It was only one person out of each couple that died," the gargoyle said.

"What the fuck?"

Max decided that next time he had to deliver news likely to upset someone he'd make sure the gargoyle was locked in a cupboard on the other side of the house. "Not straightaway, but at a young age."

"How did they die?"

"Different things; a couple of cancers, a few heart attacks, a few I just couldn't find out because they weren't reported in the press. The forge isn't the only thing linking them, Sam. The ones that died all worked for Neugent over the past ten years."

"In Pin PR?" Sam was on his feet.

"One of them, yes, five years ago, but not the others. He's worked for several companies over that time. Sam, please, sit down until I've given you all the information."

"But my wife—"

"Please."

The last thing Max needed was to have him run off into Mundanus and do something stupid. Sam sat down. "I looked into Neugent more closely. He's never been married and he's in his thirties, whereas you described him as being in his fifties, so something doesn't add up there. Every company he's worked for is owned by one massive international corporation, one I didn't know existed until I started looking into all of this. It's called CoFerrum Inc."

"I've never heard of it."

"From the name I suspect it has something to do with Lord Iron," Max said. "And I suspect he's using Neugent to interfere with your wife in some way, resulting in her change in behaviour and physical weight loss."

Sam was on his feet again. "I'm such an idiot. She wants to divorce me and it's all because of Neugent. He's been sniffing round my wife for bloody ages, he puts her in an apartment that's got an iron cage built into it and now you're telling me people who wear wedding rings made at that forge and work for him die young? That's it."

He marched to the door.

"Where are you going?" Max asked, struggling to get back on his feet.

"He's gonna break Neugent's face," the gargoyle said, cheering. "Yeah, go on Sam, you show him who's the man!"

"Be quiet," Max said, but by the time he'd turned back to Sam, he was gone. Max limped out into the hallway to see Axon closing the front door. "He left?"

"Yes, sir, Mr Ekstrand gave no instructions for him to be kept here. A message has just arrived for you from Mrs Reticulata-Iris. She's waiting in the ballroom. I understand you agreed to give her some information in return?"

Max took the small piece of paper. There was an address in London, then a sentence explaining it was the anchor property of a Mr Sinensis-Wisteria who "has been taking great efforts to hide something since the Rosas fell".

"So Cathy came through for us," the gargoyle said, peering over his shoulder to look at the note.

"She's given us a name and address. She may have the wrong person."

"But you're gonna give her that file she wanted, aren't you?"

Max nodded. "We've made a copy and if the puppet is still messing us about she'll think we've fallen for it. It'll make it more of a shock if we bring her in for interrogation."

* * *

Cathy stepped through the Way and back into Lancaster House with the file on Miss Rainer clutched to her chest. She was grateful that no one was there to see her hurry into the bedroom.

Perched on the bed, nauseous with anticipation, Cathy opened the plain manila file from the Agency. The first line on the top summary sheet made her snatch up the piece of paper to read it again with disbelieving eyes.

"Name: Miss Natasha Rainer Rainsworth"

"She's still alive!" Cathy laughed and then wept with relief. Miss Rainsworth was now a scullery maid at a house near Kew Gardens, anchor property for the Parviflorus-Ranunculus family, and had been since she'd been sacked from her position in the Papaver household. The rest of the page was a cryptic list of abbreviations so she flipped over to read the next.

There was a report on the complaint made by Mrs Rhoeas-Papaver that accused Miss Rainer of smuggling inappropriate literature into the household and giving lessons on "inappropriate topics" including social history with an "unusual focus on the Suffragettes and other such mundane matters". She scanned down to the signature at the bottom of the page: Harold Bennet.

"That bastard! He knew all along!"

A section was highlighted noting that Miss Rainsworth was under no circumstances permitted to work in any household in which Catherine Rhoeas-Papaver was resident. Paper-clipped to the report was a brief note in Bennet's handwriting outlining how he'd told the now Mrs Catherine Reticulata-Iris that Miss Rainer had died in order to avoid any further enquiries.

"Well, sod you, Bennet," she said to the signature and flipped forwards to a list of previous assignments. Rainer's first position was as a lady's maid, then she became a governess. Was that switch in career normal for Agency staff or had Rainer charmed her first employer into giving her a more challenging role suited to her intellect?

There was a knock on the door. "Not now, Morgan, I said I wasn't to be disturbed."

"It's me, Cathy," Will said and the handle started to turn.

She slapped the file shut, rolled over to the far side of the bed and shoved it underneath. She was just about back on top when the door opened.

"I told Morgan—" Cathy stopped when she saw the tray with champagne, two glasses and a bowl of strawberries.

"You're not unwell, are you?" he asked, pausing to close the door with his foot before setting the tray down on the dressing table.

"No." She shuffled to the edge of the bed. "I was just…having a lie down."

"Good." He smiled as he eased the cork out of the champagne and then poured it into the glasses.

Whilst he had his back to her she checked there weren't any pieces of paper in sight. She'd locked the camera and iPad away before going to the Arbiter.

"We have something to celebrate." He handed her a glass. "I've been accepted into Black's."

"Black's?"

His smile lost its lustre. "The gentleman's club. It's the most exclusive in Albion and I thought it would take years to get in. It only took a week."

"Oh." It was hard to fake enthusiasm when she just wanted him to leave so she could carry on reading the file. "Actually Will, I—"

He chinked his glass against hers. "Here's to the future."

She couldn't ignore the toast without being horribly rude so she smiled and had a sip. "Will, would you mind—"

"And here's to you."

The crystal rang as he tapped his glass against hers and sat next to her on the bed. They both took another sip.

"Why are we toasting me?"

"Because you won over the Tulipas. Bartholomew sponsored me into Black's and I'm sure he wouldn't have if he hadn't been so delightfully charmed by you."

"I'm not charming."

"Nonsense. You're just an acquired taste. How did it go earlier?" Her heart fluttered. "With Dame Iris. I heard she paid a visit."

"Oh that," Cathy said with relief. Of course he didn't know what she'd been up to since then. "It was bloody awful." A giggle slipped from her lips. "I probably shouldn't have told you that. I survived. Let's leave it at that." She didn't want to go into detail and prolong the conversation.

He beamed at her. "Here's to successfully surviving the formidable Dame Iris!"

Another bright ring from the crystal and another sip of champagne and Cathy laughed, feeling a rush of euphoria rising in her chest like the tiny bubbles in her glass. Miss Rainer was alive! She was working at a house a short drive away in Mundanus and there was nothing to stop her from going to find her.

Will reflected her smile. "Here's to us," he said and after tapping her glass he downed the rest of the champagne. "Now, celebratory strawberries, brought to us out of season by the magic of the mundane world!"

Cathy knocked back the last of her champagne, happy to celebrate even though it was for a different reason. She imagined running up to Miss Rainer and telling her that she'd got to university despite everything they'd tried to do to stop her, that all those lessons about freedom and the right to pursue one's own life hadn't been in vain.

Will relieved her of the empty glass and retrieved the bowl to set it between them on the bed.

She plucked out a strawberry and its sweetness exploded across her tongue. "These are so good!" Her heart raced with elation and they both laughed when they reached into the bowl at the same time. Will caught hold of her fingers and brought them to his lips. He leaned towards her, closing his eyes, and she found herself doing the same. His lips touched hers. Their warmth felt incredible and for the first time she thought only of Will. It was as if she hadn't even noticed him before, hadn't been aware of the beauty of his eyes and the richness of his voice. The kiss drew her in, seeming to last forever and then no time at all as he pulled away gently and studied her.

Cathy stared at him, wanting him so intensely she couldn't understand why she'd pushed him away for so long. What kind of idiot had she been? She threaded her fingers into Will's hair, pulling him back to her, feeling a terrific lust she'd never experienced with Josh. The more they kissed, the harder it was to remember what she'd seen in him anyway.

20

Will scanned the list of names, crossing out the ones he'd already spoken to, as Cornelius poured the sherry. He was desperate to throw himself into winning the Dukedom so he didn't have to think about what he'd done the night before. He'd hardly slept, lying next to Cathy as she was curled on her side, sleeping deeply. At first he felt satisfied he'd solved a problem, the next he even felt heroic for saving her from the impending wrath of Lord Iris. It shifted into a leaden guilt that lingered until he decided to get up and leave before she woke.

It was cowardly and he was disgusted with himself. He had arrived at the house and asked for Cornelius without his usual trip up the stairs to see Amelia. He didn't feel a need to be sated and he didn't want her to see the guilt in his eyes.

"Is that all of them?" Cornelius asked, bringing Will's mind back to the task. He crossed three more out then passed it over. "You've been busy."

Will sipped the sherry and lay the pen down. "There isn't time to waste."

"You've spoken to Tulipa, I see. What did you say?"

"That I couldn't support him because I have no choice but to stand myself."

Cornelius' eyebrows arched. "And how did that go?"

"As well as it could."

"Have you noticed anything unusual since then?"

"Like what?"

"Was it quiet on the road over today?"

Will nodded. "It's always quiet. I don't think I've ever seen another carriage. It takes some getting used to after Aquae Sulis." Cornelius still seemed dissatisfied. "What is it?"

"I don't think you should have told him. Now he'll see you as a threat."

"I could hardly do anything else. Besides, I played it down, I'm not a complete fool."

"The Tulipas are very accomplished, Bartholomew in particular. You have to be careful now, he could take action."

"What kind of action? Running me out of town?"

"Worse. Just because they're polite and cultured, it doesn't mean the Tulipas won't resort to low forms of persuasion."

"Are you seriously trying to tell me Bartholomew would threaten my person?" Will laughed. "The same man who charms my wife with debates on philosophy and thinks Freddy Viola is a grotesque idiot?"

"Will, please, listen to me. The Tulipas have been coveting the throne for hundreds of years. Just because you've had a few pleasant conversations with the man, don't think that will protect you."

"Don't be absurd."

"Don't be complacent!" Cornelius's voice rose. He closed his eyes as Will stared, taken aback. "I'm sorry. I feel very strongly about this. You must put an extra footman on your carriage and have them armed."

"Really?"

"Yes. Please take my advice. If nothing else, it will put Amelia's mind at rest as well as my own."

Will nodded and looked back down at the list. "There's a few left to talk to. No one has promised their support yet, but a couple seem more receptive than others. I wanted to talk to you about the Peonias."

They discussed the list and new approaches for most of the morning. Will decided to return home for lunch so he could consult the steward about security and see if Cathy was all right. It wasn't until he was halfway back that he realised he'd neglected to see Amelia.

"Is my wife at home?" he asked Morgan as his gloves and cane were taken.

"I'm afraid not, sir, she was collected by Dame Iris shortly after eleven. I understand they are to take tea with a friend of the Dame and then have lunch."

Will nodded. "Could you send a message to the steward to see me in my study?"

The steward was a rather dour man with angular features and an unfortunate set of ears, but he was most capable and had already proven himself to be invaluable. He listened to Will's concerns and then assured him he would give it his full attention. Will felt like a bit of a fool, but Cornelius seemed to think it was necessary and he couldn't see any harm in being cautious.

He'd lunch at home, then go to Black's to see if there was an opportunity to find Oliver's cousin. He leaned back in the chair, wondering what trouble his best friend had got himself into of late. It hadn't been so long ago that they'd been travelling together, then swanning about in Aquae Sulis, enjoying the attention as the newly returned. He marvelled at how quickly his life was turning into his father's, with a household to care for and a patron to keep happy. He wondered when Nathaniel would be paired off and why it hadn't happened already. He imagined that Imogen would soon be engaged, and Sophia, well, there was no telling what would become of her.

He had a sudden urge to see his youngest sister. He remembered Sophia's tiny kisses on his cheek, the way she'd asked to be a bridesmaid, and felt an awful twist in his stomach at the thought of her left at home with the housemaid whilst the family had been at the Oak. Sophia would have loved the wedding; in fact, she was probably the only person capable of being filled with joy at the event.

There was a scrying glass in the drawer of his desk, one he kept in case of emergencies. Will lifted it out and looked at his reflection briefly before saying, "Show me Miss Sophia Reticulata-Iris."

The surface of the glass rippled in the manner he was accustomed to, then he saw his youngest sister sitting on the floor.

She looked pale and thinner than he remembered, and far from happy as she combed the hair of a porcelain doll.

Will's stomach tightened, remembering her happy babble and the effortless affection she'd exuded whenever they were together. He set the glass down, went to the door and locked it, then went to the middle bookcase and pulled back the third book in from the left on the lowest shelf. There was a gentle click and it swung into the room, revealing a second door behind it set into the wall. Will retrieved the wooden key, as heavy as one made from lead, from the hidden compartment in his desk and put it in the lock. It sent a tingle up his arm as he turned it.

He pocketed the key and opened the door. He could just make out his old room in his parents' Aquae Sulis home through a haze that reminded him of the roads in Sicily during the heat of the day.

He held his breath and stepped through. When he glanced back he could see the door had already shut and locked behind him and the bookcase would be swinging back into place. When the Patroon had insisted on giving the Way as a gift, he'd been resistant to the idea, thinking the Patroon's generosity was a thinly veiled lack of confidence in his ability to cope in Londinium. It was nothing more than a means of enabling Will to gain advice from his father without anyone else's knowledge. Now he was grateful he hadn't expressed that opinion at the time.

His mother, ever conscious of the embarrassment of being surprised by an unexpected guest—even if it was her own son—insisted on a Charm being put in place to ring a bell down in the servants' hall should the Way from Londinium be opened. The butler was hurrying up the stairs as he emerged from his room.

"Good morning, sir, what a pleasure to see you again."

"Good morning. Is my mother here? I need to speak to her. I apologise for the lack of polite notice, but it's important."

"She's entertaining guests. Perhaps you'd be kind enough to wait in the drawing room, and I'll inform her of your arrival."

"Is my father here?"

"I'm afraid not, sir. He's expected back this evening."

Will paced as he waited in the drawing room, feeling strange now he was back in his old home. He felt younger and tense in a way he hadn't for some time. He was back on guard, ready to defend himself from his siblings and their latest attempt to ridicule or trick him.

He was brought tea, which he hadn't the stomach for, and then shortly afterwards his mother arrived, dressed in such an elaborate dress he surmised the guests were important.

"William." She kissed him on the cheek. "What a lovely surprise. Is everything well in Londinium?"

"Yes," he said. "Mother, I'm here about Sophia. I want her to come and stay with us."

It was clearly the last thing she'd expected him to say. "I beg your pardon?"

"I want her to come and live with Cathy and me. She's not happy here."

"Whatever gives you that impression?"

"I used a Glass."

"How rude!"

"She's not looking well. Is no one keeping her company? Who is looking after her?"

"Stop making such a fuss. She's fine."

"I'd like to see her."

"But that will only upset her, she misses you."

"All the more reason for her to come with me."

Mother arranged two cups on saucers, and they rattled as she did so. "William, do sit down and think about what you're suggesting. Catherine is newly married and hardly in a position to care for her, and besides, it's her first year as a new bride. She should be settling in and no doubt Dame Iris is paying her a great deal of attention."

"You're worried the Dame will find out about Sophia," Will said, sitting opposite her. "I'm not a fool, mother. We'll keep her out of the Dame's way and tell the staff she's a distant relative of mine, whose mother is sick or something."

"Is Catherine prepared to do this?"

"She'll adore Sophia, it's impossible to not love her."

Mother set the teapot down. "Oh, William. You haven't told her, have you?"

"It's not a problem," he said. "Besides, I want her to have some contact with a young child. She needs to get used to the idea of us having children and what better way to do that than see how delightful one can be?"

"William"—Mother handed him a cup of tea he still didn't want—"you've got a lot to learn."

"I can't leave Sophia here being so miserable, it's not right."

She fidgeted, stirring her tea for too long. "We have guests. We've not been able to give her as much attention as usual, it's true. And your father has been nervous about this for a while…the Patroon has been visiting more often since you went to Londinium. Perhaps it wouldn't hurt to have her stay with you a little while, just whilst we're entertaining."

"Let me have Sophia to stay for just a month. We'll see how she settles and how Cathy takes to her. Would you be amenable to that?"

"But what about standing for the Dukedom, won't she be a distraction?"

"Hardly, Mother, and I rather think having her around will keep me cheerful in the midst of all the politics."

"You really are a sweet young man, William. I hope Catherine realises how lucky she is."

Will took to stirring his tea. "I'm sure she will."

When the carriage finally pulled away from the restaurant, Cathy released a long sigh of relief. Finally she could accomplish something useful now that her obligation to Dame Iris was over for the day. She wanted to check her email and see if her tutor had responded. Cathy had been very apologetic, explaining that a family emergency had taken her away from her studies and that she'd be unlikely to return for a few months. She wanted to know if she'd be able to continue her studies at a distance in the interim. She'd ordered books from her reading list and arranged to pick them up at a bookshop only a short walk away. She'd also stumbled across information on P.O. Boxes, a remarkably useful mundane service which would enable her to have a postal address separate from the anchor property. Slowly, piece by piece, Cathy felt like she was starting to make real progress. She wished she could hurry the painting Charm along as easily.

There was also a hire car to arrange so she could sneak out to find Miss Rainer. She'd already found the anchor property on Google maps and even looked at it with the satellite view. The people of Mundanus were so wonderfully advanced! Thanks to the internet she could sort out all the logistics without having to be seen leaving the house. None of the servants had noticed her going off to the nursery, as the corridor leading to it wasn't used for anything else. She smiled. The room that had made her faint was now her favourite in the house.

The time wasted with Dame Iris had been so frustrating. Cathy's cheeks ached from the hours of fake smiling and attempts to appear animated when the Dame described various embroidery projects she'd undertaken in the last year. It had been so hard not to just grab the teapot and start pouring it all over the table cloth whilst shouting every expletive she'd learnt in Mundanus. Imagining it was the only thing that enabled her to appear vaguely cheerful throughout the tedious tea with the Dame's boring friends and then lunch at a restaurant with the atmosphere of a funeral parlour in a healthy neighbourhood.

She wondered whether Will was home and the churning over of the previous evening's events started again. She felt a flicker of hope that he would be and that they'd kiss again. "Don't," she whispered to herself. "Don't fall for him, you idiot."

Cathy tried to remember the details of the conversation they'd had, but they seemed to have been pushed out by what had followed. She felt her cheeks grow hot as she remembered how it had felt. She shook her head. What had she been thinking? Then, for the hundredth time since she'd woken up, she hoped she wasn't pregnant. How could she have been so careless?

The euphoria over finding out Miss Rainer was alive had made the champagne rush to her head and her better judgement collapse. The memories were slippery, muddied by recollections of his kisses, his touch, tempting her down mental alleyways all leading to the same rush in her chest. She needed to talk to Will and see if she really did feel differently about him. Then she changed her mind; she had to stay away from him in case she lost control again. She had to stay focused on her real goal and not be distracted by her handsome husband.

Will was likely to be running around Londinium canvassing for supporters so it was the ideal time to hide in the nursery and get things ticked off her to-do list. The only thing that stopped her worrying about his fight for the Dukedom was the sure fact that Bartholomew would win and she wouldn't have to face the awful prospect of being Duchess. Shivering at the thought, she took the footman's hand to descend the steps. The new dress hastily commissioned at the Dame's insistence wasn't the easiest to move in. Style over comfort, as always.

She smiled at Morgan despite the aching and headed straight for the stairs up to her room.

"Cathy?"

Will's voice. She gripped the handrail as her pulse soared. She tried to think of piles of horse dung, dead flies on windowsills and fried eggs, anything to take her mind from the memories he reignited.

"I'm going to have a bath, I've had a sod of a day," she called down, resolutely keeping her gaze on the stairs ahead of her.

"Come to the sitting room. There's someone you need to meet."

She sighed. "I'm not up to impressing guests. Can't it happen another time?"

"No. Sophia is here and she wants to meet you."

Cathy tried to remember where she'd heard that name, running through the list of wives and notables of the Londinium Court that she'd been given to learn by Dame Iris. It was twice as long as the list Will had given her shortly after they'd arrived.

"My sister," he added.

The conversation from the night of their first soirée flooded back. The secret child. She peered over the banister and regretted it immediately. His brown hair was slightly tousled like he'd been riding and there was a glow in his cheeks that made him look far too attractive. A flash memory of his hand stroking the curve of her hip as he kissed her throat made her blush and look away from him.

"Cathy? Are you coming down?"

"Why is she here? Are your parents visiting?"

"No. Sophia's going to stay with us for a little while." He walked round to the bottom stair, extended a hand towards her. "You'll love her. I promise."

"Does she have a nanny?" She didn't take his hand for fear of throwing herself into a passionate clinch.

"Not yet. I was hoping you could spend time with her when I'm not here. She was being neglected in Aquae Sulis."

The thought of looking after a child triggered memories of miserable afternoons with Elizabeth throwing tantrums. But those afternoons had been spent in Mundanus. The beginning of a plan formed, involving a day trip to Kew Gardens without the need to hide it from Will. "I'd be happy to play with her in Mundanus, if that's what she needs."

Will's face was made divine by a bright smile. He climbed the stairs between them, slipped a hand around her waist and kissed her firmly on the lips.

The smell of his skin rekindled the memories of the night before. She kissed him back before she realised what she was doing. "Um—" she pulled away slightly "—what about keeping her a secret?"

"I've told the staff she's a distant cousin of mine."

Hidden in plain sight all of her life and ushered away when anyone visited. Cathy almost wished she'd had the same childhood, free of the pressure of performance.

Then she knew what to paint to satisfy Lord Poppy. She would put Sophia in the painting, but not as the subject and—as in real life—tucked away somewhere unobtrusive. Poppy hadn't specified that the secret would have to be obvious, or divulged at the point of delivery. In fact, she was certain he would be happier left to wonder what it was, thereby satisfying him without betraying Will's trust or endangering the child. As long as the Charm arrived on time, there was still hope she could navigate safely through Poppy's trap.

Will was smiling at her and she realised he was reflecting her own expression. He gently pulled her back and kissed her again. "I like being like this with you. It's the way it's supposed to be."

"You weren't there when I woke up."

"I'm sorry, my love, I had an early meeting. I didn't want to wake you."

Cathy stared at him, processing what he'd called her. She felt giddy and stupid and increasingly annoyed with herself. Why—

"Come on," Will said, taking her hand and pulling her down the stairs.

"Will, about last night," she started, but when she reached the bottom he called for Sophia and picked up the pace.

He took her to one of the sitting rooms. Sophia was almost at the door when they arrived, having heard his call. Cathy saw the way she beamed at Will and how it delighted him to sweep the little girl up into his arms and bring her face level with theirs.

"Sophia, this is Cathy."

"Your Cathy?" she asked him.

"My Cathy," he smiled and they both looked at her. She could see the resemblance between them instantly.

"Hello," Sophia said, and, as much as she thought she was immune to cute children, Cathy did find herself warming to her.

"Hello," Cathy replied. "Will tells me you're going to stay with us a while."

Sophia nodded eagerly, making her ringlets bounce. "I missed Will-yum. Will you take me to the park when he has to do grown-up things?"

"Of course I will, I love parks. And there's one I've always wanted to visit where the trees are hundreds of years old. Would you like to go and see them and have ice-cream too?"

Sophia nodded enthusiastically. "Yes, please. Let's go now!"

"We'll go first thing tomorrow. I need to work out how to get there first."

"Oh. Do you want to play dolls with me?"

Cathy wrinkled her nose. "No, thanks. Maybe later we could make paper aeroplanes together."

"Do princesses make paper aeroplanes?"

"Only the best ones," Cathy said and it seemed to satisfy Sophia. She was less than five years old and already being programmed into only wanting to do "girly" things. Cathy resolved to present some alternative interests to her.

Will kissed Sophia on the cheek and put her down. She returned to the rug and the three dolls in varying states of disarray. Cathy then felt his eyes on her and looked back at him. His smile was soft and he brushed her hand. "Thank you."

She knew what he was thinking. There was the beautiful child, quiet and well-behaved. Here was his wife, and soon she would be pregnant and full of the delights of motherhood, especially after having the opportunity to spend time with the sweetest child in Society. There was no way in the Worlds Will wanted to be with her for any reason other than furthering the family line, even without the beautiful Rosa hidden away somewhere. Did he touch Amelia in the same way? Did he kiss his wife like he kissed the rose?

"I need to change and make the arrangements for our trip," she said, anxious to get away from him and the plans he had for her. She'd lost her virginity and the next time Will made overtures towards her it would be harder to turn him down. There was no way she could stay in the Nether and have babies under Dame Iris's intense scrutiny. No. It was time to find Miss Rainer and step up her plans for escape before Will had made another child to fall in love with.

21

Sam liked to think of himself as a reasonable man, one who could get through life without having to punch anyone to make a point. The concierge was challenging that self-image. Not only did he feel like punching the smartly dressed jobsworth, he also felt like knocking down anyone else who wanted to keep him away from Leanne.

"Look, for the tenth time, it's a fucking emergency," he said, slowly losing control of his voice. "She's my wife, you don't have the right to stop me from seeing her."

"I'm sorry," the man said, no longer calling him "sir". "Mrs Westonville made it very clear to me that under no circumstances was I permitted to let you see her."

"That's because she didn't know what I know now! If she knew what I know, I know she'd see me in a shot." He sounded like a lunatic. Sam pressed his hands down on the top of the horseshoe-shaped desk-cum-booth the concierge sat behind, reminding himself not to use them to wallop him. "Look, I know you're just doing your job, and you might think you're protecting a vulnerable woman, but I'm trying to protect her and you're doing more harm than good."

"If you don't leave, I'm going to call the police."

"For what?"

"Trespassing. Breach of the peace. Being a pain in the jacksy. I know divorce is hard, but you don't live here, she does, so I'm on her side." He waited for Sam to move. "Right, that's it."

The concierge lifted a phone handset from its cradle and Sam patted the air. "I'm going, for fuck's sake. But if anything happens to her—"

"Yeah, yeah, you'll hold me personally responsible. I've seen the same films as you. Now piss off. Sir."

Sam sucked in a deep lungful of air through his teeth. Now he understood why people flipped out. "Twat," he said loudly, heading for the door. He'd wait on the pavement outside until she came out. It didn't matter if he had to stand in a doorway all night, he had to warn her about Neugent.

She'd stopped taking his calls after sending a text saying, "Nothing to say, give me a break for at least a month." He left a voicemail asking her to call, saying it was urgent. She didn't. On the train up to London he'd hammered the redial button, thinking that surely she'd get the idea that this was more than just him panicking about a separation. He suspected she wasn't even using that number any more. That was what she'd do: switch it off, get a new phone and new number and get on with her job. She kept different parts of her life in separate mental boxes. For a long time he'd been in the crappy battered one left in the corner whilst she played with the big shiny work box. Now he felt as if she'd put him into one of his own, one she was soon to throw out altogether.

He rubbed his eyes. As the adrenalin from his confrontation with the concierge ebbed he became aware of the fatigue again. He'd been suffering from varying degrees of panic since the conversation with Max and the gargoyle.

Sam ducked into the doorway of a generic office building out of the concierge's line of sight and looked at his wedding ring. He still wore it, even after everything that had been said about it. He wasn't divorced yet. Taking it off seemed too premature, and too final.

At the sound of high heels clipping on the pavement he peered round and saw Leanne, handbag over her shoulder, wearing a brilliant red coat. She'd lost even more weight and her legs were starting to look too thin.

"Leanne!" He stepped out a few metres ahead of her.

"The concierge told me you'd been a pain in the arse."

"I need to talk to you, Lee, it's important."

She started walking again, eyes fixed on a point past his shoulder. "You've got until I get to the tube station."

He fell into step alongside her. "Are you OK? You've lost too much weight, you know, you're wasting away."

"Good start, Sam, offend me, that's bound to make me more receptive."

"Shit. Sorry, I'm just worried about you, that's all. Look, there's something wrong with this thing you've got with Neugent. A friend looked into the forge and there were other people who made their rings there and ten of them died before their time."

She frowned at him, not slowing. "Do you realise how pathetic you sound? 'This thing I've got with Neugent'? You mean a career? And what the hell have those people got to do with me?"

"They all worked for Neugent, Lee. It's a pattern."

"Oh, right, so after realising what you've lost you've cooked up some amazingly shit story to try and frighten me into resigning so I'll move back to Bath? That's really sad."

"Are you even listening to me? They died!"

"Of what?"

"Well, different things but—"

"Oh, so you've carried out a detailed statistical analysis of all of the people who have ever had any contact with Marcus who happened to make their own wedding rings and concluded that dying is weird? Do you know how many people work for him? Do you know how many people have used that forge? Do you know how statistically unlikely it is that a failed marriage could be repaired by husbands making outlandish claims about their wife's boss?"

"They all died too young!"

"By whose standards? Thousands of children die every day. Show me your analysis and explain to me which age you define as the correct time to die. Oh, that's right, it doesn't exist."

"I'm trying to protect you, Lee, that's all. I know you're in danger."

"I'm in danger of telling you to fuck off before we get to the station, I'll give you that."

"I'm serious. I know I can be a dick sometimes but even I wouldn't come up with something like this to try and patch things up, would I? I thought we'd just had our time together and I was happy to move on, because I didn't know there was anything else involved."

She stopped and looked at him. "What is this about, Sam? Do you need help?"

"I'm trying to tell you, *you* need help! You need to come back to Bath with me. We can talk. No, even better, we'll go somewhere else…Cornwall…Scotland, wherever you want to go, and we'll talk it all through and we'll start again."

She closed her eyes. He wanted to touch her but she wasn't giving the impression that would be allowed. "Sam," she said with a sigh, "you're assuming we have something to try to save here. We don't. I've changed, you haven't. I don't see any point in stringing this along any more. I'll get in touch with my solicitor, let's just divorce as quickly and cleanly as we can so we can move on."

"I don't want that."

"Sorry. There's nothing I can do about that. Let it go. You'll be happier without me, you really will."

"No, I won't." Sam felt like a child, powerless in the face of a diktat from a parent, something non-negotiable and world-breaking and utterly out of his control.

"I have to go or I'll be late. Get some help, Sam, talk to a counsellor or something, but don't try and suck me into this car crash."

"I'm not your problem anymore, is that it?"

"More that I don't want to be yours anymore. My solicitor will be in touch."

She walked off, leaving him standing on a London pavement with people tutting as they had to walk around him. He watched her, not knowing whether to run after her or stop believing all this stuff anyway. Filtered through her it did sound stupid. But he still believed it and he still wanted to protect her, even though she'd made it clear there was nothing she felt for him other than irritation and pity. If he pursued her, she'd get angry again and it wouldn't achieve anything. He could feel a surge of panic and impotence threatening to make him do something stupid like throw her over his shoulder or burst into tears. Neither was acceptable. He rubbed his eyes as he lost sight of her and decided the only sensible thing to do was go and get pissed.

Cathy parked the hire car a short walk away from the house where Miss Rainer worked and twisted round to check on Sophia.

"She's fast asleep," Lucy said.

"Thanks for coming to help," Cathy said, smiling, and felt the nerves catch her breath. "I'll be as quick as I can, then afterwards we'll go to Kew Gardens and wake her up. She won't even know we've been here."

"I'll keep an eye on her, don't worry," Lucy replied. "Go, and good luck!"

Cathy closed the car door as quietly as she could and looked up and down the mundane suburban street. It was lined with trees still clinging to the last of their autumnal leaves and parked cars ready for the daily commute. Bathed in the grey light of the pre-dawn, the silent street made Cathy long for Manchester again and the fresh potential that filled every early morning there.

The painting Charm had arrived late the previous evening, locked in a box, and delivered to the house by a young boy. The key had arrived by Letterboxer soon afterward. Inside the box was a beautiful turquoise bottle made of Venetian glass—she knew the Shopkeeper only used it for the most expensive Charms—with a flame-shaped stopper, along with a tiny sable brush. An accompanying note read;

> *Catherine,*
>
> *You are officially the first customer to receive such a rare and expensive Charm without having paid for it first. I trust you will come to see me to discuss the price at your earliest convenience.*

Should you have need of the Charm before then, you should know this: its effects will last anywhere between twenty-four hours and twenty-four days, depending on how much affinity your own abilities have with one of the critical ingredients. Side-effects include insomnia, mania, depression, hallucinations—auditory and visual—and becoming a bore. I beg you to arrange for private time away from guests and social obligations before you use it.

When you have your materials to hand and are ready to create, simply dip the brush into the bottle and paint its contents onto your eyelids, the skin above your heart, the palms of your hands and lastly your fingertips. You may experience the customary tingling associated with powerful magic.

I hope it is sufficient for your needs, and look forward to seeing you at the Emporium forthwith.

Yours sincerely,

S.

Cathy was eager to use it but, fearful the side-effects would render her useless in the search for Miss Rainer, she decided to wait until the day was over. Early morning would be the best time to find her. As a scullery maid it would be Rainer's responsibility to draw the water for the household's morning routine. In the past that would have involved carrying buckets to a hand pump but now that Mundanus had entered the modern age it meant Miss Rainer would be filling buckets in the anchor property's kitchen to take through into the Nether reflection of the house.

The thought of her tutor's brilliant mind being squandered on menial tasks infuriated Cathy. There was no way she would let the Agency continue to treat her this way and if they proved to be a problem then Cathy planned to help Rainer escape into Mundanus too.

The house was a detached Victorian villa on three storeys and was a rather modest anchor property. Cathy didn't know anyone from the Ranunculus family personally but she knew they weren't the most successful of the Great Families and were often overlooked.

They hadn't made Dame Iris's list of important people to know in Londinium and Cathy envied their anonymity.

After one last glance up the street Cathy hurried up the sloped driveway and darted down the side of the house. The kitchen would be at the rear, overlooking the back garden, and out of sight of the neighbours. The side gate was locked but not too high to be climbed over and Cathy dropped onto the other side feeling like an amateur burglar.

There were French doors that led onto the garden but the curtains were still drawn so she couldn't see into the house. Cathy tiptoed across to crouch beneath the kitchen window and listen for any noises within. Just as she was about to peep over the windowsill there was the muffled clank of a metal bucket being put into the sink and the sound of water splashing into it.

Cathy slowly curled her fingertips over the windowsill and raised herself up to peep over the edge of the window frame, just in case Miss Rainer wasn't the one drawing the water that morning.

But it was her! Her hair was different, now tied back in a tight bun, and she looked more pale and tired than Cathy remembered but it was definitely Miss Rainer. Cathy straightened up and tapped on the window excitedly. Miss Rainer jumped but didn't drop the empty bucket she was holding.

Cathy searched for the flash of recognition and the smile she'd imagined receiving upon their reunion but there was nothing of the sort on Rainer's face. Perhaps it was hard for her to see out into the murky dawn with the lights on inside. Cathy pointed at the back door and Miss Rainer nodded, setting down the bucket to go over and unlock it.

"Miss Rainer!" Cathy whispered as soon as the door opened.

"Can I help you?"

Cathy's exuberance imploded. "It's me, Catherine. Your student."

Miss Rainer's eyes narrowed and looked up in the way they used to when she was considering the best way to explain a difficult concept. "Catherine? That name's familiar…did we work at the same house once?"

Cathy struggled to speak as her chest tightened. "You were my governess for over ten years!"

"I'm a scullery maid, Miss Catherine. Do you want me to fetch the governess for you?"

"No! You were mine, don't you remember?" Cathy wanted to grab her shoulders and shake her until Miss Rainer looked and spoke like her old self again. It was like speaking to nothing but a physical copy of her and it was terrifying. "I was called Catherine Rhoeas-Papaver then, we lived in Bath—in Aquae Sulis—don't you remember?"

"Papaver…" Rainer whispered and Cathy thought she could see something of her governess in her features, just for a moment. "That is familiar…"

"You gave me *The Time Machine* by H.G. Wells and we talked about it for hours. You taught me about Emmeline Pankhurst and Virginia Woolf and Aphra Behn! Don't you remember any of it?"

Miss Rainer's brow creased. "You're upset."

"Of course I am!" Cathy croaked. "You were everything to me. You made me what I am!"

"Catherine Rhoeas-Papaver…" Miss Rainer said again and looked down. "The floor." She pointed at a patio flagstone. "Something important in the floor."

"What do you mean?" Cathy felt a glimmer of hope again. The Agency had done something terrible to her, but something remained, she was sure of it. Perhaps she'd been drugged. If she could get her away from the house and somewhere safe—

"Something important," Miss Rainer said and bent down to take off her shoe.

Cathy felt sick as she watched the broken shadow of her hero fumble with a stocking and peel it off her leg. She wanted to find Bennet and smash his face into a wall until he confessed what they did to make her this way. She wanted to go to Elizabeth and dangle her out of a window by her hair until she really understood how much hurt she'd caused by telling Father about Miss Rainer's unorthodox lessons.

"Catherine." Miss Rainer's voice pulled her out of her rage. Rainer was now sitting on the back step with one foot bare, her skirt hitched above her knee. She was pointing at a scar on her thigh in the rough shape of a diamond. "Something important in the floor."

"What does that mean?" Cathy crouched down. "Who did that to you?"

"Me," Rainer replied. "To remember."

"Remember what?" The vacant shrug of Rainer's shoulders made her want to cry.

Cathy pulled the hem of the skirt down to cover the scar and restore Miss Rainer's modesty. She threw her arms around her shoulders. "I'm so sorry. I'll find out what they did to you and I'll make you better, I promise. I swear it, Miss Rainer, I swear I will." She wept.

"Shhh." Miss Rainer patted her back awkwardly. "Don't cry. I'm fit as a fiddle. But I do have to go, otherwise I'll get into trouble."

Cathy released her and helped Miss Rainer to stand after she'd put her stocking back on. "Do you remember me at all?"

"You're…familiar," Miss Rainer finally replied but Cathy wasn't sure if she only said that to make her feel better. "But it doesn't matter, not as much as you think."

"What does matter?"

Miss Rainer looked up at the sky again. "The work," she finally replied and, after an uncertain smile, went back into the house and locked the door.

Cathy stumbled out of the garden and over the side gate. She walked a little way down the road before she had to sit on the kerb with her head in her hands. She let the grief take her, unable to hold it inside any more.

Cars drove past and a woman out walking her dog stopped to ask if she was all right. Cathy mumbled a lie to evade any further attention and dried her eyes as the woman carried on. Cathy watched the dog snuffling at the kerb and breathed in the morning air, steadying herself. She couldn't run away, not now, not knowing what she did. Then she was grieving for a life she knew she could never have again.

Eventually, Cathy stood and blew her nose. "Time to stop pissing about," she whispered to herself and went back to the car as her thoughts settled around a different plan of action. Sophia was still asleep and Lucy was supposedly reading a guide to flower arranging.

"How'd it go?" Lucy asked as Cathy got in and put her seatbelt on. "Did you find her?"

"No," Cathy replied. "But I found something important." She looked over her shoulder at Lucy. "You were right about me. I thought I was the only woman who doesn't fit in. I think I liked that, because I thought I was better than everyone for seeing through it all. I was so obsessed with getting out that I didn't give a sod about anyone else. That was selfish; I see that now. I've been a childish idiot."

Lucy reached forward to squeeze her shoulder gently. "You thought you were alone, but you're not, do you see?"

"Oh, I see all right. I'm not going to run away again." Even as she said the words they caught in her throat. "I can't, there's too much to be done in the Nether. It's not just the way women are treated—the Agency is dodgy as fuck and they're doing terrible things to people and I've just ignored it all. We shouldn't be treating people that way, not in the twenty-first century."

Lucy grinned. "You said it."

Cathy tried to smile back but the thought of staying in the Nether to fight the patriarchy and unearth the secrets of the Agency made her feel sick to the stomach. She wasn't cut out for this, she wasn't a great thinker or a great writer. She was just an angry woman who read weird books and couldn't handle life in Society. How could she make a difference?

But maybe that's what all of those women before her had thought before they went on to fight the system. They had found the strength and the courage to speak up and challenge the establishment despite the impact on their own lives. Rainer had taken a terrible risk to teach her things she wasn't supposed to know and had lost everything as a result. Cathy knew that if she gave in to her own fear it would make Miss Rainer's suffering worthless.

She just had to be brave and work hard. "The work" as Rainer had said it echoed in Cathy's mind. Yes, she thought, that is the most important thing. The work.

22

The potion tasted faintly of onions. It burned Cathy's throat as it went down like the rough whisky she'd tried at an awful student party in Manchester. The canvas and paints were laid out before her and she'd told Morgan to bring her tea every hour, on the hour, until she retired. She had no idea how long it would take to paint the picture for Lord Poppy, nor any idea where to start. She'd only just managed to stop crying about the state Miss Rainer was in now. She had to satisfy Poppy if she wanted a chance to help her.

Then, as the burning faded in her chest, she knew where to put the first line. Cathy picked up the pencil and began sketching out the Royal Crescent in Bath, barely looking at the book she'd obtained to guide her. By the time Morgan arrived with the first round of tea, the shape of the painting was described in faint graphite lines and she knew exactly what to do next.

"Morgan," she said as she reached for the brush, "I'm going to need cake. Lots of cake.'

Amelia listened for footsteps on the stairs, knowing that Will was expected for another late morning meeting with Cornelius. She'd wasted days and lost sleep wondering why he'd snubbed her after his last meeting with her brother. Now she was busy at the dressing table trying to hide the shadows under her eyes with makeup.

Loud thuds sounded more like Cornelius in a rush. She sighed and applied her blusher, trying not to see it as painting her face like a whore.

He still managed to knock, but entered before she'd even called him in. "Cornelius!"

He shut the door. "Will's on his way."

She twisted round to frown at him. "I know." His fist was clenched around a note. "What's that?"

He strode over to the fire and threw the single piece of letter paper onto it. He didn't answer until he was satisfied it was ash. "I'm not going to tell you what it said, only how it affects you. Darling, we must keep Will here today."

"How long for?"

"As long as we can. I can occupy him for an hour or two easily. When I send for mid-morning refreshments you must come and join us and persuade him to spend some time with you."

"He didn't seem interested when he last visited."

"There's a lot to distract him, so you must be persuasive today."

She stared at her reflection in the mirror. She did look like a whore.

"I'm sorry to ask, but it's critical." He came over and kissed the curls arranged to emphasise her slender neck. "Not long now, darling. We'll look back on this time and marvel at how awful it was, and how it never will be like it again. I promise."

She nodded as the sound of the bell downstairs made him dart to the door. "I won't let you down, Cornelius." She made herself smile at the kiss he blew to her and listened to him going back down the stairs more slowly. She heard him greet Will casually, like everything was normal.

Amelia looked down at her trembling hands. She knew why she had to keep him there: to keep him away from Catherine. It was the day everything would change for Will, for Cornelius and ultimately for her. She knew it would take time for Will to recover from the death of his wife, but not as long as someone in love would take. Amelia was used to playing the long game. She could wait.

As she checked her face in the mirror, she wondered what Thorn would do to Catherine. A frown creased the skin above her nose and she swiftly corrected it. She didn't want Catherine to suffer.

She hoped it would be quick and painless, like one would slaughter a beast for meat. She closed her eyes. What a perfectly despicable thing to think.

She thought back to the brief conversation she'd tried to have with Catherine on the night everything collapsed in Aquae Sulis. She only wanted to check that the glamours used to disguise the Lavandula décor had been done to perfection, simply to put her mind at rest.

There was also curiosity about Will's fiancée and the need to check Catherine wasn't going to be a problem. It was clear early in their conversation that she cared nothing for Will and seemed to be in a strange world of her own, incapable of having the most basic of conversations without tripping up. How the families could have decided she was the best match for Will still confounded Amelia. Will was evidently destined for great things—why pair him off with someone as plain and incapable as Catherine?

Satisfied she looked as good as possible, Amelia went to the cheval mirror and inspected her outfit. It wouldn't do. It had been selected for an average day, not one when she'd have to use everything in her arsenal. She chose another and then rang for the maid, all the while worrying about the tiny amount of perfume left in the bottle. Once she had more freedom it would be a trifling matter to obtain the Charm from the Shopkeeper again. She had no idea how long that would be and whether there would be another time she'd need it more before then. Having control over Will's affections as he grieved would be critical.

The maid arrived and helped change her clothes and tidied her hair. Half an hour had passed already. "Would you be so kind as to let me know when Cornelius rings for elevenses? I'd like to join them instead of taking it in my room today."

"Yes, ma'am." The maid curtsied and left Amelia to pace the room and obsess about the perfume. Before long, she was informed of the request for tea and after one last check of her reflection she descended the stairs and went to the drawing room.

"I thought my friendship with Oli, not to mention my helping his family, would count for something." Will sounded irritated. "I can only imagine Peonia has had his head filled with absurd promises by the Wisteria idiot."

"May I join you?" Amelia asked as the tea and sandwiches were brought in.

Will stood; she offered her hand and he kissed it. It was the first time she'd been in a room with both her lover and her brother and she didn't like the way it made her feel obliged to act in two different ways at once.

"Trouble with the Wisterias?" she asked, seating herself next to Cornelius so she could flirt with Will without her brother seeing every detail.

"And the Peonias," Will said. "They've teamed up and are being perfectly odious."

Amelia poured the tea, taking the opportunity to put herself at the centre of attention. It had worked so well in Aquae Sulis Will had positively slavered at the sight of her. But today he seemed distant and when she looked up from the teapot he wasn't even looking at her. He looked very tired. Perhaps the strain was taking its toll.

"I'm sure you and Cornelius can think of a way to bring them round."

Amelia handed Will his tea, brushing his finger as he took it, but he didn't even notice. He dropped a lump of sugar in, stirred and stared at the fire. She should have used the perfume.

Cornelius seemed unconcerned, but he didn't notice such details. "They're simply trying to feel like they're part of the game," he said, taking a sandwich from the stand. "Let them play. When it's time to commit they'll realise how foolish it would be to ignore your generosity."

"But together they're a sizeable faction in the Court and they know it." Will drank the tea in three gulps, alerting Amelia to an impending announcement of his departure. "Well," he began, putting the cup and saucer on the table, "I'll give it some thought and we'll revisit it tomorrow, Cornelius."

He stood and Amelia did the same. "William," she said, trying not to seem flustered, "could I possibly speak to you in private for a moment?"

Will looked at her, as if properly noticing her for the first time. "Of course," he said with a smile, but there was still a distance between them.

He didn't touch her as she led him up the stairs to her room, but just followed in silence. When they reached her bedroom she gestured for him to come in and then closed the door.

"Is something wrong?" he asked.

"I missed you yesterday." She said it with a smile, not wanting to make him feel guilty. "I know you're very busy, but it's good to pause every now and again, is it not?"

He looked more tired now she was closer to him. "I have a lot on my mind."

"Can Cornelius help?"

"With some of it."

It wasn't just the Dukedom that had been worrying him. Unsurprising that an inadequate wife would cause him no end of worry at such a critical time.

"Perhaps I can help you, in my own way." She approached slowly, watching every minute movement, trying to gauge whether he would accept contact. She got close enough to reach out and touch his arm before he looked at her properly.

"I'm not good company at the moment, Amelia," he said, clasping her hand briefly before letting it go.

"Only because you're burdened." She took a step closer. "Let me take your mind off things for just a little while, then you can return to your business refreshed and ready to demolish any difficulty with the silly Peonias."

She kissed him, but there was no passion so she slipped her arms around his waist, looking at the atomiser on the table and cursing her poor decision.

He did hold her, and gradually, as if remembering who she was, he adjusted his arms so that he enveloped her more fully. "I'm sorry," he whispered. "I know you're lonely, and how much you miss being in Society."

She tilted her head back and they kissed again. Better this time, but it still didn't convince her he was planning to stay. Usually he would be steering her to the bed, eager to start unbuttoning and unlacing, but he was still withdrawn.

She pulled away and looked up at him. "What is it? This isn't just the Dukedom, Will. There's something else, isn't there?"

"It's nothing." He kissed her but she knew it was simply to cut off the conversation.

"You look so tired, darling. Why don't you tell me about it? Perhaps I can help." Still nothing. "Is it Catherine?"

He broke the embrace and she knew she'd made a mistake. "I should go."

"Talk to me, Will. I can help."

"Amelia." His was not the voice of a lover. "I don't think it would be appropriate to discuss my home life with you. And if you do, you're mistaken. Now if you'll excuse me."

He headed for the door. Amelia went to the dressing table and brushed her fingertip against the mouth of the atomiser. There was enough residue to make her skin tingle and she touched it to her neck. "Will, I'm sorry, please don't leave like this."

She rushed over as his hand was on the door handle. The panic made her flushed and the heat lifted the scent from her skin to waft about him. She watched his pupils dilate and then kissed him. She was met with renewed passion, a new urgency to his kiss as he pulled her tight to him.

"I'm sorry," he whispered into her hair as she kissed his throat. "Let me stay."

"Of course," she said, drawing him away from the door. "Stay as long as you wish, my love."

* * *

Sam found Cathy where he'd left her, sitting on the bench in a children's play area in Green Park, looking at an iPad. As he approached, a little girl ran up to her and they had a brief conversation before the girl ran over to some other children playing on a roundabout.

"I'm back," he said, making Cathy jump.

She powered down the tablet and slipped it into a case. "How did it go?" She patted the bench next to her. "Take a seat. You look like you need it."

"I do." He sat down. One of the children on the roundabout started to cry and was carried off. "You don't look so great yourself."

"Thanks." She yawned. "It's the come-down I suppose, I drank more potions than cups of tea. And not sleeping for three days. What did *he* say?"

"Oh, the usual arse."

"About the painting?"

"He didn't look at it." He nodded at the amazement, then anger, that flashed across her face. "I know. All that and he didn't even look. He said it wasn't the right time to see it." He hadn't looked at it himself, as they'd agreed, fearing Poppy would take offence. All he knew was that it was a huge, heavy canvas rolled in a wide tube over six feet long. He'd had to carry it on one shoulder. "But he did say he was satisfied you'd fulfilled your contract."

She let out a loud, drawn-out sigh and looked even more tired. "Thank God for that. He didn't mess you about, did he?"

"No, he said he had something important to arrange."

She bit her lip. "I just hope it doesn't have anything to do with us."

"Cathy! Watch me!" The girl called from the roundabout.

"Who's the kid?"

"My husband's cousin."

He watched another child snivelling his way across to his mother, holding his hand out. At least there weren't any children involved in his mess with Leanne.

"So in your message you said that something's going on with your wife," Cathy said.

"I'm sorry about that. I was drunk." He'd woken in a crappy hotel down the road with a hangover that had made Exilium even more difficult to cope with. When he got the call from Cathy to say the painting was ready with only a few hours left to spare, he'd noticed the phone battery was low. He checked the call log and found he'd made repeated calls to Leanne's mobile throughout the small hours and then a call to Cathy's. He couldn't remember any of them.

"So what's this about your wife's boss killing people?"

Sam explained it all to her, from the dodgy apartment and him losing his job through to the people with the same wedding rings dying young. When he finished she rested a gloved hand over his briefly. "I can see why you're so upset."

"You don't think I'm over-reacting?"

"No. In fact—"

"Cathy." The small girl was back and tugging gently on Cathy's coat. "Please can you play with me?"

"I thought you were playing with the other children," Cathy said.

"They've all gone."

Sam had been so engrossed in spilling his guts to Cathy he hadn't noticed all the other families had left. He could see one of the mothers hurrying away, her child limpeted to her, weeping. "Did they all hurt themselves?"

The child nodded. "I didn't do anything. Cathy, can you play with me now?"

But Cathy wasn't looking at her. Sam followed her gaze to a figure approaching them wearing a grey coat with a half cape about its shoulders. It looked like something out of a film to Sam, or something worn by a student with aspirations to be a modern-day dandy. The man's face was unremarkable, his brown hair long enough to be tied back in a ponytail. Eyes fixed on Cathy, he undid the top three buttons, partially revealing an embroidered waistcoat. Cathy stood up.

"I don't like this, he's a Fae-touched," she had time to say, just before the man drew out a stiletto dagger.

"Fuck!" Sam jumped to his feet too.

"Sophia, run!" Cathy yelled and the child bolted for nearby bushes.

Sam didn't move for a second, watching the man cross the park as if he were watching a film; it felt too unreal to spur him into action.

A terrible high-pitched screech came from the child. Sam spun around to see her tangled in rose briars reaching out of the ground like the tentacles of a sea monster. Sam gawped as the thorns tore into the girl's legs, piercing her coat and reaching for her throat.

Cathy sprinted over to her, grabbed the creepers that were about to choke the child and held them off, blood blooming on her pale-blue gloves. The man was heading straight for her. The sight of the knife being raised into the air kickstarted something deep in Sam's instincts and he threw himself into the attacker's path, brandishing his left hand in front of him.

"I'm protected by Lord Iron!" he yelled.

The man shook his head, as if Sam were nothing but a stupid child. "Always where you should not be," he muttered, and grasped him by the neck with his left hand. There was a brief and terrible crushing sensation and before he fully registered he was in the air, Sam landed a few feet away on his side.

The moment after he landed Sam felt a horrific pain in his left arm and chest. Then he fell sideways like he'd been rolled off something moving beneath him. As he tried to look, his head hit one of the uprights in the iron railings marking the edge of the play area. He felt blood running down his arm and saw it dripping onto what looked like one of the iron bars, which seemed to have been bent beneath him. Then he heard Cathy cry out.

She was crouched between the attacker and the child, whose high-pitched scream sounded more like a football referee's whistle. The man had just slashed at Cathy but she'd brought up her arms to defend herself and the girl. There was a gash in her gloves, which were now more deep red than pale blue.

Not even thinking about what he was doing, Sam reached down with his right hand and grasped the iron bar. It felt warm and malleable and broke away from its point in the railings easily. The metal was slick with his blood. Its finial was shaped like an arrowhead and with every passing moment it felt more like a spear.

The assailant kicked Cathy under the chin, sending her sprawling into the tangle of thorns, and made a swift downward strike. Sam threw the spear at the same moment as he heard the sickening thud of the attacker's hand hitting her chest after the dagger was plunged in up to its hilt.

The spear curved slightly in the air and struck the man in the side, knocking him over and leaving the stiletto embedded in Cathy's chest. The man pulled out the spear but when he struggled to his feet he looked completely different. And horribly familiar. He was one of the brothers who had carried the body out of the museum that night when it all started. His limbs were far too long and thin. Thorn looked at Sam for a second, long enough for him to see the black almond eyes, then fled into the undergrowth.

Cathy wasn't moving and Sam wasn't sure he could either. Sweat prickled across his face. It was hard to breathe and he felt cold. His phone was lying in reach so he dialled 999, asked for an ambulance and police. In between short painful gasps he explained he'd been attacked, a woman had been stabbed and a child was hurt. As he gave their location he fought the urge to just close his eyes and drift off. When he was reassured help was on the way Sam hung up, planning to call Leanne and leave her a message. His hand was barely able to keep a grip on the phone and his thumb had become putty.

He let his arm drop. The girl was now calling Cathy's name with a gut-wrenching desperation. "It's all right," he wanted to say, but his lips felt like rubber and his voice was nothing but a pathetic wheeze. Cathy still wasn't moving.

His phone started to vibrate. Sam managed to lift it enough to see Leanne's name on the caller ID as his vision tunnelled to black.

23

Will kissed the inside of Amelia's thigh in a cave of lacy petticoat layers. He enjoyed the way she squirmed beneath his fingertips, the little gasps as his kisses moved higher and higher up her leg. He should have been at Black's, or at home, solving the problems that plagued him, but she had been irresistible. He just had to have her, then and there, before he could think clearly again.

The brief pain in his left hand made him prod the wedding ring with his thumb as he teased her, thinking his slightly awkward position had caused the skin to be pinched by the band. A few kisses later and it felt like it was constricting. It rapidly became too painful to ignore.

He emerged from her skirts to inspect his hand. The band looked no different but his finger throbbed.

"What's wrong?" Amelia propped herself up on her elbows. Her cheeks were deliciously flushed and her hair was a pleasant tumble around her face.

Will twisted the ring and it tingled at his touch. "I don't know." He wondered where Cathy was and whether she was feeling the same. He looked down at Amelia, her toe playfully exploring his belly button, and feared the ring was reacting to his infidelity. Was that even possible? Why was it happening now and not all the other times he'd been with Amelia?

Then he realised it was the first time he'd bedded her since he and Cathy had consummated the marriage. His lust evaporated.

"William." Amelia beckoned to him.

But Will was distracted by the sudden racing of his heart and a sense of panic that had burst into his awareness out of nowhere.

"Something's not right." He flattened down her petticoats and climbed off the bed. He pulled on his underwear and breeches hurriedly, fearing a summons from his patron any minute. Why hadn't his father warned him of this?

"Will!" Amelia groaned. "I've only just got those off you!"

He took a breath to speak but a sudden, terrible pain filled his chest, making him fall back against the dressing table in his surprise. It was excruciating, stealing the air from his lungs and making blue pinpricks of light appear at the edge of his vision.

"Will!" Amelia cried, frantically tying a robe over her chemise and petticoats. "What's wrong?"

Will squeezed his eyes shut, not daring to speak until the worst of the pain had passed. He looked down at his bare chest, expecting to see a wound, but his skin was unharmed. Just as quickly, the pain faded.

There was a loud pop and the faerie that had spoken to him in the carriage appeared in front of him. "What are you doing here?" it squealed. "You need to be with your wife! She's dying!"

"What?" Will felt like his stomach was falling through the floor.

"She hasn't had a child yet. How could you be so careless!"

"What are you talking about? Where is she?"

"In a green place in Mundanus."

Will threw his shirt over his head and fumbled with the sleeves, feeling sick. His sword was at home. What was Cathy doing in… then he remembered Sophia. "Take me to her."

"No, Will!" Amelia said. "It's not safe. What if it's a plot to draw you out and kill you!"

Sobered, Will nodded. "Find out where she is, and whether anyone is helping her," he ordered the faerie and it disappeared in a shower of iris petals. Will pulled on his socks and shoes.

"Oh, my goodness, this is so awful," Amelia gasped, clutching a sheet in front of her mouth.

"I shouldn't have stayed, I knew I should have gone home," he muttered. "If she dies…my God, she can't die, she can't die." He imagined Lord Iris's wrath, feared for Sophia who must have been with her. A 'green place in Mundanus' was probably St James's Park as that was the closest to home.

The faerie reappeared. "There are mundanes there, lots of them, filthy men all around her and it's so noisy."

Will remembered what he'd seen of the emergency services on his Grand Tour. "Are there lots of blue flashing lights?" When the faerie nodded he realised Cathy was probably getting exactly the kind of care she needed. "Is she still alive?"

"You wouldn't be here if she was dead," the faerie said. "You'd be in Exilium, begging for forgiveness. My lord is furious."

"So am I!"

"And now those mundanes have her." The faerie flitted about his head.

"Tell Lord Iris I'm doing everything in my power to make sure Cathy will be safe."

"I'll tell him you will be now, but if you hadn't been distracted—"

"Just go!" he yelled, making it scowl and then disappear with a pop.

Amelia ran to the door and called for Cornelius. "What are you going to do?" she asked.

Now he knew Cathy was being helped and that, if Sophia was with her, she'd be cared for too, he could think clearly. "She'll be taken to a hospital. I need to contact the Agency." As head of a household, he'd had a pack of information sent to him detailing other services the Agency provided outside of common knowledge. He was thankful he'd taken the time to read it. In return for a small fortune, they would extract Cathy from Mundanus, remove any mention of the incident in the relevant records and Charm any mundanes involved to forget she'd been there. It was complex and difficult, but worth it. "They'll help me clear up the mess. When I know my family is safe I'll find out who did this."

"And then what?" She was pale, still clinging to the sheet as Cornelius arrived.

"Then I'll destroy them."

* * *

"The bar was just lying next to you?"

"Under me," Sam said to the policewoman. His voice was so hoarse it sounded alien. "I landed on the railings. I think I broke them."

She made a note and then looked him up and down. "You're not the heaviest man, Mr Westonville. The assailant must have thrown you with some force."

He pointed at the bruising on his neck. "He nearly choked me to death one-handed. He was strong."

"So you picked up the bar…"

"Yeah, and I looked over and he stabbed the woman." A wave of nausea made him suck in a breath. "There was a horrible sound, when it hit her chest I suppose, and I just threw the bar at him."

"And you hit him square on."

"Yeah."

"From ten metres away, when you were injured and bleeding."

He frowned. "Don't you believe me?"

"I'm just making sure I have all the details, sir."

"If I hadn't hit him he would have stabbed her again."

She just nodded. "And then what happened?"

"I called 999 and I passed out."

"The doctor tells me you're very lucky."

Sam looked down at the two iron chunks beside him. The nurse had told him they'd pulled one out of his arm, one out of his side. Apparently they'd formed rudimentary plugs in his wounds. The nurse said they'd never seen anything like it and offered the plugs to him as morbid souvenirs. They were thicker than the railings had been, the policewoman had pointed out, and she wanted to know how they'd got that way. Sam had a working theory it was something to do with Lord Iron and the wedding ring. He couldn't say anything about it though.

"I've got a cracked rib and a couple of small holes in me apparently. And bruising."

He wondered how Cathy and the girl were. The police officer had been professionally vague, saying Cathy was in surgery and the girl was being cared for in A & E. He'd pretended he didn't know who they were, saying he'd gone to the park to get some fresh air in the midst of a marital crisis and he was passing as the man attacked.

He needed to speak to Cathy as soon as she woke and warn her that one of the Fae were after her—one of the Thorn brothers, no less. But he'd have to wait until the police had finished taking notes and she was out of surgery.

"The woman who was attacked will be OK, won't she?" he asked.

"I'm afraid I don't know. It was a serious attack. She's lucky you were there." The police officer stood and put her hat back on. "Thanks for the details. You'll need to make a formal statement when you're feeling better. We're doing all we can to catch him."

Sam just gave a weak smile, knowing there was no way in hell anyone would find Thorn. He lay back against the pillow, glad to be in a room alone thanks to the need for an interview with the police. The bandages were tight around his torso and arm and he still felt shaky but the nurse had told him that was normal.

He'd asked them to contact Leanne as his next of kin. He hoped she would at least come and make sure he was OK. She hadn't left a message and it was driving him mad that the one time she'd called him he hadn't been able to answer the phone. He felt worn out but every time he tried to relax he thought about the attack.

There was a brisk knock on the door and a man entered. He wasn't wearing a white coat nor any medical accoutrements, just a smart suit with a light jacket over it. Sam didn't recognise him.

He was carrying a clipboard and an air of importance like that of a hospital administrator or manager. "Mr Samuel Westonville?"

Something about the way he said it made the hairs on the back of Sam's neck prickle. "Yeah."

"I just need to clarify a few details about the case with you."

"Who are you?"

"DI Taylor."

"I just spoke to your constable."

"And she highlighted some details I wanted to check myself."

"Can I see some ID, please?"

The man smiled affably, plucked an ID wallet from his pocket and flipped it open. "I understand you interrupted the attack."

Sam nodded but the ID hadn't calmed the sense of there being something dangerous about the man. He thought about how Thorn had disguised himself and wondered if this was him coming to kill off a key witness. Sam's mouth went dry.

"Could you explain to me how the railings broke?"

"I landed on them. Look, I told the policewoman everything and I'm feeling rough. Could we talk about this tomorrow?"

"I understand. Could I just take a look at the bruising on your neck?"

"I was telling the truth. He picked me up and threw me." Sam nervously reached up to his throat. Now he was more concerned they disbelieved him and were going to start seeing him as a suspect.

The man's smile became false and froze rictus-like on his face when he saw the wedding ring. He shuddered and took a step back as he made a show of peering at the injury. "Yes, I can see the marks quite well from here. Well, thank you, Mr Westonville. As you said, I should let you rest."

The man left quickly. Sam looked at the ring and twisted it nervously on his finger. As soon as the doctor gave him the all-clear he was going to get out of there and go somewhere safe.

24

Will paced the length of the small room in three strides, already hating the pale-green walls and faded pastel pictures. Cornelius was perched on one of the chairs, as if trying to minimise contact with the mundane furniture. He looked strange in the casual shirt and jeans he'd changed into for the trip into Mundanus.

"You don't have to stay," Will said.

"I don't think you should be alone at a time like this."

Will managed a smile and resumed the pacing.

"I'd forgotten how unpleasant Mundanus smells," Cornelius said.

"Hospitals are particularly bad," Will replied. All he wanted to do was find Sophia. The man from the Agency dressed as a doctor had shown them into the room and told them to wait whilst he got an update on Cathy's surgery. He'd mentioned in his preliminary report that a mundane man and child had been brought in with her, but hadn't said anything more about them. Will had been relieved to hear Sophia described as such, having been terrified that the Agency would somehow identify her. Now he just needed to know how badly hurt she was.

"I'm going to see if I can find a cup of tea," he said.

"I can go." Cornelius half rose out of the chair.

"No, I need to do something," Will said. "I won't be long."

He walked away from the room briskly, planning to be round the corner and out of sight as quickly as possible in case Cornelius decided to follow him. Whilst he was grateful for the gesture of support and an extra pair of eyes in case any attempts were made to trick or dupe him, he didn't want Cornelius to know about Sophia.

Will headed back towards the accident and emergency

department they'd walked through only five minutes before, knowing Sophia would be treated there. He hated the thought of her alone in such a noisy, frightening place, and had to get her back home without the Agency clean-up team knowing.

He approached the desk and a nurse looked up from her computer. "Good morning. I'm looking for my cousin, she's almost five years old, blonde hair, brown eyes, she was brought in earlier, she was involved in an incident at a park." He didn't want to say she was his sister, just in case the enquiry ended up on a record somewhere for the Agency to find. Paranoia was the best policy where a clean-up was involved.

"What's her name?"

"Sophia."

The woman sighed. "Sophia what?"

A cubicle curtain was drawn back sharply a few metres away, and Uncle Vincent was standing there, looking most grave. "Will, she's over here."

"May I?" he checked with the nurse and she waved him on.

Will hurried over. "Uncle Vincent? What are you doing here? How is she?"

He stood aside, revealing Sophia's sleeping face. There was a gash across her right cheek held together with tiny white plasters. She was lying under a blanket but he could see she was in a hospital gown and her arms were bandaged. He went to her side and brushed his fingertips over her hair, barely able to breathe.

"You'd better have a damn good explanation for how this happened," his uncle said.

"Whoever did it almost murdered my wife," Will whispered.

"You were supposed to be looking after her."

"I don't need you to make me feel any worse. They were attacked at a park. Cathy was stabbed—she's in surgery now."

"Who did it?"

"I don't know yet."

"Will Catherine pull through?"

"I don't know. How did you know Sophia was here?"

"Your mother asked me to keep an eye on her. I saw her in an ambulance through the scrying glass and I watched until I knew where she was. I've only been here ten minutes."

"Do my parents know?"

"No. I don't think they need to yet, do you?"

Will looked back down at Sophia. She looked so small in the huge bed. "No. How badly is she hurt?"

"She's covered in puncture wounds." His uncle's voice wavered and he cleared his throat. "The policewoman said she was found in the undergrowth but they don't understand why her wounds are so bad. The doctor said she'll be scarred. They've given her something to make her rest. She was very distressed, understandably."

Will gripped the edge of the bed, wanting the one who did it to be dragged in so he could personally rip his throat out. "Do they need to do anything more?"

"No. I just didn't want to move her until I saw you. I knew you'd be here soon enough."

Will took one of his calling cards from his wallet. "Get a taxi to the Hyde Park stables in Bathurst Mews, ask for Jones and give him this card. Tell him who you are and ask him to take you to my house. Remember, they think Sophia is my cousin. I'll come home as soon as I have a full report from the Agency and know when we can extract Cathy from mundane care. Don't leave until I get home."

"Is it safe for her there?"

"Yes, damn it, of course it is. And go now, the Agency's clean-up team is here. I don't want you to be seen with her."

Vincent said nothing as Will kissed Sophia's forehead gently and returned to the waiting room.

"No tea?" Cornelius asked.

"The machine only took coins," Will said with a shrug. "I only have notes on me. Has the Agency man been back yet?"

"No."

Will sat down and rested his head in his hands, trying to drive the image of Sophia's injuries from his mind. The feeling of complete impotence made his skin itch, as if all the anger was crawling beneath it like insects. He wanted to punch someone and throw the chairs around the room and yell as loud as he could like some bestial man, but he forced himself to stay still. He would find out who did it, and kill them. The thought helped.

The door opened and the Agency man walked in, looking shaken. Will's chest felt like steel bands had been wrapped around it as he stood and looked at the man expectantly.

"There are some complications to this case I feel I should discuss with you in private, Mr Iris." The man took the stethoscope from around his neck and laid it on one of the chairs.

"Cornelius, would you excuse us?"

Cornelius gave the man a long look as he left the room.

"Let's sit down."

Will did as he suggested, noting the tension in the man's shoulders and the way he adjusted his position a couple of times once seated.

"How is my wife?"

"She's still in surgery. It's very serious, Mr Iris, she nearly died. Had the knife been removed by the attacker she would have bled to death before the ambulance could arrive. Ironically, leaving the weapon in her was the best thing that could have happened in the unfortunate circumstances."

Will ran his hands through his hair and looked up at the ceiling. "What are they doing to her?"

"I'll get access to the full details once she's out of the operating room, but from what I've gathered so far one of her lungs has collapsed and she's bleeding severely into her chest cavity. They've had to insert a tube—"

Will held up a hand. "How long will she be in surgery?"

"I can't say with accuracy. They'll have to leave the chest tube in for several days at least until the lung has healed. Mrs Iris was kicked and knocked out. She has a concussion as well as a bad bruise to her jaw and deep cuts on her arms. She must have been defending herself."

"Oh, God."

"Her hands are badly cut too, though no one understands why. There will be extensive scarring, especially to her chest, and it will take several weeks for her to recover fully if she makes it through the surgery without further complications."

"The ones you mentioned?"

"Ah, no, sir. I told you when you arrived that the initial police report was of a man and child found injured in the same attack."

Will held his breath, expecting him to say something about Sophia.

"We've looked into the man's statement and there's…something odd about what he did. I'll read you the preliminary report."

Will listened to a description of a man ending the attack by throwing an iron bar. At first, Will was simply glad he'd been there, but when he was told about the way the railings had broken, the iron plugs in the man's wounds, the accuracy of the difficult shot and no athletic background, his frown deepened.

"All of this, and the fact a very experienced colleague detected something…disconcerting about a ring he wears, leads us to suspect he's connected to the Elemental Court."

"The who?"

"We know very little about them, I'm afraid, but we know they have an arrangement with the Sorcerers. It seems a representative of Lord Iron defended your wife." He leaned closer. "Would you have any idea why?"

"No," Will said, disturbed by what he was hearing. "I've never even heard of a Lord Iron. Are they like our patrons?"

"I wouldn't like to speculate, sir. Information on them is remarkably difficult to come by."

"I'll see what I can find out. All of this will be kept confidential, won't it?"

"Of course, sir."

"What about the weapon? You said it wasn't removed. Does that mean we have a way to find the attacker?"

"The weapon was a stiletto, which is easy to conceal. It's currently held by the police as evidence but we'll recover it. From the initial report, there are no markings of note on it, but then I wouldn't expect there to be."

"Are there any leads?"

The man shook his head. "Not yet, sir. The crime scene is crawling with mundanes at the moment so it's very difficult for us to use our own methods to ascertain anything concrete. Should anything arise we'll inform you, of course. Our primary function is to prevent a breach and avoid the wrath of the Sorcerers by having the mundanes poking their noses where they should not."

Will nodded, wondering if he could hire an investigator of some kind. Then he imagined Cathy in surgery, the blood, the people manhandling her like she was a piece of meat. "The doctors…they wear gloves, don't they?"

"Yes, sir."

"When can I take my wife home?"

"I would recommend removing her to the Nether once she's out of intensive care. Mundane medicine is really quite remarkable. There's no better way to ensure her survival with such serious injuries."

"How long will that be?"

"I'll know once she's out of surgery. We have someone posted to watch her twenty-four hours a day. Once she's well enough to be nursed at home we'll start the full clean-up."

"And you can provide a nurse?"

"Yes, sir, fully vetted, as all our staff are."

Will nodded. "Please brief my steward on what will be needed."

"There's another matter I feel I should bring to your attention." The man looked nervous. "Another complication."

Will straightened. Don't mention Sophia, he thought. Don't mention—

"Your wife was carrying a mobile phone and an iPad. Both are devices used by the—"

"I know what they are," Will interrupted. "I've recently returned from my Grand Tour."

The man coughed to disguise his embarrassment. "My apologies. It's registered to Catherine Parker, with an address in Manchester."

"Manchester? What in the Worlds—?"

"Indeed, sir. We're looking into the possibility that your wife borrowed it. But my suspicion, if I may be so bold, is that your wife has a mundane alias based in the dark city. The police will look at the logged calls as part of the investigation."

"Well, you have to lock that all down," Will said, feeling sweat break out on his palms. "Immediately."

"That will be very difficult—"

"That's what you do, isn't it? That's what I'm paying you for?"

The man nodded.

"I want details of all the phone contacts, the address, everything, and I want that separate from any notes you keep on this case," Will said, lowering his voice. "I don't want any of it to be seen by your boss. I don't want anyone except you and me to know."

"That's rather—"

"I'll pay you handsomely for the inconvenience," Will added.

The man looked him in the eye and understood the bribe. "I see, sir. I'll consider it my personal priority and will exercise the utmost discretion."

So Horatio's accusations had been true. Cathy had been in Mundanus and established enough to have another identity. Why Manchester of all places? The thought of her having so much hidden from him was a shock, but it explained the way she talked and the way she'd dealt with that problem with the furniture. No wonder she'd been so keen to take Sophia into Mundanus; she was exploiting an opportunity to use the internet. But why?

Then he realised the man who saved her from the attacker was probably her lover, the one Horatio had sneered at him about. She'd probably been at the park to meet that man and Sophia had provided the perfect excuse to linger there with him.

Will twitched at the thought of it. He wanted to throttle the man, even though he'd saved his wife. He needed to find him and tell him to stay away from Cathy. Will clasped his clammy hands together and tried to find some calm in the midst of the primal rage. He had to think, not react like a caveman. The Fidelity Charm would have made it impossible for Cathy to be unfaithful to him, but it wouldn't have stopped her being in love with this man. It must have been the reason behind her reluctance to consummate the marriage; she was trying to stay faithful to a man she fell in love with in Mundanus.

The Agency man stood with a finger pressed against his ear and for the first time Will noticed a small earpiece. "My colleague has told me an Arbiter is coming in. I have to leave. I recommend you do the same."

"I haven't done anything wrong," Will said.

"I'll let you know when you can see your wife," the man said as he headed to the door. "And, as far as you can, don't worry. We'll take care of everything regarding the mundanes."

Will was left with his fears. Cathy was too stubborn to just slip away, surely. He didn't want her to die. It wasn't just the shame of not protecting his wife adequately, it wasn't the guilt or the fear of reprisals from the Fae or her family. He wanted Cathy to survive and he wanted to take care of her and find a way to have a happy marriage. Will was certain they could have one, if he just had another chance. He had to give her a reason to leave this secret life of hers in Mundanus behind.

Max sat in silence a couple of metres away from his captive, knowing it would make the Fae more nervous. He took the time to review the breakthrough the puppet had given them. Two hours after Catherine had given him the name of the Wisteria puppet, he'd told him the former head of the Alba-Rosa line was hiding in a small terraced house in South London, thankfully in the territory of the Sorcerer of Kent, who didn't have rogue Arbiters hunting him. Four hours later the truth mask had done its job and Max had confirmation that every ward in North London under the jurisdiction of the

Sorcerer of Essex was corrupt. The sobbing man had spoken of the Rosas being given carte blanche by their Patroon to do what they wished in London north of the river. His own son had arranged the kidnapping of five blonde men and women on the order of Lady Rose herself, using a modelling agency on Judd Street as a front, just as Max had suspected.

The real breakthrough came when Max had pretended the man hadn't told him enough and that he'd be handed over to the Agency. That was when Alba-Rosa, once a proud and powerful man, fell to his knees and begged to be spared in return for a means to contact Thorn himself. And it had worked. Max tricked him into entering Mundanus and took him into custody. He'd made more progress in the last twelve hours than he'd made since being shot at the clock tower.

Every time Max drew a breath, Thorn twitched. He was dressed in a grey coat with half-cape, an elaborately embroidered waistcoat and breeches. He had a sack over his head and was bound with bands of copper to an iron chair, at the centre of several concentric circles of wards chalked onto the floor of Ekstrand's ballroom. Max cleared his throat and Thorn whimpered. He was ripe.

"There are a few specks of blood on the right-hand sleeve of your coat, Mr Thorn," he said. "Would you like to explain how they got there?"

"I don't have to answer to you, dog. Under whose authority do you keep me here?"

"You were in Mundanus, Mr Thorn. You know that's not allowed."

"I only came through because I was called by one of ours. I wasn't doing anything to an innocent."

"The blood. Who does it belong to?"

The Fae sat in silence. Max gave it a minute, then unzipped the small leather case that had been resting on the table beside him. He removed the copper implements one by one, dropping them from an inch above the metal tray so they landed with a loud clink.

"I have several questions," Max said. "And I have several tools here that I can use to get the answers, if you continue to be uncooperative." He stood, picked up the first implement and limped over, using the walking stick to make his approach obvious. "I have a sickel probe here, made of copper. The mundanes use them to look for tooth decay, but I've found they're perfect for sliding under fingernails."

"You think torture will get what you want?"

"Yes, I do."

"There will be consequences if you harm me," Thorn said.

"Really? Your family has fallen from grace and you're an embarrassment to the royal family. The last I heard you were being punished in Exilium, which makes me wonder if you're not only persona non grata, but also on the run from the Prince's wrath."

"The Prince!" Thorn laughed. "You know nothing, you empty shell, nothing."

"I'm about to change that," Max said. "Are you sure you don't want to tell me where that blood came from?" When Thorn remained silent, he lined himself up with the back of the chair and positioned the probe above one of the Fae's nails. "Last chance."

"You wouldn't dare."

Max gripped the nail, shaped more like a talon, on the forefinger of the Fae's right hand and thrust the sharp end of the probe into the flesh beneath. Thorn screeched and Max counted to five, occasionally tweaking the angle of the pick. Made feeble by the copper bonds, Thorn couldn't break free.

Max pulled the probe out. "I have a pair of copper pliers too, perfect for extracting nails. Then the flesh underneath is so much easier to get to."

Thorn whimpered but said nothing so Max went back to the tray and rummaged noisily. He took his time going back, letting the Fae listen to the steady *thunk* of the walking stick on the floor.

"The blood came from Poppy's favourite," Thorn said as Max lined himself up behind the chair again.

"Catherine Rhoeas-Papaver?"

"Catherine Reticulata-Iris now." Thorn clenched his fists in a vain attempt to protect himself. "The cold one managed to steal her and plant her in his family."

"How did her blood get on your coat?"

Thorn sighed heavily and his head fell forward. "It...splashed. I would have pierced her heart but one of the blood metals interfered. Go and sit down, empty one, and I'll tell you. Damn the Prince, damn all of them. I see no reason to endure pain for them. Nothing will help my brethren now."

Max returned to his chair and tossed the pliers back onto the tray. "I'm listening."

"I didn't escape. The Prince released me to do his bidding once more. He holds my brother and sister. I had to do it."

"The Prince told you to kill Catherine Iris?"

"The Prince told me to stop the Irises taking the Londinium throne. Whatever it took. I found one of ours, hidden like a bulb waiting for the spring. He knew of the Iris boy and his vain hopes. The one we hate. The one who ruined everything for us!"

William Iris, Max thought. "Go on," he said.

"I wanted to drown his heart in grief and confusion," Thorn said. "I wanted to kill the one given to him and make his pairing imperfect. It would humiliate him in the eyes of the cold one and unleash Poppy's wrath upon him. We wanted him to think it was another in the Londinium Court, to give the Iris boy another to blame in case it was witnessed. It would have been perfect, had it not been for the blood metal."

Max knew he meant iron; the Fae couldn't even bring themselves to say the word. "You said you had to do the Prince's bidding 'once more'—when was the last time?"

"When my brother and I stole the Lavender from Aquae Sulis."

Max adjusted the way he sat, to try and ease the ache in his leg. "The Prince asked you to do that?"

"Yes. He was behind all of it. He told my sister to do all she could to undermine the cold one's grip on the city. He told us we would be protected should anything go wrong. Ha! How bitter royal lies are!"

Max reined in his own speculation. Better to take the information to the Sorcerer and discuss it with him. "Your people in Londinium have no fear of Arbiters. They've been bolder in Mundanus of late."

"The Prince had nothing to do with that. My sister made a deal with a Sorcerer—I don't know the details. In return, the Arbiters ignored our own."

"It seems your sister is willing to go to extraordinary lengths to protect the information you're so happy to give."

"What extraordinary lengths?"

"Killing Arbiters."

Thorn sat up straighter. "We've done no such thing."

"You would say that, being strapped to a chair in front of one."

"Which Arbiters? We haven't killed anyone, not even the one we planned to this morning."

Max listened carefully, alert to any tightness in the Fae's voice, but it sounded like Thorn was actually telling the truth. He had to be sure though. He couldn't risk passing anything inaccurate onto Ekstrand. "Tell me more about this deal your sister made," Max said, reaching for the copper pliers.

25

Will didn't have a chance to speak to Cornelius before a man in scruffy mundane jeans and sweatshirt came into the waiting room. Will would have thought him an average man off the street, were it not for the fact that his face wore the chilling, expressionless stare of an Arbiter. His eyes were slightly bulbous, his mouth wide with thin lips, both giving him an unpleasant frog-like appearance.

Will and Cornelius stood. The Arbiter looked at them both and then focused on Will. "You're William Reticulata-Iris."

"I am."

The Arbiter's eyes flicked to Cornelius. "I understand you're a White now."

Cornelius just nodded and the Arbiter looked back at Will. "Your wife was just stabbed in St James's Park. I understand she survived the attack."

"Yes."

"You've only been in the city for less than a month and have already caused one of the most serious breaches in the last one hundred years. A man and child were involved. Innocents. Not to mention the ones cleaning your mess up."

"It's not a breach, it's being handled by my people." Will didn't need the Arbiter to make him feel any worse. "Once my wife is out of danger she'll be removed from Mundanus."

The Arbiter sat down on one of the plastic chairs. "I know you're doing everything right, otherwise I wouldn't be being so polite. I went to the crime scene and I know who's behind the attack."

Will's fists clenched. "Who was it?"

"So you want to deal with this?"

"Yes."

"Suits me—I'd rather not have the paperwork. I only want your guarantee that you deal with this in the Nether, and involve no innocents, nor—"

"Just tell me who tried to kill my wife!" Will shouted.

The Arbiter stared at him for a moment. "Someone from the Tulipa line. Massive Charm use, most likely a powerful glamour, seeing as there were other mundanes in the area. I take it you know the Tulipas? They live in Hampton Court, you can't miss it."

Will shook his head. "You must be mistaken."

The Arbiter's stare was difficult to stomach. "I don't make mistakes about things like this. I'd be on your guard until you deal with them. And, for what it's worth, I don't care how you deal with it as long as it stays out of Mundanus. London is dangerous enough without your kind trying to kill each other."

"That's enough, Faulkner," Cornelius said and herded the man towards the door.

"I can't believe it," Will said when the Arbiter had gone. "Not Bartholomew. He'd never hurt Cathy."

"Will—" Cornelius' voice was firm "—Arbiters don't lie."

"But it must be a mistake, a—"

"Think about it. You have a wealthy, powerful family, so does your wife. You told Bartholomew you were going to stand against him and I warned you he would act."

"But why Cathy? Why not attack me?"

"To make you weak. To pull you out of the running. To make you so griefstricken that you forget your ambition. Or to make you an unattractive proposition for the Court—would a recently widowed man be a stable Duke? Any and all of those things. But it's also a statement, Will, do you see? They're showing you they don't care about being decent or playing by the rules. They'd rather destroy you than see you on the throne."

"But Bartholomew isn't the type of man to attack a woman with a dagger. It's too crude."

"He may not have wielded it himself, but he gave the order. The Arbiters don't get this kind of thing wrong."

"But can we trust an Arbiter over our own instincts?" The only other Arbiter Will had ever seen was the one in Aquae Sulis and he'd just watched him limp through into Exilium. Had they ever fed misinformation to those in Society for their own ends?

"Why would he lie, even if he were capable of it?" Cornelius replied. "He just wants us to stay away from the innocents."

Will held his head in his hands. "I can't rush into a reprisal based on what an Arbiter says. I have to wait for the report from the Agency. I need more evidence before I start a war."

Sam woke and looked around the hospital room in disorientation. A knock at the door sounded too loud and he wondered if previous knocks had woken him. "Come in." He winced at his bruised throat.

The policewoman entered who'd interviewed him before. It wasn't as if she'd been cheerful then, but there was a new depth to her grave expression. "Mr Westonville, I'm sorry to wake you, but I have something to tell you."

He sat up. "Oh, God, did she die?"

"The woman in the park? No, she's in intensive care now. The surgery went well, apparently." She came in and sat beside the bed. "Mr Westonville, I'm very sorry to inform you that your wife died this afternoon."

"What?" A faint ringing began in his ears.

"She suffered a brain aneurysm whilst waiting for a train in Paddington station. She was pronounced dead on arrival at A & E. I'm so sorry."

"What? When?"

"This afternoon. Whilst you were here."

It felt like the bruising on his throat was getting worse. He could barely swallow. "What?" he said, then again and again, as if his thoughts were stuck on a loop.

"Mr Westonville, as your wife's next of kin, you need to confirm her identity."

"When?"

"I can take you now."

"Where?"

"The morgue."

He didn't remember walking down the corridors with her, nor the lift. He was only barely aware of a couple of heavy double doors, someone behind a desk who gave him something to sign, being led into a room, a massive drawer in the wall being opened…

Leanne looked like she was asleep.

She was asleep, in the hotel on their honeymoon, a two-star pit in Bournemouth, the sound of mad seagulls coming in through the window. He watched her wake and, after smiling at him, she looked towards the window.

"Do you think the locals are slaughtering them?" he'd asked.

"Sam, we're on our honeymoon." She tickled his ribs. "The gulls are shagging, not being slaughtered." Then they were lying naked on top of the sheets. It was back when the summer came in August and it was too hot to make love under them.

"If I ever make a noise like that when we're shagging," he'd said, running a hand over her stomach, "divorce me."

Sam didn't remember leaving the morgue or reaching the steps leading down from the hospital entrance. He didn't realise he was sitting until he saw Max looking down at him.

"Are you hurt?" Max asked.

"My wife."

"Has something—"

"Neugent. Fucking Neugent."

"He murdered her?"

"She tried to call me but I was hurt, in the park. Thorn tried to kill Cathy."

"I know. I brought him in for questioning. Are you badly hurt?"

He shook his head.

"Mr Ekstrand wants to see you," Max said. "Will you come with me?"

Then Sam was sitting on the sofa in front of the fire, the smell of woodsmoke and the clatter of Axon carrying in tea and cake seeming so familiar and so alien at the same time. Petra came and sat next to him, taking his hand, asking if he wanted tea, and all he wanted to say was "I want my wife" but he couldn't get the words through his thick throat. Then he wept.

Afterwards his head felt clearer and he accepted a cup of tea as Max and the gargoyle came in and sat opposite. Sam told them what had happened at the park, everything about the railings, about Thorn and then about the policewoman collecting him to identify Leanne. The teacup rattled on the saucer as he spoke. There was silence after he finished.

"I'm so sorry, Sam," Petra finally said. "That's awful."

"Yeah," the gargoyle agreed. "How's Cathy?"

"I dunno." Sam shrugged and then winced as the movement tugged at his injuries. "Where's Ekstrand?"

"With the apprentices. I've told him you're here," Max said.

"Would you like me to ask him if you can stay here for a while?" Petra asked. "There's a room for you if you want. I can understand you not wanting to go home at the moment."

"There's no way I'm staying here again."

"Ah, our guest has returned." Ekstrand's cheeriness crashed into the sombre sitting room. "Where have you been?"

"Mr Ekstrand." Sam stood up. "I need your help."

"What with?" Ekstrand asked, beckoning the apprentices in.

Eagerboy smiled but Sam didn't have an ounce of friendliness left in him. "My wife has been killed by a total bastard and I need you to help me stop him from fucking anyone else's lives up."

Ekstrand looked at Max. "It's possible Neugent—or something connected to him—had some involvement in his wife's death," Max said. "It's not guaranteed."

"He did," Sam said. "She was losing weight, she wasn't herself, and it was Neugent's fault." He pointed at Max. "You were the one who told me about that pattern in the first place. You know it's true."

"Who is this Neugent?" Ekstrand asked. "Is he a puppet?"

"No, he works for CoFerrum Inc," Sam said. "He's got something to do with Lord Iron."

"Well, so do you." Ekstrand pointed at the wedding ring. "Were you involved?"

"Sam." Petra's hand brushed his arm. "She died of natural causes."

"There was nothing natural about it, she wasn't even thirty!"

"But an aneurysm can happen to anyone at any time, and another person can't cause it," she replied. "It's just something awful that happened to your wife. You can't say with absolute certainty that Neugent had anything to do with it and the likelihood is he didn't."

"Bullshit. Max warned me about him, he does something to people and it makes them die young. He'll do it again, I know he will." He looked back at Ekstrand. "Look, aren't you and the Arbiters supposed to protect innocents?"

"From the Fae and their puppets, yes," Ekstrand replied.

"And the likes of Lord Iron and his people?"

"There's never been any need. The Elemental Court are completely different from the Fae—they don't interfere with people or kidnap them."

"But my wife was an innocent who got sucked into some job that ended up with her living in an apartment designed to be an iron cage."

"The apartment was designed to protect against Fae," Max said. "It had a cage-like structure, but there was no sense of imprisonment there."

"Well, that sounds rather helpful and sensible," Ekstrand said.

"You don't get it, do you?" Sam yelled. "My wife is dead! I tried to warn her, I did everything I could, but she died, and I'm telling you this will happen again to another couple. Help me do something about that! It's directly connected to Lord Iron, who's presumably in this Elemental Court, and you're saying there's no need to police them like the Fae?"

Ekstrand looked at Max. "Do you think there's grounds for concern?"

Sam stared at the Arbiter, willing Max to support him.

"I do, sir," Max replied.

"I disagree," Petra said. "I think it was an awful coincidence."

Ekstrand rubbed his chin and then turned to his students. "What you see here is a rather complex dilemma."

"Don't you dare make a fucking lesson out of this!" Sam marched over. "This is none of their business. The only lesson to be learnt is that Neugent needs to be stopped."

Ekstrand's eyes were shadowed by his brow. "There's a lesson in everything. Even in watching what happens when a Sorcerer is insulted. Would you like me to make this more educational?"

"Mr Ekstrand—" Petra practically threw herself between them "—Sam is upset, please forgive him for being so emotional."

Ekstrand pursed his lips, peering at Sam over her shoulder. "I can't just leap to conclusions about people who may or may not be connected to Lord Iron. There are formal channels of communication with the Elemental Court which must be observed."

"There are important reasons why things are done this way, Sam," Petra said, now facing him with Ekstrand behind her. "I know it must be frustrating but—"

"That doesn't even come close. I've had it with you people. You've never given a shit about how you've screwed my life up, there's no way you're going to help me now. Fuck you, fuck your sorcery bullshit and fuck your ways of doing things. I'm off."

Sam pushed his way past Petra, who was begging Ekstrand to forgive him in his griefstricken state. Axon was near the front door looking at him expectantly. "I want to go home," Sam said. There was a pause as Axon listened for any contrary instruction from Ekstrand. When none came he nodded to Sam. "Take care, sir," he said, opened the door and led him down the path to open the gates onto Mundanus.

Sam stepped out, looked up at the stars and the moon and felt hollow inside. The wounds hurt and there was nothing to listen to but the iron plugs clanking in his pockets as he began the walk home.

All Cathy saw at first was light. Then a shape by her side coalesced into Will.

"My love." Will kissed her cheek. "How are you feeling?"

"Tired." She looked down at her bandaged arms and hands. There were tubes and beeps and a distinct sense of being unwell. "I dreamed you were here."

He smiled and smoothed her hair away from her forehead. "I came to you in the recovery room after the surgery but you were still waking up. The nurse said you might think you'd dreamed me."

There was another shape outside the curtain and she could hear other beeps and people talking. "Where am I?"

"You're in a hospital in London, in the intensive care unit. Do you remember what happened?"

She looked at the shape through the curtain. "Who's that?"

"One of my people. I'm so sorry I wasn't careful enough." He kissed her cheek, her forehead, but she barely registered it. "I won't let anyone hurt you again, I promise."

"Where's Sophia?"

"She's safe at home."

"The thorns, they were wrapped around her, she was hurt."

"They've bandaged her up, and my uncle is with her." Will paused. "Thorns?"

Cathy tried to nod but wasn't certain if she was successful. "I told her to run, she was grabbed by…these creepers…growing out of the bushes covered in thorns. She was screaming. I tried to pull them off her. They were trying to wrap around her neck." She looked back down at her hands, now understanding why they were bandaged.

"Then what happened?"

"The man had a dagger. He was going to hurt Sophia, so I tried to stop him." She felt exhausted just talking about it.

"He was trying to hurt Sophia?"

"Yes, I don't know why."

"Not you?"

"Why would he want to hurt me? Why would he want to hurt her though? I don't know, it doesn't make any sense. Oh, God, Will it was awful. I don't remember how I got here. He didn't get Sophia?"

Will shook his head. "The man who attacked you, Cathy, did you recognise him?"

"No."

"What did he look like?"

"I don't remember his face…I was looking at the knife." She felt tears welling. "He stabbed me?"

"Yes. Do you remember anything about him?"

"He was Fae-touched, he was wearing a grey coat with half-cape and a sparkly waistcoat. I saw it when he drew the dagger. Brown hair, in a ponytail."

"Did he look like one of the Tulipa line?"

Cathy closed her eyes. All she wanted to do was sleep.

"Cathy? I'm sorry, but I need to know as much as possible. Did he look like Bartholomew?"

"What? No, nothing like him or his family. I'm tired."

"You're certain?"

"It was a Rosa, Will. The thorns…" He said something else but it was far away. "That's a Rose Charm." There was a brush against her forehead and then sinking into velvety darkness.

26

Will sat hunched over his desk, the fire crackling in the grate as he examined what he knew. The Arbiter said there was Tulipa magic at the crime scene—how he knew that, Will hadn't the faintest idea, but there was no reason the Arbiter would lie. The thorns Cathy reported explained Sophia's injuries and those to her own hands. By the time the police arrived the Charm controlling the thorns would have dissipated, leaving a badly hurt child and no evidence.

Whilst it was some relief to know how Sophia had been scarred, it also confused him. Cathy was convinced the attacker was a Rosa and the thorn angle was damning. But it sounded like a powerful Charm, and who could wield Rose magic now the patron was broken and the Rosas rounded up by the Agency? And if there had been such powerful Rose magic there, why hadn't the Arbiter mentioned it?

His uncle was still spending every minute of the day with Sophia, for which he was grateful; he only wanted close family around her. Every time he checked on her she asked when Cathy was coming home.

Will was still haunted by the thought that the man who threw the railing was a lover meeting Cathy in the park for a stolen hour. There was a chance he could have been passing by and intervened when he saw a woman and child being attacked, but when Will considered the secret mobile phone and computer, it was clear Cathy had been up to something in her private time. Whatever it was would end now. She was his wife and his alone, regardless of what happened before they married.

A rattling in the door made him look up. By the time he'd

reached it the gilded letterbox had appeared and a note was posted through. When he saw the seal he knew it was from Amelia.

It was a Rosa, Will… Cathy's words haunted him as he went to the fireplace and opened the envelope. The note was brief and the handwriting suggested it was penned in a hurry.

> *Will, please come to me, something is wrong with Cornelius and I'm frightened.*
>
> *Please hurry, darling.*
>
> *Amelia.*

Will crushed it in his hand, disturbed by the doubts that surfaced. Before seeing Cathy earlier that evening he would have been summoning a carriage without a second thought; now he wasn't certain whether he should go at all. But he couldn't just ignore the note.

He pulled the cord beside the fireplace. "Morgan, I need the carriage, urgently, with two armed footmen. And bring my sword cane with my cape."

"Yes, sir." Morgan bowed and left.

In the carriage Will prepared himself for the worst, fearing that Amelia was luring him into a trap. He chided himself for such paranoia. Then he remembered that if he'd been more cautious, Cathy and Sophia would never have been attacked. He was never going to let Cathy leave the house alone again. He'd have to find her a bodyguard for when he couldn't be with her, but could he trust the Agency enough to provide one? He shook his head. It was getting to him.

The carriage drew up; the door was opened and the step lowered. Will climbed out and looked at the footmen. They had both been trained in the latest techniques from Mundanus, with modern pistols unclipped and ready to be drawn at their hip, the holsters incongruous with their formal eighteenth-century footmen's attire. "Come with me," he said to them. "And be ready for foul play."

Will rapped on the door with the knocker and the butler

answered as usual. Amelia was in the hallway. At the sight of him she rushed forward and threw her arms around him.

"I'm so glad you're here!"

He could see she'd been crying. He returned the embrace, remembering how much he cared for her and how much he wanted her to be safe and happy. "What's wrong?"

She glanced at the footmen and pulled him away a couple of paces. "Cornelius came back a few hours ago," she said, her voice lowered. "He was very upset. He said Catherine had almost died and an Arbiter said the Tulipas were involved. But he seemed too upset. I knew he was holding something back."

"Let's talk in here," Will said, pulling her towards the drawing room. "Guard the door," he said to his men and then closed it.

"He was very tense…as if he were preoccupied. I asked him what was wrong but he wouldn't tell me. He told me to go to my room and stay there."

Will felt nauseous. Surely Cornelius couldn't be involved? "Then what happened?"

"A couple of hours went by so I asked the maid what he was doing and she said he was writing letters and throwing them on the fire. I told her to tell me if he did anything else, and later she came to me saying he'd sent out the footman with a note. Cornelius didn't come up to take tea with me as he usually does. I heard the door about an hour ago and the maid told me a man had arrived and asked for Cornelius. He was taken to his study straightaway. I asked her who it was and she said he didn't have a calling card but Cornelius was expecting him."

She paused, biting her lip. "Go on," Will said.

"With everything that's happened, and the way he was acting, I was worried so I came downstairs. I thought I'd knock on his door and pretend I didn't know he had a guest, so I could see who it was. But when I came down I could hear Cornelius shouting. He never shouts. I heard the other man too, he said something about Tulipa, then there was a…I don't know…a scuffle and then a thud and it went quiet."

Will could feel her shivering beneath his hands. "Then what happened?"

"I knocked on the door and Cornelius told me to go away. Just like that, 'Go away', very harshly. Then I heard him weeping. I haven't been able to get into the room, it's locked from the inside. The butler said he was told not to disturb them. Cornelius won't come out." She broke down. "I didn't know what to do so I wrote to you. Do you think I'm being silly?"

"No."

"You're angry with me."

"No, I'm not. You did the right thing. Stay in here and don't worry. I'll make sure he's all right."

The thought of Cathy in hospital flashed through his mind as he kissed Amelia. He went out, checked she was remaining behind and then shut the door. "Come with me," he said to his men and headed for Cornelius's study.

"Cornelius?" he called as he knocked. "Is everything all right?" There was a long pause. Will tried the handle but the door was locked. He knocked again. "Cornelius?"

He pressed his ear to the door but couldn't hear anything. He beckoned to the butler, who'd been lingering in the hallway since he'd arrived. "Do you have a spare key?"

"Yes, sir, I'll get it for you."

Two minutes later Will was turning the key in the lock, his other hand on the sword cane. He opened the door slowly. "Cornelius? It's Will, I'm coming inside."

He peered around the door. The body was the first thing he saw, sprawled on the rug in front of the fire. It was a man, dressed in a grey coat with half-cape, just as Cathy had described.

It took him a moment to locate Cornelius. He was sitting in a corner wedged between two bookcases with knees drawn up, staring at the body. A glass paperweight was lying on the floor between his feet, smeared with blood. He was as white as a fine china cup and there were spots of blood on his cheek.

"Wait outside," Will told his footmen, then went in and closed the door behind him. "Cornelius?"

"I killed him," Cornelius whispered.

Will stepped carefully over the body and moved round to look at his face, which had been obscured by the desk. He was lying on his back, his eyes open. His hair was long and brown, tied back in a ponytail, and Will could see a heavily embroidered waistcoat beneath the partially unbuttoned coat. As he got closer, he could see the blood pooled on the rug and the depression in the man's skull, presumably made by the leaded glass ball.

"Who is he?"

"My cousin," Cornelius finally answered.

"A Rosa?"

"Yes."

"What happened?" Will stooped to close the man's eyelids. He'd never seen a dead body before nor touched one.

"He was the one who stabbed Catherine."

"How do you know that?"

"He told me."

Will pulled the one chair in the room closer to Cornelius and sat down. "Did someone take him in to protect him from the Agency?"

"No. He was in hiding."

"I think you need to start at the beginning. Let me get you a drink."

Will poured two brandies from the decanter on the other side of the room and handed one to Cornelius, who took it with a shaking hand.

"When I came back from Mundanus I started to think about the Tulipas, how you said they'd never be so crass." Cornelius took a long drink and it seemed to steady him. "So I decided to pull in a favour and make some enquiries."

"I didn't realise there was a place where one could contact the local assassin."

Cornelius didn't react to the comment. "There are certain unsavoury individuals in Londinium who always seem to know what's going on. One thing led to another and it all pointed to my cousin. He was desperate enough to agree to a meeting. He was afraid he was going to be killed." Cornelius laughed bitterly. "But not by his own cousin."

"What did he tell you?"

"That Tulipa promised to hide him from the Agency indefinitely in return for Catherine's death."

Will put his glass on the desk. Now he was starting to shake. "Bartholomew?"

"Yes."

"Are you certain he was telling the truth?"

"Yes. I…I lost control of myself. I could see you throwing Amelia and me out to the dogs because of that selfish bastard. And there was a child there, he almost murdered a woman and child, Will. One of my blood. I didn't realise I'd hit him until he fell." The glass slipped from his hand and he hid his face.

"I don't blame you," Will said. All of his rage was aimed at the Tulipas. "You and Amelia are Whites now, not Rosas. And if you were still a Rosa you would have hidden this from me, hidden him and not cared about what he'd done. It all makes sense now. Cathy thought he was a Rosa. Bartholomew must have given him some sort of Charm, that's what the Arbiter picked up on. But she said creepers covered with thorns were holding the child…that's the only thing I don't understand. How could a Rose Charm still be—"

"The dagger once belonged to one of the Thorn brothers," Cornelius replied. "It still held some power. He told me."

Will felt all the uncertainty drop away, leaving only a bright core of pure anger and the desire for revenge. "You were right about Bartholomew," he whispered. "It was all an act and I fell for it. Even though he didn't do it with his own hands, he planned it all and he paid another man to murder my wife." Will knocked the rest of the brandy down his throat. "I have to act. It's just a matter of time before my Patroon or my patron find out about this and demand to know what I'm doing about it."

"This isn't just about them trying to murder Catherine,"

Cornelius said. "This is about the throne of Londinium. Strike back and send a clear signal to the Londinium Court that you are a strong, decisive man."

Will nodded slowly, remembering the sight of his sister, thinking of Cathy lying in hospital, needing to do something to channel the rage. "If I'm to go against the Tulipas directly I'm going to do it properly. I have to see my patron."

The house smelled stale when Sam got home. He didn't bother to turn the light on; the creeping twilight gave him enough to see by and matched his mood. It had taken almost an hour to walk home and whilst it had made his wounds complain he needed the exhaustion.

Leanne was dead.

He chucked the keys into the bowl in the hallway and looked at the picture of the two of them in the field, lit by an amber shard from the streetlight outside. He wished he could remember it being taken, wished it gave him something other than a sense of emptiness. He knew the album from their wedding day was on the bookshelf in the spare room upstairs, and that he wouldn't be able to look at it for a long time. A part of him wanted to study the pictures and invite in pure grief in the hope that eventually the rock in his chest would be expelled, but more of him just wanted to switch off.

He went into the living room and saw nothing but the pictures she'd chosen, the furniture she'd picked out, the plants she'd bought. The only thing he'd really contributed was the TV and DVD player. He decided to put the house on the market the next day and move somewhere a long way away that was completely his.

Car doors slammed outside and he went to the window. The street was filled with parked cars now all the commuters were home. He saw neighbours from either side of the house and a couple of people he didn't recognise all pull out and drive off at the same time, leaving the road outside his house and his neighbour's completely free of parked cars.

Normally he wouldn't have given it a second thought, but now he knew about the Fae-touched and Sorcerers he felt distinctly unsettled. He wondered if Cathy's husband had found out about him or if Ekstrand was planning to do something that required easy access to his house. Then he realised neither party would want to do anything in the real world; they'd be sneaking through the Nether. He shivered and looked behind him at the empty room.

The sound of a car outside brought his attention back to the road. A stretch limousine was crawling down the narrow street and pulled into the space that had just been made. Sam went to the side of the window so he'd be out of sight from the road, fearing that Neugent would step out any moment. Once it was parked, a man got out of the front passenger seat dressed in a dark suit. He looked like a broad-shouldered security man or FBI mook from a silly American thriller. He even had an earpiece and a flesh-coloured curly wire reaching down beneath the collar of his white shirt.

The man looked the street up and down, spoke into a concealed mouthpiece and then moved to open the rear passenger door. Another burly guard got out, followed by another. Sam's breath sped up as the adrenalin kicked in. He considered leaving by the back door, not wanting to find out who was inside, even if it was Neugent. Nobody brought blokes that big with them for a tea party. But he couldn't tear his eyes away from the spectacle in his quiet suburban street.

The third man to get out was the one they were there to protect; his neck wasn't as wide as his head and he was at least a foot shorter than the guards. His suit was well-cut and fitted perfectly. He buttoned his jacket when he got out. He had the air of confidence that the super-wealthy exude effortlessly and appeared to be of mixed-race descent, his hair black and cropped short. He was looking at Sam's house.

He gave a nod to one of the men, who opened the garden gate and came up the path. Panicking, Sam dashed into the hallway and went into the kitchen only to see another suited guard posted at the end of the garden, so tall his head was visible despite the six-foot high gate.

The doorbell rang. Sam jumped and then winced as the movement aggravated the wounds. He could pretend to be out; the lights were off, after all. But then he realised they'd arrived only minutes after he'd got home. They'd probably followed him or could already have been watching the house.

The doorbell rang again, followed by a loud knock. There was nowhere to run even if he had been fit enough to do so. If the events of recent weeks had taught him anything it was that when powerful people made him their business, there wasn't much to be done about it.

Sam opened the door and looked up at the guard.

"Mr Samuel Westonville?" the man asked in a predictably deep voice.

"Yeah." He tried not to sound nervous.

The man stepped aside and his boss walked up the path to the doorstep. "May I come in, Mr Westonville? I have something to discuss with you."

"Who are you?"

"If I may?" He wanted to come in before anything else was said. Sam looked at the two mooks standing behind him and gestured for them all to come inside, leaving them to close the door.

Sam went into the living room and switched on the light. The guards came in before the boss, one sweeping the room with a trained eye, the other pulling down the blind and closing the curtains. "Clear, sir," the curtain-closer said and the man entered.

Sam stood in front of the TV, trying to look as calm and capable as he could with an arm in a sling. After glancing around the room, the boss came in further but didn't sit down.

"So who are you?"

"I imagine you're already familiar with one of my names. I'm Lord Iron."

Sam's tongue felt like a piece of shoe leather. "Oh," he finally said. "Yeah, I've heard of you."

"May I sit down?"

"Um, yeah, sure. I'd offer you a drink but there isn't anything in the house."

"Not even water?"

"Well there's water but—"

Sam fell silent when Lord Iron nodded to one of the guards, who left the room and headed to the kitchen.

"Firstly, I'd like to offer you my deepest condolences on the death of your wife, Mr Westonville."

"You heard about that quick. Do you visit all spouses of your deceased employees on the same day?"

"These are difficult times, but surely not so difficult that one cannot maintain one's manners?"

Sam cleared his throat and sat down in one of the armchairs. "Sorry. It's not the best time. And I don't usually get the secret service over for tea, you know?"

Lord Iron glanced at the remaining guard. "Take no notice of them." The other one returned with a glass of water. Lord Iron took it, thanked him and sipped. "Hard water in this area."

"I don't want to be rude…" Sam said.

"I'm sure you're wondering why I'm here. Well, it's a rather delicate topic. I wanted to see how you were coping first. How are your injuries?"

Sam frowned. "Sore."

Lord Iron nodded. "They could have been much worse. Mr Westonville—may I call you Samuel?"

"I prefer Sam."

"Sam, whilst I appreciate good manners, I like to get to the point. Your wife died prematurely."

"I know." Sam clenched his teeth.

"And I believe one of my employees is responsible, a Mr Neugent. Are you aware of him?"

Sam's heart began to race for a different reason. "Yes. Do you know what he's been doing?"

"I know there's a worrying pattern. And I know you and I could work well together. You've already demonstrated a remarkable ability to act under pressure."

"Look, just tell me straight, what do you want?"

"I want you to come and work for me Sam. And I want your first assignment to be dealing with Neugent."

"You own CoFerrum Inc?"

"Yes."

"Then you're his *über*-boss, you can sort him out better than I possibly can."

"There are many things I can and will do. I just thought you'd want to be personally involved." Lord Iron put the glass down. "You've been wronged. I'm offering you the chance to put it right yourself. If you're not interested, then, by all means, grieve and put your life back together in whatever way you wish. But if you want to make sure that what happened to you doesn't happen to anyone else, I'm the best person to help you."

"I'm not sure we have the same ideas about putting things right."

Lord Iron laughed. No one else in the room did. "Perhaps not."

"Right now, I want to fucking kill him."

"We can discuss that."

Sam's eyebrows shot up. "You want me to be your hitman?"

"Sam, this isn't a computer game. The way I see it is this: your wife was under my protection."

"Yeah, we need to talk about what that means."

Lord Iron raised a hand. "Indeed, we do, but suffice to say I'm deeply disturbed by what happened to your wife whilst under my protection, and I feel a personal responsibility to see this matter dealt with. I think you have a certain…affinity for things that could result in a very different life for you. One that's satisfying and would prevent other parties taking advantage of your talents."

Sam thought of Ekstrand. "I'm not very talented by all accounts."

"Nonsense. You just haven't been given the right opportunities. I'm not waving a magic wand here, Sam. I'm not promising anything other than the chance to address an injustice against you. And a salaried position, should you be in need of one."

"Do you know anyone called Mr Ekstrand?"

Lord Iron nodded. "You're concerned about how he'd react should you accept my offer?"

"Something like that."

"There's no need to worry. He and I have an understanding. Besides, you're not his property."

"I'm not yours either."

"I'm sorry if I gave that impression at any point."

Sam wondered whether to ask if he knew about Lord Poppy too but decided it would be best not to speak his name. If they knew each other, Iron would want to know why Sam did and he didn't want to have that conversation.

"Don't be intimidated by all this, Sam." He waved a hand at the guards flanking the sofa, misinterpreting Sam's silence. "These men are here to protect me, not threaten you. If you want me to leave and never seek you out again, just say the word. If you need time to think, I can give that to you, but I do want to deal with Neugent sooner rather than later. If you'd rather take the time to grieve and leave him to me, I can return in a few months' time. It's all up to you."

"And what would happen if I said yes?"

"I would invite you to come with me to my home. It's safer there and more relaxed. We'll discuss a salary, any needs you have and I'll answer your questions. Should you wish to accept my offer you'd be welcome to stay there as a guest, have company accommodation or funding to purchase a new house."

"I already have a house."

"Bath isn't a convenient location. I'd give you a generous relocation package."

Sam looked around the room. He'd already decided he wanted to sell the house. He had no job, no prospects and all he knew he wanted was to ruin Neugent's life. The man sitting in front of him was offering the chance to do that and whilst a part of him was worried about what that would entail, he mostly didn't care what happened after Neugent had been dealt with. There was very little else in his life now.

"All right," Sam said. "I'll come with you, just to talk about how this could work. I'm not promising anything. And I'm not agreeing to anything until we've had a serious conversation. OK?"

"Fine by me." Lord Iron smiled. "I think this could be the beginning of a most mutually beneficial relationship."

We'll see about that, Sam thought, but still shook his hand and managed a noncommittal smile.

27

"Mr Ekstrand, you'll be late!" Petra was at the doorway to the sitting room and smiled at Max when she noticed him.

"I'm not going to the Moot," Ekstrand said, arms folded.

"It looks like the Sorcerer of Essex made a deal with Lady Rose," Max said.

"You got that from Thorn?" Petra asked

"Thorn was angry with the Prince for not protecting them, so he was remarkably cooperative," Ekstrand said.

"I made sure he was telling the truth," Max added.

"Is that why the gargoyle is hiding in the cupboard under the stairs?" Petra asked. "I heard whimpering. Shouldn't you check on it?"

"There are more important things to deal with."

"It's all an infernal mess." Ekstrand left his spot by the fireplace to pace the room. "The Prince is involved in all of the business with the Master of Ceremonies, and Thorn said Rose made a deal with the Sorcerer of Essex. If Dante truly has made a deal with her, it could explain the stone hearts. I don't know how, exactly, but that's what my instincts are telling me. If Dante has created a foul hybrid sorcery my personal wards may not protect me at the Moot. The castle's wards only keep every living thing that's not one of the seven outside, which is useless when one of them may try to kill me. So I'm not going."

"But you called everyone together, Mr Ekstrand. If they convene and nothing happens, they'll be very angry with you."

"Petra, I would rather have a heart heavy with the need to write a few apology letters than one made of stone, wouldn't you?"

She nodded. "Well, I have something new to bring to the table. Whoever or whatever killed the people in the cloister damaged the building. I found hairline cracks in the four towers. I'm assuming they weren't there before."

"They weren't," Max replied. "What made you look for them?"

"I wasn't looking, to be honest. I needed a break, I went for a walk around the perimeter and noticed them then."

Ekstrand nodded. "Everyone was killed at the same time... cracks in the building they were inside...Max, meet me here in three hours. We'll go to the Moot then."

"When it's over?"

"Yes. And not a moment before." Ekstrand left the room.

Petra looked at Max. "Could Dante have really made a deal with a Fae?"

"According to Thorn he did. We don't know why or what the details are, but it explains why the Rosas were ignored by the Arbiters in North London—that's in Essex territory. Dante probably offered immunity for the Rosas in return for knowledge of Rose Charms."

"But why would a Sorcerer ever want to truck with the Fae?"

"I'm sure Mr Ekstrand is asking the same question," Max said, struggling to his feet. "I'm going to get some sleep whilst I can."

She touched his arm as he hobbled past. "You'll check on the gargoyle, won't you?"

"I wasn't planning to," he replied and went up to his room.

Max had just got comfortable when the door opened. He didn't bother to open his eyes, he already knew what it was.

The gargoyle came to the bedside, still silent thanks to the new formulae. "I want to make sure Cathy is all right. I want us to go to Mundanus and find out whether she made it."

"No."

"But—"

"Either she died or she's just badly injured. Either way there's nothing to be done about it."

The gargoyle couldn't argue with that. "What will the Sorcerer do with Thorn?"

"Probably post him back to Exilium when he's sure we don't need him anymore."

"It was awful, what you did."

Max opened his eyes and turned to face the stone frown. "It was a means to an end." The gargoyle said nothing. Max closed his eyes again. "I'm going to sleep. If you want to be upset go somewhere else."

"Easy for you to say." The gargoyle left him to sleep.

Will inspected his finery and checked that his hair and close shave were perfect and his sword and scabbard positioned correctly. He briefly fingered the elegant pommel, remembering the day it was presented to him by his father. A week later he'd set off on his Grand Tour with it secreted in his luggage, protected by a Charm to ensure no mundane saw it. He wore it in various Maharajas' courts in India, in the great Salon at São Paulo, at the costumed ball in New York and in the Parisian Court. He'd never had to actually use it and he'd never worn it to Exilium before, but his instinct told him he needed to make a point, and he was prepared to do whatever it took to see justice done.

On the Tour he'd seen examples of mundane justice, from people being arrested for drunken behaviour in Crete to people being beaten by a local drug lord in South America. Whilst Oliver had been laid up with a dreadful cold, Will had spent a rather interesting evening chatting to a man released from prison after a ten-year sentence in the American Midwest. The stories the man had told him would stay with Will for the rest of his life. They made him glad he was only visiting their world and not actually living in it.

In Society justice was dispensed in a variety of ways, depending on the city one lived in and the family one belonged to, and was settled by duels more often than not. The situation with Bartholomew was complicated by the fact that there was no Duke in Londinium to address the grievance. It was of such severity that Will didn't feel he could approach the Marquis of Westminster, and besides, he wanted to deal with it directly. If he was going to confront a man two hundred and twenty-five years his senior, one who was likely to be the next Duke of Londinium, Will wanted to be sure he had the blessing of his patron.

When he was satisfied his appearance was acceptable Will took a deep breath and said to the mirror, "Lord Iris, I beg an audience with you."

The glass rippled immediately, suggesting his request had been expected, and rapidly shifted from a wavering reflection of his dressing room to a view into Exilium. Will stepped through.

He'd been to Exilium twice before and even though he was expecting it the beauty of the place still amazed him. He could see the copse of trees ahead and a blue iris bobbing in the gentle breeze. The air was fresh and filled with fragrance. Will permitted himself one moment to appreciate it before moving forwards, remembering to keep the desire to speak to his patron foremost in his mind.

The path through the trees was clear and he walked purposefully, not too quickly, not too slowly.

Will heard a raised voice as he went further into the copse.

"I gave her to you in good faith. You knew she was my favourite, you knew how special she is, and yet you let this happen?"

Lord Poppy. Will hadn't expected him to be there.

"I did not allow her to be attacked. Don't be absurd," Lord Iris replied, his voice just as even and cold as it ever was. "She was in Mundanus. I'm flattered you assume everything is under my control, but it's not."

"Why was she there? Mundanus smells and she should be with your boy making beautiful babies, not amongst the unwashed and ugly!"

"Perhaps he can explain that himself."

Will entered the clearing. Lord Iris was seated on his chair carved from the tree stump, surrounded by the latticework dome. Lord Poppy was standing next to him holding his cane like a major's baton. Whilst Lord Iris looked at Will with cool interest, Lord Poppy came towards him so fast he didn't register the movement.

"You! I was there when you swore the oath to protect her in front of the great Oak. What pathetic attempt at a husband are you?" Before Will could defend himself, Poppy turned to Iris. "I demand his freedom. He will be my slave and I'll remind him of the importance of keeping oaths for eternity!"

"You will have no such thing, Poppy," Iris replied. "You know he's required elsewhere."

"I have suffered such distress, such misery!" Poppy moaned. "You don't understand what an agony it is. Let me go to her at least, let me stroke her hand and—"

"No. She's an Iris now. Either calm yourself or leave. There's work to be done."

"You have a glacial heart." Poppy sniffed and looked back at Will. "This isn't over."

Will remained silent, taking heart in the fact that Iris was protecting him. His patron beckoned him closer. Poppy stalked him across the clearing until he knelt before Lord Iris and bowed his head. "Thank you for receiving me, my Lord."

"William, do you have an answer for Lord Poppy?"

"I do, and more, my Lord." He'd predicted Lord Iris would want to know why Cathy was there in the first place and decided that a lie as close to the truth as possible was the best solution. "Catherine was in Mundanus to spend time with a child, something I arranged in the hope it would ignite excitement about our starting a family."

"Why?" Lord Iris tilted his head as he scrutinised Will. "Her excitement isn't a prerequisite. You will have a family regardless of how she feels."

"Forgive me, my Lord, but, having fallen in love with Catherine, I place a great deal of importance on how she feels." It was a gamble but he had been told by his father that Lord Poppy was a romantic. If Will appeared to be the hapless love-struck husband, it might serve the dual purpose of placating Poppy whilst convincing Iris he was committed to having a child.

"You love her?" Poppy asked, bending to peer closely at Will. "Truly?"

"I do, Lord Poppy." It seemed to be working.

"Then why put her at risk?" the Fae shrieked, his face contorting with rage. "Why not keep her at home? She could paint pictures and skip from room to room, saying funny little things and being surprising."

Will doubted Cathy had ever skipped in her entire life. "Paint, my Lord?"

"Poppy, how they choose to spend their time is irrelevant as long as marital duties are performed." He looked back at Will. "Continue."

"There was no way to predict such a brutal attack, my Lord," Will said. "I've been tireless in my efforts to identify the individual behind it and I'm here to seek your blessing in dealing with them."

"You know who tried to kill my favourite?" Lord Poppy had shifted from fury to excitement faster than Will could take a breath. "Tell me who it is and I will peel the—"

"Poppy," Iris interjected, "you will not act without my sanction. Catherine Reticulata-Iris is mine and how this is dealt with will be my decision."

Poppy's lips pressed tight together and he inclined his head at Iris. "Of course, dear Iris, of course. Forgive me."

Both of the Fae looked to Will expectantly. "The assassin was sent by Bartholomew Semper-Augustus-Tulipa in an attempt to sabotage my pursuit of the Ducal seat."

"A Tulipa!" Poppy straightened. "Really?"

"That's surprising," Iris said. "I don't like surprises."

"I positively adore them, usually," Poppy said. "But this one is simply confusing. Are you sure?"

"I wouldn't say it were I not sure, Lord Poppy. I found it difficult to believe myself but evidence from an Arbiter and a trusted third party have proved it to be true."

"This Bartholomew is the one Lord Tulip has been boasting about," Lord Iris said as he stared out into the clearing. Will felt himself relax now Iris's attention was elsewhere, as if his patron's gaze had been physically holding him. "I never thought the noble Tulipas would sink so low."

"I don't believe it," Poppy said firmly. "There must be a mistake."

"The assassin confessed to a trusted source and an Arbiter confirmed the presence of a Tulipa at the scene." Will feared he would be accused of ineptitude.

"Interesting," Lord Iris said. He looked at Poppy. "One can hardly doubt an Arbiter. You have no doubts, William?"

"None, my Lord."

"But Tulip hasn't—" Poppy began but Iris silenced him again.

"We all know how much the Tulipas have coveted the Londinium throne. They see it as theirs by right. I imagine this Tulipa would do anything to be Duke. Sometimes a desperate man does desperate things, wouldn't you agree, William?"

Will nodded, chilled.

"Even resort to stabbing a woman married into a powerful family known to be a favourite of a prominent Lord. If that doesn't embody desperation I have no idea what could." He looked at Poppy. "We have been insulted, have we not?"

Poppy nodded. "More than insulted, *wounded.* I expect compensation."

"That will be discussed." Lord Iris redirected his gaze back to Will. "I should imagine you are most aggrieved."

"Indeed, my Lord. I beg your permission to address this insult."

"It would start a war," Iris said.

"That's why I seek your blessing, my Lord. Whilst I'm keen to act, I'm also aware of the political instability in Londinium."

"I'm pleased by your restraint," Iris said. "Well-directed passion is a formidable force. See how well I chose a match for your favourite, Poppy?" Iris regarded the trees and flowers, deep in thought. "We cannot allow this to go unpunished. Catherine is important to us both, is she not, Poppy?"

"You know how I feel, as much as you deride me for it."

"William," Lord Iris said, "you will have my permission and

my help too. But you need to be committed. If you accept, once this begins you must see it through. There will be no opportunity to reconsider and no possibility of withdrawal."

Will bowed his head lower, caught between the thrill of being offered a boon without any involvement of his father or Patroon, and the fear of what it could be. "I'm yours, Lord Iris. If you believe me to be worthy of your aid, then I'll seek perfection in its execution."

"Excellent." Lord Iris rested his hand on Will's head. "This is how it will be."

28

The gargoyle said nothing as Max went downstairs to answer the summons from Mr Ekstrand. Max had slept well, like he always did, and once he'd had another dose of painkillers from Axon he felt ready to tackle whatever task the Sorcerer had for him.

Axon directed him to the ballroom and he entered after his knock was answered. The mirror was once again at the centre of concentric circles of wards. Ekstrand was wearing his cloak and held his silver-tipped cane.

"I'm going to open a Way to the castle," Ekstrand said. "You'll arrive just inside the curtain wall, in Mundanus. It's night there so it'll be locked and should be empty of innocents. Use your Peeper to look into the outer gatehouse—it will be directly in front of you. If it's empty, the Moot is over. Report back to me immediately. I'll keep the Way open."

"Yes, sir," Max replied and pulled the Peeper from his pocket.

He stepped through once Ekstrand had opened the Way. The air was fresh and cool against his skin after several days of being in the Nether. Max walked as fast as his limp permitted towards the wall of the inner gatehouse. The high limestone curtain wall kept him out of sight of the town and any innocents still on the street.

Rushden Castle had been the location of the Moots for centuries but Max had never actually been there. It was the first time he'd set foot on the Isle of Man. It was independent of any of the seven kingdoms in the Heptarchy and therefore considered neutral enough to provide a location for the Sorcerers to meet. The medieval castle was remarkably well preserved because none of the Sorcerers wanted the mundane anchor of their meeting-place to degrade. The innocents got a museum and heritage site and the Sorcerers had one fewer thing to squabble about. On balance, Max considered it to be a good deal.

Max placed the Peeper against the wall and twisted the soapstone circles that housed its lenses in opposite directions until the deep amber glow of torchlight shone through. He peered into the small stone room and didn't see anyone at first glance. He was about to pull the Peeper away when it occurred to him to move it down the wall. When he saw the dead apprentice lying near the door he removed the Peeper and stepped back through into the ballroom. Ekstrand closed the Way.

"The Moot's over," Max said. "There's a dead apprentice in the gatehouse."

Ekstrand said nothing as he stood there, staring at the tip of the cane. "We go through," he finally said, "the three of us, to the reflected castle."

"Yes, sir," Max replied and the gargoyle came closer as another Way was opened.

They followed Ekstrand through into the inner bailey, this time in the misty grey light of the Nether. The building looked exactly the same, both it and the curtain wall made of the same limestone; the only difference was the torchlight shining out of the arrow slits and tiny medieval windows.

The gargoyle went to the corner of the keep, nose to the ground and sniffing like a hound on the trail of a fox. It ran its heavy claws lightly over the stone. "There are cracks here."

"Just like at the Cloister," Max said as Ekstrand inspected them.

"I need to know whether the Sorcerers are still here," Ekstrand said. "I expect they're already dead, and that whatever foul sorcery Dante worked here is done, but I won't take the risk of going inside."

"I understand." Max headed towards the door.

"Wait. The wards on the Keep will kill anyone who's not one of the seven ruling Sorcerers of the Heptarchy. It will take me a long time to break them alone."

"They would still work against an Arbiter?"

"Absolutely. Security would be horribly compromised otherwise. The wards aren't dependent on the illegal entrant having a soul, they're dependent on there being critical differences in parameters we use to identify ourselves and the person trying to enter. However…"

He looked at the gargoyle, which stopped sniffing the wall and then shrank against it. "What?"

"The gargoyle might be able to go through."

"Might?"

"If it isn't possible, you'll simply be unable to progress. There's no risk."

"Oh, good. So at best I'll be able to go inside the building of doom. Brilliant. I'm so thrilled."

"We have to try," Max said. "We need to know now."

"And it isn't as if you have to worry about your heart being turned to stone," Ekstrand added. "You don't have a heart and you're already made of stone. Perfect. In you go."

With a wrinkled muzzle and quiet grumbling the gargoyle made its way towards the door. Ekstrand unlocked it with a huge key covered in formulae and then stepped back. The gargoyle gave Max one last look before it reached for the handle, opened the door and went inside.

"Well, I'm not dead," it called out after a moment. "Or…less animated than I should be. I can't hear anyone either."

"Go to the Lord's Presence Chamber," Ekstrand said. "That's where they'll be if they're still there."

As they waited Max inspected the cracks in the limestone and Ekstrand paced. It wasn't long before the gargoyle came back to the entrance.

"Do you want the good news or the bad news?"

"What?" Ekstrand marched over.

"OK, the bad news is that they're all dead. Maybe that's good news, I don't know."

"What's the good news?" Max asked as Ekstrand covered his eyes and sagged a little.

"It isn't all of them."

Ekstrand dragged his hand down his face. "Who's missing?"

"I don't know, I've never seen them before. But there are only five."

"It makes sense," Max said. "Dante killed them and left."

"Bring the bodies out to us," Ekstrand instructed the gargoyle and it went back inside the keep.

"We shouldn't stay here too long," Max said. "Dante may expect us to return."

"If he'd left a trap, we would be suffering already," Ekstrand replied. "Check for any residues whilst the bodies are brought out."

Max wound the Sniffer as the gargoyle deposited the first body at Ekstrand's feet. "Northumbria," he said, and crouched down to close the dead Sorcerer's eyes. "Could be jolly on a good day. Excellent watchmaker."

Max kept an eye on the Sniffer as it whirred gently and sucked the air through the funnel on its top. Before it returned the results the second body had been brought out and laid next to the first.

"Sussex." Ekstrand closed the eyes with some reverence. "Strange fixation on tadpoles and astute mathematician. I won't miss his bad breath."

Max read the Sniffer at the sound of the tiny *ping*. "Rose, sir, like before, very strong."

Ekstrand nodded, grim-faced, and the third body was carried out to him.

"Kent. Cantankerous old fool with very strange ideas about underwear. Never should have been one of the seven, in my opinion." His eyes were still closed gently.

Once the Sniffer had retracted and was in his pocket Max looked at the dead Sorcerers. They looked like sleeping old men, not some of the most powerful individuals in Albion. All had grey hair, all were grey-faced, all had large noses and ears with bunches of wiry hair growing from them.

The fourth body was laid down and Ekstrand closed his eyes. He was younger than the others and had more hair, mostly brown.

"East Anglia." Ekstrand sighed. "Young pup, only held the throne for three hundred years or so. Fascinating chap, if you're interested in coastal defences. Which I am, on Thursdays."

Max had never heard Ekstrand talk about the other Sorcerers like people before. He knew there had been wars over the centuries and as a result practically no trust existed, but somehow they still functioned as a collective. Now there would be Chapter Masters all over the country without the guidance and resources of a Sorcerer. The only party who could benefit from the inevitable chaos would be the Fae.

"Why would Dante do this?" he asked Ekstrand, but received no reply.

"This is the last one in that chamber," the gargoyle said, and eased the body off its shoulder onto the ground.

"This can't be right! That's Dante! That's the Sorcerer of Essex."

"So Mercia is behind this," Max said.

"I should have known!" Ekstrand pressed his balled fists into his temples. "Bloody Mercia! It all makes sense now—he's always coveted Wessex, he knew I'd call a Moot and that he'd kill me here. He just didn't count on me staying away."

"But why kill all the others?" Max asked. "And why would there be corruption in London and nowhere else?"

"That we know of," Ekstrand replied. "For all we know, the puppets may be running riot in Mercia too!"

Max looked down at Dante. His dead eyes were still open, reflecting the silver sky. He struggled to reach down and close them as Ekstrand cursed the Sorcerer of Mercia in several languages without drawing breath.

"There's no one else inside the keep," the gargoyle said but Ekstrand didn't hear it.

"Look again," Max said. "We need to be certain." The gargoyle sloped off. Eventually Ekstrand paused to draw a breath. "What now, sir?"

"Well, that's obvious, isn't it?" Ekstrand replied. "War."

* * *

Will stepped through the Way Lord Iris had made for him at the edge of the clearing. "I expect nothing less than perfection," his patron had whispered in his ear moments before and Will felt the pressure acutely.

The Way closed once he was through and he was alone in a wide corridor, in front of impressive wooden doors. It sounded like a large gathering of people was in the room on the other side of them. Will took a moment to look around and then went closer to listen before entering.

There was a round of polite applause and a call for quiet. "My first act as Duke of Londinium—"

Will leaped away from the door. That was Bartholomew's voice, without a doubt. There was over a week left, how—

Then he realised Lord Iris had chosen the time and place of his arrival back in the Nether. Several days had passed during the few minutes he'd been with his patron and he'd been sent back into the Nether reflection of Somerset House, the location of the Londinium Court. The reason behind it was clear; Lord Iris still wanted Will to take the throne. He'd just given him a different means to do so.

He stifled a burst of panic as the full extent of how he'd been used became apparent. After a few moments focused on his breathing, Will concluded that nothing had actually changed; Lord Iris had always intended him to make a play for the throne. The only thing that had altered was the way he was going to do it and the fact that Bartholomew was already Duke.

He had to focus on what Iris and Poppy had gifted him. There was no going back and no other option. His patron demanded perfection.

Will opened the doors onto the throne room. The air was hot with the press of people and filled with a riot of perfumes. It was a grand space, two stories high, used by the mundanes as an art gallery. The walls in the Nether room were filled with framed mirrors instead of art as a precaution against the use of Charms in political discussions.

At the far end of the room was a low dais with two gilded chairs upon it, one smaller than the other. The Tulipas sat as Duke and Duchess, and the head of the Digitalis family stood next to Bartholomew, holding the sceptre that indicated he'd thus far retained his position as Marquis of Westminster.

"You're late, Will!" Freddy's voice boomed across the room, making everyone turn and look at him. "Shame you missed the best bit. I thought you planned to stand. Would have been a damn sight more interesting."

He chuckled and the rest of the room fell silent as they watched Will enter, his eyes fixed on Bartholomew. He thought of Sophia's perfect skin scarred forever, he thought of the terror Cathy must have felt and the sight of her lying in the hospital bed, her jaw black, her chest in bandages. He distilled it all into a single sharp point and the men and women of the Court parted as he made his way towards the throne.

"William." Bartholomew smiled. "I was wondering when we'd see you. I too thought you'd be here earlier. I hope nothing untoward has delayed you?"

Will suppressed a knee-jerk response to Bartholomew's feigned ignorance. Instead, he walked up to the lowest step and said, "Bartholomew Semper-Augustus-Tulipa, I accuse you of the attempted murder of my wife Catherine Reticulata-Iris and demand your immediate resignation from the Ducal seat you obtained by foul means."

As his wife paled Bartholomew's face was the perfect picture of shock and indignation. The crowd burst into a gabble of gasps, commentary and a burst of expletives from Viola, but Will ignored them all.

"William, what are you saying?" Bartholomew finally replied. "What happened to Catherine? Is she well?"

"She almost died. You sent an assassin to kill my wife and it's my right to demand you step down and answer for your crime."

Bartholomew stood, rested a hand briefly on Margritte's shoulder and went to the edge of the dais. "William, I did no such thing. I have no idea what madness has possessed you to walk in here minutes after I've been declared Duke and accuse me of an utterly despicable act, but I beg you to withdraw to a private room with myself and the Marquis to discuss what has happened."

"There is no need to discuss anything. I know you're responsible and, if you will not step down, then I claim the right to challenge the throne by combat."

Bartholomew's eyes were wide with horror as Freddy muscled his way to the front. "What is this nonsense?" he boomed, dropping his huge hand on Will's shoulder. "Has the devil taken you? You're making a fool of yourself, even I can see that. The Duke has been generous enough to give you a way to withdraw. Be grateful, young blood, and take the offer."

"Remove your hand, sir," Will said through his teeth. "This has nothing to do with you."

Viola tutted, shaking his head. "I just don't like to see a young lad lose badly."

Will rounded on him. "He tried to kill my wife!" His voice rang off the mirrors, amplified by the dreadful hush of the assembled. "It's my right, damn it." He looked at the Marquis. "You know this is true!"

Digitalis tugged at his cravat, his face pink at the sudden attention. "There is a precedent," he said to Bartholomew. "If a challenge to the throne is made in open Court, the Duke must respond. If it's resolved by combat and the challenger is victorious, he has the right to take the Dukedom."

The words elicited a roar of speculation. Will shut it out as best he could to study Bartholomew's face. His forehead shone with sweat and he was determined to maintain his act of the innocent wrongly accused. Bartholomew looked back at his wife, whose eyes were shining with tears, and then looked down at Will. "Is there nothing I can say to dissuade you from this course of action?"

"No."

"Then I must respond to your accusation. I did not send an assassin to kill your wife, William. There is nothing in this world that would make me commit such a heinous act. But whoever has convinced you of this has been most persuasive. I have no choice but to accept your challenge."

"Bartholomew, don't pay attention to the whelp," Freddy said, but the Duke held up his hand.

"I cannot ignore this." He looked at the Marquis. "Here and now?"

"Yes, your Grace. A direct challenge to the throne requires an immediate duel to the death."

Margritte was on her feet. "William, think of your wife, she needs you."

"Don't assume I'll lose," Will said. He tossed his frock coat aside, drew his sword and stepped towards the centre of the room.

The crowd drew back to the edges as Bartholomew lifted off the heavy ducal livery collar of golden oak leaves and laid it reverently on the throne. He then went to Margritte, bent down and kissed her. The tenderness of the act irritated Will. He carved a figure-of-eight in the air with his rapier and the whooshing of the blade through the air satisfied him.

Will tried to ignore the fact that he hadn't trained properly for several weeks. He did his best to block out Freddy's pitying look and Bartholomew's total confidence as he removed his jacket, drew his rapier and came down into the centre of the room. He looked sad, as if he had to put a favourite pet down, rather than fight off a serious contender to the throne and defend his honour.

"I'm sorry it's come to this, Will." He took his position opposite. "We could have been very good friends."

Will remained silent. He had to use his boons wisely or he was going to die. He held up the hilt in front of his face, tip of the sword pointing to the ceiling, to indicate he was ready. Bartholomew shook his head sadly and then mirrored the movement before easing into a comfortable on-guard stance. His back was straight, shoulders relaxed, sword in his right hand.

There was a predictable exchange. Bartholomew was limbering up and testing his responses. Will remembered countless sparring matches with Nathaniel, who accompanied every one of his mistakes with an insult. Nathaniel was an expert in ridiculing whilst fighting, something Will had always wanted to be able to do with the same aplomb. He'd found it impossible to develop such a skill when constantly on the receiving end. What it did teach him, however, was not to be distracted by anything said once the fight had begun.

Seeing an opening, Will went in with an attack. Bartholomew anticipated it and parried expertly, answering with a riposte that sliced into Will's shirt.

"Excellent, Barty!" Freddy shouted.

Bartholomew backed off and Will stole a glance at the cut fabric. There was a tiny amount of blood and no pain. That slice should have cut him badly. One down, two left.

Bartholomew had moved far more quickly than he should have and Will knew he had employed a Charm, no doubt one of many at his disposal. Will just had to hit him once, just once, but every time he moved to strike he was parried or his blade thrust into air after Bartholomew had expertly side-stepped.

"Regret it now, boy?" Freddy heckled.

"Quiet, Freddy," Bartholomew said. "This isn't the time."

Will parried an attack, evaded another and very narrowly parried a third. He was working at the peak of his ability whilst Bartholomew was just warming up.

"I didn't send anyone to kill Catherine," Bartholomew said. "How you could think I would do such a thing I will never understand."

"Don't worry, you won't have much longer to ponder the question," Will replied and Freddy roared with laughter.

Bartholomew smiled and then his blade was slashing Will's chest. It happened so fast Bartholomew was withdrawing before Will even realised he'd been hit. Again, his opponent gave him the chance to see the wound. His shirt was so badly cut his chest was mostly exposed along with a pale red mark, like a scratch from a cat.

A single drop of blood was running towards his belly button. He only had one more left.

Bartholomew raised an eyebrow. "Your patron favours you, it seems."

"He understands my desire to protect my family and see justice done."

"Is he cheating, Barty?" Freddy boomed.

"No," Bartholomew replied. "He's fortunate, that's all."

Another flurry of attacks and parries. Will felt his shirt clinging to his back as sweat rolled down it. He tried to recall all the times he'd managed to strike Nathaniel; there'd been so few of them he could usually remember them with little effort. Now his life was in the balance it was harder, but one did surface.

It was, on the face of it, no more than a traditional feint. It was the lead-up that had snared Nathaniel and it wasn't something that Will had intended. He'd got angry, slashed ineffectually and then decided to give up. Then he'd noticed Nathaniel lowered his guard, just for a second and he exploited it. Nathaniel gave him a gash on the arm and a good beating in return, but it had been worth it.

Will waited for the next attack and defended himself but pretended to foul up his footwork.

"You've got him scared, Barty!" Freddy called out, just as Will predicted he would, and in response he launched himself forward with a flurry of furious attacks. None got through Bartholomew's expert defence but they were enough to give the impression of desperation.

Will retreated, letting himself pant audibly. Freddy jeered and Will concentrated on letting his shoulders drop, making his stance loose and his expression hopeless.

Bartholomew looked like a man who wanted to be elsewhere. "This is pointless." He glanced up at the ceiling as if searching for an answer in the heavens. It was the moment Will had been hoping for and he lunged forward with the perfect strike. Any other man would have been run through but Bartholomew twisted in time to reduce the injury to a cut on his stomach.

It was enough.

To everyone else Bartholomew would just look shaken, natural when injured for the first time in a duel, especially one in which the abilities were so mismatched. But Will could see his eyes glaze and his grip on his sword altered, as if he was doubting the feedback from his hand. Poppy had promised an instant effect and he hadn't exaggerated.

Bartholomew blinked rapidly, adjusted his stance and made an attack but it was slower and Will parried it easily. It was like fighting someone of his own ability instead of a man with over two hundred years of experience on him and Charms to speed his reflexes. Will felt a rush of confidence, then reined it in. The duel wasn't over yet and he could only survive one more strike before he was completely on his own.

He lunged and Bartholomew parried, but he had to work hard to do it in time. Attack, parry, riposte; Will could see Poppy's opiate charm taking hold. Will feinted then stepped in and ran Bartholomew through, just as his blade skewered Will an inch above his hip. They were caught on each other's blades briefly, then Bartholomew staggered backwards and Will pulled his blade from his gut.

Margritte's screams filled the room as her husband collapsed, his sword still stuck in Will's side. Will pulled the blade out and laid it at Bartholomew's feet, marvelling at the lack of pain.

As Bartholomew's blood pooled Will felt his thigh muscles twitch, his heartbeat deafening. The Marquis rushed to Bartholomew's side and both Freddy and Margritte pushed people out of the way as they closed in around him and Will.

The Tulipa's rattling breath could be heard when Margritte reached him, her screams dying in her throat as she fell to her knees at his side.

"Will." Bartholomew reached towards him with a hand covered in his own blood.

Will approached, taking care to keep away from Freddy, who looked ready to throttle him.

"I'm here."

"I didn't send anyone to kill Catherine. I swear it. On my family's honour, on the life of my wife and children."

Will clenched his jaw as a flicker of panic rose up from his gut. "My sources say otherwise."

"Lies," Bartholomew whispered and his head lolled towards Margritte.

Will stepped back, not wanting to overhear the last words spoken between man and wife. Freddy was glaring at him and Will faced him fully.

"Say it."

"You've done a terrible thing, William Iris," Freddy growled. "A terrible thing."

A guttural moan from Margritte told him Bartholomew had died. He straightened. "I acted with my Patron's blessing and I saw justice done for my family. If you or anyone else here has a problem with that, you're setting yourself against not only me but the entirety of the Iris family."

Freddy was a social oaf, but it seemed he was no fool when it came to picking fights. He knew that if he took his grievance further in public, he would drag his family into a war without the support of his elders or his patron. Freddy settled back into a steady glowering, then wrenched his gaze away from Will to Bartholomew and his face twisted in grief.

The Marquis cleared his throat and made his way back to the dais. The assembled watched him in stunned silence as Margritte's awful sobbing filled the room. Will looked at the throne and tried to think only of Lord Iris and how pleased he would be, anything to try and block the sound out.

"In accordance with ancient law," the Marquis began in a tremulous voice, "the Ducal seat of Londinium passes to the successful challenger who proved his right to rule with victory in combat."

He beckoned to Will who walked up the steps. Bartholomew's blood was drying on his blade, his shirt was slashed and he smelt of sweat.

"I, the Marquis of Westminster, do hereby recognise William Reticulata-Iris as the Duke of Londinium, granting him the rights and privileges of the rulership of Londinium. If there are any here who will not recognise his right to take the throne, speak now."

Will held his breath as the Londinium Court stared at him in silence. A man bearing a strong family resemblance to Freddy was in close conference with him; Will assumed he was counselling Freddy to remain silent. He looked at the Peonia who had been so stubborn, now looking at the floor uncomfortably. The Wisteria contingent were frantically whispering to each other.

But no one spoke out. Will was under no illusion that he was being welcomed by the Court; they all knew Iris had personally supported his challenge.

Satisfied that form had been kept, the Marquis retrieved the collar from the throne and placed it on Will's shoulders. It was reassuringly heavy and Will appreciated that he had succeeded.

"Long live the Duke of Londinium," the Marquis hailed as Will sat on the throne. The Court echoed the call but Will suspected they'd cheered louder when Bartholomew had ascended earlier that evening. He looked out over their faces and saw no warmth, no respect. He watched Margritte being guided out of the room as Freddy laid his cloak over Bartholomew's body. Will knew the battle for Londinium had only just begun.

acknowledgments

I'd like to thank Jennifer Udden of DMLA once again for great feedback on an early draft of this book and also Lee Harris. Both of you made this book so much better.

I remember, with love and grief and gratitude, the hours that my late best friend, Kate, listened to me read this book aloud. She laughed at the right bits, gasped when Will did something she didn't expect and believed in this series with such passion that it helped me believe in it too. I miss you and will always love you.

I'd also like to thank my husband, Peter, for…well, everything really.

Lastly, but certainly not least (I so want to say leastly but I must resist), I'd like to thank my Mum for spotting a rather glaring error—the sort that would have come back to haunt me a thousand times over on the internet, no doubt. Thanks Mum!

More from Emma Newman

EMMA NEWMAN writes dark short stories and science fiction and urban fantasy novels. She won the British Fantasy Society Best Short Story Award 2015 and *Between Two Thorns*, the first book in Emma's Split Worlds urban fantasy series, was shortlisted for the BFS Best Novel and Best Newcomer 2014 awards. Emma is an audiobook narrator and also co-writes and hosts the Hugo-nominated podcast 'Tea and Jeopardy' which involves tea, cake, mild peril and singing chickens. Her hobbies include dressmaking and playing RPGs. She blogs at **www.enewman.co.uk** and can be found as **@emapocalyptic** on Twitter.

If you want to go deeper into the Split Worlds, go to **www.splitworlds.com** where you can sign up to a newsletter and find over fifty short stories set in the Split Worlds!

Read the next installment!

Book Three in the Split Worlds Series,

all is fair

Caught in the insidious designs of powerful puppet-masters and playing a life-or-death game for control, Cathy and her comrades face their greatest challenge yet: changing the balance of power in the Split Worlds.

Now at the heart of the Londinium Court, deceit and murder track Will's steps as he assumes his new role as Duke. Faced with threats to his throne and his life, the consequences of his bloody actions are already coming back to haunt him…

Meanwhile, Cathy, wrestling with the constraints of the Agency and Dame Iris, comes to terms with her new status in Fae-touched society and seeks others who feel just as restricted by its outdated social rules. As Max works with Cathy to uncover the horrors that underpin Fae-touched society, he bears witness as the final blow is struck against the last Sorcerers in Albion…

Darkly imaginative, vividly detailed, and genre-defying in scope, *All Is Fair* is at once a thrilling and intellectual journey into worlds beyond sight.